Vocations

Also published by Handheld Press

HANDHELD CLASSICS

1 *What Might Have Been: The Story of a Social War* by Ernest Bramah

2 *The Runagates Club* by John Buchan

3 *Desire* by Una L Silberrad

HANDHELD RESEARCH

1 *The Akeing Heart: Letters between Sylvia Townsend Warner, Valentine Ackland and Elizabeth Wade White* by Peter Haring Judd

2 *The Conscientious Objector's Wife: Letters between Frank and Lucy Sunderland, 1916–1919*, edited by Kate Macdonald

Vocations

Gerald O'Donovan

with an Introduction by Chrissie Van Mierlo

Handheld Classic 4

First published in the UK in 1921 by Martin Secker.
This edition published in 2018 by Handheld Press Ltd.
34 Avenue Heights, Basingstoke Road, Reading RG2 0EP
www.handheldpress.co.uk

ISBN 978-1-9998813-3-7

1 2 3 4 5 6 7 8 9

Series design by Nadja Guggi and typeset in Adobe Caslon Pro and Open Sans.

Printed and bound in Great Britain by TJ International, Padstow

Cover image: 'A Nun' by Joaquin Sorolla (1863–1923) from The Mary Evans Library. While the Mercy convent dominates the action in the novel, the Dominicans who might have received the Curtin sisters may be considered as being represented here by Sorolla's Dominican nun.

Contents

Chrissie Van Mierlo took her degrees at the University of Nottingham, Birkbeck College and Royal Holloway, University of London. She is the author of *James Joyce and Catholicism: The Apostate's Wake* (2017, Bloomsbury).

Introduction

BY CHRISSIE VAN MIERLO

Background

Jeremiah O'Donovan, who would later take the first name Gerald, was born at Kilkeel, Co. Down on 13 July 1871. The son of Jeremiah and Margaret (née Regan), his father's job as a local government official took the family around the country, resulting in a fragmented education. Despite this, O'Donovan entered Ireland's famous national seminary at Maynooth in 1889. His progress was not altogether straightforward, and he left the college briefly during a flirtation with the Jesuit order. He was readmitted shortly thereafter, and ordained into the priesthood on 23 June 1895. Following a couple of brief appointments, he was moved to the parish of Loughrea in Co. Galway in 1897. There he encountered many of the social issues that would later be tackled in his writings: the absenteeism of the landlords, excessive clerical control, and poverty. In fact, life in Loughrea is mercilessly skewered in his first novel, *Father Ralph*, where the town appears under the thinly veiled guise of Bunnahone.

It is worth examining this period in his life, as his experiences in Loughrea fuelled much of his later fiction. The young priest's sympathies with Ireland's cultural revival and 'nation building' were now apparent; during this period, he became a notable proponent of the Irish language movement (though he did not speak Gaelic himself),[1] the Irish theatre, and the Irish co-operative

1 In 1903 he was elected to the Gaelic League's *Coiste Gnotha* and held the position for two years. He put himself forward in 1905 and 1906 but was not elected again, possibly because of his decision to resign from the priesthood.

movement. The diary of the prominent Anglo-Irish politician and agricultural reformer Sir Horace Plunkett (1854–1932) records that by February 1899 O'Donovan had joined Plunkett's Irish Agricultural Organisation Society (IAOS), a body that was primarily concerned with establishing agricultural co-operatives, although it soon became associated with nationalist political activity. O'Donovan's position at Loughrea also allowed him to put other burgeoning social ideals into practice. Responding to the resurgence of the temperance movement in Ireland at the end of the nineteenth century, he founded St Brendan's Total Abstinence Society in 1900.[2] The society, which was located in rented rooms at a military barracks and possessed a gymnasium and library, had a considerable membership of around 300 men (Lally 2008, 33).

O'Donovan's involvement in the building of St Brendan's cathedral in Loughrea reflects another preoccupation, the promotion of the Irish arts. The enlightened Bishop of Loughrea John Healy was of a similar mind to O'Donovan when it came to the importance of engaging Irish artists and craftsmen, and in 1901 the bishop appointed the younger man to be administrator of the parish, enabling him to commission works for the new building (Ryan 1993, vii). O'Donovan also had the support of scholar, playwright and co-founder of the Abbey Theatre Edward Martyn, the man who provided most of the funds for the project. By April 1901, O'Donovan had commissioned sculptor John Hughes to create an unconventional statue of the Virgin and Child for the cathedral (Frazier 2000, 325). The building also features banners

2 The temperance movement gained great popularity in Ireland in the middle of the nineteenth century under the guidance of the charismatic friar Father Theobald Mathew but floundered after the death of its leader. Jesuit James Cullen gave new life to the temperance campaign by founding the Pioneer Total Abstinence Association in 1898, an organisation that survives to this day.

designed by artist Jack B Yeats (brother to the poet) and his wife Mary Cottenham and sewn by the Dun Emer Guild (founded by the Yeats sisters with Evelyn Gleeson in 1902). Windows by stained glass artists Sarah Purser and Michael Healy also contribute to the distinctly Celtic flavour of the decoration, a contrast to the trend for Italian and German ornamentation in Irish churches of the period. Despite his relative youth and inexperience, O'Donovan's talents were apparent, and in 1902 he undertook a lecturing tour of the United States of America in order to raise funds for St Brendan's. He would return the following year as part of an IAOS delegation (Candy 1995, 57).

By 1901, O'Donovan's sphere of influence extended considerably beyond the parish of Loughrea. He made trips to Dublin as often as twice a week, delivering public lectures and visiting the well-known novelist George Moore and his circle, with whom he had become friends. As Adrian Frazier observes, the company he kept in Dublin illustrates 'how far out of the grooves of the Catholic clergy O'Donovan had already run by 1902' (Frazier 2000, 325). O'Donovan was garnering a reputation as an intelligent cleric of action and a 'patriot priest', but crisis was soon to arrive. In *Father Ralph* the protagonist's decision to give up the priesthood is shown to be, in part, a response to the anti-modernist excesses of the Catholic hierarchy in the first years of the twentieth century. In reality it seems likely that O'Donovan's clash with his superior, Bishop O'Dea of Clonfert (who had succeeded the sympathetic Bishop Healy in 1904), precipitated the split. While the details of what occurred between O'Dea and O'Donovan remain unclear, it is likely that a combination of personal, social, intellectual and spiritual concerns ultimately led to O'Donovan's decision to leave. Undoubtedly his shocking decision to abandon the priesthood influenced George Moore's well-known novel *The Lake* (1905). Although the novel is not strictly *à clef*, Frazier further notes that 'Moore was writing the final section of *The Lake* just as O'Donovan was throwing up his parish duties in Loughrea and seeking advice on how to support himself by his pen' (Frazier 2000, 553, n. 145), and these literary ambitions are mirrored by the novel's protagonist, the renegade priest Father Oliver Gogarty.[3]

After his departure from Loughrea, O'Donovan spent four years in Dublin and in London. He took with him to London letters of introduction to publishers from Moore. Like Kitty in *Vocations*, and several other O'Donovan protagonists, fleeing to the city from the 'provinces' equates to a certain kind of freedom, albeit a freedom that is compromised by practical realities. These were certainly not easy or settled years, and 1910 saw O'Donovan working as sub-warden at Toynbee Hall in East London, a Christian socialist educational settlement. Like the protagonist in *Waiting*, O'Donovan fell in love with a Protestant, Beryl Verschoyle, who was of Northern Irish and English descent. The couple were married at Whitechapel Registry Office on 15 October 1910 and would go on to have three children: Brigid was born in December 1911, Dermod in June 1913 and Mary in April 1918.

The early essays and short fiction that O'Donovan had been writing now gave way to the semi-autobiographical, intensely realist *Father Ralph* (1913). A *succès de scandale*, the novel sold extremely well and was positively received in many of the literary papers, though it naturally provoked the ire of the Catholic press. *Father Ralph* was swiftly followed by *Waiting* in 1914, at which point the outbreak of war brought O'Donovan's burgeoning career to a halt. He initially joined the British army and was stationed in Hull, then at the Ministry of Munitions. In late 1917 he was working in the Italian section of the Ministry of Information in London, where he met the Italian-speaking Rose Macaulay, and they began a secret and long-standing affair that would continue until the end

3 Frazier also suggests that O'Donovan was the model for the idealistic priests who appear in two of Moore's short stories, 'The Way Back' and 'In the Clay' (Frazier 2000, 325).

of his life (Lefanu 2003, 134). Details of the relationship between O'Donovan and Macaulay were lost forever when her flat was bombed during the Blitz and his letters to her were destroyed. Macaulay enjoyed her single, non-domestic life as an increasingly well-known literary figure in interwar London, but she accepted the moral consequences of her adulterous relationship and withdrew from receiving holy communion in the Church of England until long after O'Donovan's death (Smith ed. 1961, 42, 61–62). O'Donovan may have remained married to Beryl for the sake of their children, perhaps also because of his affection for her. It is possible that a lingering sense of Catholic morality endured long after he had left the Church, a character trait that can also be discerned in some of his fictional creations.

Work was scarce in post-war London, and the O'Donovans moved back to Italy for a short time. While there, Gerald published *How They Did It* (1920), concerning the ineptitudes of the British war effort, and *Vocations* in 1921. But his literary career was about to come to an abrupt and premature end. In the year when James Joyce's monumental portrait of Dublin life *Ulysses* was published, to be hailed the world over as *the* great modernist novel, O'Donovan's last work, *The Holy Tree* (1922), was brought out by Heinemann. Written in an Irish 'peasant' style, the 'Holy Tree' in question is a symbol of the author's complex philosophy of love. O'Donovan stopped writing in the year that Ireland made a decisive break with Britain with the inception of the Irish Free State, and it is possible that the dramas of the nascent state, which developed along decidedly Catholic lines, no longer held his interest.

In contrast to the vigour of his early years, from this point on he lived a life of relative isolation. In the 1920s, O'Donovan briefly worked as Plunkett's secretary. He also refused an offer to write George Moore's biography. His daughter Brigid remembers him as 'lying on a sofa all afternoon reading his way through the *Cambridge Ancient History* and endless detective stories, one a day' (cited in Candy 1995, 60). In the Second World War he took up new political interests, including work on a committee for Czech refugees. This was abruptly halted when, while on a discreet holiday with Macaulay in the Lake District, he suffered serious head injuries as a result of a car accident, for which she blamed herself. The death of his youngest daughter Mary in 1941 was another devastating blow. Following surgery for cancer, O'Donovan died at the family home in Albury, Surrey on 26 July 1942 aged seventy-one. Macaulay wrote the short, anonymous obituary for him that appeared in *The Times*.

Vocations

O'Donovan's interest in the role of the convent in Irish life can be traced back to his days as a young priest. At Loughrea, he rented rooms in the Mercy convent in order to establish St Raphael's Home Industries Society, a society that taught women practical skills like embroidery and lacemaking. These interests are reflected in one of his early articles; in the *Irish Ecclesiastical Record* for the second half of 1898, O'Donovan contributed a short essay entitled 'Two Pioneer Convents'.[4] Both these Galway convents were, like the convent in *Vocations*, Mercy communities: The Sisters of Mercy of Portumna and The Sisters of Mercy of Gort. O'Donovan is concerned with the practical role convents might play in raising the standard of living, because, as he optimistically notes to his readers, 'The priests of Ireland have always shown themselves in sympathy with the temporal as well as the spiritual interests of their flocks' (O'Donovan 1898, 503).

With this in mind, he praises the efforts of both convents in drawing upon available funds to establish Technical Schools. At Portumna the nuns concentrated their efforts on agricultural endeavours, such as butter-making, as well as training girls to

4 O'Donovan also took up the subject in the short piece 'Practical Schools for Girls' (1901).

be cooks; at Gort local girls were taught weaving, lace-making, hosiery and embroidery. As well as raising agricultural standards and spreading the spirit of co-operation, these endeavours were intended, in O'Donovan's view, to help stem the flood of Irish girls emigrating to Australia and America. The descriptions of the Mercy establishments contained in the piece echo some of the physical descriptions of the convent grounds in *Vocations*; but, by contrast, in these instances the appearance of 'sweet do-nothingness' betrays 'the hives of industry within' (O'Donovan 1898, 509–10). O'Donovan the parish curate naturally focuses his attentions on what convents *should* be doing, rather than making explicit the many failings that he would later explore in his fiction. A piece he published in the *Leader* on 10 January 1901 entitled 'Dishonouring Irish Saints' levels more direct criticism of the French influence on Irish convents (Candy 1995, 64).

Concerns about the standards of Irish education, and particularly about excessive clerical control over schools, is an abiding theme in O'Donovan's life and work, something that is most pointedly depicted with the schoolmaster Maurice in *Waiting*. These concerns clearly extended to the fate of Irish girls. While his views on the 'woman question' are hardly progressive by contemporary standards, the fact that he pronounced publicly on this issue at all is comparatively unusual, and his concerns appear to be genuine and grounded in practical experience. In the O'Growney Memorial Lecture that he delivered in 1902, he suggested that women could play a larger role in the revival of the Irish language (O'Donovan 1902). A further public pronouncement came at the 1904 meeting of the Maynooth Union, where he criticised the clergy for the inadequate training of women in domestic affairs (Anon, *Record of the Maynooth Union* 1905, 12). Another pet project was the introduction of district nurses into rural Ireland.

The outspoken priest's concern that Irish girls were trained 'to be accomplished rather than to be accomplishing' (Candy 1995,

57) is the very frustration that emerges with the Curtin family in *Vocations*, although this was written almost two decades later. As we have seen, *Vocations* was born out of the productive post-war period in O'Donovan's writing career, which saw him turn back, yet again, to the experiences of his early life. By the time he finally came to revisit his experiences of the Irish convent, he was father to two daughters (as well as a son) and it is perhaps natural that he now turned his attention away from the larger questions of nation and state that he had addressed in the 1920 work *Conquest* and towards the fate of the individual girl or young woman within an excessively repressive and coercive religious society.

Father Ralph (1913) and *Waiting* (1914) were both published by the popular and well-established Macmillan press. The publication of the highly controversial first novel was by no means straightforward, however, and Macmillan's New York office was not prepared to issue the novel owing to Catholic objections. The press must have hoped that *Waiting* would prove as popular as *Ralph,* but unfortunately the second novel did not live up to expectations. Disappointing sales may have been a result of the fact that the initial shock of the tell-all priest *cum* critic had worn off, and O'Donovan's relationship with Macmillan appears to have ended. Subsequently, O'Donovan would issue *How They Did It* with Methuen and *Conquest* with Constable in London and Putnams in New York. By the time O'Donovan published *Vocations*, he was now working with Martin Secker of London, the house that, at around the same time as issuing *Vocations*, was taking some considerable risk by publishing the first UK edition of D H Lawrence's *Women in Love*. O'Donovan's novel appeared priced at 8s. 6d.

O'Donovan's old associate George Moore had every reason to be sympathetic with the subject matter of *Vocations* given that he had himself tackled the issue of celibacy in works such as the 1895 short story collection *Celibates* (he would go on to revisit the subject in the 1927 work *Celibate Lives*). Moore used his influence to smooth the way for the US publication of the novel. Although he was unable, with characteristic concern for his own interests, to commit to writing a positive review himself, he wrote to Horace Liveright in New York:

> I have just read a book which I think very well of. It tells the truth in so interesting a way that I could not put the book down, but kept on reading it for three or four days [...] If it were not for my own work I could write a prodigiously favourable article about it (cited in Candy 1995, 168).

Vocations was subsequently advertised with Moore's endorsement, which also appeared on the paper jacket of the 1922 edition.

The novel came out initially in two editions: the 1921 UK edition with Martin Secker and the 1922 US edition with Boni & Liveright. Given typical minimum print-runs of 1,000 copies, it is likely that 2,000 copies appeared between the UK and US editions. While these numbers are unimpressive when placed against an Irish sensation like Charles Kickham's *Knocknagow* (1870), or even *Father Ralph*, they are nonetheless suggestive of the fairly solid readership that O'Donovan had built up over the course of his short career and are similar to print numbers for comparable works from the period.

In a 'Letter to the Editor' in the *Observer* on October 30 1921, O'Donovan responds with disdain to a letter from one 'Girl from a Convent' criticising *Vocations*.[5] He notes of her apologies on behalf of the convent system, 'Only a nice girl from a convent would confess to not having read the book she criticises; or be satisfied that she had got a fairly good idea of its contents from a review'. His letter contains scathing humour through his sarcastic suggestions, and reveals something about the status of a novel like *Vocations* in his native country:

5 The *Observer*'s own reviewer was sceptical about the novel. They suggest that a better title for the book would be 'Vows' and concludes that the story is 'effective as propaganda but not so convincing as a work of art' (Anon 1921, 4). O'Donovan responded scornfully in his 'Letter to the Editor', retorting cantankerously that 'it was not written about vows (or about cows or gateposts, or cabbages, all of which are mentioned in the book)' (O'Donovan 1921, 17).

> Even in Dublin it [*Vocations*] is to be had; though, in the bookshops patronised by convent girls, by some slight finesse. I am told that, in those wonderful shops, although it shares popularity with the lives of the saints and other less edifying works of fiction, it is not displayed, and can only be purchased (promptly, however), by a whispered conversation with the shopman (O'Donovan 1921, 17).

The 'under the counter' existence that O'Donovan suggests for his book is unsurprising, given its contents. Equally unsurprising is the fact that the most striking and opinionated reactions to the novel came from the Irish Catholic press. The Jesuit C C Martindale was highly critical in the Catholic *Dublin Review*, opening his review by comparing 'Donovan's' [*sic*] novel to the 'the swamps of some Maria Monk' (Martindale 1922, 139), a reference to the sordid and salacious escaped nun's 'memoirs' that had created a publishing sensation in the middle of the nineteenth century. Martindale is keen to call attention to many small factual 'slips', but his more substantial criticisms are that characters in the novel behave too much like authorial mouthpieces (or in Martindale's terms 'megaphones'), that 'Mr Donovan is not very good at writing about women', and that the author's 'false perspective' pushes out of sight more positive characters like Father Brady (139). For Martindale, O'Donovan views things through 'two eyes slit' (141) and is unable to see anything but the vulgar and corrupt in the religious life, a worldview that smears not only the Church but the Irish nation as a whole (140). In summary the reviewer questions 'Why is it that we have learnt, by now, to rely on these modern and anti-clerical Irish novelists having an appetite for the sordid?' (140-1). The remark might just as easily have been prompted by Joyce's *Ulysses*, a work that, incidentally, would also dismay and disgust Martindale, in his review that appeared in the *Dublin Review* that same year.

Reviewing for the *Times Literary Supplement*, prominent Catholic convert Aodh de Blácam also finds the accounts contained in

Vocations to be unbelievable. As he puts it, 'Some authors have seen nothing in life but sex. Here Mr O'Donovan closes his eyes to all but rampant superstition' (de Blácam 1921, 611). While the reviewer is willing to admit that some of the extremes portrayed by O'Donovan might exist, it is their depiction 'not as exceptions, but as the rule' that 'unbalances' the novel. By way of a conclusion, he asserts that 'Drumbawn does not exist in Catholic Ireland because it could not exist on the globe, so the real sins of Ireland go unscathed' (611). The more positive *Times* reviewer again saw that O'Donovan had neglected the possibility of true religious callings, but, on the whole, he or she is impressed by the 'very human' quality of the novel (Anon 1921, 8). In their estimation, O'Donovan writes with 'discrimination and, needless to say, with a fine sense of humour' (8). For this reviewer, anyone who is able to approach the work with the necessary detachment will be in a position to appreciate its fine qualities.

Across the Atlantic, H L Mencken mentioned *Vocations* in *The Smart Set* but credited it only as an example of a book that provides 'civilized entertainment' (Mencken 1922, 143). A more unambiguously positive review was penned by Louise Maunsell Field for the *New York Times*. Maunsell Field echoes Moore's endorsement of the novel and remarks that 'an Irish novel which never touches on politics, even for a moment, is something for which to be grateful' (Maunsell Field 1922, 14). For her, 'the author's psychology is excellent' and the characters 'deftly drawn' (14). The reviewer emphasises that the book is not about doctrinal questions but rather the convent life, and in her view 'the author's understanding of human nature, and his talent for characterization, give *Vocations* a much wider appeal than its theme would indicate' (16). She is also keen to emphasise the vitality of the characters, who appeal strongly to the reader. This is particularly true of the 'intelligent, sensitive, life-craving Kitty Curtin, so clean natured and strong willed' (16).

Set like most of O'Donovan's works in a fictional Irish locale, *Vocations* opens on a strained domestic scene. The small town of Drumbawn is home to the Curtin family: prosperous publicans Tom and Johanna and their daughters Winnie and Kitty. Owing to their financial success, the Curtins have been able to provide their children with an expensive convent education. Conscious of her social position, Johanna has therefore instructed the girls to distance themselves from their humble roots and forbids any mention of 'the shop', although as Sister Eulalie reassures them 'The ways of God are wonderful [...] and even public-houses enter into the divine economy' (8). Educated 'out of their class', the two young women, their schooling now complete, are left with nothing to do but stare out of the upstairs windows, indulging in romantic fantasies about passing neighbours and visiting priests.

As the story begins, Winnie is determined to enter the Drumbawn Mercy convent, because there she will be able to spend more time with the subject of her infatuation, her confessor Father Burke. For Johanna this is a thoroughly desirable choice; she has promised her daughters to God and considers this particular convent to be suitably *élite*. By contrast, Kitty is nurturing a passion for Dr Thornton, to whom she has never even spoken. *Vocations* returns to several ideas that preoccupied O'Donovan in his earlier fiction: clerical avarice and sexual misconduct, the dominance of the Church over the rural economy and the system of Irish education, and the fate of the individual who has been ensnared by the Catholic establishment. Uniquely, however, in *Vocations* these subjects are seen from a female perspective.

In the early 1970s, American historian Emmet Larkin transformed our understanding of religious culture in modern Ireland. As Larkin saw it, under the religious stewardship of the zealous Cardinal Cullen, in the second half of the nineteenth century Ireland underwent what he terms a 'devotional revolution' (Larkin 1972, *passim*). This included the promotion of Rome-sanctioned devotions such as rosaries, novenas and triduums,[6] as well as an expansive programme of church and convent building and a startling rise in the number of religious vocations. As Larkin notes, in the twenty years following Cullen's return to his homeland from Rome, the number of priests rose by some 700 (twenty-five per cent), reaching a total of about 3,200. The number of nuns saw an even steeper rise; in 1850 there were only around 1,500 nuns in Ireland, but by 1870 there were more than 3,700 (644–5).

The clergy-filled landscape of O'Donovan's fiction is perhaps then more accurate than it might at first appear—a reflection of the cultural geography of turn of the century Ireland as much as the author's own preoccupations. Indeed, the rise in clerical numbers must be offset by the fact that the population of the nation of the whole was in decline during this era, meaning that the ratio between clergy and laity became ever smaller. Understood in the context of a nation where these changes had fully taken effect, Winnie comes to represent the quintessential example of an Irish girl whose mind has been supersaturated with the rites and rules of Rome. She will therefore be led, docile, into a life of celibacy behind the convent walls. Her superstitions are fused with rituals like novenas and rosaries, the saying of which becomes a competitive sport among the nuns. Inculcated as she is in the way of thinking, her physical desires are ripe for exploitation when articulated in a spiritual idiom by the predatory Father Burke.

6 Novenas are a formal mode of devotion, prayed publicly or privately over the course of nine days in order to obtain special spiritual favours. A novena might ask for the intercession of the Blessed Virgin Mary or a particular saint and be prayed with particular intentions in mind. The triduum denotes three days of religious devotion in preparation for an important feast day in the Roman Catholic Church. The best-known example is the Paschal or Easter Triduum, which consists of Maundy Thursday, Good Friday and Easter Saturday.

In chapter 18 Father Brady, a character who frequently appears to offer a mouthpiece for the author's own views, declares that 'There's something wrong with the whole system. The natural calling of women is to have children' (295). As contentious as these words might be to modern ears, Brady, and by extension O'Donovan, had reasonable grounds for feeling that modern Irish girls were being denied their 'natural' rights to marriage and children. Feminist historian Maria Luddy has commented upon the high levels of permanent celibacy in post-Famine Ireland: 'In 1871 43 per cent of all women aged 15 to 45 were married, but by 1911 this percentage had fallen to 36' (Luddy 1995, 5). Marriage also began to take place later in life: 'In 1841 the average age of marriage for an Irish woman was from 24 to 25 years, but by 1911 it was postponed to 28 years. For Irish men, the average age of marriage had risen to 33 years in 1911, from 28 years in 1841' (5). This last trend might account for Father Dunne's view that there simply aren't enough husbands to go around. As he says of the convent, 'It's a pleasant enough sort of an asylum for a disappointed woman. They can't all get married' (155). *Vocations* deals primarily with the effect of these social changes upon the fate of the individual, but the trend for later marriages and high levels of permanent celibacy, along with high levels of emigration, would continue to impact the future of the nation well into the twentieth century.

Coupled with the renewed religious fervour that dominates in *Vocations*, various economic factors might also account for this state of affairs: the process of farm consolidation that occurred after the Great Famine of 1845–1852, and the shift towards a system of inheritance by which estates could not be easily divided, may have made marriage appear a less attractive option, and the struggle to accumulate a sufficient dowry could also have been a factor (Luddy 1995, 5). These struggles are the subject of the short story 'An Irish Peasant', which O'Donovan published in the *Saturday Review* on 14 September 1912 (O'Donovan 1912, 329–30). Set like *Father Ralph* in the fictional town of Bunnahone, the peasant in question, John Joyce, has signed his farm over to his middle-aged son in order to ensure that his heir is able to secure a wife with suitable fortune. Ultimately the miserly wife in question drives the old man out, leaving him to die alone in the workhouse.

Mr Joyce might have made a 'bad' business decision in signing his land away, but Mr Curtin is determined to make a 'good' one. Where Johanna gives voice to the culture of religious indoctrination that flaunted the romantic, spiritual appeal of the religious life, for her husband Tom, his daughter's future life represents nothing more than a sensible business transaction. Regardless of the mismatch between Kitty and the oafish Joe Duggan, the latter is viewed as the ideal husband simply because he is best placed to continue the family business. Ultimately Mr and Mrs Curtin represent two sides of the same coin when it comes to a young woman's choices, or lack thereof, in turn of the century Ireland. For the senior Mr Duggan, 'It's a queer fad to leave an important business like this hanging on the whim of a young girl' (31). But in reality, the 'free choice' (23) that Tom offers his daughter is no choice at all. Forced to choose between a miserable marriage to Joe Duggan and a marriage to God, Kitty is led, inevitably, to the convent gate.

For O'Donovan, rural Ireland is dominated by a 'gombeen man economy', a system in which the interests of prosperous merchants and shopkeepers take precedence over those of the poor, and where the local clergy are in the thrall of the businessmen who keep their collection plates full. The social hierarchy of the towns depicted in the novels infects the character of the priests themselves. *Vocations* represents a spectrum of priestly life—ranging from the down to earth Father Brady to the gluttonous and hypocritical bishop—but it is the preening and pretentious Father Burke who is the most prominent priest. Where the girls renounce their substantial fortunes to the convent and embrace the veil, Burke, who routinely calls upon the most prosperous families in the parish, will have everything of the best. As the narrator tells us, for Burke the '[p]riesthood was a career and not a vocation. He was an average prudent man of the world who managed a small business with care' (220). Just as Mr Curtin sees marriage as an economic transaction, for Burke a 'vocation' is also a business that must be sensibly handled. So long as he is not too indiscreet in his dalliances with women, he will continue to prosper.

Despite the outrageous comedy of some of O'Donovan's more vivid satirical portraits, a bitter and tragic edge always lurks beneath the prose. Winnie's fate at the hands of Burke is a consequence of the fact that he treats the nuns as his playthings, knowing that there is little chance that he will be held to account for his actions. The full ramifications of these kinds of abuses are, however, brought to life through the brief story of 'Poor Sister Christina!', 'the nearest squeak [Burke] ever had' (223). After conceiving a child with the philandering priest, the ruined nun had her baby in the workhouse hospital and is now (probably) a prostitute on the streets in Liverpool.

'I want—I don't know what I want. Have you ever felt like a human being?' Kitty asks her sister in chapter one (10). At the opening of the novel she is unable to even articulate her own desires, resorting instead to petty squabbles with her sister. The development of Kitty's psychology, her 'coming into consciousness', is the most important journey of the novel. Kitty is hardly a New Woman and the novel's attempt at female psychology is severely limited by the fact that almost all of her major life decisions are precipitated by the actions of men: Dr Thornton's decision to marry another girl, Father Bernadine's counselling in favour of the convent life, and the look in George Lynch's eyes that inspires her rebellion. All the same, *Vocations* constitutes an important inversion of the traditionally masculine *bildungsroman*, typified in modern Irish literature by Joyce's *A Portrait of the Artist as a Young Man* (1916).

Following what she thought was a conversion to the religious life after the onslaught of guilt and coercion of Father Bernardine's retreat, Kitty is, like Joyce's Stephen Dedalus, able to break free of the convent walls. If there is any real spirituality or Godliness to be found in the novel, this is not in the man-made institutions of the Church—which are so mercilessly skewered by O'Donovan—but rather in the natural drives of the body and the beauty of the world outdoors. Upon realising her dreadful mistake on the day of her profession, Kitty imagines '[h]er real self', a newly freed soul 'ranging the far hills while her comic ghost was playing a part in an inexpressibly funny comedy' (238). The appeal of the distant hills and the singing of the lark comes to represent the 'life calling to life' (304) that ultimately awakens her from her sleep, finally allowing her to fly free.

Conclusion

O'Donovan is a unique modern Irish writer. A member of the Catholic majority raised outside of the nation's capital and an ordained priest, he possessed an insider's view of a rural Ireland that was frequently approached from the outside by writers associated with the Anglo-Irish Literary Revival. However, far from being in opposition with the leading lights of the Revival, his association with influential figures like Moore and Martyn demonstrates a certain amount of collaboration. His rebellion also sets his novels apart from the domestic 'priestly fictions' produced by Canon Sheehan and Canon Guinan, for example (cf. Candy 1995). Observing from the other side of the water, this former priest was free to explore the failings of Ireland's Catholic institutions with an up-close and unflinching eye.

Some early readers of *Vocations* found the novel to be overly one-sided, or found that the book privileged its political agenda ahead of fictional artistry. A contrary view suggests that the very strength of the novel lies in its ability to fuse the high drama of a compelling narrative and a sympathetic heroine with a savage social critique. For all the book's despair at Ireland's 'vocation factory', however, the climax of the story is not so straightforwardly pessimistic as readers might have anticipated, and Kitty is spared a tragic end.

As she boards the train to Dublin, musing that 'Bessie Sweetman would know lots of nice men' (346), there is a least the possibility of a brighter future in sight.

References

Anon, *Record of the Maynooth Union* (Dublin, 1905).

—'Vocations', *Observer*, 16 October 1921, 4.

—'Vocations', *Times*, 20 October 1921, 8.

Candy, Catherine, *Priestly Fictions: Popular Irish Novelists of the Early 20th Century* (Dublin: Wolfhound, 1995).

De Blácam, Aodh, 'Vocations', *Times Literary Supplement*, 22 September 1921, 611.

Frazier, Adrian, *George Moore, 1852–1933* (New Haven: Yale University Press, 2000).

Lally, Bernadette, *Print Culture in Loughrea, 1850–1900: Reading, Writing and Printing in an Irish Provincial Town* (Dublin: Four Courts, 2008).

Larkin, Emmet, 'The Devotional Revolution in Ireland, 1850–75', *American Historical Review*, 77.3 (1972), 625–52.

Luddy, Maria, *Women in Ireland, 1800–1918: A Documentary History* (Cork: Cork University Press, 1995).

Martindale, C C, 'Some Recent Books', *Dublin Review*, 170.1, 139–41.

Maunsell Field, Louise, 'Latest Fiction', *New York Times Book Review and Magazine*, 7 May 1922, 14 & 16.

Mencken, H L, 'The Intellectual Squirrel Cage', *The Smart Set*, 68: 4 (August 1922), 138–44.

O'Donovan, Gerald, 'An Irish Peasant', *Saturday Review*, 14 September 1912, 329–30.

—'Letter to the Editor', *Observer*, October 30, 1921, 17.

O'Donovan, Jeremiah, 'Two Pioneer Convents', *Irish Ecclesiastical Record*, Fourth Series (July–December 1898), 503–512.

—'Practical Schools for Girls', *Leader*, 9 February 1901, 385–6.

—'An O'Growney Memorial Lecture, No. 26' (Dublin: Gaelic League Pamphlets, 1902).

Ryan, John F, 'Introduction', in *Father Ralph*, by Gerald O'Donovan (Dingle, Co. Kerry: Brandon, 1993), v–xiv.

Smith, Constance Babington (ed.), *Rose Macaulay, Letters to a Friend 1950–1952* (London: Collins, 1961).

Further reading

LeFanu, Sarah, *Rose Macaulay* (London: Virago, 2003).
Macdonald, Kate (ed.), *Rose Macaulay, Gender and Modernity* (London: Routledge, 2017).
Murphy, James H, *Catholic Fiction and Social Reality in Ireland, 1873–1922* (Westport, CN: Greenwood, 1997).
Ryan, John F, 'Gerald O'Donovan: Poet, Novelist and Irish Revivalist', *Journal of the Galway Archaeological and Historical Society*, 48 (1996), 1–47.

Gerald O'Donovan's works

Father Ralph (London: Macmillan, 1913).
Waiting (London: Macmillan, 1914).
How They Did It (London: Methuen, 1920).
Conquest (London: Constable, 1920; New York: Putnams, 1921).
Vocations (London: Martin Secker 1921; New York: Boni & Liveright, 1922).
The Holy Tree (London: Heinemann, 1922).

The text of this new edition has been prepared from the 1922 Boni and Liveright edition, cross-checking with the 1921 Secker edition. Where found, typographical errors from these editions have been silently corrected.

Chapter 1

Winnie Curtin pounded the keyboard of the shining Bechstein.

At school she had chosen as her motto *age quod agis*. It was written under her name in her many prayer books. It stared at her in large blue letters from the end rail of her bed. It was worked in blue silk on the linen cover of her dressing-table, and in blue wool on the reed matting at the back of her washstand. It was inscribed on the inner case of her watch, on the flaps of her purse and handbag. In spare moments she printed the words in blue on slips of white cardboard which she kept in the corner of her workbox, awaiting suitable use.

The motto was pasted on the first page of the overture to the Huguenots, arranged for four hands, now in front of her, and inspired her treatment of the treble. Her lower nature preferred to play bass, but her motto impelled her to choose the more difficult part. Kitty preferred the treble; but Kitty did not realize the sacrificial uses of music. She played because she liked playing and not for the good of her soul.

Winnie thumped, counted, frowned and wriggled. She struck a wrong note, gave an impatient exclamation, bit her lip and glanced apprehensively at the motto. She said an ejaculatory prayer to St Stanislaus, to obtain for her the grace to do her allotted task wholeheartedly, but calmly. '*Age quod agis*' she muttered fiercely through her white teeth. It was a favourite saying of St Stanislaus, her favourite saint. Some day he would make her calm and collected like himself. Work and prayer were the great means; always to keep her hands busy; to keep her mind fixed on the things of God, and off the vanities of a wicked world … One, two, three. There, wrong again. She frowned petulantly, pushed back off her damp forehead a strand of limp, fair hair, craned her neck upwards so as to see her reflections in the mirror hanging on the end wall of the drawing-room. She patted her hair, a faint smile puckering the corners of her lips. What a mercy it did not easily get out of curl! Her blue eyes glowed. She moved her head in order to get the most attractive view of her slightly tip-tilted nose. She sighed. It wasn't straight like Kitty's. But, then, Sister Eulalie said that, in the world, snub noses were very much admired. She blushed, glanced apologetically at her motto on the neglected music sheet, shut her eyes and said three Hail Marys as a penance for vain thoughts.

'Winnie. Winnie, Father Burke!' in a mocking voice cut off the third Hail Mary in the middle.

'Where, Kitty, where?' Winnie said excitedly, bounding off the music seat and rushing towards the window, near which her sister Kitty was seated in a low arm-chair.

'He has just crossed the street,' Kitty said, her brown eyes staring idly at the market crowd chattering in groups on the road.

Winnie clutched the red rep curtain, drew it forward a little to shield herself from prying eyes, and peered at the crowd.

'I don't see him,' she said dolefully.

'Of course, he's standing in the street for you to look at him.'

Winnie blushed and pouted her pretty lips. She stood up straight and listened. After a few seconds she said in a disappointed tone: 'He hasn't knocked.'

'Oh, bother him,' Kitty said, taking up the open book which lay on her knees. 'He! Him! as if he were the only man in the world.'

'You're a cold fish,' Winnie said angrily.

Kitty smiled with closed lips, her eyes fixed on her book.

'You've no heart,' Winnie added, snatching at the book; 'sitting there, pretending to read.'

'He's only a priest.' Kitty, with a shrug, yielded the book without a struggle.

'Such a way to speak of a holy man,' Winnie said, pouting.

Kitty gave a low, rounded laugh, stood up lazily and stared at the street.

'There's blind Lanty passing,' she said, with a bored sigh.

'Poor, dear old Lanty. I gave him his sixpence yesterday.' Winnie pushed Kitty aside and eagerly watched the old man thread his way carefully helped by a black-and-white, blear-eyed mongrel and a heavy blackthorn stick, through the thinning crowds.

Kitty laughed again. 'Lanty is a holy man, yet you aren't gone on him,' she said, with a quizzical look at her sister.

Winnie blushed a vivid pink. 'You're a horrid girl; I won't speak to you again this evening.' She stalked to the piano, her head in the air. 'It's all those novels. Hiding all day behind the curtain and pretending to read! Just to get a look at Dr Thornton. You won't practise your pieces or do anything. Sister Eulalie is right. Your heart is too much in the world. Remember how she warned us against novels. A slippery path to sin and hell, she called them. I can see you sliding down deeper every day,' she added vengefully, flopping on to the music seat and running her fingers over the keyboard.

Kitty yawned and continued to watch the street. The dust was a golden brown under the slating eyes of the July sun. Home-going, empty carts lumbered along in a quivering haze, the harness, the painted wood of the carts, the bronzed faces of the drivers reflecting reddish lights. At the edge of the pavement a group of men chaffered beside a crib of unsold calves. The crowds dispersing to their homes, to shops or public-houses seemed to take away with them all the energy of the few remaining bargainers. The strident voices of the morning had sunk to a dull 'take them or leave them' monotone.

Winnie's anger faded away at the sight of her motto, which reminded her again of her soul and of her duty to God.

She accused herself of 'horridness' towards her sister and murmured words of sorrow under her breath. She must make it up with Kitty. Of course, Kitty meant nothing wrong about Dr Thornton. No nice convent girl ever did. And there really was nothing much for her to do except to look out of the windows. She did her share of the dusting; and even if she had the whole of the dusting as her charge it wouldn't take long. It was a pity that she didn't care more for devotional books, but Kitty was like that. And as Sister Eulalie said, one must leave her to God who would speak to her heart in His own good time. She couldn't help seeing Dr Thornton who passed so often on his rounds. What if—Winnie took her fingers off the keys, sat bolt upright on the music seat, turned sideways and looked at Kitty. It would break her own heart, but that was nothing if it made Kitty happy. She couldn't wish it for her, for at the best it would only be a second best, and Kitty deserved the best in the world. Of course, Kitty must be a nun. As Sister Eulalie said, they would storm heaven for the grace of a vocation for her. Sister Eulalie was praying, and all the Mercy nuns—they had just finished their third novena. And the Dominicans were praying hard—it was very good of them, though they knew that if God heard their prayers Kitty would enter the Mercy convent to which she, Winnie, had already dedicated herself. And the dearest Sacred Hearts, to whom her own vocation was due, prayed daily that Kitty should have light. But if all their efforts failed—of course, they couldn't fail, aided as they were by the weekly Mass Father Burke said for Winnie's intention, and the candles she offered every evening at the Blessed Virgin's altar in the parish church—but supposing they did fail, Dr Thornton would be splendid. He was so good-looking, so well dressed ... Her narrow forehead puckered and she stared at the back of Kitty's head with a troubled look. He was a relation of the Thorntons of Thornton Grange. A distant relation, but still he was a Thornton. And the Curtins were only shopkeepers. Even the dearest Sacred Hearts were always put out when one spoke of the shop, and insisted that the girls at St Margaret's were never on any account to be told of it. But, perhaps, Dr Thornton wouldn't mind? He had such a pleasant smile for everybody; and blind Lanty said he was the grandest gentleman and the humblest man on the face of God's earth. And she had often seen him look at them when she and Kitty passed him in the street. One wasn't supposed to notice that, and she always kept her eyes down or straight in front of her when they met him, but somehow she knew. What a pity they didn't know him. If only old Dr Timmins retired or went to heaven or something, then they could have Dr Thornton as their doctor. Of course, she meant no harm to Dr Timmins, but he was aggravating. God forgive her for having such thoughts. Besides, marriage was a subject one should not think about. She would leave it all in God's hands and pray. If God wouldn't have Kitty as a nun, He would surely do the best for her in the lower state of marriage. In some way He would bring it about that they should know Dr Thornton and He would move the Doctor's heart towards Kitty. She said an ejaculatory prayer. These were dangerous subjects and she must not dwell on them. Besides, it was all nonsense, as Kitty was sure to be a nun. She played a few bars with hard mechanical correctness and said in a conciliatory tone:

'Kitty, dear, will you play our piece now? I think I know it.'

Kitty withdrew her eyes from the struggle of two obstinate pigs with their driver, and turned round with a sigh. 'Haven't we had enough of it for one day?' she said.

'Duty, dear,' Winnie said firmly, holding up a warning finger.

'No. I won't play. I hate it. I hate everything. I wish I was dead.'

'Kitty, darling,' Winnie said in a horrified voice, her eyes raised towards the ceiling. Her lips moved in prayer to avert immediate punishment of such blasphemy.

Kitty shrugged her shoulders. 'Haven't you ordered tea?' she said, with a frown. 'Father Burke went straight into the shop. He must have delayed talking to mother, but he's sure to come up.'

Winnie jumped off the music seat, her eyes glowing with pleasure. 'Oh, Kitty! And I've been sitting there doing nothing. Why didn't you tell me? Aren't you excited? It will be such a treat.'

'Anything for a change,' Kitty said morosely. She moved Winnie's music stool to the centre of the piano, sat down and began a Chopin waltz.

'Could I dare ask Peggy to leave the shop? She's sure to be helping there as it's market evening,' Winnie said doubtfully.

'If you don't hurry he'll be up before you're ready. And Peggy won't have her apron on or anything. And she may have to go out for cakes,' Kitty said ironically.

'And he likes cherry cake. Oh my, I'm so flustered. And we must get cigarettes out of the shop. Do, Kitty, help. Fix up his arm-chair by my window. Perhaps we ought to say we're not at home. It's not a lie, Sister Eulalie says. I know papa won't like us to take Peggy out of the shop on such a busy evening. Can't you advise me, Kitty?'

'As if your mind wasn't made up!' Kitty mocked her.

'I'm not gone on him you needn't be hinting at that. I'm only fond of him as a good priest. Sister Eulalie says that's quite allowable. And you know you said yourself he has beautiful eyes.'

'Poor old Winnie,' Kitty said softly, her eyes shut. Her body swayed to the rhythm of the waltz. Her pale cheeks took on a faint tinge of pink. Her breath came quickly, and once or twice her fine nostrils twitched as if from pain.

Winnie left the room and Kitty played on, passing from Chopin to César Franck and back again to Chopin without a break.

Winnie came back and busied herself about the room.

'He's still in the shop. Do help, Kitty,' she said impatiently. 'I can't move this bureau out of the way alone. I thought you hated playing?'

Kitty stood up. 'This? No,' she said, with a frown, helping to move the writing-desk.

A small tea-table was placed near the window by the fireplace. The best lace tea-cloth was spread on the table. Father Burke's arm-chair was drawn near the table. The blind was lowered half-way to keep off the sun from Father Burke's face, and the curtains arranged so as to give him a view of the street. A low footstool was placed on the spot where, after several experiments, Winnie decided his feet would rest.

Peggy Delaney, rustling in a clean starched apron, brought in the tea things, bread and butter, an iced cherry cake, a plate of mixed cakes, and a box of cigarettes. Her face and hands shone from a recent application of soap.

Winnie laid the table.

'And, Peggy, the tea and hot water the very moment he comes up,' she said impressively.

'Of course, miss. Sure and don't I know my business. I had a look into the shop on my way up and it's still deep in the talk himself and the missus is over the counter. But I'll keep an eye on the door in from the shop and keep the kettle on the boil.'

Peggy Delaney left the room. Kitty stood at the window near the door and watched the street. A frieze-coated countryman lurched with careful steps along the pavement opposite, an anxious-faced little woman urging him forward by the arm. He stopped with a jerk and stared across at Curtin's shop.

'It's no use, Nora, no use at all,' he said, in a loud maudlin voice. 'Sorra step home I'll go till I bid the time of day to my friends, Mr and Mrs Curtin. There they are over there. Can't you read the signboard? Thomas Curtin and Co.; not but what that signboard is a damn lie, and it's often I told it to Tom Curtin. It's Thomas Curtin and wife and daughters it should be. What do I care who hears me? Aye, there's one of the daughters peeping out of the window. The high stepper of the two it is. Good luck to you, miss, and a fine strapping husband. It's the run of a fine pub he'll have.'

He waved his hat, but Kitty had precipitately flown.

'The pub—always the pub,' she said angrily.

'Teas, wines and spirits and general merchants,' Winnie corrected.

'I wouldn't mind if I were let serve in the shop,' Kitty said passionately.

Winnie dropped the duster with which she was polishing the already speckless piano, her mouth wide open.

'Kitty, dear, are you mad? The shop, of course, is the will of God and we must accept it. But to be a shop girl, a barmaid? It's dreadful even to think of it.'

'Mother is,' Kitty said doggedly.

'That used to worry me too,' Winnie said, looking thoughtful. 'But Sister Eulalie gave me a most beautiful explanation of it. Unless father and mother had the shop they would never have been able to send us to such a high-class school as dear St Margaret's; and perhaps we— that is *I*, should never have got my vocation. The ways of God are wonderful, she said, and even public-houses enter into the divine economy.'

'Mother has a good deal of fun in the shop,' Kitty said, unmoved by Sister Eulalie's gloss on the purpose of pubs.

'It's the cheerfulness of the obedient soul, Sister Eulalie says,' Winnie said, in a hushed voice. 'Mother doesn't really enjoy it. It's dreadful for her mixing up with all these rough men and women. But she offers it up as a willing sacrifice before the throne of God for our sakes. We ought to be very grateful to her, Kitty, and do everything she wishes us to do.'

She looked keenly at Kitty, nodding significantly as she said the last words.

'Fudge,' Kitty said, with a toss of her head. 'Mother enjoys every minute of it. She'd be lost without the gossip from morning till night. She's restless if she's out of the shop for half an hour. She'd be ill if she were kept out of it for a day. It's no use your hinting at the convent for me. I'm sick of nuns. I don't care what mother wants. I won't do it.'

'Kitty, darling! the will of God?' Winnie said, deeply distressed.

'The will of mother and Sister Eulalie,' said Kitty recklessly.

'That's blasphemy. May God forgive you, Kitty.'

'I'm just as fond of mother as you are,' Kitty said. 'I know she's fond of us and that she slaves in the shop for us. She sent us to St Margaret's to make ladies of us. All she has done for me is to make me bored to death. We dress up in the morning and sit here all day without seeing a soul. If I look out of the window it's not because I like the street or find much to interest me in it, but because I hate the room.'

'What's come over you, Kitty? It's a beautiful room.' Winnie looked round with admiration at the shining mahogany furniture, the spotless blue silk upholstering, the red rep curtains, the coloured statue of the Blessed Virgin in one corner, the bamboo whatnots laden with countless china ornaments in the other corners, the light blue walls almost concealed by copies in oils, heavy gilt frames, of popular pictures which had appeared in Christmas coloured supplements of the *Graphic* and *Illustrated London News* for ten years past.

'Beautiful!' she repeated ecstatically. 'All our beautiful pictures and embroideries.'

'Even Father Burke knows they're rubbish,' Kitty said contemptuously. 'It was bad enough to have to do them, but it makes me sick to have to look at them every day.'

'You know you're talking nonsense.' Winnie gave an uneasy laugh. 'You're just pretending to be clever. All the nuns admired them. And Mother Davoren said they were really choice. It's that talk you picked up from the man who took Mother Davoren's place when she was ill that month.'

Kitty blushed. 'And if we don't sit here where have we to go?'

'Well, there's our walk every day. And we are allowed out twice if it is fine, and our boating in summer, and our little visits to the church and to the convents.'

'And you're twenty-one and I'm nineteen and a half,' Kitty said hysterically. 'My God, what a life! Never allowed to speak to anyone but blind Lanty and a few beggars. Everyone we pass on the street is either someone we're not allowed to speak to or someone who won't speak to us. We're either "the stuck-up Miss Curtins", or "those dolls, Tom Curtin the publican's daughters".'

'You shouldn't listen—'

'Oh, I don't mind. But I can't help hearing the remarks people make. That's just what we are, dressed-up, clockwork dolls. No wonder people set their watches by us. "There are the Miss Curtins going for their walk! It's eleven o'clock." That's what they say.'

'Sister Eulalie says fixed hours are everything. Regularity is —'

'Do shut up, Winnie,' Kitty interrupted desperately. 'It's all getting on my nerves till I'm nearly half mad. I want — I don't know what I want. Have you ever felt like a human being?'

'I wonder what's keeping Father Burke,' Winnie said, with a blush.

'I haven't even a Father Burke.'

'You're very wicked, Kitty.'

'If you say another word I'll take him from you,' Kitty said contemptuously.

Winnie burst into tears. 'You're a horrid, nasty girl,' she said, between sobs. 'You took Mother Davoren from me and you didn't care a pin for her. And I can see that Sister Eulalie likes you better than she likes me. It's not fair. And you hate her and I'd die for her. You've always had the best of everything with your brown hair with that gold in it, and your brown eyes and your nose and chin. And a complexion that never gets mottled. Even holy people are attracted by these things. You make me miserable.'

'Whatever I want it's not Father Burke,' Kitty said, with a shrug. 'I won't even hand him his tea, if you like. You can light his cigarette and everything.'

'He's such a perfect priest,' Winnie sobbed inconsequently. There was a loud knock at the door and Peggy Delaney came in with a tray on which were a teapot, a hot-water kettle and a muffin plate overflowing with hot buttered scones.

'What's wrong, Peggy? He hasn't—?' Winnie cried, in a horrified voice, pausing in her efforts to dry her eyes.

'Gone he is without a doubt of it,' Peggy said dramatically. 'If I looked in once I looked in ten times and there he was in the thick of the talk with your mother. And the next time there she was weighing out a pound of tea for Mrs Gallagher of Cluny and no sight nor tidings of him. I rushed round to the front door, thinking he might have gone round that way, and if I didn't see him half-way down the street, going in the Muldoons' door.'

'He'd never go and have tea with *them*,' said Winnie fiercely.

'Is it with them trapesers?' Peggy pursed her lips as she put the tray on the table. 'Father Burke is a real quality priest.

Sorra wet his lips with tea he would in any house round here, but at Thornton Grange and maybe at Lawyer Finnegan's and here with yourself and Miss Kitty.'

'I suppose mother couldn't come up?' Winnie said, with a relieved sigh.

Peggy threw up her hands in despair. 'Thronging ten deep in front of the counter the people are with the delay Father Burke put on them. She'll not be able to stir out of it before nine or ten o'clock this night except for the cup of tea I'll smuggle into the snuggery for her now and again.'

Winnie and Kitty sat down to tea in silence. Winnie poured out the tea with trembling fingers. Kitty uncovered the scones and held out the plate to Winnie who said in a whisper: 'I can't eat anything.'

'He's sure to come to-morrow,' Kitty said unsympathetically, helping herself to a scone.

Winnie took an occasional sip of tea and an occasional furtive glance at a photograph of Father Burke in a silver frame on the top of the piano. Suddenly a worried look overspread her face and she got up.

'I think I'll print some of my mottoes,' she said.

'Do, dear,' Kitty said mechanically.

Winnie sat at her desk and absorbed herself in the delicate lettering. Kitty ate steadily, her eyes fixed on the pavement across the street. She ate hot scones, bread and butter and two small cakes. Once she looked unhesitatingly at the open box of cigarettes.

'I wonder if I might?' she said.

'What, dear?'

'Take a cigarette. I often think it would be a help.'

'Oh, Kitty,' Winnie said, putting down her pen hastily. 'What would mother say and Sister Eulalie? Only fast women do that.'

Kitty shrugged her shoulders. She stood up and walked listlessly to her usual seat by the window next the door. She took up a book and held it open on her knees, but her eyes were fixed dreamily on the opposite pavement.

Winnie's pen scratched lightly on the cardboard. The slanting sun fell directly on the upper part of the windows, heating the room through the thin, half-drawn blue blinds. The faint breeze coming through the open lower sashes was hot.

'The room is suffocating,' Kitty said drearily.

'Shall we have our evening walk, dear?' Winnie asked, holding up a completed motto and regarding it with critical admiration.

'No. I hate walking.'

'Then I'll do another motto,' Winnie said, with alacrity.

A tall, broad-shouldered man in boating flannels passed up the street. Kitty held her breath. He nodded with a pleasant smile to someone hidden from her on her side of the street. She drew back to the shade of the curtain. John Thornton! What a fit name for him. Jack, his cousin, Daisy, at St Margaret's, called him. Jack Thornton. He was doctor to the convent, too. Winnie would know him there. Nuns weren't so badly off, after all. He was going on the river.

'It's so hot I think I'll go out,' she said, rising.

'You are a fuss-pot. First you won't and then you will,' Winnie said, putting aside her pen reluctantly.

Kitty rushed ahead to their joint bedroom, but was last to reach the hall door.

Winnie stood hesitating on the pavement. 'The Hill or the river?' she said doubtfully.

'The river.'

They walked along the street towards the bridge with the precise, even step they had been taught at the convent.

They held their sunshades exactly as they had been taught. There was something girlish about their print muslin dresses and blue sashes, their broad-brimmed straw hats with blue ribbons. But their fresh young faces, cool under the glowing sun, were girlish too.

From their house to the bridge they passed without recognition a dozen people whom they had known by sight all their lives. They did not know them. A few men raised their hats. The girls made little stiff self-conscious bows and blushed prettily. Winnie made as if to cross the bridge, but Kitty, with a quick movement, succeeded in heading her down the road along the river-bank.

'I thought we'd pay a little visit to the Blessed Sacrament,' Winnie said, in mild protest.

'There's more air here. We can go to the church later,' Kitty said, eagerly scanning the few boats on the river.

They spoke in a low tone, little above a whisper, as befitted conversation on a public road. As they approached the old black-and-white boathouse in which the half-dozen boats of the town were kept, Winnie said daringly: 'Shall we go on the river for half an hour?'

'Without special permission?'

'Oh, let's,' Winnie said, half fearfully. 'On a market day when mother is busy we can presume it.'

A boy rode past them on a bicycle, and jumping off at the door of the boathouse, called out: 'Are you gone yet, Dr Thornton?'

'Think of *him* being here!' Winnie whispered, with excitement.

'Imagine,' Kitty said coldly.

'That call you were expecting to Gralla,' the boy said, through the open doorway.

'That puts the lid on this evening, Conlan. Put back my boat again. Better luck next time.'

Both girls blushed at the sound of the deep voice echoing among the rafters of the boathouse. They blushed still more deeply as Dr Thornton almost brushed past them on his way out. He gave them a keen glance and hesitated as to whether he should raise his hat. Their 'eyes front' were not encouraging. He muttered 'nice kids' against his teeth, jumped on the bicycle and rode off.

'I don't think I care for going on the river this evening,' Kitty said, turning back from the boathouse door.

'One never knows from one minute to another what you want.'

'I might want to enter the convent,' Kitty said sneeringly.

'God hasn't spoken to your heart? Has He, Kitty?'

'He's better employed.'

Winnie thought this a very wrong expression and had to press her lips tightly together to prevent herself from saying so. Kitty's frequent references to the convent to-day were, however, a good sign, she thought. It was as if God was at last calling her and she was resisting. But if God was calling her resistance would be useless. A little visit and some extra candles at the shrine of the Mother of Good Counsel would be a help.

'Where shall we go now?' she said timidly.

'Anywhere.'

'A little visit to the Blessed Sacrament? We both owe one.'

'No.'

'Sister Eulalie will be disengaged. Shall we see her for a minute?'

'No.'

'The Dominicans?'

'They bore me stiff.'

'What else is there to do?' Winnie asked helplessly.

'To go home and go to bed.'

'But it's hours yet to ten o'clock and mother will expect to see us when the shop closes.'

'That's true. Let us walk on and on and on, for miles and miles and miles to the end of the world,' Kitty said recklessly.

'You're mad,' Winnie said, terror stricken.

'Not quite—I think. But when I am I'll enter the convent. Come back and let's take out the boat. I'll wet you to the skin.'

Winnie followed meekly, murmuring ejaculatory prayers under her breath.

Chapter 2

'Thank God, that's all done,' Mrs Curtin said, with a sigh of relief, resting her arms and part of her ample body on the grocery counter.

She had worked hard since half-past eight in the morning, but the clock above the whiskey counter, now declaring half-past nine of the night, looked down on a fresh, florid face, bearing no trace of fatigue. Not a hair of the mouse-coloured pile that crowned her head was disarranged. Except a switch that hardly showed it was all her own hair. The thin spot on top and the few grey hairs at the sides were a secret between herself and her mirror, careful arrangement concealing them even from her daughters. Her face, her flowing bosom, her huge cameo brooch, her heavy gold watch chain breathed contentment. Leaning on the counter she took a last look round and nodded with satisfaction. Not a sign left of one of the busiest market days she had experienced for thirty years. The floor was swept clean of sawdust. Pewter and glass shone, clean and polished, on their appointed shelves. Stainless counters reflected from their polished surfaces the light of the powerful gas lamps. Not a bottle or tin was out of place. The shop windows had been shuttered. The shop door was half shut. Closing hour was ten o'clock, but it was well known in Drumbawn, and for miles around it, that stray customers were not welcome at Curtin's after nine o'clock. Two white-aproned assistants, with frequent glances at the clock, flicked imaginary dust off the silvered taps of the spirit barrels. The only worker was Tom Curtin who sat absorbed, his spectacles low down on his nose, at his desk, counting the day's takings.

'Harry! Owen!' Mrs Curtin called out in a muffled tone which was supposed not to disturb her husband, almost at her elbow.

'Yes, ma'am,' both the assistants answered with one voice.

'You can take off your aprons now and have a breath of fresh air. As it was a hard day you can stay out till a quarter-past ten. I'll shut the shop myself.'

The young men bobbed, muttered thanks and hurried away.

Mrs Curtin took out from a drawer that day's unopened copy of the *Drumbawn News*, put on her spectacles, glanced carelessly at a few of the headings, refolded the paper and replaced it in the drawer, murmuring, 'I could write a better paper myself with far fresher news in it. It's so stale that 'twill keep till Sunday, when I'll have my leisure.'

She fumbled with a pocket underneath her skirt and drew out her rosary beads. Settling herself comfortably on the counter she prayed, with an occasional look at her husband. The bald patch on his crown was getting worse. That last stuff she got from the chemist was no good at all. And all the fine words he said about it. What robbers some people were. Thank God she never sold a drop or an ounce of stuff that wasn't up to its warranty. The grey hair only made him more handsome. She must trim his beard again to-morrow. What were the girls doing?

Tom Curtin shut his desk and locked it, whistled inaudibly, stood up and stroked his beard.

Mrs Curtin watched him out of the corner of an eye. It must have been a great day. But sure she knew it was from what passed through her own hands. And when Tom whistled like that and rubbed his beard it was always for something very extra. What a fine upstanding man he was. It was from him Kitty got her nose. And they were both a bit hot in the temper. She replaced her beads in her pocket and waited patiently. You couldn't rush Tom, but if you only gave him his own good time he'd let out as much as was good for you to know. He was leaning back now against the well-stocked shelves. She half turned towards him, leaning heavily on one elbow.

'Not tired, Johanna?' he said, working his lips ruminatively and examining the shelves on the opposite side of the shop.

'Nothing to speak of, a little, maybe, in the feet. The legs aren't as young as they were.'

'Tut-tut. You're as young as ever you were. But I think we can run to a chair for you to rest your legs. Yes, Mrs Curtin, I think we can afford a chair for you. The girls been enjoying themselves?'

'What else have they to do but to enjoy themselves? Sure you give them every comfort and pleasure that young girls could wish for, Tom agra.'

'We keep them select, Johanna. We keep them select,' he said moodily.

'Sorra more ladylike young ladies could you find in the whole county, or the next one either, though I'm their mother as says it. They're a pattern to town and country.'

'Happiness is the great thing, Johanna. To have them happy as well as good is my great aim. A dress or a hat, now? Anything up to ten pounds or so. It was a good day—a very good day. Three new wholesale accounts that promise well. Seventy pounds paid in that I struck off as a bad debt ten months ago. And better over-the-counter business than we ever did, even during the great fair. And don't forget a hat with a bunch of cherries in it for yourself. Big, fat, red ones they become you.'

'You are too good to us all, Tom.'

'Tut-tut. I tell you the young ladies' bank account is mounting up. They'll be warm girls for a man to marry, Johanna Curtin.'

'Winnie is as good as promised to God already.' Mrs Curtin shut her lips tightly, hard lines showing at the corners of her mouth.

'It's the one weak spot in you to be a voteen, Johanna. I don't doubt but you've soft sawdered Winnie into the convent, but what about Kitty? Tell me that now?'

'I see signs of it in her, too.' Mrs Curtin dropped her eyes and fingered with some uncertainty a twine-box on the counter.

'And what'll become of the shop and the land?' Curtin said harshly, rubbing his lip with the nail of his right thumb.

'We have a long life before us yet, please the Lord,' Mrs Curtin said evasively.

'And where,' said Curtin vehemently, 'will the business go when we're under the sod?'

'Into the hands of God Himself and of His holy nuns, I hope and trust and pray,' Mrs Curtin said, with some spirit.

Tom Curtin frowned and then laughed. He pulled his beard and patted his wife on the shoulder. 'You're a great hand at the praying, Johanna. And I'm all for it ... in reason,' he said seriously. 'You've done wonders with them girls. But if you had an eye in your head for that sort of thing you'd see that it'll take a great deal of praying to get Kitty behind a convent wall. I'll let you have Winnie, as she's built that way, but Kitty is another pair of shoes.'

'It'd be a grand thing in our declining years to have the both of 'em up there on top of the hill, praying for us,' Johanna said, in a wheedling tone. 'And think of the comfort it'd be to us and we dead. Safe they'd be from all the wickedness and trouble of the world. If I picked a good man out of the basket itself it's not every woman has that luck.'

'It's a wicked world, surely,' he said, picking at his beard.

He straightened a pile of tea-paper.

'Tut-tut, a girl must take her chance, and there's the shop and the land and what we have laid by to think of,' he added.

'It's a tidy penny, I've no doubt,' she said.

'So, so.' The movement of his hand expressed indifference.

'Mrs Muldoon was boasting that they have twenty-five thousand laid by,' she said, turning round and facing him.

'The Muldoons! I know people with twice as much that boast so little that even their own wives don't know of it.'

'As much as all that?' she said, with emotion.

'And there's the stock and good-will and the book debts and the three farms,' he continued, with a calculating air. 'When you get to a certain stage, Johanna, it rolls up on you and you asleep.'

'The hand of God was in it all,' she said impressively.

'No doubt, no doubt. But our own hard work was in it, too. They say a watched pot never boils, but it was by dint of watching and working from morning till night that we are what we are. It was a struggling business, without a penny behind it, when I got it with you, Johanna, twenty-two years ago. See it now. And think what it might become if we got the right sort of man for Kitty.'

'Take my word for it, Tom, that sort of man isn't to be got twice running,' she said, in a cajoling tone, with an admiring look. 'The young men now are different to what they were in your day. If you had ten eyes in your head it's someone you'd get that'd make ducks and drakes of our business in a twelvemonth.'

'The pair I have never failed me yet, though I have to wear spectacles itself,' he said sharply, drawing himself up to his full height.

'It's not one of them counter hands, Henry or Owen, you have your eye on?'

'And what was I when you were glad to get me, Mrs Curtin?' he said, with a jocose grin.

'I might have known you had too much pride in you to demean your daughter.' She spoke with relief, reading him in the light of a long experience.

'What would you say to young Duggan, now?' he asked, gazing, with a questioning look, at the ceiling.

This was a blow and hit her hard. She bit her lip and gave him a fierce look through half-closed lids. She stepped across to the shelves, moved askew a green tin, that proclaimed in gilt letters, 'Finest China Tea', and set it straight again. She went back to the counter, supported her back against it and crossed her hands over her bosom.

'And it was for that Whipper-Snapper you made a lady of your daughter and sent her to the most elegant school in all Ireland, with the finest quality of the land,' she said, with cold deliberateness.

'If it goes to that, he was at college,' he defended himself.

'College inagh!' She snapped her fingers with withering contempt. 'Nothing but a hedge school, though it's run by priests itself. Mrs Duggan that was, God rest her, once tried to boast of it to me, but I soon put her in her place. The pride of the school was a son of them wholesalers in Capel Street, with such rotten stuff that you wouldn't let it inside your door, even if the whole world was drained dry of all but what they had. "Tell me your company, and I'll tell you what you are, Mrs Duggan" I said to myself. And my own daughters hand-and-glove with the daughters of three Sirs and a General, not to speak of half a dozen landlords and high-up doctors and lawyers and the like up in St Margaret's. Don't "college" me with your Joe Duggan. He's a counter-jumper, nothing more nor less. Wasn't he three years behind the counter in Arnott's above in Dublin?'

Tom Curtin heard her through impatiently. He glanced at the clock and compared it with his watch, shrugged his shoulders, muttered 'tut-tut,' and added sharply, 'The whole world knows he was apprenticed to the wholesaling.'

'And what does he want to know drapery wholesaling for if he's going to run his father's retail drapery in Drumbawn?' she asked, with a mixture of contempt and curiosity.

'You'll know more about that before you're many minutes older,' he said, with another look at the clock.

'It's now four minutes to ten o'clock. His father said he'd come in for a chat just as we were shutting. I wouldn't be at all surprised if it was to broach openly what he has often hinted at to me. Mike Duggan doesn't waste his time paying visits that haven't something important behind them.'

Mrs Curtin took a handkerchief from under the belt of her black apron and dabbed at her eyes.

'Come, come, woman,' Tom Curtin said sternly.

'I'm beyond all that, Tom.' She gave a dry sob. 'You have broke the heart in me this night. I had it set on them two girls going into the convent. 'Twill break Kitty's heart, too, marrying her off like this agin her will.'

'Who's talking of marrying her off agin her will? I'm not going to force her to it. It's bad enough for yourself and the nuns to be trying to delude her into the convent, and she not wanting to go. She can marry Joe Duggan or go into the convent, whichever she likes best, but she must have her free choice.'

'You won't settle anything, then?' Johanna said more brightly, putting away her handkerchief.

'Certainly not. The girl must choose for herself.' Mrs Curtin gazed thoughtfully at the tea-tins.

'She's a headstrong girl, mark my words for it, Tom. She's dainty in her ways, like them blood-horses that are particular about their food. If it was a gentleman, now—Dr Thornton, or the like—I wouldn't be saying that she wouldn't be foolish enough—'

'Pooh, pooh,' Curtin said angrily. 'I want a man that'll keep on Curtin and Co.'

'It's Joe Duggan then, or no-one?' she said hopefully.

'There isn't another man I know I'd trust with the business,' he said.

Johanna smiled at the worn wedding-ring on her finger. With the help of God Tom might give Kitty the last push into the convent. Tom had a great notion of freedom. How well she knew it all her life: to give you the choice of two things both of which you disliked. Kitty'd be sure to see the beauty of the convent when that grasping lout, Joe Duggan, came after her. The ways of God were wonderful. If He couldn't lead a soul to grace by the straight road He took advantage of it on a by-road.

'Fie, fie. Thomas Curtin and Co. open for the sale of drink at five past ten,' a harsh voice said jocosely from the door.

'Come in, Mr Duggan. Come in. It's not every night we expect the Chairman of the town Bench to visit us,' Tom Curtin said, with a welcoming laugh. 'The door, Johanna. But if the peelers have us up before the court itself, you'll let us off light, Mr Duggan?'

Mrs Curtin lifted a flap of the counter and shook hands with the heavy-jowled, clean-shaven man whose keen grey eyes, under heavy lids, seemed to appraise everything in the shop in one quiet glance. While her husband was welcoming Duggan she shut and barred the shop door.

'We mustn't keep Mr Duggan on his feet,' she said, bustling back to the counter. 'Come this way into the snug, Mr Duggan, and don't forget we have mouths on us, Tom.'

Duggan lumbered behind her through a small door at the end of the counter, near the front window, to a recess partitioned off from prying eyes in front of the counter. He settled his cumbrous body in a low arm-chair beside the small mahogany table. Mrs Curtin sat in a high chair, and rested her elbows on the table.

'It's the first time I've really rested my feet this day,' she said, with a sigh of contentment.

'The whole world knows how you mind the business and what a power of business you have to mind.' Duggan rubbed a thin lock of white hair across his bald forehead.

'Now we can make ourselves comfortable,' Tom Curtin said cheerfully, coming in with a tray laden with bottles, a siphon, a jug of water, glasses and a box of cigars. 'Which will it be, Mr Duggan? Brandy that's as old as ourselves, or whiskey that's about half our age? And there's some port for the woman of the house that'll raise the cockles of her heart.'

'Sure, how could a man choose between the angels out of heaven,' Duggan said, with a sigh. 'But the brandy might be kinder to a man of my years. I'm fifteen years nearer to my grave than you are, Thomas Curtin, and it's thinking of winding up my affairs I must be.'

'Tut-tut,' Curtin said, as he drew the cork of the brandy bottle with reverent care.

'You're a young man yet.'

'I'm within a year of seventy.'

'And what's that to a hale and hearty man with a good son to take a lot of the burden of life off him?'

'The best son in the town of Drumbawn, though it's myself that says it,' Duggan said proudly.

'You're only saying what the whole world is saying,' Tom Curtin agreed heartily, as he poured away the top of the spirit into a spare glass.

'A drop of this will make you feel younger even than you look,' he added, as he helped Duggan liberally.

'Stop, stop. No, no soda, thank you. I wouldn't be insulting the good liquor by showing any fear of it. As I was saying, I'm drawing near to my end, and it's time I was making my soul. Your health, Mrs Curtin, and yours, too, Mr Curtin, and the young ladies, God bless them. A long life and handsome husbands to them.'

Tom Curtin helped his wife to a half-glass of port and himself to a glass of soda water.

'Thanks, thanks, and for the girls, too,' he said. 'Though it's the divine spouse one of 'em'll be having. She's booked for the convent.'

'Which of'em might that be now?' Duggan asked, smacking his lips.

'Winnie, the eldest one.'

'Ah,' Duggan said, with satisfaction, and wagged his head impressively at his glass. 'And it's a good handsel she'll be taking in to them, no doubt.'

'We must deal generously with God,' Curtin said, pulling his beard.

'A couple of thousand now, and maybe a couple more when I'm gone. But the bulk must go to the girl that has to bear the brunt of the world and who'll have, I hope, children herself to provide for.'

'That's generosity and justice both in the one breath,' Duggan said, nodding a fervent approval, 'and worthy of the high name you have, Mr Curtin, in town and country. It's many a man'll be setting his cap at Miss Kitty. There's many of the gentry that'd like to have the handling of her money,' he added meditatively, sipping his brandy with appreciation.

'Every penny of my money was made by myself and Johanna there, and it won't go to any waster if I can help it,' Curtin said emphatically. 'I want a man for her that can look after her business, and, maybe, add to it.'

'That's sound sense if ever I heard it spoken.' Duggan leant back in his chair and supported his hands on the arms. 'You give me courage to speak up. I can point out that very man to you.'

'I'll hear you, Mr Duggan.'

'And that man is my son, Joe,' said Duggan slowly, staring at the table.

Tom Curtin gazed at the ceiling and said nothing.

'First and foremost I may tell you that the boy has a liking for her. If she hadn't a penny to her name, he'd be strongly tempted to ask her to marry him to-morrow. It's lucky for him, though, with the big schemes he has in his head, that his heart and his head can go the one road. For if Miss Kitty is the purtiest girl in the town, she's the one girl, too, that can help Joe to what he has in view. You have a fair idea of my standing, Tom Curtin, but you can learn it all any day you like to come up to the bank with me. There's the business, and a warm wad of ready money, and the land. I'll make over everything to Joe the day he marries, except one farm at Clogheen that I'll live on myself, but he'll have that, too, when I go. Now that's what he is; and he's no bad prize even for a warm girl like Miss Kitty. But it's nothing to what he hopes to be. You know he served his time up in Arnott's at the wholesaling. But no-one in Drumbawn, except myself and himself, knows that he spent a year of it as an improver in a big shop in Kensington, London, where they sell every known thing under the one roof. It's the John Barker of Drumbawn Joe intends to be one day. I made a start for him to-day by buying out Kerley, the ironmonger, next door to us; and Dooley, the chemist, above you is open to an offer, I know. Joe couldn't buy you out, nor would he dream of it, but you'd come in on your own terms. You're a young man yet and won't want to retire. Joe's own words to me were "Mr Curtin must give me his name if he gives me the finest girl in Drumbawn!" If you see eye to eye with us, the whole business'd be called Thomas Curtin and Co.'

For the first time since he began his explanation Duggan looked at Tom Curtin and surprised a faint smile of satisfaction in the studiously set face. He paused, took the cigar Curtin held out to him, and put it on the table beside him. He sipped at his brandy, said it was famous stuff, and sweeter to the smell than new-mown hay. He looked again at Curtin, whose eye was fixed in a questioning stare on the brandy bottle. Tom was biting. Better give him time to get the hook well into his gills. Duggan took up his cigar, fingered it softly, bit off the end, and settled down to a luxurious smoke.

The ticking of the clock above the whiskey counter beat like the hammer of fate through the silent shop.

Mrs Curtin moved uneasily in her chair. Twenty-two years' experience of Tom Curtin told her that not only had he bitten, but that he had swallowed the hook. She had her own ways of managing him, but he was past her interference, now. If she crossed him it would only make him the more stubborn in following his own bent. Them Duggans were clever without a doubt, but somehow or other she'd put a spoke in their wheel yet. They were thinking only of themselves, but she was thinking of God; and she'd have God on her side. As long as she had breath in her body, Thomas Curtin and Co'd never go to make a great man of Joe Duggan. To think of him spending that year in London and she never to know of it! She prided herself on her knowledge of the doings of Drumbawn, and this was a severe blow. But it also impressed her. There was no craft or guile them Duggans weren't capable of. Tom, with all his conceit of himself, 'd be putty in their hands. But with the help of God she'd be able for them. She listened to a faint grating of the house door and the sound of stealthy footsteps along the hall-way. Twenty-five to eleven and she had said quarter-past ten. She'd give a tongue thrashing to them gallivanters of shop-boys in the morning. Poor fellows! they had a hard day of it. But she'd let them know that nothing escaped her. She smiled with pleasure, her confidence in herself confirmed. And if that limb of a Peggy didn't tell on them she'd give her a lambasting with her tongue.

'The bottle is near you, Tom. Won't you help Mr Duggan to another little drop?' she said, with a smile.

'And if I don't give in?' Tom Curtin said, with a deep frown at the soda siphon.

'That's the very thing I said to Joe. Where would you be, Joe, I said, if Tom Curtin gives you the go-by? "I'd develop the wholesale side of our own business in any case," he said, "with the twenty thousand you're giving me. I might either spread it out into Kerleys, or build on to the back of our own shop for the extension of the drapery and keep Kerleys for ironmongery. With the prosperity that's coming on the country there's a great future for agricultural machinery. It'd be a lopsided sort of business, though, and I'd drop entirely the idea of Dooley's. Without Mr Curtin," he said, "I'd be like a pricked bladder!"'

'How much do you want with her?' Curtin asked fiercely of the brandy bottle, after a long pause.

Duggan pulled hard at his cigar. 'I'd do up that house on the river-bank for them that the Resident Magistrates used to have of me. In view of Joe marrying, I made up my mind not to let it to the new man. Miss Kitty was brought up tender and must have her comfort and her piano and maybe a pony and trap to drive about in. All that'd be a present from myself. You know what I'm giving Joe besides. But the scheme is a big one and to give it a fair chance it'll want a power of money. Would ten thousand be too high a figure?'

There was a tentative note in Duggan's voice and he was a little taken aback at Curtin's questioning scowl.

'Ten thousand? Hum-hum: pooh-hooh!'

'It isn't as if it was coming into an empty pocket,' Duggan said stubbornly.

'Nonsense, man, nonsense,' Curtin said, with a sweep of his hand.

'What would you rise to, then?'

'Ten thousand. A mere trifle.' Curtin moistened his dry lips. 'I may not be in politics, Mr Duggan. I'm not a JP like you, or Chairman of the Town Board. But I'm known to the trade, sir. Thomas Curtin and Co. has a reputation with the wholesale houses in Dublin and Belfast at least as high as Michael Duggan and Son. Ten thousand, pshaw! The day my daughter marries your son, if she marries him, I'll put down pound for pound with you. Have another drop of brandy, Mr Duggan?'

'Twenty thousand!' Duggan's jaw dropped open and displayed his straggling teeth.

'There isn't a headache in a gallon of it,' Curtin said gaily, 'and to show what I feel this minute I'll break the custom of a lifetime and join you in a thimbleful.'

'Stop, stop,' Duggan interjected. 'I'm that drunk with pleasure that another drop of that brandy'd put me off my feet, good and all as it is. I'm glad of the money for Joe's sake. But, honest to God, I'm gladder to find a man that has so much belief in my own son.'

'That'll be her fortune,' said Curtin heartily.

'But there's as much more where that comes from, and if Joe can convince me about the soundness of his plans there's no reason why it shouldn't all go into the business. I'd give Joe his head but I'd look after my own side of the business, at least for a few years to come, and keep some kind of general control. But we can go into all that after. And in any case they'd have everything when the wife smuggles me into heaven with her. Take another half of port, Johanna. Here's to the happy couple.'

Mrs Curtin helped herself to a good half-glass of port and smacked her lips.

'How like men ye are, to be sure,' she chided, as she put down her glass, 'to settle the poor girl for life and not so much as to ask her leave.'

'Of course she must be asked,' Curtin said hastily. 'Not a word about all this, Mike Duggan, except to Joe, till the little girl gives her consent.'

'I suppose it's all right?' Duggan scratched his head doubtfully. 'Will you tell her yourself, Tom Curtin, or must I go and see her? I'm shy-like with young females, and Miss

Kitty looks so very stand-off when I pass her by in the street. It would be easier for me if you'd tell her what we decided on.'

'Oh, no, no.' Tom Curtin gave a superior smile. 'We're living in new-fangled times, Mike. And young girls like to think they're having their own way. Joe must court her, just as if we had never agreed to anything. And when they've made it up between them, then we'll give them our blessing.'

'Isn't it dangerous to leave so much in a young girl's hands?' Duggan said, with a worried frown. 'You never know what maggot'd get into her head. Couldn't we just tell her it's all settled and let them do the courting after?'

'No, that wouldn't do at all,' Curtin said. 'It's a lady you'll be getting for a daughter-in-law, Mike Duggan,' he added pompously. 'They learn ways in them grand convents that are a bit different from what we were used to. Besides, I've passed my word that she'd have a free choice. Ask Joe in to have a cup of tea, Johanna, and throw them together now and again. Beyond a priest, once in a way, it's the first time a man'll have come inside their drawing-room. Kitty is sure to fall head-over-heels in love with Joe. He's a bit of a lady-killer, with all his grand business ideas. You'd better get Winnie out of the way, ma'am, or she'll be losing her vocation on the head of him,' he added jocosely.

'It's a queer fad to leave an important business like this hanging on the whim of a young girl,' Duggan said doubtfully, levering himself out of his chair.

'Oh, Kitty has her head screwed on all right. Too long her mother has kept her tied up. She'll be glad enough to jump the traces. But she's a sensible girl for all that and knows which side her bread is buttered. And I'll let her know, too, what I think of Joe. There's no fear but she'll make the right choice. Eh, Johanna?'

'God is sure to direct her to the best,' Mrs Curtin said as she shook Duggan's extended hand.

Chapter 3

As a child Johanna Curtin—then Johanna Mahoney—was pretty and vivacious, and a favourite pupil of the nuns who taught in the elementary school attached to the Drumbawn Mercy Convent. She could hardly have been called religious in any of the senses of that word of varied meaning; but she did everything that was necessary to gain and keep the favour of the nuns. Outside school hours the Muldoons, the Duggans, the Rafters and the Devines tried, as she said, 'to crow' over her. Their fathers were prosperous shopkeepers: her father was poor. If Helena Rafter got a new dress or a new hat, the Devine girls, the Duggans and the Muldoons appeared in new hats or new dresses within a week. When Johanna suggested a new hat to her father, Tim Mahoney growled that she ought to be thankful she wasn't in rags or in the workhouse, where her extravagance was driving him. She soon came to know that drink was driving him there.

Her mother died when she was ten, and things then grew worse at home. Sometimes there was a slatternly servant, often there was none. Meals were uncertain and a hot meal an event. Davie Joyce, the meek shop assistant, who had been a part of the shop as long as she could remember, left, and was succeeded by a grumpy elderly man who stayed a month. For a long time there was no assistant. She and the servant, when there was one, helped in the shop on market and fair days.

She saw her father in all the stages of maudlin intoxication except absolute collapse. Once when she mustered a frightened courage to remonstrate, he became furiously angry, cuffed her out of the shop and ordered her never to set foot in it again. Other assistants came and went. They remained in her memory as nice men who tried to keep her father from drink, or horrid men who drank with him; but nice or horrid he quarrelled with them all, and they invariably left after a month or two.

She had a miserable time, but there were compensations. In her hearing Josie Muldoon might snigger and ask Helena Rafter what shopkeeper in Drumbawn was his own best customer; and Helena might snigger and answer as often as she liked, 'a name that begins with an M and ends with a Y.' For wasn't Mahoney's shop, on the outside at least, far finer than the Muldoons and the Rafters? Wasn't it double-fronted with twenty-two shutters while theirs were single-fronted with only thirteen shutters between them? And if they went to the sea in the summer and had picnics and excursions, she beat them hands down at their lessons when they came back to school. They might make game of her dress in the street, but once they were inside the convent school they had to sing very small. They might look down on her outside, but there they had to look up to her. She got her green and red ribbons before them; and the coveted blue ribbon of a child of Mary a full year before Josie Muldoon, who was a year older. The convent was heaven. It was the only place in the whole world where one's merits were recognized. Nothing she did or didn't do pleased the Rafter girls or the Muldoons or the other snobs; but by industry and a guard over her tongue and temper, by being respectful and obedient, by piety, she won and kept the regard of the nuns. Josie Muldoon called her a voteen and a hypocrite, but that was only jealousy. And if she didn't like praying as much as the nuns thought she did, what harm did it do to anyone? She never did anything really wrong whether the nuns were looking or not, except to hate Helena Rafter and Josie Muldoon, and a saint out of heaven couldn't stand them. By dint of hard praying she always forgave them when she went to confession; but somehow or other a new feeling of hate sprang up again at the very first sight she caught of either of them.

At seventeen she had been three years in the sixth class and two years head of the school. Josie Muldoon was then a year married to Mike Duggan, the draper, a man old enough to be her father, and had just had a son. Helena Rafter was at a boarding school in Dublin. Tessy Devine was a novice, but, thank God, she hadn't dowry enough to be taken at Drumbawn, and had to enter a cheaper convent at Lisakelly. Johanna should have left the school a year before, but she hung on, hating to leave the scene of her many triumphs. The thought of spending the whole day and every day at home filled her with horror. She had no particular desire to be a nun. The acts of piety and obedience which had always brought her rewards every nun had to perform as a matter of course. Yet if she could only be a nun in Drumbawn, what a triumph it would be over the Devines with Tessy having to go to Lisakelly! She could even look down on Josie Duggan.

The nuns were sympathetic, but prudent. The manner necessary for Drumbawn convent could only be acquired at a high-class boarding school; and a vow of poverty was possible only when backed by a comfortable balance at the bank. Alas, Tim Mahoney was unable to pay his debts. He had neither money nor credit. And not even if he were smothered in piles of gold would he 'waste a penny of it on them bitches,' he declared angrily, when Johanna timidly opened the question. Johanna knew nuns who had no manner and nuns who had had no money, and still hoped. But one of the Superiors explained kindly but firmly, that a lack of manner was sometimes compensated for by an abundance of worldly goods which the convent could transmute into the greater glory of God; and money could, less often, be dispensed with for important family connections and high accomplishments. But the lack of both money and manner was an almost certain sign of the absence of a vocation to such a convent as Drumbawn. To make matters worse, there was the notorious Tim Mahoney to be lived down. This could be done, of course, through the grace of God, but not as Johanna was situated. God, however, was wonderfully merciful, and far-sighted, and had provided for such difficulties as Johanna's in the Little Sisters of the Poor and foreign missions. There vocations were tempered by the difficulty of getting postulants.

For a whole week Johanna stormed heaven by prayer for a vocation to one of these more lowly orders, but her heart remained unmoved. They were worse even than Lisakelly. After triumphing for ten years over Josie Muldoon, Helena Rafter, Tessy Devine and all them frights of big girls she should simply disappear. The mere thought of being hidden away in London or in some savage land while the other girls were shining in the full glare of Drumbawn publicity made her consider the thought of home. What if she could turn her father from the drink? With tears in her eyes she told Reverend Mother that she felt a call to work a mission on her father. And she could always be near at hand in case the effective signs of a vocation to Drumbawn Mercy Convent, with the help of God, materialized. The nuns were enthusiastic in their approval and promised their help in unremitting prayer.

Within a week she had got rid of the incompetent servant of the moment, who pilfered drink, and had secured the services of a decent widow who was glad to work for her food and a few shillings now and again for clothes. Johanna promised both with an assumed cheerfulness, but with secret misgivings. Her father never noticed the change of servants and swore at her when she asked money for food; but, by wheedling Durkan, the latest shop-assistant, she managed to provide regular, if meagre, meals.

When she had established order in the house, one morning, before anyone else was down, she stole into the shop with trembling limbs, bringing with her a Windsor chair from the kitchen. She seated herself in front of the battered desk in the curtained recess beside the snuggery from which there was a view of the whole shop. Narrow beams of light struggling through the shuttered windows gave a ghostly look to barrels and tins. Her courage was oozing away at her finger-tips, but she tightened her lips and kept back her tears with an effort. She took out her rosary beads and prayed fervently. The regular ticking of the shop clock first excited and then soothed her nerves. But she jumped in her seat when the clock gave a wheezy groan and began to strike seven. Durkan ought to be down to open the shop. She'd see to that. At a quarter-past seven she heard shuffling steps in the hall, much fumbling and the clinking of glass at the handle of the door leading into the shop. She turned in her seat and watched the door, fascinated. At last it was kicked open. Her father, unshaven, in shirt and trousers, came in laden with three or four empty soda-water bottles and an empty whiskey bottle. So that was why he was never quite sober, even in the mornings. She clutched her beads, prayed hard under her breath, and watched him kick the door to. He did not look at the desk, but made his way, coughing and spluttering, towards the whiskey counter. He got rid of the empty bottles under the counter, muttered in a hoarse whisper, that carried through the silent shop, 'I'm as dry as a limekiln,' stared at the row of barrels, sighed and murmured, 'Just one three fingers not a drop more. Not another drop to-day. Not till the night, anyway.' He opened a bottle of soda water, held a long tumbler under the tap of a whiskey barrel, filled it about a third, held the glass up to the feeble light, again put it under the tap and filled it halfway to the top. He added a dash of soda water and drank the mixture off in a series of gulps. He smacked his lips and said, 'That's better.' He recorked the soda-water bottle, but, on second thoughts, withdrew the cork and poured the liquid into the empty glass, added a long draught of whiskey and, leaning back against the counter, drank it leisurely. He drained the last sip from the glass, sighed and said, 'That's better. Now I'm feeling equal to the day.' He put away the empty bottle and glass carefully and shuffled back towards the door giving on the hall. Halfway he stood still and peered at the desk. His mottled face went pale in streaks. He stumbled back a pace or two, clutched his head with his hands and cried aloud in a frightened voice, 'My God, it's the jim-jams.'

'It's not. It's me, father,' Johanna said, rising, and clasping the back of the chair.

He stepped back another pace and stared at her wildly.

'It's me, Johanna,' she repeated.

'What? What? What the devil are you doing here?' he muttered feebly.

'I'm going to work in the shop from this out,' she said, gaining courage from his seeming weakness.

'The devil you are,' he muttered vaguely. 'The devil you are,' he shouted angrily, after a short pause, a hot flush mounting to his forehead. He sprang towards her with his fist raised.

'Be off to hell out of that this minute!' he said, waving his fist.

She trembled all over, but the rosary beads, which hurt her fingers as she clasped the chair, gave her courage. 'I will not,' she said, moistening her dry lips with her tongue.

'Take that, you bloody bitch,' he said thickly, jamming his fist in her eye. She stumbled backwards, but the chair helped her to keep on her feet.

'Are you going?' he asked fiercely, pointing to the door.

'I am not,' she answered, with blazing eyes.

He rushed at her again unsteadily, but she lifted the chair

by the back and the legs caught him in the shoulders. She gave a slight push. He stumbled against the counter and slid on to the floor, where he lay flat on his back.

For a few seconds she was afraid that she had hurt him, perhaps killed him. The chair fell from her hands, and she stared at him, wild-eyed.

He moved, clawed the floor with his hands and levered himself into a sitting posture. He burst into tears and whimpered in a maudlin voice: 'You devil, you. You devil out of hell. I'll never do a day's good again. You've broken every bone in my body.'

'The whiskey is beginning to tell on you. It's drunk you are. Get up out of that and up to your bed with you,' she said, with a show of more courage than she felt.

A look of fear overspread his face, and he muttered in a terrified tone: 'There's snakes climbing all over your face. They'll ate you alive. There they are now climbing along the air at me. Give me a drink. Just one drink for the love of God and His blessed saints. Save me, save me,' he shouted, struggling to his feet.

She did her best to hold him down, but he had succeeded in getting his hands tightly about her neck, when Durkan, hurried by the shouts, rushed into the shop and released her.

'What's on him at all?' she asked helplessly, as her father again began to weep.

'Keep them off me. Keep them off me. Don't you see them rushing at me like a cloud of gulls?' Mahoney shouted wildly, beating back the air with both hands.

'It's only the DTs. He had a touch of 'em once before,' Durkan said lightly.

The fortnight her father had to stay in bed gave her an assured position in the shop. Durkan tried to make fun of her, and failing in that, tried to make love. The consciousness of a disfiguring black eye gave strength to her open hand.

She helped him to sense and prevented the loss of overmuch of the blood that streamed from his nose by slipping the big shop-door key down his back.

On her father's return to the shop he accepted her as the inhabitants of a defeated country accept an enemy army in occupation. She opened the shop every morning, shut it at night, and kept the keys, but she had at times to relax her vigilance with inevitable betrayal. Durkan was cowed, but unfaithful. He drank himself and helped her father to drink the moment her back was turned. She could have got rid of him, but she was afraid to face a possibly worse man.

For five years her life was a constant struggle. There were rows and defeats and set-backs. Each new day concealed a disappointment or some lurking terror. But each year saw an advance. Trade recovered and the fear of bankruptcy disappeared. The mountain of debt gradually grew less and less. Travellers trusted her; customers liked her. Business men would have laughed at her books, at her elaborate system of checks and safeguards, but they worked. She took no hours off and no holidays. Most of her meals were taken in the snuggery, often with both eyes on the shop. Her only relaxations were her rosary beads three times a day, Mass on Sunday mornings, and a visit to the convent on Sunday afternoons. To these she attributed all her success. Some day she would pay God back for all He was doing for her, by entering the convent.

Meanwhile, she had her small triumphs. Mahoney's became known as Johanna Mahoney's. A good-for-nothing brother of Josie Muldoon asked her to marry him; and the thrill of refusing him was the greatest pleasure she had experienced since she became a child of Mary. When she was able at last to buy decent clothes, she decided to give up going to early Mass on Sundays and hiding herself away in a side aisle. For the first time in her life she entered Duggan's shop next door and ordered the best of everything. It somewhat marred her joy that Josie wasn't in the shop, but she consoled herself by the thought that Josie was sure to hear of her purchases. But, in any case, she'd see the result at the last Mass on Sunday. Hat, boots, gloves, umbrella, were worthy of the dress and dolman; and she'd say that much for Duggan's, much as she disliked Josie, the dress and dolman were worthy of the great reputation Mike had for sound stuff.

Five of the old sixth class she counted out of the corners of her demurely cast-down eyes as she walked up by the centre of the nave to one of the front seats of the parish church, two minutes after the clock had ceased striking twelve on Sunday morning. Surprise, envy, blank amazement she noted all their expressions with a swelling heart.

For the first time for several years she was unable to improve the minds of Durkan and her father at the Sunday dinner by a recapitulation of the sermon. Had there been a sermon at all? She couldn't remember. Her father fumed at her extravagance. She grudged him a glass, and there she was wearing a decent man's drink for a twelvemonth on her back! Durkan was so much impressed that in the afternoon he mustered up courage to propose marriage. She explained to him the method by which she could now detect the surreptitious consumption, from stock, of even one glass of whiskey. More in sorrow than in anger, he gave notice. Outwardly calm, but with a sinking heart, she accepted it, but omitted for the first time in five years her Sunday visit to the convent. Happily for her comfort, a whiskey traveller, early on Monday morning, recommended her a new man; and on Wednesday Durkan had gone and Thomas Curtin had taken his place.

From the first she was a little afraid of him. He was handsome, but a little stern. He had a grand accent when he liked to put it on. He didn't drink, and he knew his business.

For the second time she missed her visit to the convent on the following Sunday. She and Curtin went over the books together instead, and he explained to her the defects in her methods of book-keeping and stocktaking. Next day he opened the shop and shut it, and insisted that she should go for a walk in the slack hour. She gave him the key of the desk. He was a most knowledgeable man and understood about her father without being told. The next Sunday she never even thought of the convent and spent the afternoon boating with Curtin on the river. They talked of the business, and he told her that he had a couple of hundred pounds laid by.

Often, when she was supposed to be making up the books, she found herself watching and admiring his manner with the customers. She sometimes thought uneasily of her vocation, but never on Sunday afternoons, which were now given up to improving conversation with Mr Curtin. Even on busy weekdays she consulted him in her simplest difficulties. By his advice she put her father on a strict ration of two glasses of whiskey a day; and when the old man tried to increase it by stealing a bottle of whiskey from the shop, Curtin took it from him firmly, but respectfully, in the hall. Tim Mahoney foamed with anger. He began by calling his daughter and Curtin unmentionable names, but ended by offering to make over the shop to them if they'd marry and make him an allowance.

'Would that suit you, Miss Mahoney?' Curtin asked, in his most dignified accent.

'It would, Mr Curtin,' she replied timidly.

Three days afterwards they were married in the early morning, with no witnesses except the clerk of the church and Johanna's servant, opened the shop an hour later and worked as usual. Johanna would have liked to make a splash, but she felt that the opportunity had not yet come. A shop-boy, in the eyes of Drumbawn, was no great things of a match. But one day she'd show to the whole world that she hadn't made a mistake.

Then began a year of happiness. She saw the last debt paid without touching Tom's money. His praise that it was all her own doing, that another woman in Drumbawn, or in all Ireland either, couldn't hold a candle to her, was the sweetest music she had ever listened to. He had his faults who hadn't? He had a liking for his own way; and maybe, at times, was firmer than he might have been, but having domineered for five years over men she despised, she loved him all the more for his masterfulness. The business advanced by leaps and bounds; and when she was forced to remain out of the shop in expectation of her child, an assistant was engaged.

She suffered agonies in childbirth. In moments of relief she felt that God was angry with her. Perhaps she was too happy for this world? And was she unfaithful to God in not having become a nun? If He'd forgive her now, she'd make it up to Him. If she had a son she'd make a priest of him. And if it was a daughter, she'd make a nun of her. If He'd only spare her and the child, all the children she'd ever have'd be given to God.

When Winnie was born both the agony and the promise were forgotten. God smiled on her in every way. The child was the prettiest child that ever drew breath. The business was so flourishing that a second assistant had to be engaged. There was no cloud in her life but her father, who still occasionally gave trouble. He was particularly troublesome just as she was expecting the birth of her second child. In a moment of anger she prayed that God would relieve her of him by taking him to Himself; but was very much upset when God appeared to take her at her word. She went straight from his peaceful death-bed to her labour in an agony of fear. If God would only forgive her she'd bring both the children up in the ways of God from the very moment the second one'd see the light. She sent for Tom and clutched his hands, her eyes wild with terror, sweat oozing from her face and down her dank hair. She begged him to vow Winnie and the coming child to God. He soothed her and told her there was no fear of her. The doctor had told him out on the stairs that she was doing beautifully.

'You'll vow them to God, Tom?' she repeated fiercely.

'I'd do anything in life for you, Johanna, but I don't think it's fair like to do that,' he said, with a stare at the wall paper. For the moment he was not thinking of her, but of the son who was to inherit the big business he and Johanna were about to build up.

'God might take me if you don't,' she shrieked, again in the lock of pain.

He was deeply moved and hesitated. God didn't do things that way. But still, one never knew. It was horrible to see her in such pain. Still, women were like that, and the doctor had sworn that she was doing fine.

'Sorra bit of Him,' he said soothingly; 'you'll be as right as a trivet in a whileen.'

She gave him a look that frightened him, a blend of pain and hatred. In so far as she could think of anything at that moment except her own suffering, she hated him.

'You be off now.' The doctor came to the bedside, and pushed him aside.

'Is there any fear of her?' Curtin asked doubtfully. He had no intention of giving in to her whim. A promise was a promise, but there might be some way, if he could only collect his scattered wits, of easing her mind.

'None whatever. Be off. You're disturbing her, standing there.'

Johanna's hatred was transferred instantaneously to the doctor. Tom'd given in—she saw it in his eyes—if the doctor hadn't driven him from the room. Them doctors had no religion. But God saw into the heart and didn't need the spoken word. He'd take Tom's unspoken intention for the deed and she'd be all right.

Her confinement was a difficult one. Even the doctor admitted it when she was convalescent. 'There was a moment when I was sure the child was gone, and when you ran a poor chance yourself. But I did the trick,' he said complacently.

She pressed Kitty to her breast and smiled mysteriously. Doctors thought a great deal of themselves, but what fools they were! 'Twas God did it all. And He did it for her because of her promise. And she'd never forget it for Him. Now that the danger was past Tom was forgetting that he was on the verge of promising, too—had as good as done it. He was that disappointed at not having a son that she wouldn't worry him now; but with God's help she'd work him to do the will of God some day or other. He'd be easily led if only one day she'd give him a son. The doctor said she could never have a child again. But then doctors didn't know everything, and knew nothing at all of the ways of God.

Johanna dismissed the nurse she had for Winnie and got a real holy girl that the nuns recommended. When her month was up she again began her Sunday afternoon visits to the convent, always taking the children with her. She confided her plans to Reverend Mother, who was only moderately encouraging. No doubt God would help her faith, but one could never be sure of those things. One might lead a horse to water, but it was the horse who had to drink. Still, there was a great deal in the leading, and if it was done continuously the horse was pretty sure to drink some time. But Sister Eulalie, who had been Johanna's special friend among the novices as a girl, was enthusiastic. She saw the hand of God in everything, in Johanna's marvellous recovery, in the success of the shop, with its promise of fitting dowries for the girls. Johanna should have been a nun herself, but the girls would more than make up for her lapse into marriage. It was hardly even a lapse if God so clearly intended to use it for His purpose. Sister Eulalie saw vocations in the children's eyes already. Little Kitty never cried when she fondled her. And Winnie played with a veil and guimpe as if she loved them. And they were both as good as gold when she took them into the chapel. The great thing was to keep them apart from worldly children and to surround them with religious emblems.

When Kitty was three and Winnie four and a half, Sister Eulalie was in charge of the infant school. It wasn't as select as it might be, she explained to Johanna; but, unless a governess was possible, something of the kind might suit the children for a start. A governess, of course, was the thing for children marked out for such a high destiny, but if that wasn't feasible, she'd do her best to keep them select. Johanna was very much taken with the idea of a governess. The shop would run to it; and it would be such a slap in the face to the Rafters and the Duggans and the Muldoons and the rest of them. The children already had the best clothes of any children in the town, and a pram, the same as was made for the queen's own granddaughter, the traveller said; and a nurse that was a real nurse; anyway, she had nothing else to do except to mind the children, and wasn't just the hired girl taking a turn at driving the pram, which was all Josie Duggan ever had in spite of all her attempts at grandeur. Still, the stuck-up pieces who once looked down on her had clothes and prams for their children, and nurses, even if they were only of a sort. But a governess! Except for Lawyer Finnegan, and the Resident Magistrate, and a few of the like, the thing was unknown in the town of Drumbrawn. As for a shopkeeper having one, it never happened within the memory of man. Thomas Curtin and Co. was already taking its place in the town, but a governess'd put to the keystone to the arch.

Tom liked the idea, too, when she proposed it to him. He was no longer known in Drumbawn as 'that shop-boy, Curtin, that Johanna Mahoney married,' but as 'Mr Curtin.' He wore his grand accent more often than when Johanna first knew him, and cultivated a manner in harmony with it and his neatly trimmed beard. 'They looked down on us once,' he often said pompously, 'but one day they'll be craning their necks to look up at us, and it won't do them any good for we'll keep ourselves to ourselves. Except Mike Duggan there isn't one of 'em I'd be bothered bidding the time of day to.' 'Him! with that streel of a wife,' Johanna would say contemptuously. And Tom would say with a smile that only half escaped through his beard, 'Oh, the wife. Well, she's no great things.' They talked over the governess often and earnestly. They even papered a bedroom for her. But when Sister Eulalie had at last heard of one who had, as it were, stepped straight out of heaven, she was so suitable, Johanna showed signs of doubt, and Tom hummed and hawed. 'To tell you God's truth, Johanna,' he said, dropping his dignity, 'I'd never have a minute's ease with a woman talking French and the like hanging round the house. Sister Eulalie must teach the children anything in the way of trimmings that's within her reach, and the minute they're fit for it we can send 'em to the best boarding school that money can pay for.' Johanna sighed with relief and admitted that a great fear of the woman was beginning to gnaw at her own heart.

With rather complex feelings Johanna saw the children start for school every morning. In her mind they never had an independent existence. They were a part of herself. The complement of her own purposes and ambitions. They were a weapon of offence against Josie Duggan, who had no daughters, against Helena Rafter, now Helena Dowd, who, despite her grand boarding-school education married Jamesy

Dowd, the rate collector, and could ill afford to overdress her string of plain children. Winnie and Kitty, their burnished pram, and Peggy Delaney their nurse, were a daily triumph over the mothers who had looked down on Johanna in her youth. Sister Eulalie continued the triumph in school. Peggy Delaney had strict instructions that the children were not to be allowed to speak to other children on their way to school; and at school Sister Eulalie saw that they were kept apart from the common herd. They sat at the same little desk, did all their lessons side by side; and Peggy Delaney was always waiting in the hall to pounce on them at playtime and when school was over.

When Johanna had these thoughts of pride and vanity too often, or too long, she put them away and convinced herself that all her care was for the safeguarding of the children's vocation. For it was as a sort of extension of her own soul that Johanna chiefly regarded her daughters. They were that part of herself which she had offered to God in atonement for certain of her own vaguely explored defects. They were akin to her daily attendance at Mass, her visits to the Blessed Sacrament and Our Lady of Good Counsel. And, when she saw them off from the door every morning, though she hoped that Josie Duggan and Helena Dowd would see them and envy her, what most profoundly moved her was the thought of the spiritual gift of herself she was making to God.

When Winnie was nine and a half and Kitty eight, Sister Eulalie wrote a note asking Johanna to call on her on the afternoon of Reverend Mother's feast without the children. Johanna was very much disturbed. What in the world could Sister Eulalie want to take her away from the shop on a market day for? And Reverend Mother's feast, too, when Sister Eulalie herself and all the nuns were up to their eyes. Sister Eulalie met her at the gate and led her to a seat in a remote part of the grounds, under the shade of a walnut tree.

'It is here I make all my great spiritual decisions,' the nun said impressively, as they sat down.

'My heart is going this way and that. A market day and Reverend Mother's feast and all ! What in the world is it, dear Sister?' Johanna asked eagerly.

'We can't give important things too much significance. It's the children,' Sister Eulalie said, with a mysterious sweep of her veil.

'To be sure it is. And it isn't Winnie—that I go bail. What has Kitty been up to, the little limb—may God forgive me for saying the like of one of His own chosen.'

'She will talk to Johnny Dowd. I found her sucking a bull's-eye that he gave her yesterday' Sister Eulalie said severely.

'What are we to do at all, at all?' Johanna was deeply distressed. 'There's no fear of her, do you think, Sister?'

'Not from him,' Sister Eulalie said. 'He was packed off to the boy's school this morning. But Kitty is a difficult child and needs guarding. She spoke to Sarah Higgins last week,' she added, pursing her lips.

'Them Higginses!' Johanna lifted her eyes despairingly to the dappled leaves.

'It must be a boarding school at once,' Sister Eulalie said firm but regretful.

'The sooner the better it seems to me.' Johanna's tone conveyed liking and respect for Sister Eulalie, yet a shade of resentment for her carelessness.

Sister Eulalie understood, and her extraordinarily youthful and pretty pink-and-white face flushed a little.

'In a way it was my fault keeping them so long in the infant school,' she admitted meekly. 'It was dearest Winnie, you know,' she added, in a defensive voice. 'She's so engrossed with the things of God that her mind wanders from secular subjects. To say the least of it, she was slow with her reading and writing. And as for her tables and sums—' She shook her head. 'I've kept Kitty back as much as I could. But they'd both be better now in a school where they could mix freely with other children. Apart from external difficulties, they are thrown too much together in class, and dearest Winnie sometimes feels hurt at Kitty's superiority.'

'I wish she was half as biddable as Winnie. It's the heart that God looks to and not the wits,' Johanna said.

'God gathers both brain and heart into His net.' Sister Eulalie gave a self-satisfied smile. 'Kitty is all right—a little childish ebullience, perhaps. The lives of the saints are full of records of children's wilfulness. It's the direction of the spirit into the proper channel that matters. I'd advise St Margaret's.'

'They're not too swell entirely there?' Johanna asked complacently, putting up a ninepin that it might be knocked down.

'Nuns are always the servants of the servants of God,' Sister Eulalie said primly. 'At St Margaret's they train for the world it is true. But their chief desire is to train for God. They are the most fruitful moulders of hearts I know of. I was there myself.'

'And a good warrant you are for them, I'm sure,' Johanna said. 'I often say to Tom there isn't in this world a better guide to God than Sister Eulalie. You're sure there's no fear of Kitty getting a drift for the world with all the high-up girls she'll be coming across?' she added uneasily.

Sister Eulalie smiled reassuringly. 'I will tell dear Mother O'Neill your intention for the girls. She will take them as a sacred trust and will watch and pray. I've no fear at all of Winnie. Kitty has a wayward spirit and inclines to the lower life. But not radically, I'm convinced. She couldn't with all our prayers. But there are a few small points I must mention. You won't mind my being quite open with you, Johanna?'

'My skin is fairly thick by this with all I went through,' Johanna said proudly.

'Darling Johanna,' Sister Eulalie said, feelingly pressing her hand. 'High and low, rich and poor, are all equal in the sight of God and His holy nuns,' she confided. 'They make no distinctions of class. But in deference to the prejudices of some worldly parents they have to take up a certain attitude in regard to the class of pupils they take. This is especially true of St Margaret's, where they confine themselves solely to the gentry. The retail trade is unknown there.'

'We're starting a little in the wholesaling line,' Johanna said, with a shrewd questioning look. She wasn't much disturbed, as experience had taught her that there was always, in religion, a way round seemingly insuperable difficulties.

'Not enough.' Sister Eulalie shook her head emphatically. 'A brewer or a distiller or a big wholesale house in Dublin, with the owners living, say in Rathgar, is, of course, different. But a mixed wholesale and retail in a country town—and living over the shop, too! It's unheard of.'

'They're nice ladylike little girls and Tom Curtin is growing to be a warm man,' Johanna said, with spirit.

'They are; though their accents still need a little pruning. And I impressed on Mother O'Neill that they were in a position to take all the extras—I saw her when I went to Dublin last week with Reverend Mother about her teeth.'

'I hear the new set is real beautiful,' Johanna said, biting eagerly at such a delicious morsel of gossip.

'The subject is never mentioned.' Sister Eulalie gave a slight frown.

'It'd be quite easy, too, to pretend that the shop wasn't there.' Johanna's retaliatory laugh had in it a shade of malice.

'Oh, no, no. No pretence, Johanna. That would be sinful. In view of all the special circumstances, however, Mother O'Neill thought the rules of the convent could be relaxed if the shop were never mentioned,' Sister Eulalie said hastily. 'They needn't be ashamed of the shop or anything like that—just silence and a discreet tongue, with now and again, perhaps, a little mental reservation. I'll give them a little warning and instruct them carefully on what is allowable. Though I think in any case they'd respond to the atmosphere of gentility which will surround them.'

'It'd be no bad thing in a way if they were ashamed of the shop,' said Johanna thoughtfully.

Sister Eulalie smiled with all the shrewdness of which her childlike face was capable. 'It would turn them towards the convent,' she said artlessly. 'I thought of that in choosing St Margaret's for them. I wouldn't try to make them ashamed exactly—it wouldn't be quite religious. But by encouraging gentility in them in every way the result would be the same. Perhaps for a year or two they might even spend all their vacations at the convent. At their age the atmosphere would then sink thoroughly into their natures. Mr Curtin?' she added doubtfully.

'He's as anxious as myself to put the girls above them other riff-raff of the town. But he wouldn't have a word said agin the shop on any account. But yourself and myself can manage it all, Sister agra. There's the bell and you must be going, I suppose. I leave everything in your hands. As for Tom, leave it to me to get round him.'

The children went to St Margaret's and stayed there for ten years. Winnie got all the good conduct prizes, never mentioned the shop, but was secretly proud of the source of the postal orders that enabled her to give superior presents to the nuns on their feast days. Kitty told everyone about the shop, defended it and hated it.

They were ten years of pride for Johanna, not unmixed, however, with fear. She saw Winnie and Kitty grow into perfect ladies. No daughter of her generation of Muldoons,

Devines or Rafters, no matter what her name or station, could even pretend to the gentility of her daughters. Their gentility, indeed, oppressed her a little at times, especially Winnie's, who was zealous for converts even in manners.

Johanna made efforts to manage her cup, to eat, to sit, to enter a room, after the rule of St Margaret's; but she tried to escape the penance of eating with her daughters as often as possible; and made an offering to God of her sufferings on Sundays when no excuse could be found for eating alone. Kitty was more sensible about 'them pernickety things' and met her mother's apologies for lapses by advising her to be natural.

Johanna shepherded her daughters to daily Mass, walking behind them so that Winnie could not afterwards criticize her. But her keenest pleasures were the walk to and from twelve o'clock Mass on Sundays and the Sunday afternoon walk with Tom and the children in their best Sunday clothes. The solid prosperity of Curtin and Co. was manifest in herself and Tom, while the children demonstrated its grace and refinement. Those walks, too, were useful lessons for the children in filial respect. The cordial greetings of the priests, the gracious salutes of Lawyer Finnegan, of the bank manager, of the more important shopkeepers, ought to show Winnie and Kitty what a high position their father occupied in the town. And all this though he never condescended to politics beyond subscribing liberally, had refused to go on the Town Board or Board of Guardians and had never been on a race committee in his life.

Johanna always cried when she saw the children into the train on their way back to school after the holidays, but she invariably walked back to the shop with a brisk step and a pleasant feeling of relief. She could now walk into the parlour at her ease and sit as she liked, admire their beautiful paintings and dream of their future. Not that dreaming was much in her way. The counter with its gossip, its respectful but pleasant badinage, had become more and more her life. But always hovering in the background was her relation with God. Behind the shop, in the prosperity of which she rejoiced and expanded, was God from whom all its prosperity sprang and on whom it rested. And the children were the connecting-link between God and the business. In moments of weakness she was tempted to think that the success of the shop was due to the hard work and good management of herself and Tom, but she at once repented these base thoughts and asked God's pardon. God was faithful to her because of her promises about the children. She must be faithful to God else some ill-luck would happen to her. She was the least morbid of women and had no nervous fears or fancies. But she honestly accepted this view of the Divine government of the world and worked for her salvation with the same assiduity which she gave to her daily work in the shop.

On the whole her spiritual projects were shaping fairly well. Kitty was silent and secretive at home, though the nuns said she was the most popular girl in the school. Johanna longed to know at times what Kitty was thinking of, but was, on the whole, half glad, from some remote fear, that the girl was uncommunicative. It might be only the girl's dissatisfaction with the shop and her surroundings. That was all to the good. It might be other things but there, God would look after His own. It was thus she thought of sex. It had troubled herself very little, and that little she had almost forgotten. It was something not to be spoken of, not to be acknowledged, to be put entirely out of one's thoughts, to be prayed against, to be overcome. It was a temptation of the devil, and all temptations of the devil, sooner or later, yielded to prayer. Young girls had to be careful of men, of course. They were the form in which the devil mostly tempted them. But Johanna had nothing to reproach herself with in this respect. She had kept the girls entirely apart from men except a few harmless priests. Some priests were gay enough and needed a strict eye as well as another; but she flattered herself on her judgment, and was sure that no wolf had entered her fold. If Kitty was a little sullen-like it was just the way of young girls to kick against the snaffle. Johanna herself hadn't been obedient to her father, but then her father hadn't been a good father to her. And to give Kitty her due, she was obedient; and so well she might with the good mother she was to her.

The year the girls had spent at home, when their education was finished, was a trial to Johanna. Winnie was a nuisance with her crotchety whimsies, her manners, and her sulks at not being allowed to enter the convent at once. And Kitty had suddenly developed a stubborn temper. She was pleasant enough, but she was as obstinate as a mule. She would take no hints about the convent; and flatly denied that she had the intense desire to be a nun, with which Sister Eulalie, several times a week, credited her. Johanna meditated putting down her foot and ordering her into the convent, but Sister Eulalie advised against it. As the advice coincided with Johanna's own judgment she agreed to try more and still more prayers and masses. She'd put her through the mission at Carrickdhu; and get a score of masses said for her by Father Eusapius, the holy Carmelite of Kensington, who had more vocations to his credit than any other priest in the world. Then, one could never tell how Kitty would take an order of the kind. And if she refused?

When Tom threw at her head his bomb of marriage for Kitty, Johanna soon recovered from the shock. By the time she had completed the round of her beads, with which she prepared for bed, she had fully made up her mind that Tom was an instrument of Providence. What a dozen missions couldn't do, nor hundreds of masses, and thousands and thousands of prayers, Tom and his laddy-da of a Duggan might do between them. If Kitty had a leaning that way—Johanna asked God's forgiveness for even thinking it—the best way to cure her of men was to give her the offer of one that was sure to sicken her.

She put out the light and listened to Tom's snoring. Her mind wandered back over the past. She had done her duty by the girls from the day they were born; and she'd go on doing it to the end. In the convent they'd realize all their mother had done for them. And God would continue to smile on her. She pictured a long and peaceful life, with quiet in the house after Winnie was gone; Tom by her side she hoped all through, and, in any case, for a long time to come; with the faithful Peggy Delaney, who from being the best nurse in the world, had become the best cook and general servant. And she'd enjoy the girls more visiting them in the convent than having the bother of them in the house with all their uppish ways.

Chapter 4

The drawing-room was saturated with heat. The shining surfaces of the mahogany furniture and the blue of the upholstery gave a deceptive appearance of coolness; but the smudgy copy of Millais' 'Bubbles' seemed hot and oily and uncomfortable, and 'Carnation Lily Rose' gave the effect of grease paint under a high temperature. Flies droned lazily as if the moisture in the air weighted their wings. Even Winnie had given up struggling with the overture to *Il Trovatore* and sat, gasping for breath, by one of the shaded windows, open at the top. The high collar of her cool, blue tussore dress was a little limp. Moisture like tiny dewdrops glistened on her narrow forehead, near the roots of her tired hair, in the hollows of her pretty nose, and in little dissatisfied lines at the corners of her mouth and eyes. Her fingers twitched spasmodically. Her face was slightly flushed—more deeply where the soft cheeks rounded the graceful curves of her jaws. Her bright eyes gleamed.

'Five people passed in half an hour,' she spat resentfully at Kitty, who sat, facing her, beside the window near the door.

'Only three,' Kitty said listlessly. 'Two were the same people coming back.'

'Oh,' Winnie said peevishly.

She drummed her fingers on the arms of her chair on which she sat as if about to spring from it. She examined Kitty critically, with quick, nervous darts of her eyes, sighed enviously, jumped up and dabbed her face with her handkerchief, in front of a mirror, the lower end of which was a lake where swans disported themselves among water-lilies and cool green wild irises.

'I don't think I ever painted anything better than that,' she said, distracted for a moment from the demands of her complexion.

'Than what?' Kitty said mechanically, continuing to gaze at the street.

'My swans, dear.'

'It used to be a nice old glass,' Kitty said, with a yawn.

'I don't know what you mean, I'm sure,' Winnie said, firing up.

'You old dear.' Kitty looked at her with a lazy smile. 'It's just a nasty, hot, crotchety old day.'

'It's easy for you that can look so cool no matter what heat there is,' Winnie said, half angrily, half appeased.

'I haven't your delicate skin,' Kitty said, with the faintest shrug of her shoulder, looking again at the street, up which a cart was now lumbering.

Winnie smiled, looked at the glass, arranged her hair, tried one or two changes of expression, smiling the while, half turned so as to get a view of the line of her neck and shoulders.

'You'd be surprised what a difference it makes to the fall of the veil,' she said complacently.

'What?'

'The set of the head, neck and shoulders, stupid. I tried everything on one day. Sister Eulalie let me. I was simply perfect behind, or in a side view from the back.'

She sighed, went back thoughtfully to the seat and stared out of the window with a worried frown.

'I accept myself as God made me, and I'm not in the least bit jealous,' she jerked out at a dog, who was nosing dirty garbage on the opposite side of the street.

'What on earth are you talking about?' Kitty, tired of watching the dog, said, looking up with a slight show of interest

'It's the front view or the straight side view. I'm just ordinary there,' Winnie said dolefully. 'My hair helps me out in the postulant's cap—the sun catches it so. Really pretty, with a distinction all my own, Sister Eulalie said. But that will be only for six months. And with my hair hidden under the white veil I'll be just pretty and no more.'

'I sometimes wonder whether you ought to.' Kitty looked thoughtfully at Winnie's worried face. 'I don't think you want to one bit. You're so proud of your hair, too.'

'I'm not. I'm not. It's horrid of you, Kitty,' Winnie said angrily. 'I care for it as a gift of God, but I'm quite ready to hand it back to Him the moment He asks for it. And I do want to go more than anything in the world—more than my life,' she added excitedly.

'I'll have Father Burke all to myself when you go. I'll light his cigarette for him and he'll stroke my hair and my fingers,' Kitty said, with malice.

Winnie glared at her furiously and mumbled incoherent words, as if she were choking.

'You beast—you horrid beast,' she said shrilly, in a wild burst of sobbing.

'Oh, don't be a little fool.' Kitty gave a wondering look at the disturbed face. 'I was only joking. He's a slimy beast and I wouldn't let him touch me. If you go I'll never see him.'

A smile struggled with anger on Winnie's tear-stained face. She wept more quietly, dried her eyes after a while and said ingratiatingly: 'I know you don't mean the horrid things you say. Though I'd rather you'd mean them itself than that you'd take him from me. You'd never understand his beautiful soul. And what's harmless for me might be a danger to you. Of course, he never means anything but the greatest holiness. But it's different with girls who haven't all the safeguards of a holy priest. Nuns have them, too, of course. But while we're in the world we must be on our guard. Even holding hands is a danger unless one has schooled oneself against the world, the flesh and the devil. I consulted my confessor and he said I'm quite safe.'

'But Father Burke is your confessor,' Kitty said, with a smile.

'Of course he is,' Winnie said serenely. 'You miss a lot by not going to him. He's simply beautiful. I wouldn't mind your going to him in the least. For, of course, he's the same as God Himself in the confessional and never pretends to know you. He's more spiritual than any spiritual book. I'm not sure that he'd allow you to hold hands or things like that. That's a privilege of special souls. In fact, I think, dear, it would be safer for you not to. I don't think it's spiritual pride or anything; but I really do believe that *I* could live in the world and not be of it. But *you*, no. You need the protection of the convent. Good looks are a snare to oneself as well as to others,' she said sententiously, with a judicial nod of her little bird-like head.

'Have they snared Father Burke?' Kitty said jeeringly.

'I think you're horrid to him,' said Winnie. 'I don't want you to be too nice to him, of course,' she added hastily. 'He must always be my friend. But there is a just mean, as Sister Eulalie often says. It hurts me when you snub him. You might show an interest in him as my sister, you know—hand him his second cup of tea, and praise his sermons and things like that. He'd like you a little, in spite of your standoff ways, if you only gave him the chance.'

Kitty smiled down at the long slender fingers resting idly in her lap and moved them, one after another, as if admiring the trim pink nails.

'The whole world knows you have beautiful hands,' Winnie said pettishly.

'You'll miss him when you go to the convent,' said Kitty, her eyes still fixed on the firm white hand which she slowly turned back and front.

Winnie frowned. 'I did think of that,' she said, with a glazed stare at the window. 'Indeed, I cried my eyes out often in bed. I never told you, dear, for it was a sorrow I couldn't share with anyone. He was beautiful about it,' she added, in a thrilled tone, turning ecstatic eyes towards Kitty. 'What was it he said? I mustn't miss a word of it, it was so holy and original. "Sorrow is the crown of sacrifice," he said. "And sorrow's crown of sorrow is remembering happier things." I'll never forget that much of it. There was a lot more, but I can't remember the exact words. It all happened when I was giving him a list of all the sacrifices I was prepared to make for God in proof of my vocation. There was our happy home and all its comforts with as many kinds of cakes as we liked for tea, and the pleasant walks with papa and mama on Sunday afternoons, and our duets, and morning mass, and our little visits, and my painting and the view of the gaiety of the street from our windows here on market and fair days; and the boating, but I couldn't make much of that as I felt bound to tell him I was always afraid in a boat. I didn't mention parting from you, not that it wouldn't hurt me awfully, darlingest, but because it would show a want of faith in prayer. I *know* you'll come with me, so there won't be a parting. He made light of many of my sacrifices. There would be cake in the convent on feast days; and what with all the nuns and novices there would be so many feast days that I'd never feel the want of it, especially as I seldom eat cake for fear of getting fat. Mass and visits and painting and music I'd have in the convent. The happy home he admitted counted for a good deal. Indeed he painted it so beautifully that I began to feel that I was giving up something real. But you should hear him on the convent as a happy home! When he had done with that I felt I was giving up nothing at all. But all the time there was the sacrifice I hadn't mentioned and that I didn't intend to mention but which I was forced to unless I was to appear naked before God without any offering at all. I never knew how great a sacrifice it was until I tried to tell it as openly as I could. He was ever so tactful and nice about it all. Not a word was said about names, but of course he understood it could be no-one but himself. He admitted it was a real sacrifice. And it was then that he became inspired. No missioner I ever heard was equal to him. I was so much moved and carried away to the seventh heaven that I can't rightly remember. But, anyhow, the memory of him sitting there in the arm-chair with his feet on the foot-stool, holding my hand, smoking the cigarette I had lighted for him and talking brilliantly, would remain with me through life as an exquisite sorrow by means of which, in the end, I'd mount to perfect happiness before the throne of God.'

'He wanted you to go then?' Kitty jerked out, with a tightening of her lips.

'He as much as admitted that it was the hardest task he ever had to do,' Winnie said, with glowing eyes. 'That it was not only the girl who was going into the convent in such cases that made a sacrifice. Other people, even priests, had feelings too. He felt bound not only not to stand in my way, but to urge me to go. Sacrifice, as he beautifully put it, was the law of the life of the soul,' she ended, with a sob.

'Ah,' Kitty said harshly, through her teeth.

'I ought to have felt happy, but somehow I didn't,' Winnie began again, wiping her eyes. 'And in my despair, I mentioned leaving you. I half promised mother to stay till you got your vocation—'

'It's on its way from a wholesaler, I suppose,' Kitty said, with a sneer.

But Winnie was too much and too miserably interested in her story to allow herself to be interrupted.

'So that we could enter on the one day,' she continued. 'But he didn't make much of it. In fact, he thought I'd pray better for you in the convent.'

'So that's that,' Kitty said, making an attempt at a cat's cradle with the fingers.

'At last I agreed to go in on the eve of the Assumption,' Winnie said, with another breakdown.

'Poor old Winnie,' Kitty sympathised. She moved towards Winnie's chair, and, sitting down on the arm, drew Winnie's head to her breast, murmuring under her breath 'the crooked beast.'

'I'm awfully sorry you're going, dear,' she said aloud, fondling the shining hair.

'I'm sorry, too. That is, I'm glad. Of course I'm glad,' Winnie said brokenly, between sobs. 'I don't know what's come over me. Of course I always wanted to go. And everybody wants me to go. Everybody but you. And you don't know what you want. God has spoken to me over and over again, and I know. And I know what's good for you, too, if you'd only listen to me. Oh, Kitty, darling, come with me.'

'Poor old Winnie,' Kitty said, with set teeth.

'I haven't told mother yet. I won't until the last minute. I can't bear talking about it except to you—and to him, and Sister Eulalie. I told her. I went straight up to her last night after it was all settled and had a good cry. She was beautiful—full of consolation. So was Father Burke himself for that matter,' Winnie said, smiling through her tears. 'It isn't as if I had to give him up altogether,' she went on happily. 'It won't be the same, of course, as having him here all to oneself, giving him his favourite cakes and cigarettes and everything. But he'll manage somehow to see me every day. Sister Eulalie was as kind as kind could be. She *understands*. She told me her own story. *He* was a Dominican—a real saint. He died. And the human side of her heart is like a stone since—for herself. She never even once had the slightest inclination to a real 'particular' since he went to God. But she has sympathy—oh, so much—for others. She's sacristan now, you know, and she'll take me on as her assistant from the very first. It's an unusual privilege for a 'cap'—no-one less than a white veil ever had the duty before. But she *feels*. It will be such a happiness to prepare his vestments and his chalice. And I can give him the best chalice and the best vestments as often as I like. You may be sure it will be always. And I can come in to clear away just before he has finished his thanksgiving, and there will be a little minute. Oh, it's too beautiful. And she'll take me in to help in the infant school, too, where are endless opportunities. Sister Eulalie says he's sure to be very attentive in looking after the children. And she'll try to arrange for me to take in his breakfast. One must be discreet, of course, as Reverend Mother is very particular with caps and white veils. And several of the black veils are sweet on him and might be cattish. Not really, you know—just talk. But it would never do for a cap to be talked about. Only the mothers or old nuns like herself can afford that, Sister Eulalie says. Besides, it wouldn't be fair to him, who must be, like Caesar's wife, Sister Eulalie says, above suspicion.'

Kitty's calm but expressive face underwent several changes while Winnie was speaking. A look of sympathy hardened into disgust, but after a while softened into pity.

'Don't do it, Winnie. You mustn't, you mustn't. Surely you can't even think of it. Such—'

'My dear, I can do even more than that,' Winnie said proudly. 'I haven't told you the supreme sacrifice. I'm going to give him up as my confessor.'

She looked at Kitty for some sign of admiration, but finding none, made a half shamefaced qualification; 'at least for the present. A lot of the nuns wanted him to be confessor to the convent, but Reverend Mother and the bishop preferred that dry old stick, Father Brady. Oh, I forgot, dear, that he's your confessor. But you must admit that he's dry. I went to him once when he was on his holidays, and never a word of consolation or beautiful spirituality. He wasn't in the least interested in my difficulties. In fact, if he weren't a priest, I'd say he was almost offensive. I'm sure people outside the box could hear him shouting at me, "have some common sense." He wouldn't even listen to my acts of mortification and self-denial and threw an absolution at my head as if I was nobody.'

'I'm glad, anyway, that he'll be your confessor,' Kitty said, with a shrug.

'You've no real sympathy in you,' Winnie said, pouting.

'I feel for you more than I can say,' Kitty said, fondling her hair. 'Just as if you were a little child and I were your mother,' she added vaguely, staring at the window with troubled eyes.

Winnie shook her off and said pettishly, 'That's the kind of sympathy that I hate—it's so superior. Sister Eulalie, who's miles older than me, says I'm wonderful, and you only try to pick holes. Though you got prizes and things itself I'm older than you and naturally have the most sense. Besides, as Mother Ogilvie used to say, "the best brains in the world are mere dross without the divine guidance." *I* never act without it.'

'I wish I could find it,' Kitty said harshly.

'My dear, you don't pray enough,' said Winnie, forgetting her grievance in her zeal. 'I've found the greatest difference since I started saying the Little Office of the Blessed Virgin twice a day instead of once—in English in the morning and in Latin in the evening. It's the Latin, I'm sure that does it. And the small print that tries my eyes is an additional help—a little extra mortification, you know.'

'But you don't know Latin?'

'It's the intention, my dear, that matters,' Winnie explained. 'It's the language of the church and of course, must be the language of Heaven. That's why it's so powerful.'

'Anyway, I hope you'll be happy,' Kitty said, with a sigh.

'Of course I'll be happy,' Winnie said lugubriously. 'With all I'm giving up I couldn't be anything else. Never mind, I don't say that I'm giving him up as a confessor for ever,' she added more cheerfully. 'God wouldn't expect that of me. I could get him the very first day by special application to the bishop. But Sister Eulalie said that might be too marked. He was against it himself, too. So I'll pray for guidance and wait a few weeks after going in before I act on the promptings of divine grace. My! it's all hours—there's four o'clock.'

She stood up hurriedly. 'Come, Kitty, our duet. We can fit it in nicely before tea.'

'There's a better view out of your window than mine,' Kitty yawned.

'By keeping quite close to the side you can see as far as Dr Thornton's front door; but I'm not sure that I don't prefer mine with the view of Miss Fagan, the dressmaker's,' Winnie said judicially. 'I'll give up mine to you, if you like.'

'No, thanks, I prefer my own.'

'There's no pleasing you.'

'There. That's the seventh wasp to-day,' Kitty said, killing a wasp with a book on the tea-table.

'There now. I must polish the table again,' Winnie complained.

'Nonsense. You know it's a godsend to have something to do. Let me do it.' Kitty snatched a pad from Winnie. 'Another thrill in our exciting lives,' she went on, polishing vigorously. 'Hullo, there's a bluebottle. Let's hunt him.'

She threw the pad on the table and started in pursuit.

Winnie took up the pad with set lips, finished the polishing of the table to her satisfaction, put away the pad in its drawer and said firmly: 'Our duet, dear.'

'Duet be hanged. There, I'm glad he's escaped. Heighho, I wish I could fly away through the window.'

'Bad language again! How your guardian angel is blushing for you. You know I wouldn't be true to myself unless I showed disapproval.' Winnie emphasized a horrified look by pursing her lips.

'Pheu, it's hot.' Kitty dropped into her chair. 'Bad language? Why, that's nothing to what I can do and will if you look at me like that. Stop, or I'll say damn in a second.'

'Oh, Kitty, pray. Pray at once,' Winnie besought her.

'Murder? I could do it, I think; I can kill a wasp without a qualm. But, no. I don't want to die. And jail would be no worse nor better than this. If a man would only run away with me, I'd go like a shot.'

'A man!' Winnie blushed furiously. 'What would mother say? And Mother Ogilvie, and Sister Eulalie? What God feels I can't even think—and your guardian angel and the Blessed Virgin!'

'I hate men. I hate every man that ever was born,' Kitty cried passionately.

'Ah! But not hate, say dislike. That is sometimes a sign of a vocation.'

'I'm so lonely. And 'twill be worse when you go.' Kitty wiped away a tear that trickled down her pale cheek.

'There—that's another sign,' Winnie said excitedly. 'And Kitty, dear, it would be a sin against the Holy Ghost not to enter with a face like that,' she went on admiringly. 'To be able to cry without going red and having swollen lids is a great gift of God. You'd look like a holy picture—Mater Dolorosa or Blessed Margaret Mary Alacoque—with a background of the black veil and the white guimpe and dimity. I try not to be jealous, though I have every reason to be—front and back and sideways you'd look magnificent. Oh, do come with me, Kitty. It would be flying in the face of providence not to. When God gave you that face He marked you out for His own.'

'Fudge,' Kitty said impatiently. 'If He bothered about us at all, you wouldn't be going into the convent to play the fool, and I shouldn't be moping my life out here. I—'

They both heard the loud creak which the stairs—the

third step from the top—made under their mother's heavy tread. Winnie's eyes, which were raised to heaven in angry protest, turned towards the door, while she shook a warning finger at Kitty and said, 'Ssh, mother.' Kitty shrugged her shoulders, got up and shook the cushion in her chair, a look of pleased anticipation in her eyes, though she said grudgingly, 'Mother is all the excitement we have. However, she's better than nothing.'

Winnie's strangled whisper, 'Dearest mother! How could you, Kitty!' was cut short by the pushing open of the door and the boom of Mrs Curtin's voice: 'Well, girls. It's you're lucky to be sitting there at your ease on a hot day like this.'

The girls were standing in that attitude of respectful attention proper to the reception of superiors according to the ritual of St Margaret's as instilled by Mother O'Donnell.

'Yes, mother,' they both replied in unison.

'It's a terrible villain of a day, glory be to God,' Mrs Curtin said, forcibly expelling her breath, 'but if I could sit at my leisure in a nice cool room like this, I'd be as happy as a queen.'

She mopped her face with a handkerchief and looked around admiringly. 'Well, well, to be sure, it's the great painters you are, thanks be to God.'

'Artists, mother dear,' Winnie said primly.

'Think of that now. And whose chair am I to have today? Your father often says to me, "We must get another arm-chair for the girls' drawing-room, so that you needn't be taking their seat." But I say to him, sure, if they took it into their heads to leave us it's wasted it would be. By the same token there's no cooler rooms in Drumbawn on a hot day than up at the Mercy Convent.'

Kitty pushed her chair forward a little. Mrs Curtin flopped into it with a thud.

'Oh, not that way, mother. You should sink down gracefully—your feet a little more back. The third rule of modesty, you remember,' Winnie said, holding up a warning finger. 'But you're dressed up, mother,' she added excitedly. 'What in the world is it for? Mother is dressed up, Kitty. Think of that and never giving us notice. Is it—is it Father Burke is coming to tea?'

'Oh, one thing and another,' Mrs Curtin said, with a secretive smile. 'And I down behind the drink counter I saw a whiskey traveller—Jamieson's it was—come in at the door. He's a stuck-up young fellow, with a fancy waistcoat and a diamond pin in his cravat, so I just slipped my apron on to the floor, and there I was dressed up to the nines.'

'Yes, but what had you your new dress on under it for?' Winnie persisted. 'It is—it must be because you've asked Father Burke to tea. I must run and tell Peggy to get some cakes.'

'The cakes is all got. You needn't stir hand or foot. Sorra one of you'd hit on it if you were guessing for a month of Sundays.'

'It's not the traveller?' Winnie asked haughtily, but doubtfully.

'The Muldoons might do the like of that, but you can trust your mother not to demean herself or her children,' Mrs Curtin said, with a frown. 'Not but that's a presentable young man enough, and might rise to something with time and the grace of God. But there's no call on me to lift him from the level where God put him. A traveller, indeed! It's the most high and mighty young man in the town of Drumbawn.'

A growing curiosity at last broke down Kitty's expression of studied indifference. She steadied a slight twitching of the lips and asked coldly: 'Who is it, mother?'

'Someone you'll like a great deal. Your father is always on the look-out for some fresh gaiety to give you. "Ask that nice young man in to tea to see them," he said, and sure enough I asked him, and he's coming. If he's not a gentleman itself he's next door to one.'

Mrs Curtin, having completed the smoothing of her skirt, paused, looked up at Kitty and caught her fleeting look of disappointment.

'It's Mr Joe Duggan,' she added, with contemptuous emphasis on the 'Mister'.

'The young man with the boots.' Kitty's low laugh did not entirely conceal her disappointment.

'He wears 'em loud, I've no doubt, to call off attention from his legs. But sure them itself are as God made 'em,' Mrs Curtin said. 'He's a fine young man for all that one of his shoulders is a bit sunk. His warped chest is a bit agin him, but sure it comes by nature from the Muldoon side of him and they aren't given to consumption, though one of 'em died of it. He has fine manners, I'm told, but what else would you expect, and he a shop-boy above in Arnott's.'

'And you never asked Father Burke,' said Winnie dolefully.

'I did, then. Not that he liked at all to be coming with the same Joe Duggan. Run, Kitty, and open the door. There's Peggy, and she might spill something if she has to put down the tray on the landing.'

But it was Winnie who got to the door first. She examined the tray anxiously. Her mother might have made a mistake. She gave a sigh of relief. Everything was there—even the eclairs that he sometimes liked.

'Father Burke must have his own chair.' She pointed excitedly, when she had arranged the table, to her own arm-chair by the upper window.

'Then I suppose I must yield up Kitty's to Joe Duggan,' Mrs Curtin said.

'Indeed, you shall not.' Kitty pushed her mother back into the seat. 'What in the world put it into father's head to ask that man?'

'Who knows?' Mrs Curtin gave a sly look at Kitty. 'Still, I don't at all like putting a man of his awkward build on a high chair. It takes an unfair advantage of him, in a way. Your father thinks the world and all of him. Not but that his wife'd never die in the workhouse. He's a commanding man, though you wouldn't think it by his looks; any more than you'd think he was college bred. Close is no name for a Duggan and Josie Muldoon had a poor time of it with his father. Sorra lace for her shoe she could take out of the shop without his leave, and it's often she didn't get that for the asking. But by all accounts Joe is a good business man, and if his wife won't have the spending of the money itself she'll know it's behind her. He's not a man I'd choose for a husband myself, but young girls don't know what's good for 'em. And who knows but he might be better than he looks? and maybe reports belie him. Your father is sometimes right in his judgment of a man, though he thought well of that villain, Carty, that we had who stole the money out of the till. There's a knock at the front door. Give me a hand up, Kitty, I'll have to rise to bid the priest the time of day, though I'd be long sorry to go out of my way to do the same for Josie Muldoon's son. If he comes in while I'm on my feet, well and good; and he's sure to be in time, he's that eager. I wouldn't put it past him even to knock at the front door, though it's more like a Duggan to be currying favour with your father by coming in through the shop. They can be humble enough when they have anything to gain by it, though in the bottom of their hearts they think they have only to look at a girl and she'd run after them and offer to marry them.'

There was no pause in the flow of Mrs Curtin's words as Kitty helped her out of the arm-chair and moved the chair to a suitable position near the tea-table. Winnie had long ago decided that her mother could not be trusted to pour out tea. Mrs Curtin had gladly acquiesced, but insisted on a whole side of the little table for herself, with a clear space in which to manoeuvre her cup and saucer and plate.

'The burthen of entertaining Joe Duggan'll fall on yourself and myself, Kitty,' she said, in a mysterious whisper, as Winnie rushed out of the room to greet the priest. 'Winnie won't have an eye in her head for anyone but Father Burke. I hope you'll like him for your poor father's sake, he's so set on it. And often there's more good in a man than meets the eye.'

'I'll not insult him,' Kitty said coldly.

But she felt by no means cold. Long experience of her mother's expository methods taught her the meaning of the situation. Little thrills of pleasurable excitement shot through her, quite independently of her thoughts, which were in a conflicting whirl. If she could only not think at all, but just merely feel! An overwhelming sense of relief possessed her—relief from the threat of the convent. Her body felt so light, almost without weight, that it seemed as if she could fly off through space, full of a deep peace ... A vague picture formed itself somewhere beyond her consciousness. She had seen it often during the past year, but always before she had had the feeling of looking at it through prison bars, fettered and helpless. Now, with this new freedom in her heart and limbs, she could draw near and explore the mystery that somehow held the realization of all her longings. But, Joe Duggan? It was all too horrible. It was the mere thought of him that gave her that stab of pain. She mustn't think at all. It wasn't necessary to think of him. They had given up the idea of the convent for her. That was enough to think about, with its feeling of unutterable joy. There was Winnie jabbering on the landing with Father Burke, and her mother going forward to greet him, and behind them, coming sheepishly forward from the stair-head, that loutish young man from next door, with the awful, bright magenta tie and the striped waistcoat. She looked for the sickly yellow boots, but couldn't see his feet. They all felt so far away from her in this new exultation which had taken possession of her. She pressed her hands to her sides to find out if she were real, and glanced at the mirror to see her face. She wasn't even blushing, though she felt so hot. And now they were coming in. She pulled herself together and glanced again at the mirror. Her cool, firm skin, the ivory pallor faintly tinged with colour, the calm, brooding, brown eyes, reassured her. Her mother's half-sneering introduction:

'Here's Mr Duggan, who's anxious to make your acquaintance,' found her prepared.

She gave him her hand mechanically and judged him by the strictest St Margaret's standard. His 'Happy to meet you, Miss Kitty—delighted, I'm sure,' was dreadful, but it was in keeping with his slouching gait and smirk. This man, who reminded her of one of the big monkeys at the Zoo, had nothing to do with her—could have nothing to do with her. How Daisy Thornton and Bessie Sweetman would have shrieked at the idea! He had nothing in common with Dr Thornton—even with any ordinary man. She smiled as she withdrew her hand from his possessive clasp. Nothing escaped her: the clamminess of his hand; the reddish red hairs over the bluish red skin, dappled with unsightly freckles, of his coarse hand; the detestable white cuffs, which showed a flannel shirt underneath; the white dicky, which also failed to conceal the shirt ; the impossible tie, which, however, had a kinship with the colour of the skin of his neck and face; the long bony nose on which the skin was stretched too tightly; the immense Adam's apple bobbing up and down in his long crane-like neck; the thick blue lips half hidden by a straggling red moustache; the fishlike eyes which, with an offensive mixture of shyness and insolence, seemed to be sizing her up; the brownish red hair which was flattened with oil far down on his forehead; the ready-made grey suit with the creases of the shop-shelf still conspicuous. The boots were just as she expected, worse indeed, for the laces didn't match; and, of course, he brought his hat into the drawing-room.

'You might say, "How do you do", to me,' Father Burke said pettishly.

She gave him her hand with a sigh of relief and a smile that brought one to his face. He at least looked like a man. He pressed her hand. She withdrew it with a slight wrench, and said drily: 'Your usual chair is ready for you.'

'Two cushions to-day or only one?' said Winnie, with a coy, excited smile.

'Thanks, thanks,' Father Burke said, with a morose look at Kitty.

'Take your seat, Mr Joe, between myself and Kitty,' said Mrs Curtin affably to the sweating young man.

'Cherry cake and eclairs. And Peggy is just coming in with the scones. Are you quite sure there's nothing else you'd like?' Winnie whispered, as she took her place behind the teapot.

'Nothing, thanks,' Father Burke snapped, his eyes fixed with a contemptuous smile on Joe Duggan, who, with a face like a turkey cock, was gazing at his hat in angry helplessness.

'Let Peggy take that and put it in its proper place in the hall,' Mrs Curtin said, with a smile at Kitty.

Father Burke sniggered. Kitty blushed. He had really no right and he prided himself, too, on his good manners. And her mother shouldn't ... One could dislike a person without showing it. Even a dreadful person shouldn't be hurt. She took the hat, passed it on to Peggy and smiled invitingly towards the empty chair beside her mother. Joe Duggan gave her a grateful look and sat down awkwardly.

There was a long silence while Winnie poured out tea. Father Burke's nose lent itself readily to sneering, while Joe Duggan, unused to teas in drawing-rooms, gave him ample opportunity of exercising its powers. He spilt his tea and got into such confusion with his cup and saucer and plate that he could neither drink nor eat. Kitty's sympathy was aroused partly by his helplessness, but more by Father Burke's manner. She soon put Duggan at his ease and restored his confidence in himself. His first awkwardly muttered thanks changed to ogling glances. Father Burke's sneer, from being smilingly contemptuous, became angry as he watched with a speculative frown. Winnie made several remarks to him in a low voice, but he answered her shortly. Winnie's temper was quickly rising, but as she could not possibly be vexed with Father Burke, she vented her anger on her mother in several reproving looks preceded by sharp coughs. Mrs Curtin, however, resolutely refused to meet her eyes and ate scone after scone with placid enjoyment.

'It's a very chick little room very chick, indeed, the young ladies have, Mrs Curtin,' Duggan said, with an appraising look around, while he wiped his moustache elaborately with a red silk handkerchief.

'It cost a power of money,' said Mrs Curtin, making a dive for a particularly well-buttered scone.

'I believe you, ma'am. We had that very line of chairs at Arnott's, and they ran to three, seventeen, six. Very chick, indeed, but extravagant, ma'am. I oughtn't to give away things and I in the trade, only I have such an interest now in the family. But I could put you up to a tip on another line, more flash if any, and just as chick, at one, eleven, nine. On six chairs it would save—let me see—'

'I dare say you could buy the girls' dresses cheaper, too?' Mrs Curtin said drily.

'You might bet your life on it, ma'am. I was sizing 'em up, by the way of no harm, and they run to a pretty penny. I could save a five-pound note on Miss Kitty alone this minute, from head to heel, judging everything by what I see. And ten pounds and more as I've often seen her dressed in the street. The great secret in the drapery trade is to save in the quality without altering the chick.'

'Hear that now, Kitty?' Mrs Curtin gave a comfortable laugh.

'Mr Duggan has such exquisite taste.' Father Burke spoke with an elaborate expression of sarcasm.

'I had to work hard for it,' said Duggan, with a satisfied smile. 'By the same token I must be off,' he added, with a glance at the clock. 'With a big, growing business I haven't much time for frillings, but I'm sure Miss Kitty'll understand me.'

'You'll wake up poor old Drumbawn,' Father Burke said, with a pleased smile at Duggan's preparation for leaving.

'You bet, your reverence. It's been only a one-horse town up to this, but with the right kind of wife behind me and as soon as the excitement of her is off my mind, I'll make it hum. Good-bye, Miss Kitty, and now as I've broken the ice pleasantly, I'll drop in as often as I have the leisure.'

He shook hands all round, giving Kitty an extra pressure and a special leer all to herself. Mrs Curtin shook the crumbs off her dress with a sigh at the remaining scones, gave Kitty a scrutinizing glance and seemed pleased with the result.

'I'll see Mr Duggan out of the front door,' she said, with alacrity.

Half-way across the room Duggan turned round and said impressively: 'It's a pleasant day entirely they're having for the Carrickdhue steeplechases.'

'I didn't know you added racing to your other accomplishments,' Father Burke said, with an offensive laugh.

'I don't. But a man must make pleasant conversation, and I forgot it before,' Duggan said, with some dignity. 'Good evening all, Miss Kitty.'

'Pheu,' said Father Burke, with a look of disgust as the door closed. 'Now let's have more air.' He pulled viciously at the end of the blind and allowed it to spring up.

'What did your mother mean, Winnie, by asking me to tea with such a boor? I've never been subjected to such ignominy.'

Kitty laughed happily. 'After all, he's one of your parishioners.'

'Oh, Father Burke, dear Father James, I'm so sorry, I'm so sorry,' Winnie said penitently, with clouded eyes.

'Officially, perhaps—though even that's more Brady's matter than mine. But socially—my God!' said Father Burke in a disgusted tone, with a frown at Kitty. 'And to make you girls suffer all this. There's nothing whatever in it as far as you're concerned, tell me that? The hulking brute!'

'Give him a cigarette, Winnie,' said Kitty calmly.

'Dear Father James, I'm so sorry. Do sit down and lie back, and I'll put the footstool under your feet,' Winnie said, fussing round him.

'I don't admire your taste,' he said bitterly to Kitty, ignoring Winnie.

'It's a good negative taste,' she said pointedly.

He bit his lip and laughed. 'Your sister is an extraordinary girl, Winnie dear,' he said moodily, rubbing Winnie's cheek with the back of his fingers. 'She quarrels with her friends and can tolerate a guy like Joe Duggan.'

His eyes moved towards the mirror. He gave Winnie a fatherly pat on the head and then smoothed back his own already smooth hair from the side parting. He smirked at the general effect of his slim body, the long narrow head tapering down gracefully to a slender neck which was delicately poised on rather sloping shoulders. He set his lips more firmly to counteract the slight weakness in the mouth and chin.

'You ought to be ashamed of yourself, Kitty,' Winnie said, 'to go on like that with Father James, who would be nice to you if you'd only let him.'

Kitty smiled enigmatically.

'You're a horrid girl, that's what you are,' Winnie went on, still more incensed. 'She tries to be clever. Don't mind her, Father James. I couldn't make head or tail of what she was saying to you. I don't think she knows herself. Do sit down and enjoy yourself now that horrid man is gone.'

'Don't speak badly of your future brother-in-law.' Father Burke gave a short laugh, his eyes fixed on Kitty.

The indirect reference to marriage thrilled Kitty. Ever since her childhood the word had intrigued her, but all discussion of it was taboo. Often in walks under the elms at St Margaret's, when they could make a three, she had spoken of it with Bessie Sweetman and Daisy Thornton, but always (so great was their shame and fear) indirectly ... vague thoughts still more vaguely uttered. And now she was face to face with this wonderful mystery. She even felt a sort of gratitude to Joe Duggan for having opened a way for her. Father Burke's reference to him made her smile contentedly.

Winnie stared at the priest, her mouth half open in stupefied amazement.

'Yes, your brother-in-law,' he said, in angry derision. 'The haughty Kitty's husband! I can understand a woman selling her soul to the devil for a man,' he went on furiously. 'But to marry Duggan! to live with him night and day! Kitty, your worst enemy couldn't wish you a worse hell—to have to listen to his talk, to sit opposite to him at meals, to bear him children.'

He clenched his hands and his lips writhed. It wasn't a nice face now, but Kitty liked it. The smooth sneering smile had gone, and the lisp in his voice. Passion burned in his eyes. She stared at him, fascinated. Every nerve of her body was strung with emotion. Her breath rose and fell in quick, short pants ... She liked him as she had never liked him before, but it was not he but what he said, that made her heart beat quickly, gave her a feeling of exquisite pleasure. The horrors he painted did not touch her at all. She saw, not Joe Duggan, but Dr Thornton. The hell with which she was threatened was heaven—a heaven of which she had dreamed, but of which she had hardly dared to think. Like Duggan, Father Burke was an occasion, an instrument for unfolding the secrets of her heart, for disclosing the road to bliss.

'You won't do it? You won't do it, Kitty—for me?' he said in the old lispy drawl that was merely an affectation but had the effect of adenoids, his eyes fawning on her.

The change jarred her, but she gave him a smile in which there was now no repulsion. A man slumbered somewhere in him behind all his affectations and philandering. She could understand him now, hate him, but she could no longer quite despise him. She could respect the man behind the distorted face of a moment ago; even be grateful to him. But this puppet, with his half-derisive, half-ingratiating and wholly vain smile? As she stood before him, an inscrutable smile on her lips, she was callous in her analysis of every line of the weak, obstinate face.

'You'll do it for me? I'll help you,' he said, with a furtive glance at Winnie, who was weeping quietly, bent over the back of an arm-chair.

Kitty's eyes followed his. Her lips tightened and her smile gave way to a frown. If he hurt Winnie she'd be ruthless with him.

'You're making a mountain out of nothing. In any case I can manage my own business,' she said coldly.

The priest frowned with vexation. Winnie rushed forward and threw her arms around Kitty's neck. 'Oh, listen to the priest, Kitty darling,' she sobbed hysterically. 'He's all for your good. Father James, who's so fond of us both! I never could stand the disgrace of Joe Duggan. What would

Sister Eulalie say? A man like him! Dear papa looks quite a gentleman. And people don't mind one's father so much. But Mr Duggan's hands, and his face—all of him! His talk! And I was just seeing you in the black veil and all. God has deserted me—may God forgive me for saying anything of the kind. If it was God's will that anything so dreadful was to happen, I wouldn't mind a gentleman so much—but that man! And he'd have to be asked to my reception and profession dejeuners—how could we ever explain him away to the nuns and visitors? A lot of the old girls might come—we'd be disgraced for ever.'

'Don't, Winnie, don't!' Kitty patted her head. 'It's all in Father Burke's imagination.'

The priest laughed. 'Perhaps later you'll regret this attitude,' he said bitterly. 'I know you, and you'll hate it. But I'd better leave you to come to your senses.'

'Oh, don't go, Father James,' Winnie cried, and rushed towards him and caught his coat. 'You haven't had your cigarette yet. I know I'm looking a fright. But you won't mind it for once, will you?'

'Good-bye, good-bye, child. I've some duties to attend to,' he said, and pushed her roughly aside.

Winnie stared helplessly after him. As the door banged behind him she turned towards Kitty: 'It's bad enough to marry Mr Duggan, but to offend the priest!'

'Poor Mr Duggan,' Kitty said gaily. 'There, he's off down the street now. Look! His eyes as usual looking for cigarette ends or stray coppers in the gutter.'

'If he is to be your husband, you shouldn't speak of him like that—indeed, whether you are or not, it's not nice,' Winnie said primly.

'You little fool!' Kitty gave a happy sigh. 'Who's thinking of niceness? I'm so happy I can be cruel without hurting.'

Chapter 5

On the forenoon of the eve of the Assumption at eleven o'clock Winnie and Kitty walked in silence down Bridge Street and across the bridge.

For some days Winnie had been in a state of weeping. A word, a look, a touch, a memory, an anticipation led to floods of hysterical tears. Only the incentive of a last confession to Father Burke nerved her now to come out of doors and face the danger of a public breakdown. She walked along the accustomed pavements with her eyes half shut, her lower lip held tightly between her teeth, the lower part of her face hidden in a fluffy white feather boa. She made a special effort to control herself as she approached the corner of Paradise Lane, where Moll Creany, from behind her stall of delisk and green apples, was sure to offer sympathy. The whole town must know by now that she was entering the Mercy Convent in the evening; and Moll was sure to condole with her. Winnie held a shilling between her fingers and relaxed the hold on her lip in order to rehearse the smile with which she was to present the coin, and the reply to the almost certain expression of sorrow. 'You mustn't say sorry, Moll. You must be glad, for this is the happiest day of my life.' In front of Kelly's grocery when she lifted her eyes for a moment and saw that Moll wasn't in her place, the tears almost came. She had to clutch hard at the shilling and bite into her lip to counteract the feeling of disappointment.

'The priests are sure not to be there either,' she whispered brokenly, as they turned down the lane towards the church.

'Who? What? Oh, the priests. They're sure to be,' Kitty said, snatched unexpectedly from her own thoughts.

'If you were going in to-night, I'd show more sympathy,' said Winnie, letting a tear fall now that they were past the houses and had no onlookers but the church railings. 'You haven't cried even once.'

'Haven't I?'

'I haven't seen the tears, anyway,' Winnie said, looking at her with interest. 'There's not a sign on your face though it's as pale as a sheet. Paleness becomes you, though. Everything becomes you,' she went on fretfully. 'I know my nose is red and my eyes are puffy. It's not fair. I can't even show my feelings without looking dreadful.'

'If you could only get over to-day everything would be all right,' Kitty said, with an effort at hopefulness.

'I don't want to get over to-day. It's the only pleasure I have. No-one takes any notice of me. It's the first time Moll Creany wasn't at her stall for a year. And we never met blind Lanty nor anyone. No-one is a bit sorry I'm going not even father and mother. They never even offered me Mr Duggan, and I'm the eldest, too.'

'I wish to God they did.'

'Thank you for nothing,' Winnie said huffily. 'I don't want a husband. The devil may have tempted me sometimes in that way, but I always overcame him. He is very trying now and then, and I have to use the scourge Mother O'Brien made for me, the one with the seven knots in honour of the seven sacred wounds. And he's always worse, of course, with those who are dedicated to God. But the scourge drives him away. And St Winifred is very helpful. And St Anthony is a real angel—not the Padua one who's all right for finding things, but the desert one, you know, that used to be so much tempted himself by the devil.'

She was so interested in her subject that she became cheerful and stood in the centre of the gravelled drive to delay their entrance to the church. 'If ever you want a real friend I'd advise you to take him on he doesn't need bread or anything. Though naturally he'd be more friendly if you wore his medal.'

She stamped her foot with a sudden force. 'All the same, though I'm nearly sure I don't want one, I should have had the chance of refusing,' she said angrily. 'The other novices are certain to boast of having had offers, and I've never had a single one. Why, everybody at St Margaret's said that Mother Curdon refused a lord. What a romance that would be to have in one's life!' she added, with a sigh of regretful awe.

Kitty blushed vividly through her pale skin. If only her lord should one day propose, she wouldn't refuse him. She forgot Winnie, and her worry over Joe Duggan, and pursued a day-dream in the tired Portugal laurel at the side of the drive. Some day she'd get to know him, somehow or other. They said marriages were made in heaven. Surely he'd have feelings like hers. For the last couple of weeks, since she had allowed herself to think of him freely, he must have known. Bessie Sweetman used to speak of something called telepathy—she must find out more about it. He must have felt her eyes fixed on him from behind the curtain as he passed up and down the street, and the beating of her heart that threw a mist over her eyes so that she saw him only as a blurred figure. If only Daisy Thornton would ask her to stay—he often visited there. The Finnegans were no good. They were only on the fringe of the county, and would be afraid of the shop. He played tennis there often, but it would be easier to get to know the Lord-Lieutenant himself than the Finnegans, who were neither one thing nor another. And Stella Finnegan, too, only a Loretto girl—nothing at all compared with St Margaret's. It was disgraceful how Stella made eyes at him in the street. But Daisy Thornton was real county and might be different though even she had given her up since they left school. The shop!

'You're not listening to a word I say,' said Winnie pettishly. 'I see some people coming along by the railings. Let's get in before the rush.'

In the half darkness of the church porch a whoop of woe from blind Lanty restored Winnie to a tearful cheerfulness. She was a holy martyr going up among them nuns and 'd be sure to work a mission on some few of 'em who had hearts of stone for blind Lanty. She'd be a shining jewel among them and 'd mount up to be Reverend Mother in no time.

She gave him the shilling and he 'lighted her soul to glory' with a vehemence that brought a little russet-faced priest, in a temper, through the swing door from the side aisle.

'I can't even read my office in peace with you, you ruffian—disturbing the house of God like this,' he said angrily.

'It was only praying I was, your reverence, Father Brady,' Lanty whined.

'Is it deaf you think that God is?' the priest said, with a gleam in his grey eyes. 'Oh, the Miss Curtins! I thought someone was spoiling the villain. Be off with you now.'

'Sure I couldn't but have luck with the sixpence your blessed reverence gave me this morning.' Lanty said ingratiatingly.

'Be off with you of this, and do your robbery and blasphemy somewhere else,' the priest said sternly. 'What's this I'm told about you, Miss Winnie? The last person in the parish to hear anything is the parish priest. Still, I manage to know things somehow or other. This evening? Well, well. You might very easily do worse.'

His grey eyes were fixed on her speculatively, and not unkindly.

'I'll be very happy,' she said.

'It's what we're all hoping for day in and day out,' he said, with a smile. 'When we're young we like changing our toys, always hoping the next one'll be the lasting happiness. I suppose it's only by cutting ourselves often enough that we learn how to use a knife—if we ever learn at all. I cut myself badly the day before yesterday, and I sixty! and, would you believe it, Miss Winnie? for the last seven years I'm sticking to an old briar pipe with a hole in the bowl of it, that's a daily penance to me, all for fear that the next one mightn't taste as sweet. If I could only grow young again now, I'd be more sure of things. But this is only an old man's meanderings.'

'Oh, there are eleven people around Father Burke's box. Do, please excuse me, Father, I must hurry.' Winnie, who wasn't listening, rushed excitedly in through the open door.

Father Brady laughed. 'She'll beat out the woman running from Our Mother of Good Counsel. What? No. She's lost the race. Well, well, with the two in the box that's fifteen for Father Burke. And Father Dunne has four. And there's no-one at all at my box—unless you're going to me?' he added, with a dry smile.

'You can't get rid of me.' Kitty laughed.

'Dry bread—and stale and hard at that—is all I have to give 'em, and they don't like it,' he said, with a tolerant shrug of his shoulders. 'Young people can't endure using their teeth. Father Dunne gives 'em good wholesome bread, and a few people come to him for the trifle of butter he puts on it. But Father Burke is the man for them—the very latest cakes and plenty of jam and honey and butter and treacle—golden syrup, they call it now—to suit every taste. Well, well, the world is made up of all kinds. What's this they tell me about you that you're going to marry Joe Duggan?'

'I am not.'

He busied himself in fixing the marker in the breviary which he had been holding partly open with his finger.

'It'll take Miss Winnie a long time to get in to Father Burke, and, maybe, longer to get out of him,' he said drily, as he slipped the book into a torn pocket of his old, greenish soutane. 'If you don't want to go to confession right off we might have a stroll round outside in the sun. It'll save you a headache, maybe, from the bad air within.'

'I want a talk with you badly,' she said.

'Tut-tut. All you want is sunshine and fresh air,' he said cheerfully, leading the way out of the church. He seemed to forget her as he strode along by the side of the church towards a white wooden gate in the shrubbery at the back, a thoughtful frown on his fresh face.

'We'll be quieter in here.' He held the gate open for her.

'How peaceful!' she said, with a sigh, as the old two-storied presbytery embedded in roses almost to the roof came into view round the corner of a wide-spreading copper beech.

'It's all right for the old or the unhappy—all they want is to be left quiet with something maybe for their hands to do,' he said absentmindedly, his eyes fixed on a wooden seat under a shady elm on the lawn in front of the house.

'But you work from morning till night,' she laughed ironically.

'Tut-tut. I think we'll sit here, after all, and not in the sun. I was thinking of something else. Do you think Winnie'll be happy up there?'

He indicated vaguely with his hand the direction of the convent on the hill.

'I don't know,' Kitty said, sitting down. 'That is, I'm afraid she won't. She's not old enough, nor unhappy enough,' she added, looking up at the frowning face with a half-sad, half-mischievous smile.

'Some people have a lot to answer for. Fools of women, that's what they are,' he said fiercely. 'Religion! They have as much religion as my old shoe.'

He held up a dusty, down-at-heel brogue with a contemptuous smile. 'There's Winnie going into the convent with her heart half-broke. Mind you, I don't say it's not the best place for her—now. And then there's you. Well, well. So you won't marry Joe Duggan?'

'I won't.'

'And if your father puts down his foot?'

Her lips quivered a little. 'I'm perfectly miserable,' she said bitterly. 'If you speak to me like that, I'll have to cry.'

'Poor child, poor child,' he said. 'There, there, now. Don't give in to it,' he added hastily. 'The only way to meet trouble is to laugh at it. They've done their best to made a fool out of you, and you've managed to keep some sense up to this. Nuns are the best people in the world in their own way, though it often passes the wit of man to know what way it is—many of 'em, anyway. They taught you to get in and out of a carriage up at St Margaret's? Tell me that now and other fal-lals like it?'

Kitty smiled.

'Painting and embroidery and other rubbish that turned young girls into perfect ladies when the old Reverend Mother up there was at school herself. I may be a bit old-fashioned myself, but I use my eyes. If you cram a girl with that sort of thing in these times, the only place for her is in a glass case or a convent. If she turns her back on both—seeing the sort of religion they stuff her with—it's not unlikely in nine cases out of ten she goes headlong to the devil.'

'It's a pleasant prospect for me,' Kitty said demurely.

'It was the salvation of you that you could see through it,' he chuckled. 'But I wouldn't be too sure of myself, if I were you. Some of that truck always sticks. Why won't you have Joe Duggan, now?'

'I couldn't.' She shuddered.

'There now,' he said triumphantly. 'That shiver that went through you was more than half of it St Margaret's. Poor Joe has no drawing-room manners, and what he has he'd be better without. And he's no Adonis, I admit. But he's decent poor gom. Not half as clever as he thinks, maybe, though that's a failing we all have. He's no better and no worse on the whole than any other man of your own station in Drumbawn.'

'Do you want me to marry him?' she asked rebelliously.

'I don't think you'd be much of a catch for him,' he said. 'He's taken now by your father's money; and, maybe, a bit by your looks. But after a while you'd jar on him just as much as he'd jar on you. And you'd be useless to him in his business.'

She flushed a little. 'You don't spare me, but I know it's true,' she said, with a sigh of relief.

'Then there's someone else?' he questioned, with a shrewd smile.

'I wish you could get father to see things,' she said, with a still deeper flush. 'First, it was mother about the convent. Now, it's father about Joe Duggan. He doesn't give me rest or peace. And mother is hinting again at the convent as a way out of Mr Duggan. I don't know which I'd hate the most. Oh, can't you do anything?' she added appealingly.

'You poor child. Of course I'll do everything I can.' He sat down beside her on the seat. His eyes took on a worried look and he stubbed the earth with his shoe. 'It's a queer, cantankerous world and you have struck a bad corner of it,' he said gloomily. 'I suppose I ought to tell you to obey your father and mother. Still, you can't very well marry Joe Duggan and become a nun at the same time. The difficulty with many fathers and mothers is that they're thinking of themselves and not of their children. If the children's inclinations run with the parents', all goes well. But if they don't, there's the devil to pay. Your father is thinking of his business and your mother of her soul; and yourself and Winnie are a pair of dolls they have dressed up to deck out one or the other. I wouldn't say this if I thought you had a splinter of the timber of a nun in you, or if a marriage with Joe Duggan was anything but a danger of lifelong misery for you both. God unfitted you for the one and your mother and father, in the way they brought you up, for the other. They'll never see this, not if I bellow it into their ears till doomsday. Your father'll be a rock of sense about the convent and your mother about Joe Duggan; but let me cross them in their own desires and they'll both be as obstinate as mules. The most hardened sinner on earth is the father or mother that is certain sure it is doing right for its child. They are so full of the feeling of virtue they have no room for any thought of sin. Every fresh wrong is another step up the ladder of grace. It's a queer world, glory be to God. Good people, too, that wouldn't throw a lump of soft clauber at a cat, for fear of hurting it, will torture a soul or two without turning a hair.'

Kitty listened to the soft drone of his voice with only half her mind, and even that half was not deeply impressed. A few moments ago her father and mother had seemed real obstacles. But now something in the air, the drowsy hum of bees as they flitted from flower to flower in the narrow strip of herbaceous border in front of her, the cool green of the grass and leaves in the shadow of the tree, the smiling face of the house, seemed to freshen her blood and give her a new vigour. Her father and mother might have their desires and purposes, but she, too, had her own purpose. And this wonderful feeling that it gave her held in it a new consciousness of power.

'I can go away and live my own life,' she said.

'There would be that, of course. That'd be a way out that is, if you could do it. You have no money except what your father likes to give you.' He doubtfully pursed his lips.

'I could work anything,' she said vaguely. There was no weakening in her confidence in herself, in her power to achieve even the impossible. But she remembered that it was here in Drumbawn she must work out her destiny. He was here. To go away would defeat her purpose.

'If they made a good clerk of you, now, up in St Margaret's, or a doctor, or a nurse or a good sempstress, or put you through the Intermediate itself,' he said, rubbing his chin with his forefinger. 'Or even fitted you to cook a dinner. But no they were too grand to teach you anything useful for man or God. You used to wear gloves, I'm told, when you came down to see your mother in the parlour? And your mother herself boasts that she never once allowed ye to set foot in the shop. All they made of you between them was a nice young lady who could twirl her thumbs all day and do as she was bid. The sort of music and painting you know is waste in the market. I can see nothing in front of you that'd bring you in a pound in a twelvemonth.'

She was busy drawing a head with the point of her parasol in the beaten clay in front of the seat, and made no reply. The chin wasn't strong enough. Of course she could do things, a thousand things, and earn money, too. But it wasn't necessary now. She was going to stay at home. She'd just wear out her father over Joe Duggan. And he'd help her against her mother and the convent. Her father might even jump at Dr Thornton. Father Brady could help in many ways.

'Is that my photograph you're drawing there?' he said, with a grin. 'You might earn a few pence at that, but it would hardly keep you from the workhouse.'

'I might marry,' she said suddenly, after a meditative look at a flower-bed in which she seemed to have discovered the solution.

'Ah!' he said quietly. 'Now we're coming down to bed-rock. I was asking myself all along who the other man was. When a girl is so determined in refusing a man she generally has another up her sleeve. It can't be Jasper Rafter, for he has a crooked nose,' he went on, his eyes on the drawing in the clay. 'Nor Tim Devine, who has a moustache. And it's just as well, for I doubt if your father'd look at either of 'em. It might be John Thomas Muldoon, but he'd be a poor exchange even for Joe Duggan.'

She made a little movement of disgust.

'Ah,' he said, with a shrug. 'Sure, I ought to know a St Margaret's girl better than to think that she'd stoop to her own level. It's some prince out of a fairy book, I'll be bound.'

'No. It's a real man.' She blushed.

'Think of that now! Soaring up to a lawyer or a doctor you'll be. It's not young Farrel, the solicitor? He's on the look-out for a wife with money, I'm told.'

'That fat little tub,' she said, with an intolerant smile. 'No, it's someone you like very much.'

The priest looked puzzled. 'I can't think of anyone else in the town that's free to marry that's at all likely.'

He gave a slight start and said with a frown, 'It couldn't be—it's someone you know well, of course?'

'No, it's someone I've not met yet,' she said shyly, 'I know him well by sight, of course. And his cousin Daisy used to be my greatest friend at school. It's Doctor Thornton,' she added, in a whisper, blushing deeply.

He hid the look of pain in his eyes by running his fingers through his shaggy white eyebrows, muttering under his breath, 'My God—them nuns—them nuns.' He stood up and tried ineffectively to kill a wasp with his handkerchief.

'There must be a nest of 'em somewhere about,' he said, blowing his nose.

'It's trying to take a rise out of a simple old man you are,' he said, with a little hollow laugh, taking unnecessary pains to replace the handkerchief in the pocket of his soutane—'How in the world could you be in love with a man you've never spoken a word to? The like was never heard of.'

'Oh, but it is true,' she said tremulously. 'It must have been for the last two years at least. For a year, I'm certain. Though I didn't really know what it was—that is, I didn't admit it to myself till about a fortnight ago. Perhaps I ought to have told it to you in confession, but there was nothing at all to confess. You see, I prayed and prayed and kept the thought away from me till—and I haven't been to confession since.'

'Tut-tut. There's nothing at all in it. A man you never

even bid the time of day to. Pheu, pheu! A dose of castor oil you want, or a pill. Girls often have them day-dreams or nightmares. A man you just saw passing in the street. You'll forget all about him in a week.' He puffed and blew and pushed back restlessly his thick white hair with his open palm. 'Rubbish. In a few days—maybe, before night.'

She smiled up at him confidently, her brown eyes glowing in their calm depths. 'No. I may not know much, but I know about myself. I love him. If he died to-morrow, or if I never met him to speak to, I'd never love anyone else. I've lived on him for a year—a sort of pleasure and pain that kept me from going mad. I didn't know—most of the time—what it meant. And it often hurt me as much as it helped me. But for the last fortnight it has been heaven. I'm worried, of course, with that dreadful man coming to tea, and father dragging at me one minute and mother and Winnie the next. But nothing really matters now, except him. I—'

The priest's frowning, twitching face made her hesitate.

'You're not vexed with me for allowing myself to think so much of him? I'm afraid it must be sinful—I'll tell you all about it in confession. But I can't be sorry. I don't know what you'll think of me. I'm just happy; happy.'

'Nonsense, nonsense. Why would I be vexed with you?' He frowned at the trees. 'It's just indigestion. It'll pass off. I'll tell you what I'll do. I'll speak to your father. I'll make him listen to me. Even if he's a fool itself, he's a decent man. And your mother, I'll give that woman, with all her religion, the talking to of her life. I'll nun her … herself and her convent. We'll put the kybosh on Joe Duggan. I'll make your mother take you to Lisdoonvarna or to Malahide or to Bray where you'll meet plenty of young men in one of them big hotels. You'll soon find that the world isn't made up of only one man. Don't bother your head, child, about a man you don't know. There's many a nice young girl takes a magrim in her head over an actor or the like that she only sees on the stage. But it vanishes like smoke before the first likely young fellow she has a dance or a senachie with.'

Kitty's eyes clouded. She sighed and said a little stiffly, 'I'm sorry, Father, you take me like that. It's not like you. I hoped so much you'd understand and help me. I don't want to go to Lisdoonvarna or to any big hotel. I don't want to meet young men. I only want to meet the one man who is in my heart day and night. You may call me a bad girl for talking to you like this. But if you could only know how I feel. He is more to me than my life—than my soul even. Don't look at me in that strange way. I don't want pity, I want help. You're a great friend of his and could do something in some way. I don't care if you think me forward and unladylike. You won't? Well, I must get Daisy Thornton to help me. I'm sorry I troubled you. Winnie will be waiting for me.'

'No, no, child, not that. You entirely misunderstood me,' he said, pushing her back gently on to the seat from which she had half risen.

She looked up at him with a hopeful, confident smile, but he nervously shifted his eyes. The whirr of a mower came faintly across the lawn.

'There's that damn man using that damn machine again, and we can't bear our ears,' he said fiercely, as he turned his back on her and stared in the direction of the unoffending gardener with a troubled frown, muttering under his breath, 'My God, my God, the poor child, the poor child. Did anyone ever hear the like?'

He wet his dry lips with his tongue and swallowed hard. 'I can't stand that noise,' he said aloud. 'Come away into my study for a minute, and we'll finish our talk there.'

He led the way quickly across the few feet of grass and the broad gravelled path, as if he wished to escape from her. She followed with an expectant smile, pulling as she passed through the door a rosebud from a cluster hanging low down over the lintel. It was her favourite rose, and she took it as a lucky omen. She felt a thrill of extraordinary happiness as she pressed the flower to her lips.

'That's Father Burke's sitting-room in there,' he said in the tone of one who is thinking of something else. 'Full of fal-lals and gramophones and a piano and things. A great man entirely for the ladies. I have to put my foot down agin tea-parties or he'd never give Father Dunne opposite—a studious man—a moment's ease with his books. I'm away to the back here myself, behind Father Dunne, out of the way of the clatter.'

He threw open the door of a shabby little room and bowed Kitty in. Though the window was open there was a strong odour of stale tobacco smoke. An old pipe, a tobacco box, a match-box and ash-tray stood on a mahogany table near the fireplace. The carpet was worn to the thread. Two bundles of papers in wire files and a calendar were the only ornaments on the faded yellow wall paper. A high, standing desk of plain deal, furnished with a penny bottle of ink, a pen, a ruler and a tattered sheet of ink-stained blotting paper, stood in front of the uncurtained window. An old glass-fronted bookcase was hidden away in the darkest corner. Kitty noted every detail : the few stiff chairs along walls, the broken coal scuttle. The high hard arm-chair would be Father Brady's own. He'd give the comfortable leather one to visitors. Dr Thornton often sat in it! What if he should come in now just by accident? Of course she knew it wasn't likely, but it was pleasant to feel that he might.

'Won't you sit down there?' the priest said gently. She slipped off one of her gloves so as to feel the leather with her bare hand. She nestled back so that the chair should touch her at as many points as possible. She shut her eyes in order to breathe in its full joy.

'I brought you in here that we might be less public,' the priest said in a tone that made her open her eyes with a start. There was pain in it and pity. He was leaning forward a little in his chair. The light, falling sideways on his eyes, showed a network of little lines under the lids and at the sides. All the freshness seemed to have gone out of his face. He looked tired and old. Something was hurting him. She felt sorry for him. If he could only feel as she felt, to whom even the cool leather pressing against her arms was a joy!

'It's an uncomfortable sort of room to bring a young girl into, but when I'm not trapseing about the streets I'm out tending the flowers. I seldom sit in it,' he said, with a sigh, closely examining the tips of his fingers.

'You wished to say something to me?' she asked eagerly. 'It's a great year entirely for the roses,' he said, and moved the tobacco box and pipe from one position to another. 'They're all over the—'

A little spasm of pain shot over his face. He pushed the ash-tray away from him restlessly and sat upright. 'I'm only a diddering old man and you're a brave girl. If I have to pull out a tooth on you, you'll bear it, won't you? And as I have to do it, I'd better do it straight off without any beating about the bush.'

She gripped the corners of her chair with her fingers and had the cold, grating feeling in her blood which the approach of the dentist's drill always gave her. There was no fear, merely an uncomfortable expectation of something disagreeable.

He paused and looked round the room as if seeking inspiration from the bare walls.

'Well?' she said, with a smile.

With his eyes fixed on the empty grate, he said tonelessly, 'Dr Thornton is going to be married to his cousin Daisy in a couple of weeks. They're just within the forbidden degrees, but I have the dispensation for them there in my desk. They were only waiting for an appointment he's just got at the Mater Hospital above in Dublin where they're going to live.'

He pushed his hair back from his forehead and paused as if listening. There was no sound but the chirp of birds through the open window. With a deep sigh he looked at her. She was leaning forward in her chair, her hands still gripping the arms, the smile still on her lips which had fallen slightly apart. There was no trace of colour in the clear pallor of her face. Her eyes had the filmy glazed stare of the sleep-walker and seemed to look through him and beyond him.

'It's not public yet, so you'll say nothing about it,' he said helplessly.

His voice seemed to wake her. The strained figure relaxed. A warm flush suffused her face. The smile deepened and she looked at him eagerly.

'What?' she murmured, with a twitching of her lips. She passed her hand over her forehead and pressed her eyes as if trying to remember. 'Say nothing about it? Of course not,' she said, with a feeble smile. 'The room has got so hot, don't you think?'

'A little glass of wine now,' he said miserably. 'I have some in the bottom of the bookcase, and glasses and all, or soda water?'

'Winnie will be waiting for me. It must be an age since I came in.' She held on to the edge of the table and stood up. 'It is such a beautifully cool room. And the view through the window—the river and all the trees. The apples are getting red already. We must be going, mustn't we? They'll be waiting for you in the church.'

She looked with a half-frightened stare at the crushed rosebud which she still held in her hand. Her fingers closed over it.

'I don't think I'll go to confession to-day after all,' she said apologetically.

'And why would you? All this'll pass. Everything passes.' He held open the door for her.

'Everything passes,' she said, with a wan smile.

All power of thought seemed to have gone from her. She felt as if all life had been emptied out of her. Empty and hollow like a drum. 'What a queer feeling,' she murmured with a little shudder. That was Father Burke's room and the other Father Dunne's. It was all a dream about Dr Thornton. What had Father Brady called it? That horrid lawnmower was grinding out her soul. Though the sun was shining, it was cold, so very cold.

The priest had to hurry his steps to keep pace with her.

'You'd better go home and have a little rest,' he said, holding out his hand when they reached the church door.

She shook it listlessly and muttered, 'I'd better go home and have a little rest.'

Half-way to the gate she turned round and looked at the church clock. Only ten minutes to twelve and she had thought it must be nearly night. Winnie was still in the church. Winnie was a religious girl and said her prayers. Prayers and prayers, ever so many of them. And she said no extra prayers. That was why she was so miserable and unhappy. God deserted her because she deserted Him. She must pray, pray. She turned round and walked rapidly towards a side door of the church. Under the gallery, near St Joseph's altar, where there was no confessional ... It would be quiet there and she could pray.

She crept noiselessly into a dark corner, huddled down over the back of a pew and tried to smother her sobs with her arms. The world was nothing but wretchedness and misery. Prayer was no good. There was no God at all, only some beast who tore at one's heart.

Chapter 6

Mrs Curtin wore her black apron as a concession to the shop; though, since the day of Kitty's birth, the shop had never been more remote from her mind. If there had been no other cause her clothes alone would have accounted for her scant attention to the nice weighing of tea; her silk petticoat, hitherto reserved for twelve o'clock mass and the more formal visits to the convent, rustled agreeably beneath her voluminous black satin dress; her Sunday switch and her best tortoiseshell combs adorned her hair which towered up, a formidable headdress, over her crown; heavy gold pendants, barbaric in their splendour, weighted down the lobes of her ears and threatened, at every movement of her head, to seek a more secure resting-place on her broad shoulders. Respect for her corns forbade the wearing of her best boots in the shop, but her comfortable elastic-sided slippers of soft leather, hidden by the counter, gave her peace of body with only a slight sacrifice of her aesthetic sense; indeed, by a little manoeuvring of her long skirt, they were invisible even to visitors to the snuggery. Her face glistened with soap and contentment. Her gift of Winnie to God had never been in any real doubt; but she was a careful woman who graduated the extent of customers' credit to a pound and preferred regular payments in full to running accounts, and her own debt to God had for years, during retreats and missions, and even at less searching times of spiritual stocktaking, burthened her conscience. To-night at ten minutes to nine, so as to give ample time to all the nuns to kiss Winnie on both cheeks before night prayers at nine, her first-born was to be deposited in the front reception room of the convent, with a last worldly good-bye. It was not exactly the payment in full she had intended, for Kitty was still to be paid in. But there had lately been such cumulative evidence of Divine favour for Kitty that a clear receipt was as good as in her pocket. Winnie's sudden announcement of 'going in,' with its threat to the upsetting of her plans, had at first rushed her off her feet, but she soon saw in it a direct manifestation of the Divine will. It coincided almost to an hour with Kitty's separate and independent outbursts against Joe Duggan and was followed by a persistent moodiness in her younger daughter which Sister Eulalie, after anxious consultation, interpreted as final disgust with the world, though as yet only in its primary stage. Winnie's entrance, with its consequent loneliness for Kitty, would be the torch that should set the tow afire and bring Kitty at last to God. Yet that no accident might intervene, a special novena was to be begun by the nuns within a few minutes of Winnie's arrival for the purpose of fanning the flame.

As Johanna leant her heavy weight on the counter, her arms carefully resting on a quire of white tea-paper, she felt that God was beaming on her. She thanked Him fervently for fixing Winnie's departure on a slack day when she could give way to pleasant thoughts without any neglect of business. Out of the corner of her eye she could see the two shop-boys chatting idly behind the whiskey counter. She checked a frown and smiled. They well knew, the ruffians, that there was tea and sugar to be weighed in a slack hour. Still, poor fellows, let them enjoy the day that was in it. If Tom himself would only not be coming in and out with a worried face on him like a clucking hen. Men had no religion in them at bottom and one'd think it was to the scaffold Winnie was going from the looks of him. When Kitty went he'd be in a tantrum entirely. Still, the worst of his tempers was no more than a squall on the river and God'd be sure to give her the grace to cool him. If he had an eye in his head he'd have seen at dinner-time how the wind was blowing with Kitty;

but he was always a narrow man that couldn't see much outside his own business. More like a corpse Kitty was than a living being; and she didn't even look at the toothsome victuals Peggy spread as a send-off for Winnie, let alone taste anything. It was God working His will on her; and if she'd last the night before throwing herself at His feet it was the most she'd do. The ways of God were wonderful surely. If Winnie was a little trying itself for the last few days, with all the airs and consequences she put on, she was well within her rights and she as good as on the doorstep of the convent already. And it would only be for a few hours more in any case ... It was very right-minded of the nuns to pay herself the compliment (out of respect for her devoted piety, was what Sister Eulalie said) of breaking the rules and letting Winnie enter so late at night. The like was never done before as long as she could remember, and people couldn't help but remark on it. She was a humble woman, God knew, but He had blessed her out of the ordinary and she knew her deserts where He was concerned. Joe Duggan might handle as much of the money as Tom liked. He'd take good care of that so long as any of his own was mixed up with it; and he might make it grow for God faster even than Tom would. But the handling of a daughter of hers he'd never have. She sighed at the interruption of her dreams by the entrance of a customer, but she stood upright, her usual business smile on her lips.

'It's you that's looking fine, Mrs MacMahon,' she said as they shook hands. 'And what can I be doing for you to-day ?'

'I can return you the compliment, ma'am,' Mrs MacMahon said, with an acid smile on her thin, sullen face. 'A pound of tea and a quarter stone of sugar and the other things as usual.'

She gave a hostile look at Mrs Curtin's earrings, and added, 'It's only the shopkeepers is making any money these times.'

'Hear that now,' Mrs Curtin said pleasantly, 'and you with

a daughter a nun up in Stephen's Green and another over with the Dominicans, praying for you at your own door as one might say. And to tell me that a big farmer is making nothing. Smell that now,' holding a packet of tea under Mrs MacMahon's nose, 'and tell me where the profit is in it at the price.'

Mrs MacMahon sniffed, and said ungraciously, 'I've smelt worse, ma'am. By their own account shopkeepers ought to be in the poor-house—they're that fond of giving away things for nothing. And they sending their daughters to St Margaret's and all! It's hard set poor farmers are to lift their eyes as high as the Lorettos even with the run of five or six hundred acres.'

'They're very decent nuns, I'm told,' Mrs Curtin said complacently. 'I hear it said they take in likely young girls cheap that have the makings of teachers in 'em. Did you say currants only, ma'am?'

'*And* raisins, ma'am,' said Mrs MacMahon angrily. 'Thank God, we're not drained as dry as that yet, seeing the price of 'em and all. And we never docked a daughter of ours of a penny that was her due because God gave her the brains which isn't a gift that He scatters everywhere. Lizzie got the same going into the Green that Mary Kate took into the Dominicans, and the whole world knows the lowest tariff there. Cheap, indeed! If we wanted to scrape on 'em, wasn't there Mercy convents for them to go into?'

'Beyond at Lissakelly, no doubt. I think that's all now, ma'am.' Mrs Curtin moved parcels from side to side on the counter, murmuring, 'Tea, sugar, Van Houten, raisins ... But there's Mercy convents and Mercy convents. You never can believe a word you hear, but I did hear it said that Lizzie made a try for Drumbawn above and that for one reason or other it didn't come off. If the side-car is at the door one of the men'll take out them things for you, ma'am.'

'Anyway, they went in of their own free will,' said Mrs MacMahon, with an increase of heat to cover her change of position. 'And that's more than is said of some other people's daughters that I know. Good evening to you, ma'am,' she added triumphantly at the evident signs in Mrs Curtin's face that the blow had gone home.

A gleam in Mrs Curtin's eyes, however, made her retire quickly, with a muttered, 'I'll send in my own man for the things.'

'That was hitting you below the belt and no mistake,' Tom Curtin said gruffly from his desk behind the screen.

'Oh, you're there, are you?' Johanna said, biting her lip. 'The jealousy of that woman bangs Banagher! To hint at the like of that to me. There's not one in the whole barony'd say it or think it either but herself. I wouldn't send a daughter of mine into the Dominicans, not if you paid me for it. And them Lorettos live on their pickings out of examinations and the like. You should hear the St Margaret's nuns on them and how they demean themselves, sending their girls in for the Intermediate. And with a bill agin her as long as my arm, too! I'll send it in to her this very night.'

'You'll do nothing of the kind,' said Curtin sternly. 'I only wish it was ten times as long and then we might come to terms about that slice of James MacMahon's land that's spoiling the look of mine the way it butts into it.'

'There's something in that, to be sure. Still, I'll find some way of getting back on the woman. I who wouldn't interfere with the will of God, not for my own weight in gold.'

'Winnie is very miserable, anyway, up there now,' Curtin said, with a gloomy wave of his hand towards the ceiling. 'She's crying her eyes out.'

'She'll be as happy as a queen in the hands of God in a couple of hours,' said Johanna cheerfully. 'She was bent on the convent all her life. "I'll go in for the Assumption," she said to me, as firm and as bold as you like it, and nothing that I could say or do'd stop her. If she's crying itself I'm sure it's because it's glad she is—it's a way young girls have. But I won't have anyone say I had hand, act, or part in it. It was all God's doing.'

'What was all God's doing?' Father Brady asked grimly, from the doorway.

'Oh, Father Brady.' Johanna was somewhat abashed. 'It's you took the start out of me. But sure no-one is more welcome. It's a cure for sore eyes to see you.'

'How are you, Mr Curtin? What's all God's will?' the priest repeated, as he shook hands.

'Talking about Winnie, we were, and how God is taking her to-night.' Mrs Curtin gave a warning look at her husband.

'I didn't know the poor girl was dead yet? I thought ye were only putting her into the convent?'

'It's one and the same thing, I have my doubts,' Tom Curtin returned moodily.

'You and your long face.' Mrs Curtin shook at him a half-playful finger, but with the light of battle in her eyes. 'A person'd think it was murdered the girl was going to be instead of taking a front place on the outskirts of heaven. If I had her chance, and I a young girl, I'd have lepped at it.'

'You took good care to leap at Tom Curtin instead,' the priest said.

'Troth, she did that, and it's little signs of the convent I saw in her then. You see, your reverence, she was free to follow her own devices and had no good mother to guide her,' Curtin said with a grin. 'If she'd only keep her hands off Kitty,' he added gloomily, 'I wouldn't mind so much. Though from my heart out I pity that poor girl above that's going into jail this night. She's that miserable she'd move the heart in a stone.'

'I was thinking of the convent long before ever I saw you,' Johanna said, tossing her head.

'It's little you thought of it after you saw me, anyway. I just threw down the ball and you whipt it up at the first bound,' said Curtin, with an admiring look at her coiffure.

'It's romancing he is, Father Pat,' she said hastily, vexation and pleasure in her flushed face. 'Come away into the snuggery, your reverence. If he must be raking up our private affairs, it's better he'd do it there than across the counter in the face of the whole world, though it's lucky it's a slack day with no-one at all within earshot.'

She went round by the desk, and held the snuggery door open for the priest. 'One'd think from hearing him talk that I put pressure on the girl. Take the arm-chair, your reverence. But sorra bit of it. "I'm going into the convent on the eve of the Assumption," she said. "You're doing nothing of the kind," I said, fairly flummuxed at the suddenness of it. But there she stood as firm as a rock, with that stubborn look on her face that she has from her father. And I could do nothing less than give way to the grace of God.'

'That's the sort of truth that they hoodwink the magistrates with below in the court-house,' Curtin said. 'Sorra word of a lie in it as far as it goes, but you'd have to look close before you'd catch a glimpse of the truth in it. You might tell his reverence what you were beating into the child's head from the day you suckled her.'

'Is it to hamper the grace of God you'd have me?' Johanna enquired indignantly. 'I put no obstacles in her path to God. If that's the sin you want to accuse me of then I'm willing to stand my trial on it before God and his reverence.'

'It's not what you didn't do, but what you did,' Curtin said, with a helpless look. 'Did you ever hear the like of a woman arguing, your reverence? It'll be me that wanted the girl to be a nun next.'

'There was every sign of it,' said Johanna serenely, fixing the folds of her satin skirt so as to cover her slippers. 'The sort of life that was good enough for me, wasn't good enough for your daughters. You wouldn't let them stand in the shop, and there was no-one in the whole town good enough for 'em, and you were set on sending 'em to a grand school.'

'The unfairness of it, your reverence!' Curtin despairingly threw up his hands. 'I gave in to her at every turn. I might have wanted to keep them a trifle select—not to mix with riff-raff and the like,' he added, squaring his shoulders, swelling out his chest and pursing his lips with an air of importance.

'He's the proudest man in the town of Drumbawn,' Mrs Curtin said, with complacency. 'And I'm sure there's no man has a better right to be with what he has made of himself and all. But you see how it is, your reverence. If he made the girls look down on the town, where else had they to look to but to God? Not that I want to be unfair to him, for they had a natural turn that way from the very start. All he did at the most was to encourage them. And it's proud he ought to be to be the means of carrying out the will of God.'

'It was a happy day for your reverence when you escaped a wife,' Curtin said, with a frown and a helpless sigh. 'There's no straighter woman of business from here to Dublin, but let her once get on religion—' He shook his head gloomily. 'But sure you know what they are there better than myself. A rock of sense, too, in everything but that. I often wanted her to go to confession to yourself that you might lay the rod on her. But, not she. It must be that dandy, Father Burke, that's more of a young lady than a priest, may God forgive me; or some missioner that draws a string of women after him by flattering them into thinking they're saints. She's been dinning the convent into them children since they were in long clothes; and all she has for it is Winnie in hysterics above stairs this minute. Kitty has more sense in her, thank God.'

'Poor Winnie is that happy that she must let of a little of it in a good cry now and again,' said Johanna placidly. 'In all your born days, Father Brady, did you ever hear a woman worse misread? And by her own husband, too—not but they're the worst when the blind fit takes 'em. They—'

'Winnie is done for, anyway,' Curtin interrupted. 'I tried to reason with her after dinner, but whatever little wits she has are turned in her head. I offered her everything—to send her to the sea or to the Spa; and to give her as much freedom as she'd like to have, no matter what her mother'd say or do. But no, nothing'd do but the convent; though she cried her heart out over it like a flustered child over a bottle that it didn't want.'

'And I'm driving her in?' Johanna derided him. 'And she going in with her eyes wide open!' She shot a hostile look at her husband. 'Why don't you tell the priest some of your own good deeds? Maybe I'm driving Kitty, too, into marrying Joe Duggan?'

'You did your best to drive her into the convent, but you failed in that,' Tom said, with a heavy frown. 'But haven't we bothered the priest enough with our private affairs?' he added uneasily. 'He'll think we're always fighting, though we never had a word between us, except on the head of them girls.'

He gave his wife an ingratiating smile, and said to the priest, with forced cheerfulness: 'You never take a holiday at all, Father Pat. A quiet week at the sea now would do you good.'

'A quiet week at home'd do me better.' The priest examined a crack in the side of his right shoe. 'But my fools of parishioners never let me have it. Well, well. What's all this about Kitty?'

Curtin eased his throat by pulling hard at his stiff collar. He looked severely but a little doubtfully at his wife, who seemed to be engrossed in smoothing her apron, the remnant of a smile on her tightly shut lips. He coughed, but she didn't look up. He cleared his throat and said nervously, in his most pompous accent: 'I'm all against this driving girls into convents, Father Brady. Though you're a priest itself, I know you for a man of sense, and you're sure to agree with me. Still, if they want to, I say, in the name of God, let 'em.'

'You say that then?' Johanna exclaimed.

'Of course I say that,' he replied, gaining courage. 'I'm never the man to stand in the way of the will of God. But it's nowhere laid down that every young girl must be a nun. Common sense is agin it, and the population, and the like, and a young girl's nature. Some fools of nuns'd like to put an end to the whole world, your reverence, and the same maggot has got into Johanna's head, for her own family at least. It reminds me of the king in the readamadasy who thought he could stop the sea from rising by lifting his hand. It's agin human nature, I say. The only fair thing by a girl is to give her a chance to get married. The sight of Winnie up there now'll make me regret to my dying day that she hadn't a fair chance. She was driven into the convent like a pig you'd be driving to market.'

'Did you ever hear the like,' Johanna said, appealing to Heaven through the ceiling. 'She's so bent on the convent that the priest himself couldn't head her off it no matter how hard he tried.'

'Because between ye all ye have put a warp in the poor girl's mind,' said Curtin angrily.

'If you will talk of unwilling pigs it must be your daughter Kitty is in your mind. And it's yourself is the cruel driver, and you trying to force her to marry Joe Duggan,' Johanna cried.

'Nonsense, woman. Is it me to use force? I only put common sense and sound reason before her. And as I know Kitty is no fool, I naturally expect her to follow my advice.'

'There you have him and his freedom now in a nutshell, Father Pat. The only man he'd trust with his business and his money is Joe Duggan. The only man he'd consent to Kitty marrying is Joe Duggan. There's freedom for you—a scarecrow of a man that'd frighten away any girl who wasn't in the last ditch of desperation. No wonder Kitty'd be reduced to a thread the way he's nagging at her. It's to fall in a faint I thought she would every minute to-day at dinner-time, and little wonder with the thought of spending her life with that man and her heart dragging her in the opposite direction to God and His holy convent.'

'And you nag her with the convent, I suppose, eh?' Father Brady said grimly.

'I don't blacken it in the poor girl's eyes like some other people,' said Mrs Curtin, with an angry nod towards her husband. 'All my life I've been an obedient slave to that man there. I do my duty by him whether I think he's right or wrong. Don't I ask Joe Duggan up to tea and try to force him down the throat of that poor little girl? But that's what a wife has to expect seemingly from the best of husbands. I praise Joe Duggan to her to the limit of telling a lie, till the look of distress on her face is a stab in the heart to me. But though I can be true to Tom to the point of sacrificing my daughter, I can't be entirely false to my God. Run down the convent I will not, and I knowing her heart is set on it.'

'It's wonderful what we know about everyone but ourselves,' the priest frowned. 'So it's a nice kind of monster you are, to be sure, Tom Curtin. What have you to say to all this?'

'It's women, women,' Curtin muttered, with a stupefied look at Johanna. 'Not till you're taken out feet foremost will you be able to plumb the depth of unfairness in the best of them. It's all a bad dream of Johanna's. I don't want to make the little girl miserable. Beyond a word in season, I don't want to push Joe Duggan on her. I'm as sure as I'm sitting here that he's the only man for her, but I won't put what you'd call force on her. If she doesn't see the good in him to-day, with a little help she'll see it to-morrow. He has a heart of gold and a sound business head, though I could wish him a better outward covering. But what is a face, after all, to a sensible woman?'

Mrs Curtin sniffed her contempt.

'The long and short of it, then,' Father Brady said briskly, 'is that neither of you want to force the girl to do anything, and that's as it ought to be. She's to go into the convent or stay out of it, marry Joe Duggan or not marry him, or marry, within reason, of course, any other man she sets her heart on.'

Both Curtin and his wife nodded a doubtful and reserved approval of the priest's first sentence. By the time he finished speaking they were both staring with hostility at the polished table.

'Eh? That's it, isn't it?' said Father Brady, looking from one to the other.

'A girl has a right to please her father in the man she marries,' Mrs Curtin said, with a frown.

'Excepting Joe Duggan, who's the only man he'll let her marry!'

'A man must look to his little business, and I know it'd be safe with him,' Curtin said doggedly.

'There ye sit now the most obstinate pair in the town of Drumbawn,' said the little priest fiercely. 'If I was to give ye your due, I'd call ye a pair of wicked sinners.'

'I go to morning Mass and do my duty regular as the clock.' Mrs Curtin resentfully took a handkerchief from under her apron.

'I must say I'm surprised at this—this outbreak,' Curtin said, with dignity. 'I may be a little—well, maybe, negligent in my own duties, but the whole town knows what a shining example Johanna is. I must say, Father Brady, I don't understand it.'

'Thank you, Tom,' said Mrs Curtin, making a display of the handkerchief. 'If my parish priest misunderstands me itself I always have my good husband to fall back on.'

'The last thing I'd ever accuse either of ye of being is a fool, though I'm strongly temped to do it this minute,' Father Brady remarked, with a shrug. 'I've know you, Tom Curtin, since you first set foot in the town and Johanna long before. Ye know how to run a shop—none better. And I admire and respect ye for it. And I hope nothing'll ever come across the feeling of friendship I have for ye both. But not if ye headed the list of Christmas and Easter offerings twenty times as generously as ye do, would I keep my mouth shut when I think it right to open it. I ought to have done so long before, and I wouldn't doubt but the bulk of the harm is done now. Ye have hurt both of them little girls—likely for life. There's no use in lifting your eyebrows or throwing up your hands about it. You can see it yourself, Tom Curtin, clear enough in regard to Winnie. Johanna says the child's vocation is the work of God. Vocation, inagh! And where does God come into it at all, unless Johanna carries Him round in her pocket to work her will for her? Blasphemy, I call it, helped out by your vanity and pride of purse, Tom Curtin. It is mostly, no doubt, Johanna's fault; but you can't escape from the blame yourself, giving your daughter a foolish bringing up that made her dissatisfied with her home without giving her mind anything real to grip on. I wouldn't misname a good word by calling it education. She thinks she has a call to the convent. She may or may not; but she's no more fit to judge than a child in arms. And no-one else can judge for her. Anyhow, she's going in—and that's harm enough for the both of you for one lifetime. A young girl that has never waked up to the meaning of life. Let us hope that she won't end by cursing ye both.'

'I never heard the like, never, never.' Johanna was weeping freely, but with a steely glitter in her eyes. 'My conscience is as clear as a well of spring water. And every confessor that ever I had lavished praise on me for the way I was bringing them girls up. A model I was to all the women of the world, Father Gaffney, the Passionist, said. And to be called out of my name by my own parish priest is more than flesh and blood can bear. Can't you tell his reverence he's maligning me, Tom, even if he's a priest itself?'

'Nonsense, woman. You're too thin-skinned.' Curtin pursed his lips doubtfully. 'I think his reverence is mistaken in some things. "Purse-proud" and "vain" are hard words now. All I wanted was to keep the girls a bit select. But there's a lot of truth in what the priest says. I always thought you were pushing 'em too hard into the convent, Johanna. It was agin nature. And that's why I'm determined to give Kitty her freedom.'

'If you don't leave that poor girl alone, both of ye, ye may give her her death,' said the priest. 'For God's sake, try to realize that a girl of her age has a mind and a will and feelings of her own. She isn't like Winnie, all on the surface. There's some depth in her; though she's as ignorant of herself and the world as ye have done your best to make her. Still, St Margaret's, though it has left its mark on her, hasn't crushed all the life out of her. You say it's agin nature, Tom, to make a girl a nun who doesn't want it. It's just as much agin nature to try and marry her to a man she doesn't want. Not that she'd give in to either of you, and more power to her for it. But ye might easily add the last straw to her misery by worrying her any more, and she walking the town like a ghost this day.

How would you like, Johanna, to be forced into the convent the day you wanted to marry Tom here? Or you, Tom, to be driven to marry a girl you disliked instead of Johanna? Try and remember that your children are flesh and blood the same as yourselves and not coins or chattels to be invested for your own selfish ends. Give the girl her freedom, in God's name, and try and take her out of herself. Show her the world a bit and let her choose for herself. As likely as not she'll choose wrong, but then, at least, she can't blame her father and mother all through her life for her misfortunes.'

'That's hard doctrine, Father Pat,' Curtin said, in a worried tone. 'I know the man is the best man she's ever likely to get.'

'If you don't throw him at her head she might even see that. Give her the chance you gave yourself. It's she's got to marry him and put up with him, and not you. In God's name let her choose her burthen of her own free will.'

'I never intended to force her. I laid it down with Mike Duggan that she was to be free to choose. But it's dangerous to give young girls with all their ignorance of the world so much freedom as all that. How am I to know but she'd refuse Joe, and I've advanced him money already?'

'You must risk that, I'm afraid—unless you want the girl's death at your door,' Father Brady said, with a shrug.

'And Johanna'll promise him a fair run—no working on Kitty for the convent in the meantime?' Curtin said doubtfully.

'I never interfere between either of the girls and their God.' Mrs Curtin calmly replaced her handkerchief. 'Am I to understand then, that I'm not to push Joe Duggan on the poor child any more?' she added, with a resentful look at Father Brady.

'Take her up to Bray for a change of air. But let her be, both of ye, or you'll have me on your tracks,' the little priest said with smiling fierceness as he rose to leave.

Johanna's and Tom's eyes met for a moment in a common, indignant look.

'It'll be as your reverence says,' Tom said, shaking hands with the priest, but avoiding his eyes.

'It's the great tyrant you are coming between a mother and her child,' Johanna said. 'But sure I always put my trust in God.'

They both stared thoughtfully after the priest, sighed with relief as he crossed the threshold of the shop door, glanced at one another, but by a common impulse dropped their eyes evasively.

'He always had the name of being an interfering man,' Johanna said meditatively.

'He is all that—still, he's the priest of the parish,' said Tom.

Tom moved books to and fro on his desk and thought over the future of the business with Kitty married to Joe Duggan.

Johanna stroked the tea-paper on the counter and wondered how long it would be till Kitty followed Winnie into the convent.

Chapter 7

Tea had been prolonged to its utmost limits, and all pretence of eating had long since ceased. Father Burke, leaning back in his arm-chair, was smoking his eleventh cigarette, and vaguely watching the smoke as it rose and dissolved in the warm air. Winnie, sitting sideways on a high chair beside him, hung over him with anxious attention, and held an ash-tray on the arm of his chair within easy reach of his hand. Kitty sat rigidly upright, her hands clasped on her lap, and stared vacantly at a closely drawn blind. Mrs Curtin, on the edge of her chair, was hot and restless. Since the clock on the mantelpiece had struck six, no-one had spoken, and the hands now pointed to twenty-five past. Mrs Curtin was worried by the silence and the slow passage of time. She was afraid to speak lest she should remind Father Burke of the lateness of the hour. He was due in church at half-past six for confessions, but she wanted him to stay on, as Winnie would be sure to break out again the moment he left. It was an unnecessary worry, however, for Father Burke, fully conscious of the time, was determined to sit her out. Indeed, his neglect of the church gave him a pleasant sensation. Brady and Dunne were sure to be there, and would be jealous of the growing queues of penitents patiently awaiting him. He moved to a more comfortable position in his chair, and Winnie silently readjusted the cushions at his back. She was a faithful little soul, he thought, as he gave her a perfunctory smile which she acknowledged with a deep sigh and a deeper blush. It was a pity, though, that she looked so dreadful after crying. If she only looked like Kitty now! But then no-one ever looked like Kitty, and to-day she was more wonderful than ever. All the afternoon she had been almost gentle with him. Was she thawing at last? She looked a little unhappy, poor thing, and pale, and the proud look had almost gone; but she was ten times more beautiful than ever, impossible as that seemed. What was she thinking of with that far-away look in her eyes? Perhaps she was looking forward, like him, to when Winnie should have gone and they would have tea alone together. He smiled contentedly at a smoke ring. Winnie gave a deep sigh. He looked up at her with a lingering smile. This was Winnie's day and he must try and forget Kitty. Poor old Winnie was one of the best. Not nearly as much fun as the Muldoon girls; but her innocence was an attraction and her devotion quite extraordinary. Except Bedelia Rafter, he didn't know any girl in Drumbawn who was quite so fond of him. He must give her some really special sort of a good-bye. Was she ripe for a kiss? How incredulous some of the other girls would be if they were told that he had never really kissed her. But they didn't know her pernickety scruples that worried the life out of him. If it weren't for her pound a week Mass-offering, and the opportunity of seeing Kitty, he'd have given her the go-by long ago. It would never do to endanger the Mass-offering which she was sure to get her mother to continue. He gave her a languishing glance to which she responded with a sigh that shook her breasts. Oh, a kiss'd be all right. She'd be sure to give it some sort of a religious meaning, anyway. If only Mrs Curtin would go, he'd get it over. The pleasant warmth, the dim light filtering through the closely drawn blinds, the silence, save for the regular ticking of the clock, had a somnolent effect and he dropped off into a doze.

Winnie raised a warning finger and said 'Ssh' in a low whisper. With a sigh of relief Mrs Curtin settled herself well back in her chair for sleep.

Kitty continued her examination of the blind. Though her eyes stared at it unblinkingly it disturbed her. The world was a vast desert stretching out around her on every side, and she was alone with her misery at the very centre of it. While the blind remained still she, too, was at rest … almost happy with her parched lips and aching heart. So it must feel like to be dead. She was dead. She set her lips firmly against a horrid threat of being reawakened into life that came at intervals from a fitful breeze which disarranged the sash pattern made on the blind by the westering sun. The noiseless bellying of the soft linen set her teeth on edge, and she held her breath fearfully till the blind sank back quietly into place.

Winnie removed the smouldering cigarette from Father Burke's fingers, and said in a sibilant whisper: 'Don't, mother. You'd be sure to snore. The poor priest must be dead tired. I was the thirteenth at confession to-day, and there were several after me.'

Mrs Curtin nodded a vigorous assent. 'Be careful Winnie, that you don't wake him yourself with your talk,' she whispered, putting her fingers to her lips.

Father Burke's jaws fell slightly apart, and a series of jerky little snorts distressed Winnie. She moved a cushion and smiled happily when he again breathed quietly through his nose. What beautiful eyelashes he had! And that little smile on his lips. What was he dreaming of? Perhaps of her great sacrifice? No, it couldn't be that, for that would make him sad. He was just happy to be there near her and to feel that she was watching over him. What happiness it would be to sit for ever just watching him like this. But of course that couldn't be. At nine o'clock—but she wouldn't think of it. She was just happy, happy, happy.

Mrs Curtin kept herself awake by sitting in an uncomfortable position. Not that there was much danger of sleep, she assured herself, with all her grand clothes on her, and her new boots pinching her corns. Would Winnie take it to heart, on the last night and all, if she slipped down for a while to the shop? If there was no-one in the snuggery she might manage two minutes in one of the arm-chairs there in spite of her clothes, just by easing the boot laces. Poor Winnie! she looked more settled now. God was giving her the grace to bear the last wrench. And the priest was a great godsend. What had come over Kitty at all, sitting there like a stuck pig? It couldn't be anything else but the grace of the convent at last—thanks be to God for all His mercies. Father Brady was a fool of a man, near as big a fool as Tom, and that was saying a great deal. She smiled with satisfaction, conscious of her own superior knowledge of the ways of God, and dozed quietly.

Suddenly the sash pattern disappeared altogether, and for a moment Kitty had a sense of overwhelming desolation. The whole world was blotted out and she no longer existed. She blinked her eyes. She could do that. And she could feel a clutching at her throat and a numbness in the fingers clasped on her lap. And there was the blind sucked out by the draught through the opening at the top of the window. It must be late as the sun had gone from both windows. It all felt so funny and hot and choky. A quarter to seven. How like a wake it all was: Father Burke stretched back in the chair; Winnie bending over the corpse; her mother's nodding top-knot; the waning light. She laughed shrilly.

'There now. You've awakened the priest,' said Winnie indignantly.

'Not at all. Not at all. I wasn't asleep,' Father Burke said. 'I was just thinking. The quiet, the calm, the peace, the dim religious light. What a fitting prelude it all is, my dear Mrs Curtin, to a great and solemn occasion.'

'It's all that, to be sure,' Mrs Curtin said doubtfully, flicking the remnants of sleep out of her eyes with her best handkerchief to the accompaniment of a tearful sigh.

'An insufficient anodyne though for the depth of a mother's grief,' Father Burke sympathized.

'It's a cruel blow altogether.' Mrs Curtin had recourse to her handkerchief to cover some uncertainty as to his meaning.

Winnie sobbed aloud. 'I'm miserable. I'm perfectly miserable. I don't want to go at all,' she moaned.

'And Winnie has shown such splendid courage,' Father Burke said briskly, ignoring Winnie's tears. 'Wonderful, wonderful. "If you want to see the stuff the Christian saints are made of", I said to Brady at dinner to-day, "just look at Winnie Curtin!" He's not a spiritual man, but you will appreciate it, Mrs Curtin. Such steadfast devotion to a high ideal. Such joy in its accomplishment, no grief, no sorrow, marching breast forward cheerfully. Why, she infects us all with her spirit of holy gladness.'

Mrs Curtin, who had put away her tears with her handkerchief at Winnie's first sob, broke into a lyrical antistrophe:

'A wonderful girl entirely. Why, instead of feeling any sorrow myself, I've been lepping for joy all this day. And how could I be else with the courage she gives me? Holiness oozing out of her. A pattern of a saint for town and country.'

'It's her motto,' Father Burke said gravely. 'That wonderful motto of hers that will be found stamped on her soul in heaven, so faithful to it has she been. Simply "do what you are doing". The quintessence of the spiritual life in a nutshell. I carry one worked by her own hands in silk in my breviary as a daily reminder. She enjoys our little teas and other simple recreative amusements because some relaxation of the body is helpful to the growth of the soul. But if called upon she could shed her blood as a martyr with the same simple pleasure with which she eats cherry cake. To-night she will walk into the convent with the cheerfulness with which she eats her breakfast or goes to confession.'

Winnie's sobs had gradually died away. Little pictures of herself as a saint flitted through her mind. If only she should be found worthy? Yet what was Blessed Margaret Mary but a nun? And St Teresa and St Brigid? If she were only true to her motto she might be hanging up yet in every convent in the world with *age quod agis* in old English lettering stamped on her exposed heart. Her nose would not look as well as Kitty's in a picture, but the artists would be sure to manage that. And that horrid sinking feeling had gone again. It always did when Father Burke spoke so beautifully. Indeed, one had only to think of him—he gave one such delightful feelings. He was a saint if ever there was one. Just as she felt when she once drank port, only nicer—little thrills of happiness all over her. Only port, of course, was bad for one, and he could be nothing but good.

'I'm so happy, so happy,' she said, looking at Father Burke with glistening eyes.

'Thank God for that. Thank God for that,' Mrs Curtin said heartily. 'And you, too, Father Burke. 'Tis you're the comfort of the soul. If she'd only stay like that for the next couple of hours,' she added doubtfully, under her breath. 'What a comfort it'd be to everyone.'

Father Burke patted Winnie's hand. She shut her eyes, to enjoy to the full the exquisite sensation of his touch.

Their voices and actions seemed very remote to Kitty, like a play she once saw acted behind a gauze screen. She was no longer part of the world—it had passed her by. Human love was always so. It broke one ruthlessly, leaving a bruised heart as an aching memory. The saints weren't so foolish as she had thought. They must have known. In God only could one rest securely. He alone never disappointed, never deserted one. Pain, and an emptiness and desolation that were harder to bear than pain, were the penalty of following one's own wicked inclinations.

There was a difficult knock at the door and Tom Curtin came in rubbing his hands together, with a half pompous, half apologetic look.

'Hope I'm not intruding. Just took a look in—the last evening you know—just to see how we were getting on,' he said sheepishly.

Father Burke sat upright in his chair and pulled down his cuffs. He was a little annoyed with Curtin. If people came in like this instead of going out he should never get away. And Brady might cut up rusty if he was too late at the church. The sight of his sleeve links appeased him. It would please Winnie that he was wearing one of her gifts. He held up a hand, smiled meditatively at the link and noted Winnie's blush.

'We were having a little spiritual conversation appropriate to the occasion,' he lisped.

'Hum, hum, we'll throw more light on it. Them dark blinds are keeping out the little light there is,' Curtin said, fussing round the windows as if he were glad to find something to do. 'What about the gas now? Or is it too early?'

'Oh, no, no. There is too much light now. It was beautiful as it was,' Winnie said pettishly.

'For goodness sake, sit down, Tom, if you're going to sit.' Mrs Curtin gave a frown at her husband and an anxious look at Winnie.

Kitty gave her chair to her father and sat on the piano stool. Curtin sat twirling his thumbs and whistling silently.

After a long silence he said abruptly: 'Ye none of ye seem too happy, with all your spiritual talk. If you don't want to go, Winnie girl, you've only to say the word.'

'Did anyone ever hear the like?' Mrs Curtin said indignantly. 'If that's the way you behave in a drawing-room! Trying to throw a wet blanket on us and we all so happy. Tell him how you're feeling, Winnie darling.'

'I'm happy oh, so happy.' Winnie gave an ecstatic look at Father Burke.

'What's come over the girl at all?' Curtin gazed at Winnie's radiant face.

'If you weren't a worldly-minded man you'd see the grace of her vocation shining out of her eyes. But sure what's as plain as daylight to them that can see is a hidden secret to the likes of you,' Mrs Curtin said triumphantly. 'It wasn't to-day nor yesterday it came there neither, as I often told you. Amn't I right Father Burke?'

'Quite right. You are always right, ma'am,' Father Burke said, with an annoyed look at the clock. 'But I'm afraid I must be going. Duty is a stern taskmaster.'

'Oh, Father!' Winnie's lips were tremulous.

'No, no,' Mrs Curtin said anxiously. 'A few more extra words of consolation now, and she disturbed by her father and all. I'll take Tom away with me so that he won't bother her again.'

'Well, ten minutes then.' Father Burke smiled at Winnie. 'Though I have crowds waiting for me in the church.'

Mrs Curtin levered herself out of her chair and tapped Tom on the shoulder. He stood up, with a start, a puzzled look on his face.

'You'd better say good-bye to her now,' Johanna said.

'Maybe I had,' he said shyly. 'Good-bye, girl,' he added, holding out his hand.

Winne shook his hand, stood up, pecked him on either cheek and said primly, 'Good-bye, papa.'

'If so and you don't like it, there's always a comfortable home for you to come back to,' he said thickly, taking her hand again.

'As if I'd do such a thing.' Indignantly she wrenched her hand free.

'Even to hint that a nun could leave a holy convent—to be so lost to God and shame and decency,' said Johanna angrily.

'Is it to insult your little girl you came in to make such an exhibition of yourself? I'm heartily ashamed of you, Tom Curtin. And before the priest, too.'

'Whist, woman.' Curtin made a scowling nod towards Father Burke, and followed Johanna out of the room, his head bent between his shoulders.

'Poor, dear papa is a little rough in his manners,' Winnie gave a sigh of relief as the door shut behind him.

'We don't choose our fathers,' Father Burke said, with a shrug.

'What beautiful consolation you always give—but you're beautiful in everything. Oh, I nearly forgot. Mother will continue my Mass on Tuesdays. You'll have to remember me then,' she said archly.

'As if I needed any reminder,' he reproached her. 'The Mass will be all right, of course. But we needn't talk of that now.'

'No,' she said unsteadily.

She stroked lightly with her finger the petal of a rose in a bowl on the piano.

'I feel so happy, dear,' she said, in a low voice to Kitty. Getting no reply she said in a louder tone, 'Wasn't dear papa horrid to say such a thing, Kitty dear?'

'Papa? I didn't hear,' Kitty said, with a feeble smile, resting her hands, as if to steady herself, on the open keyboard.

'It's nice of you to mind my going so much. I've noticed it all day. God is very good to me,' said Winnie. 'As for Father Burke, he has been an angel out of heaven. Do have another cigarette, Father?'

Her fingers trembled as she tried to light it for him. He caught her hand to steady it.

'It's getting late. I ought to go and get out my dress,' she said nervously. 'My postulant's dress, you know. I'll put everything on here except the cap—Peggy has taken that up in a bandbox.'

He was interested in the evidence of his power. She was a nice little thing, after all, he thought, watching her tremulous lips and eyelids. He pressed her hand again and blew out the match with a short laugh. The complete surrender in her swimming eyes moved him to a sneer at Kitty.

'I've to be off in a few minutes, and I shan't see you again. Can't the admirable Kitty help?' he said, looking over his shoulder at Kitty, his teeth bared as if to bite her.

'Yes, of course, I ought to be doing something,' Kitty said, smiling gratefully at him. 'They're in your top drawer?'

'Everything—all together. Just lay them out on my bed,' Winnie said, trembling in all her limbs.

She stood as still as she could, her head bent, her eyes shut, waiting. If this was a foretaste of the convent, the convent would be heavenly. Would he give her a fatherly kiss on the forehead? Or—but that would be too wonderful—a warmer, brotherly kiss on the cheek, or maybe, on the lips? Sister Eulalie said that was allowable.

He leant back against the piano and watched Kitty move slowly to the door. He drew hard at his cigarette and expelled the smoke with a curl of his lip and nose. Was her air of tragic meekness a pose, or was she yielding?

Winnie sighed deeply. He frowned and smoked short, quick puffs. Once he had Winnie out of the way he'd very soon find out. He kept his eyes fixed moodily on the door long after it had been shut behind Kitty. Winnie sighed again. He looked at the half-smoked cigarette regretfully, drew another long puff, rolled the smoke round and round in his mouth as he leant across the tea-table and threw the cigarette into an ash-tray. He flicked some ash off his coat, blew the smoke through his nose with a contented sigh and said, 'Now, little girl.'

'Oh, Father James,' she said 'breathlessly. 'The last time and all.'

'The beginning, really. You'll see lots of me. You'll bear up now for my sake,' he said, laying his arm on her shoulder.

'I'm too happy, too happy,' she panted, clinging to him.

He fondled her hair, smiled tolerantly, turned her a little on his arm, pushed back her forehead with his free hand and kissed her lips.

'Oh, oh,' she said fiercely, clutching his head with her arm, and pressing his lips to hers. She clung to him with her whole body.

'There, there, now, child,' he said gently, trying to release himself. 'That's enough now. I must be going.'

'No, no. I don't want you ever to leave me, never, never,' she panted.

'There, there. Have sense now. I hear someone on the stairs. This would never do.' He pushed her away from him, a worried look on his face.

'It's only mother going into her own room,' she said, after hesitating for a moment. 'But I don't care, I don't care.'

'Oh, yes, you do care,' he admonished. 'And I care very much for your sake. You're going to be a very holy little nun. And a very circumspect little nun, too. Your vocation is a great blessing. How often do I see you here? Once—twice a week at the most. And now I'll manage to see you practically every day—sometimes several times a day. Now, you're going to sit down there quietly, and I'll smoke another cigarette. Then I must go. But there will be to-morrow, and to-morrow, and to-morrow.'

He led her to an arm-chair and she sank back into it with a half-dazed look. She stared at him with unseeing eyes as he lit a cigarette.

He blew a smoke ring and said gaily, 'Make me a stock—a plain ribbed silk one. Or two would be better. I'll send you a pattern. And a biretta. You'll like to work for me, won't you?

It will keep us in touch even when we can't see one another.'

She started up in her seat, clasped the arms with her hands and leant forward, a look of terror in her eyes. 'Oh, I didn't do wrong—I didn't do wrong? Did I—did I?'

He laughed. 'My dear child, my dearest Winnie,' he said gently. 'Do you think I'd allow you to do wrong? A mere brotherly kiss—a mere nothing. If you go on like this,' he added more sternly, 'and make mountains out of molehills, I can't see you at all.'

'I don't know—I don't know,' she said miserably. 'It was lovely—it was horrid. It was so beautiful. No, it wasn't. It was like hell and heaven mixed.'

'Then you mustn't kiss me again if it was only a sort of Purgatory,' he said, with a dry laugh.

'Oh, but I want to—I want to.'

'So you can, often and often. But you must be sensible and not run to confession to Father Brady about it.'

'You're sure it's right?' she said eagerly. 'It makes me feel so queer. It's all over me still.'

Mrs Curtin bustled in. 'I'm sorry I was so put upon in the shop as to keep you a few minutes extra, your reverence,' she apologized. 'But sure you couldn't be occupied in a holier work of mercy. How is she doing now, the poor thing?'

'Beautifully,' Father Burke laughed. 'I've given her a good talking to and she's going to be very good. No more scruples, eh, Winnie?' he said significantly.

'N—no,' she said, hesitating.

'Is that how you trust me?' he asked, with a frown.

'Oh, I do trust you, I do, I do,' she cried.

'A little pick of supper now before you go, my petteen,' Mrs Curtin said heartily. 'Peggy has it all ready for you.'

'Oh, no, mother; I couldn't bear to look at it.' Winnie shuddered.

'Good night, now, my dear child and may every blessing attend you. I won't say good-bye, for there is no goodbye,' Father Burke said suavely.

Her fingers clung to his, but he firmly released his hand. 'I'd leave her alone for a while just to meditate on what I've been saying to her,' he added quietly to Mrs Curtin. 'The less she's worried the better.'

'The trumpet of an archangel couldn't sound the praises of all your reverence has done for that little girl,' Mrs Curtin said gratefully, as she accompanied him out of the room. 'Put that envelope in your pocket. If you say twenty Masses or so for what you'll find in it I'll be well satisfied, knowing the power you put into them. This is extra to our other little arrangements—just to keep her heart fixed firm on God.'

At that moment Winnie's eyes, at least, were fixed on the priest's back. She kept them there till he disappeared. Then her hands fell listlessly to her sides and she tottered towards the sofa behind the door, stumbling against a chair in the gathering dark. She threw herself face downwards on the sofa and broke into a fit of dry sobbing. She no longer thought of God or sin, but of something she had missed—something wonderful that she had been on the brink of and had missed. Something that would have been cheap at the price of torments here and hereafter. Hunger she had experienced, and thirst and fever, but not all of them combined could be as painful as the aching want that oppressed her now. It was as if she had been half through the gate of heaven and had then suddenly fallen straight into the depths of hell. Oh, not hell, she thought, with a shudder. He said there was no harm in it, and he knew. Of course, it was all right. And to-morrow she should see him again. Would Sister Eulalie be able to arrange about the sacristy for the morning? It was so stupid of her not to have asked him if he were saying Mass at the convent. She must leave it all in God's hands. She jumped up restlessly and made her way to her own window. Both windows would be Kitty's now, she thought, with a sinking heart. And there was Derry, the lamplighter, lighting the gas in the street. It was a pity to light the lamps with that beautiful colour in the sky. And Kitty could watch it all go—not to-night, perhaps, but other nights. It wasn't fair … Poor Kitty. She looked to-day as if it was she who was going into the convent. How miserable she'd be without a Father Burke or anyone. For he was to be her own only. Hers, hers, and she'd see him every day. She drew the blind reluctantly and lit the gas. On her way round the tea-table to pull down the blind of the other window she caught a glimpse of herself in the mirror on the mantelpiece. She turned fully round to get a better view. God was very good to her. After all she had been through, she had never looked so well—pale and interesting. Not a trace of redness even in her nose. How lucky the tea things hadn't been removed, she felt so ravenously hungry. She munched a cream cake, pulled down the blind, came back to the table and poured herself out a cup of cold tea. As she was putting down the empty cup she gave a little start. How funny, she had actually taken his cup by mistake. It wasn't funny at all, it was Providence. She raised the cup to her lips and kissed it passionately. She bit into the thin china till it cracked. She didn't care, she could eat it. But that would be sacrilege—a cup he had drunk out of. Thank God, she hadn't broken it. With a reverent kiss she put it down gently. She looked around with a blank stare. It would never be the same anywhere else. She was a fool to go into the convent. Could that wonderful thing ever happen anywhere else? Perhaps it was only here she could have that heavenly feeling. She threw herself on her knees in her own arm-chair, clasped the back with her arms, and kissed passionately the lace antimacassar on which his head had rested. She sniffed in with a satisfying breath the faint odour of the oil he used on his hair.

'Winnie, Winnie, it's coming on the time,' in her mother's voice, made her heart almost stop and snapped the delicious feeling.

'Well, to be sure. On your knees in the parlour! As if you won't have enough of it above in the convent. 'Tis you're the nun already. But be coming along now and change into your things. Kitty has 'em all ready, and everything else has gone up. I've nothing to do but to slip into my bonnet.'

Winnie sought the floor carefully with a foot. Why did her limbs feel like lead?

'Hurry on, child. There isn't a minute to spare.'

She turned round and stared at her mother resentfully. The cheerful, smiling face quickened her anger.

Mrs Curtin's jaw dropped. 'Why are you looking at me like that?' she stammered. 'You're not drawing back at the last minute, are you?'

The anger died quickly in Winnie's eyes. She looked round the room desperately, hopelessly. 'No, I'm not,' she said feebly.

'Then hurry on like a good girl,' said her mother, in a relieved tone.

'And we'll have our last talk going up the hill.'

'I'd rather you wouldn't come, mother. Let Kitty come. She won't talk. I couldn't stand any more.'

'Did anyone ever hear the like? To the mother that bore you, too—'

Mrs Curtin stopped short at the threat of weeping in Winnie's eyes and lips. 'Sure if you like,' she added hastily. 'Though the nuns'll think it queer. And I prepared for it all the day. Good-bye, then, agra, and the Lord love you. But sure He will for you're His own … though you are hard on your poor mother itself.'

She kissed Winnie's upturned unresponsive lips. 'There now, there now, 'tis you're the good child,' she said brokenly. 'Though it's like a lump of ice you are. Run away with you now. It's late you are already,' she added, with a half-frightened look. 'I'm as happy as a queen.'

Had Winnie looked back on her dazed way to the door she would have seen her mother drop limply into an armchair and weep the first real tears she had wept for many years. But Winnie didn't look back, nor did she hear the muttered, 'Oh, my dear God, I hope I done right. My O, my O, the face of her!' She climbed the stairs wearily to the large room she shared with Kitty at the top of the house. At the door she began to take off her dress. Kitty, who had been sitting listlessly on the end of Winnie's bed, got up and said, 'It's late.'

'It's late,' Winnie repeated.

There was a long pause broken only by the ticking of the alarm clock on the mantelpiece and the swish of Winnie's clothes.

'Did you set the clock for Mass?' Winnie asked.

'No. But you won't be here, and I think I'll have a sleep.'

'I won't be here,' Winnie repeated dully.

'You can have all my lace chemises,' she added, putting down regretfully the one she had taken off.

'What will you do with your silver and things?' Kitty said, toying with hatpins on Winnie's table. 'I have too much.'

'I don't know.'

'It's a quarter to nine already,' Kitty said after a long silence, putting on her hat.

'I'm ready. Run down before me and keep everyone out of the hall. Mother isn't coming,' Winnie said wearily. 'I want to see no-one.'

'Isn't she?'

Kitty crept down the stairs noiselessly and held the hall door half open till Winnie reached it in a breathless run.

Winnie stood for a moment half-way across the bridge and looked at the broad water shimmering in the light of the newly risen moon past its full.

'What are you thinking of?' Kitty asked.

'I'm not thinking at all.' Winnie moved away quickly. 'I'll be late.'

'What does it all feel like?' Kitty asked as they mounted the short hill.

'I don't know. I'm not feeling at all,' Winnie said listlessly. And, after a pause, 'What are you going to do, Kitty?'

'I don't know.' Kitty frowned. A few paces further on, she added, 'It's a horrid world.'

'I don't know,' Winnie said, as she rang the bell of the convent gate-house. 'Maybe the convent is the best after all,' she added, without enthusiasm.

When they had got free of the welcome of the gatewoman, Kitty said, with a slight shiver, 'I don't know. It might.'

'Three minutes to nine?' a pleasant-faced old nun said with mock severity, from inside the open door of the convent. 'A nice business keeping all the nuns waiting in the corridor. That you, Kitty? Where's your mother? Say good-bye on the doorstep. You must see her in her cap another time.'

They clung to each other passionately.

'There, that's enough' Reverend Mother called out impatiently.

'I wish I was back at home,' Winnie whispered.

'I half wish I was coming in,' Kitty said, and turned reluctantly away.

Chapter 8

Up to his thirty-second year Father Bernardine had been regarded by his Order as a failure, had been unable, in the expressive words of his Superior of the Colmanites, to earn his keep. He had been put on the teaching staff of the Order because of a vague attachment he was supposed to have to literature. He had an accent and manners which attracted parents. His pupils recited 'My name is Norval', and Mark Antony's speech over the dead body of Caesar with a depth of feeling that charmed the Superior himself. But success as a teacher under the Intermediate Education Board was the success of pupils in written examinations. There Father Bernardine was a lamentable failure. He was interested only in the sounds and emotional effects of words while the dull examiners demanded a knowledge of certain dry facts which Father Bernardine could neither acquire nor impart. He explained to the Superior that the Examiners were all wrong, that the soul of words was more important than the body. The Superior admitted that it well might be so, but as the soul-value of words in pounds, shillings and pence was small, he would appoint Father Bernardine to the Mission staff, where he might contribute more to the upkeep of the Order.

Within a few years failure was entirely forgotten in a spectacular success. Father Bernardine, the Colmanite, was a household word. Jesuits smiled cynically and murmured 'a mere voice', 'a husk', 'Adonis', 'plagiarist', 'actor'. The Superior of the Colmanites retorted 'jealousy' with a shrug; and smiled complacently when Father Bursar presented his balance sheet. The school hardly mattered, the mission field had become so productive. The magic of Father Bernardine's voice captured Jesuit strongholds, routed Franciscans and Dominicans, Redemptorists and Vincentians. Though every possible man was added to the Mission staff, the Colmanites were forced to refuse more missions and retreats in a month than they had been offered in twelve before the advent of Father Bernardine. Commonplace Colmanites were tolerated even in Cathedral parishes in the hope that the star of the Order might come, perhaps, the next time. For, of course, it was physically impossible for him to be in a dozen places at once, which was what the demand for him meant. He was so deeply engaged, years ahead, for retreats, anniversary sermons and special appeals that he could attend only the most important missions. Carrickdhu, his native parish, within three miles of Drumbawn, was an exception. Here he came every year for the last fortnight in August and stayed with Father Tobin, the parish priest. He gave a week's mission single-handed, in the third week of August, if the harvest was early; during the fourth week if the harvest was late. That he might not interfere unduly with work in the fields he preached only at night. Though it was his only holiday he worked hard. His daily hour before the mirror for the practice of gesture was increased to two. He made new experiments in voice production, and recast his old sermons for the coming year. In the early days of his mission work his Superior dryly suggested that he might try writing a sermon of his own. 'Why?' he asked modestly, 'when there are so many excellent sermons lying idle. And if it comes to that they really are my own. I take only the bits that suit my voice. A sentence from Cardinal Newman here, from Dalgairns there. Bishop Hedley comes in very useful. And for appeal no-one can beat Father Faber. For hell and the Divine wrath, I made a great find in an old Spanish Jesuit. They are half my own by the time I have them arranged and committed to memory. They are all my own when I have practiced them a few times before the glass. I once heard Bishop Hedley deliver a bit of one of my sermons—a bit of his own, I mean—and it nearly made me cry. It's all delivery, Father Superior, and I've got the secret of it.' He had a flexible voice of great range and variety. He was tall and thin and dark. The pallor of his ascetic face was accentuated by his dark hair. Nor did his long thin hands, his graceful gestures, his mobile mouth, his white teeth, his regular features and large, expressive brown eyes lessen his effect in the pulpit. The effect he produced in the pulpit was continued in the confessional. Of a naturally gentle disposition, he left nothing to chance. He had carefully selected passages of his favourite writers memorized ready for every emergency; and delivered them, as the occasion arose, in a low voice as soothing as the throaty gurgle of a nightingale. Almost every convent he visited asked him to be extraordinary confessor; but the many calls on his time compelled him to limit the number to twenty. Drumbawn Mercy Convent, which had been the first to invite him when he was comparatively unknown, always continued to be his favourite.

Kitty had heard of him often from the nuns at St Margaret's and Drumbawn and from her schoolfellows as a 'regular saint'. 'And so handsome, my dear. Such eyes.' Bessie Sweetman had been in love with him, for a month from hearing him preach once; and Mother Delaney, the music mistress at St Margaret's, had declared with tears in her eyes that the only thing in nature that reminded her of heaven or of a full orchestra was Father Bernardine's voice. The whole school—except Winnie, who took praise of any other priest as a reflection on Father Burke—was thrilled when he had to break his one engagement to preach at St Margaret's in order to preach the dedication sermon of a great Cathedral in presence of the Papal Legate. Girls who had never seen him developed a 'particular' for him. His photographs, introduced surreptitiously in bulk, and given away at an immense profit in money or in kind by Becky

Royston, a day girl, had a great vogue as prayer book markers till one was discovered by Reverend Mother, who promptly confiscated all and deprived the whole school of jam for tea. When it was found out that the confiscated photographs were being used by the nuns as markers for their Office books, a rebellion in the school was happily averted by the timely visit of an ancient Royal Personage. The awe of the hurried preparations; the tense expectation at the approach of the landau with outriders; the bewilderment when the Venerable Lady, who had to be nudged by her lady-in-waiting from profound sleep, merely glanced out of the corner of a blinking eye at the illuminated address and bouquets, muttered, 'Eh, is this the lunatic asylum?' and dropped off to sleep again; the indignation that followed the rapid departure of the carriage, finding expression later in forcible comment, put Father Bernardine for the moment out of everybody's head. When this excitement wore off a few girls reverted to the row over the photographs, but Kitty, who took only a passing interest in nuns and priests, was tired of the subject.

During the following holidays she heard of Father Bernardine several times at the Drumbawn convent. Once she saw him drive by in a trap with Father Tobin, and said to Winnie what a handsome man he was. Winnie sniffed and said that nothing would induce her to go out of her way to hear him, though from the way their mother talked one would think he was the only priest in the world. Winnie's sneers made Kitty take a languid interest in him. She had half wished during two successive Augusts to attend the mission at Carrickdhu, but Winnie was resolute against it. For months his name had not been mentioned, and Kitty had not once thought of him. Yet as she left the convent, after saying good-bye to Winnie, she thought of him vaguely as a possible help in her trouble.

Her feet dragged as she walked down the drive. The silence, the dark shadows under the elms, gave some ease to the feeling of unutterable loneliness that oppressed her. The moonlight flooding the grass and glistening on the laurel shrubbery brought her peace. She stood at a turn of the short avenue, and looked back at the convent. It seemed so quiet and restful. A light was switched off in the front reception room. The long row, rambling creeper-covered, Queen Anne house, looked ghost-like in the moonlight. A smiling, sleeping ghost that wouldn't hurt. And the big modern school buildings at the back, the orphanage that flanked it on one side and the chapel on the other, towered over it sternly but protectingly.

A bell disturbed the silence and startled her for a moment. She looked eagerly at the convent as if expecting some change. The sound died away, but everything was as before. The house smiled back at her. The glow in the northwest was the lingering farewell of the sun. The nuns were at night prayer now—Winnie, too. In there was peace and quiet. She shivered a little in her thin clothes. Soon the nuns would go to their cells—to rest. Reverend Mother's cheerful voice came back to her. How happy it had sounded, and confident. Winnie would be like that soon. They knew what happiness was. The very look of the house proclaimed peace; with the moon smiling down on it benignly, and the sun leaving it with regret. And she was out here in the cold shadow of the trees, cut off from all happiness, alone with her misery.

The gatewoman rattled a bunch of keys and coughed. Kitty turned round regretfully and hurried to the gate.

'So you've left her within?' the woman said.

'I'm afraid I've kept you waiting. Good night. Thanks very much.'

'It's a queer taste entirely they have, the poor things. But sure you have more sense.'

Sense? She had no sense, Kitty thought bitterly as she hurried down the steep pavement. Winnie had sense to leave the world before she discovered how hollow it was. There was Brigid Waldron. When she was crossed in love she entered a convent. But, of course, she had a vocation. It was Father Bernardine who advised her. How she blessed him when Kitty went to see her in the little convent in Drumcondra Road. And how happy she was. Such a spiritual looking man, too.

She lingered in crossing the bridge. The sound of laughter floated up the river, and the splash of oars.

'If you kiss me again I'll smash you with the oar,' came in a muffled voice, followed by a merry giggle.

She leant against the parapet, a hot blush suffusing her cheeks.

'Oh, oh. Isn't six enough for you? They'll see you off the bridge.'

'If that's all that's troubling you, we'll come over into the shadow.'

Young Muldoon and Bedelia Rafter, she thought with an aching feeling of loss. And they said Bedelia was going to be a nun, too. What did it feel like to be kissed? She should never be kissed—now. Never. Never. And he had often kissed Daisy Thornton. She felt a choking sensation, half shame, half bitterness. Daisy Thornton whom she had loved and trusted. She couldn't hate him—she could only try to forget. It was all her own fault she was a fool. But Daisy she'd never forgive. Deceitful was no name for her. And to have pretended to be her friend all these years. All Daisy's virtues stood out clearly as heinous faults. Then, with a shudder, she seemed to be gazing at a blank wall. Daisy didn't know. No-one knew. She must see Brigid Waldron again. Brigid had been miserable and had got over it. And Father Bernardine had helped Brigid. Could he do anything for her ? He looked so kind. Father Brady was kind. No-one could be kinder than he was to-day. But sooner or later he was sure to laugh at her. She couldn't stand that now. Father Bernardine was sure not to laugh. He couldn't with his great solemn eyes. And he had so much experience, Brigid Waldron said. Why, he'd soon be at Carrickdhu. Didn't her mother say something of the mission beginning there to-morrow, the harvest was so early? Very likely he had come down to-day.

She walked slowly across the bridge. The coming of Father Bernardine was almost providential, she thought, with a more hopeful feeling. She could never tell Father Brady all she had been thinking about—about that man for the last fortnight. It would be easier with a stranger.

At the corner of the bridge she almost ran into Joe Duggan.

'What in the world has you out at this time of night, Miss Kitty?' he said, with surprise, removing his hat from the back of his head and struggling with a lighted cigarette and a stick in an effort to shake hands.

'I've been seeing my sister to the convent. Good night,' she said.

His nervousness and trembling voice moved her. She could feel sympathy for anyone who was in love. She had seen before that he loved her; but, then, it had made her hard and critical. Now she knew the horrible feeling of having the gift of oneself rejected; or, what was worse, ignored.

'Don't go yet. There's something I want to say to you badly,' he said, laying his hand on her wrist.

It moved her strangely. She withdrew her hand and a momentary vision of Dr Thornton in boating flannels gave place to Joe Duggan, nervously grinning at her.

'Can't you come up to the house?' she said, in a harder tone. She looked at him a little resentfully. If only he were different.

It was as if he had done her a wrong by having such an ugly face, such a vile accent, such a shambling, awkward pose. His hat, poised jauntily on the back of his head, made her shudder.

'I can't talk of it in the house. It chokes me,' he said excitedly. 'I want the air. I came out now to work it off me. And by the luck of the world you came by. Come along down by the boathouse. It's quiet there—and I'll tell you.'

The earnestness of his voice held her. Her mother would be angry. What matter? She turned down by the side of the bridge. There was some dignity about him to-night. She felt a thrill of curiosity, of expectancy. For a few seconds she walked with her eyes shut, buoyant, as if on air.

'It's this way, you see,' he began, and brought her back to earth again. She couldn't do it. She couldn't do it. And she wanted to in a way. But it was only because he made her think of the other—of the other whom she had put entirely out of her heart. And here were all the old feelings coming back again. She listened with growing resentment … Love … the shop … extension of trade. After all her dreams she'd be just a help to push this horrid little man on in the world. And she'd have to sit and listen to him talking of 'tride'—he must have picked up that horrid pronunciation of the word in London.

'And we'd be as happy as the day is long,' he wound up.

The look in his eyes moved her to pity. He was suffering, too. Oh, if she only could. But she couldn't. It wasn't piggishness. She didn't mind the shop, anything. She'd scrub floors, wear herself to the bone if—It was just he himself.

'I can't. It's impossible. I'm sorry—very sorry,' she said, with feeling.

'But, my God! and your father and myself have it all arranged. You can't mean it? What'd become of our big business plans—and we started in on 'em already?'

She hardened again. So it was the business he was thinking of, and not of her. 'Mother will be expecting me. I must go home,' she said.

He hurried after her, bewildered. 'But, my God, I love you. You keep me awake at night,' he muttered.

She walked quickly towards the bridge, her heart throbbing. Why should he talk to her of love, remind her of it again, make her feel like this, tortured and miserable? If he spoke of it again, degraded it in that horrid whine, she'd hate him.

'You'd not turn your back on a business the like of which Drumbawn never dreamt of?' he cried.

Her laugh was harsh. So she was to be bought and sold like a bundle of cloth.

'Your father'll have a word to say on all this,' he said, angry now. 'The whole town is talking about it … and me going in to tea and all. I'd be made a laughing-stock of.'

'Then speak to father and not to me. Good night.'

She rapidly crossed the road. Thank God, he wasn't following her. The horrid thing was that she felt an inclination to marry him. No, it couldn't be that. It was just that she was upset, and didn't know what she was feeling or thinking. Father Bernardine must advise her. If she could only see him to-night. But not her mother. No, not her mother … One of the shopmen was putting up the shutters. The hall door was open … Perhaps she could get upstairs without meeting anyone.

'It's very late you are,' her mother said, coming out of the dining-room at the back.

'The blood is near turned in me, fearing some figaries in that poor child. She's all right then, and you able to leave her?'

'I left her at the convent door.'

'And where, may I ask, were you gallivanting ever since?' Mrs Curtin asked, with a sigh of relief.

'Walking with Joe Duggan down by the river.' Kitty smiled.

'Well I'm bet!' Mrs Curtin, horrified, clasped the stair rail for support. 'You, my own daughter, and a convent-bred girl at that!'

'He asked me to marry him, and I refused him,' Kitty said tonelessly.

'Come into the dining-room and have a drop of cocoa,' said her mother, in a low, thrilled tone, with a suspicious look at the connecting door to the shop. 'The cheek of them Duggans is past belief. I was just making some for myself. And a slice of cake with it'll help you to sleep after the trying day we all had. Had I better break it to your father to-night or take him leisurely to-morrow? Sure I might have known a daughter of mine'd have the grace of God about her if she was out late itself.'

'I can't eat. I must go to bed,' Kitty said, with a thoughtful frown. 'Did you say, mother, that the mission at Carrickdhu was beginning to-morrow?'

'I did then. And Father Bernardine came down by the night train,' Mrs Curtin said questioningly. 'It's the Donlevys have the right to be proud of that son of theirs. Father Tobin came in himself to meet him.'

'I'd like to go to it,' Kitty said dully.

'Well, well, to be sure, think of that now!' Mrs Curtin gave a pleased look at the ceiling. 'Your father was saying something about a little trip to Lisdoonvarna,' she added doubtfully. 'The waters are very good there, they say, though I'm not set on truck of the kind myself.'

'I don't want to go to Lisdoonvarna. I don't want waters. I want to go to the mission. You'll manage it, won't you, mother?'

'Is it me to refuse anything to a daughter of mine?' Mrs Curtin said heartily. 'I'll send out this minute and hire Teige Dillon's covered car for the whole week. And I'll get round that father of yours later. Joe Duggan, indeed! Cock him up. It's the good God Himself was your guardian angel this night. If you won't eat anything run away to bed with you, and I'll be setting everything in motion.'

Kitty climbed limply up the stairs. She looked round for Winnie in the drawing-room, then, after a vacant stare, put out the gas with a sigh. Winnie would never be there again to quarrel with …

She went slowly up to her room on the next landing and turned on the gas. It was so unlike Winnie to leave her clothes scattered about. She gathered them up and put them away on Winnie's arm-chair. She must have been very much worried. But she'd be happy now up there. It was so quiet and restful with the moon shining on it …

She took off some of her clothes, put on a light kimono and let down her hair. It wasn't fine like Winnie's, with beautiful gold lights, though there was more of it. There was no-one now to care what kind her hair was. No-one—and there never would be anyone. She brushed her hair mechanically and watched the movements of her bare arms in the glass. Her lips trembled.

If he had only known her he might never have gone to Daisy.

She dropped the brush on her lap, clasped her fingers behind her neck, pressed her elbows tightly against her breasts and stared desolately at the glass with set lips. What should she do? She couldn't stand it—this intolerable aching longing. Was that really she in the glass? What did that queer look in her eyes mean? She was bad, bad, bad, and God had deserted her. To-morrow she'd go to Father Bernardine. Could she even confess without falling again into sin? Could she ever give up thinking of him? Never, never, never. She stood up, threw back her hair, and looked wildly round the room. How lucky Winnie had gone. She would not have anyone in the world see her like this—Winnie above all. Poor child! What did she know of sin? The empty bed made the room so lonely. If only—God, what was she thinking of? How could she be so wicked? She mustn't think of him at all—and never like that. Where had her strength gone? What made her will like water? To-morrow—to-morrow she'd be strong. But now—oh, God, oh, God! …

She threw herself face downwards on Winnie's bed and pressed her head against the pillow. He must be hers. He was hers. No-one could take him from her. She had only dreamt about Father Brady … about Daisy. She had never been to see the priest at all. They'd live … where would they live ? Feverishly she tried to build up a future. Only by keeping her eyes shut and every muscle tense could she keep off some horrible danger that threatened her. In spite of everything, she'd have happiness. She stretched out her arms as if to seize it. They fell limply on the bed, and she lay inert … without hope, without feeling, waiting engulfment by the black walls that were inexorably closing in on her.

She woke and blinked at the dreary flicker of gas, ghostlike in the warm, golden sunlight that flooded the room. She had a number of detached impressions: Winnie's motto at the foot of the bed, a numbness in her arm, birds singing in the strip of back garden, dew sparkling on the leaves, the river flashing in the sun through the break in the houses of Daunt's Terrace. Why was she dressed like this? And in Winnie's bed—not really in bed at all? And the gas still lighted? She noted the time by the alarm clock on the mantelpiece. Twenty-five minutes past seven. Her memory awoke. A warm blush suffused her face. She jumped out of bed with a set look. It was a temptation of the devil to which she had listened. There was nothing—there never had been anything but her own wicked heart. What a fool she had been, too. If only she didn't feel so miserable. But that was her sin—a mountain of sin. She put out the gas, knelt for a moment before the little altar in a corner of the room, shut her eyes and vehemently said an act of contrition. She tried to work herself up to some warmth of feeling, but there was none, only a cold lethargy that gave her muttered words a hollow mocking sound. God was still angry with her. Her mother would soon be calling out to ask if she was ready for eight o'clock Mass. She got up briskly, smoothed the clothes on Winnie's bed, and stood for a few seconds at the back window. Why was everything so beautiful, and she so wretched? Even the backs of the old houses in Daunt's Terrace were beautiful in this light. The birds were happy, while—but she mustn't think. She dragged a sponge bath from the alcove, poured into it a jug of cold water. How she hated cold water, but Peggy wouldn't bring hot water unless she was asked for it. She couldn't ask her to-day. Besides, cold water would be a punishment. She took off her clothes and hesitated over her chemise. Was Father Brady wrong, after all, in saying it was all nonsense to wear a covering in one's bath, and the nuns right? Winnie always did; Winnie never sinned. Perhaps her own self-indulgence was the cause of ... but it was too horribly uncomfortable. She compromised by slipping off her chemise and stepping into the bath with her eyes shut. The first thrill of the cold water drove away her morbid fears. Her skin tingled pleasantly as the water fell on it. What had come over her last night and all yesterday? She had been just playing the fool. The birds were shouting it at her. The sun was mocking her, dancing there on the looking-glass. The only remedy was not to think. One could keep those thoughts out of one's mind by fighting against them and praying. She stood up, got out of the bath, and scrubbed herself dry with a rough towel. What beautiful skin she had ... like soft velvet. There was nothing like cold water to give it that warm glow. She shuddered, dropped the towel and began to dress quickly. She mustn't think of her body. That only pulled one down. It was the soul that mattered, and hers was stained and ugly. She'd say her morning prayers while she dressed. It wasn't right, of course, but it would keep her mind off things, and she could say them again in the church. She looked at her dress with horror. She had forgotten her prayers last night. No wonder …

A heavy step on the stairs made her throw on her clothes anyhow.

'Are you ready, Kitty? Are you ready?' her mother shouted from outside the door.

'One minute.' Kitty made a dive for her hat.

'Well, well, if you haven't your bed made and all,' Mrs Curtin said, throwing open the door. 'And a bath, too. 'Tis you have the courage on a holiday. Peggy spoke of a cup of tea, but I said you'd be sure to be going to the altar.'

'Not to-day,' Kitty said, with a vivid blush.

'It's that man last night I don't doubt. 'Twas enough to disturb any girl,' her mother said, looking at her keenly. 'I'm off communion myself this morning, with all the back talk I had with your father over it last night.'

'Oh, Joe Duggan,' Kitty said, with a dry smile. Her mother didn't suspect then. 'I haven't even thought of him,' she added.

'And why would you? But he weighed heavy on me till near two o'clock this morning. I never seen your father in a more cantankerous temper. It took me near four hours to reduce him to sense. Not but what he has a black fit on him this morning, and he's placing the hall below now like a tiger in a cage. Take no notice of him and 'twill wear itself out. Us going to the mission was the last straw,' Mrs Curtin said, with a note of triumph, as she led the way down the stairs.

'Oh, the mission?' Kitty said vaguely. She had forgotten all about that too. And Father Bernardine! He'd make her friends again with God, she thought, without enthusiasm.

'Good morning, father,' she said, addressing the back of Tom Curtin's grey, Sunday, summer suit.

'Gallivanting off to missions on a holiday—one of the busiest days in the shop,' he said, with a glare at Johanna.

'It's a fine day we'll have for it, glory be to God,' Mrs Curtin said cheerfully.

'I'm disappointed in you, Kitty, bitterly disappointed,' he said.

'There's the last bell. Do you want to have us late, Tom? Didn't we talk it all out to the dregs last night? If you have no respect for your wife itself, you might keep your word to your priest,' Mrs Curtin said, with a virtuous toss of her head.

Kitty was conscious of his disappointment as he strode along, a few paces in front of herself and her mother. She had resented his plans for her, but now she felt bitter with herself for having given him pain. She had no sympathy with his views, and no regret for not conforming to them, but his pathetic, forlorn gait gave her a new weapon against herself. She had offended God and hurt her father. She must atone in some way for her wickedness. She had a vague, but not unpleasant sense of being unutterably wicked, and a vague wish to please everyone. Then, for no cause at all, or because the river, in the shade of the bridge, flowed dark and ruthless, she had a sudden feeling of revolt. She was tossed to and fro in a current of cross purposes. No matter what she did she was certain to break her head against a rock. Self-pity came to her aid, and she had begun to taste the pleasure of seeing herself as a mangled corpse, when her mother said in an impressive whisper:

'There's Dr Thornton turning in at the chapel gate. What a fine figure of a man he is, to be sure.'

A whole train of feelings seemed to have been set afire in her. Mass was a torture. No matter how she shut her eyes, set her lips, clenched her hands and prayed, his image came; and a disturbing feeling persisted behind her most determined, No, no. The devil was in possession of her soul and God could give only a temporary respite. It was hardly even a respite. It was more like a lull in a violent toothache, with its constant fear of the next throb of the nerve. When a dazed forgetfulness came for a moment she was sure to look unconsciously at the second seat under the gallery, and the mere sight of the back of his head made the pain begin anew. Oh! if she could only go to confession to Father Bernardine at once, he would give her some peace.

She escaped breakfast with her father and mother on the plea of a headache, but vehemently rejected her mother's suggestion that they should defer their visit to Carrickdhu till the evening when the mission would really begin.

'But Father Bernardine will preach at twelve o'clock Mass,' she said.

'A kind of start-off because of the feast that's in it, but not the real beginning,' Mrs Curtin explained lucidly.

'Then, of course, we must go. My headache was nothing at all, and went away with a cup of tea.'

''The tea is great, glory be to God,' Mrs Curtin said piously, and added, with a complacent look at Kitty's haggard face, 'God had a hand in it, no doubt. He couldn't let you have a headache, and you wanting to hear that saintly man.'

She would not let her mother out of her sight during the few hours before the start for Carrickdhu. She mustn't be alone, nor think. She initiated conversations and spoke feverishly. In the stuffy covered car she never allowed the talk to lapse.

'I don't know when I enjoyed as pleasant a morning out of the shop before,' her mother said graciously, as they got out of the car in the chapel yard at Carrickdhu. 'I doubt if I could give you up to anyone but God, and you having such a lively turn for the talk.'

The heat of the little church, the smell of frieze, the buzz of innumerable insects, the drone of Father Tobin's voice soothed Kitty into a half sleep. God was no longer angry with her. She heard His pleased voice in an occasional bird note that pierced joyfully the drowsy hum of bees and bluebottles, in the tinkling of the little handbell at the Sanctus and Consecration. Everything seemed so holy and homely: the whitewashed walls with little rivulets of green mould beneath the windows; the Stations of the Cross (their gaudy colours subdued by damp stains) askew in their dilapidated black frames; the worn red carpet on the altar; Father Tobin's long white hair; the crumpled surplices of the two dishevelled servers; the hoarse whisper of prayer from the crowded congregation; and the calm, beautiful figure of Father Bernardine, in black soutane and white bands, kneeling at a *prie-Dieu* inside the altar rail. His big brown eyes seemed to see into infinity with calmness and certainty. He would be sure to know … to be able to guide her.

The first notes of his voice thrilled her. 'Mary, mother of all purity.'

He was preaching at her. He seemed to know all her sin and her shame. He abased her to the depths, lifted her up gently, poured oil into her wounds, consoled her so tenderly that she was almost glad she had fallen …

She woke with a start to her mother's:

'We'd best be going now or the beef'll be spoiled.'

The church was empty save for an old woman in a blue hooded cloak, who petitioned God with raised hands and a swaying body.

'He was wonderful,' Kitty said breathlessly.

'What with the heat and one thing and another, I didn't hear him as well as I might—I doubt but the sleep overcame me. But he sounded grand entirely,' Mrs Curtin said with content.

Her mother had to bear the burthen of the conversation on the way home, for Kitty was hugging her new-found hope.

With a few lapses she managed to cling to it till Father

Bernardine plunged her into despair by his evening sermon. She had heard many sermons on sin during her life, and they had left her unmoved. But this showed her herself in all her black hideousness. He was terrible. Anger, contempt, loathing were hurled at her as she sat cowering beside her mother. She had defiled her body, torn with anguish the hearts of God, His blessed Mother and all the angels and saints. He drew a dozen pictures of her, one viler than the other.

But worse was to come. On three successive nights he painted in lurid colours, death, judgment, hell. Her death—the death of a depraved sinner. Her judgment. Her hell.

She hated coming to the church, but Father Bernardine drew her with the fascination of a basilisk. The accusing, menacing figure with glowing eyes, more beautiful than man, was, she felt, God's avenging angel. He had no pity, no softness in him. He was hard and ruthless as the angry God she had offended.

The journeys to and fro with her mother were torture. She had to sit through long discourses on the family history of the Donlevys for three generations, the shortcomings of the MacMahons, the oddities of Father Tobin's niece and the happiness of Winnie, while, all the time, she was preoccupied with her soul. She envied her mother's placidity, her detachment from the harrowing sermons, her spiritual serenity, her idea of confession as a mere incident to be got over at the most convenient opportunity. 'He gave it to them to-night and more power to him,' was Mrs Curtin's comment on Father Bernardine's fiercest denunciation. If her mother only knew that every word the priest said was directed against her sinful daughter!

Her mother's questions invariably found Kitty in the middle of acts of contrition, and she could only reply with a vague, 'Yes, mother.' Mrs Curtin advised her to take the mission more lightly. There was reason in everything, even in a mission, and there was no call to let it interfere with a pleasant talk in and out in the car. But with sin, death, hell and judgment staring her in the face, Kitty wanted to talk to no-one except Father Bernardine, and she was afraid to talk to him. She avoided her mother as much as possible, refused to go and see Winnie at the convent, and spent several hours every day in the church at Drumbawn. Prayer brought her no consolation. She alternated between an active fight against temptation and a numb hopelessness. Her only moments of peace were when physical and mental fatigue broke down her watchfulness, when she forgot all about prayer and temptation and indulged in day dreams. But when she was about to clutch at happiness, she remembered Father Bernardine's sermons and realized that she was on the brink of the abyss—another step and she should be lost for ever. Twice she walked out to Carrickdhu alone, with the intention of going to confession, but each time she shirked it and almost enjoyed the walk home by the short cut along the river bank. With the half-fearful sense of relief with which she once escaped a necessary appointment with a dentist, she pulled loose-strife and cornflowers and watched the salmon at rest below the weir near Cluny bridge.

Father Bernardine's sermon on heaven on Thursday evening revived hope; and on Friday morning about eleven o'clock she was inside his confessional, awaiting the opening of the slide with a fluttering heart. Shame, despair, fear, pride moved her in turn. She could hear the murmur of her mother's voice, making her confession at the opposite side of the box. What a long time she was. She tried to pass her sins again in review, but it was all a confused medley. She must be the blackest of sinners to feel like this. She half rose from her knees and dropped down again with a sigh. She could not escape God in the end, and might as well face Him now. Besides, her mother would be sure to notice. And if one's sins were as red as scarlet, they would be made whiter than snow.

The slide was pushed back with a little click. She asked a blessing in an agonized whisper. She was conscious of the long slender fingers that imparted the blessing, of the beautifully modulated voice, so calm and tender now. As she said the Confiteor she stole a glance at his face. The austerity had all gone; and the eyes that could be so harsh expressed infinite kindness and sympathy. She faltered through her confession, hesitating and stumbling over words. He would never understand, she thought despairingly.

'Help me, Father,' she said brokenly.

He put one or two, questions to which she replied doubtfully. She tried to explain but he stopped her.

'But you don't understand,' she said.

'Perfectly,' he said, with decision. 'Put it all out of your mind now. The past is a closed book. But you must be careful—very careful. The descent to hell is pleasant and easy. God has providentially rescued you now—miraculously almost.'

'God has forgiven me?' she asked.

'You are firmly resolved never to sin again?'

'Yes, yes, yes,' she said emphatically, hoping by the force of her voice to drive away a vision which his words evoked. 'But I need help, oh, so badly.'

'If I am to help you you must tell me more about your life. I've noticed your devotion to the mission. It was your good mother who accompanied you every evening?'

'She has just been to confession to you.'

'Ah!' he said, with a meditative smile. 'Let us begin with school.'

He listened patiently and attentively. 'You have much to be grateful for,' he said, with a sigh, when she finished. 'Your most excellent mother—the good nuns—everything.

Naturally the devil would do his best to enter into such a paradise. He first took the form of that man at school. An art-master, you said? Male teachers are always a danger and should never be allowed in convent schools. And this doctor? An admirable man, I have no doubt—that is the subtlety of Satan. He takes the most attractive shape in order to entrap the senses. And the result was what always comes of those temptations of the devil if we neglect the safeguards with which God has provided us—sin, remorse, pain, misery.'

'What am I to do?' Kitty asked meekly.

She had a horrid desire to live over again these temptations of the devil and could only overcome them by clenching her finger-nails against her palm.

'We shall come to that,' he said. 'It wasn't your real self that submitted to these temptations. That is strong and pure. Your whole life has shown it. But the strongest of us have some less well-defined spot—our heel of Achilles—a chink in our armour through which the devil enters if we neglect our guard for a moment.'

'I am weak and sinful throughout,' Kitty said miserably.

'Humility is a good sign,' he said, with an encouraging smile. 'And your remorse is a proof of how you really treasure holy purity. Now for the remedy. You would be absolutely safe in a convent.'

'Oh, not that,' she shuddered.

'Where else will you have such safeguards? Routine, the regular life, will bring ease to your bruised heart. Prayer will ward off temptation. A little mortification, perhaps, to strengthen you against the wiles of the devil. And the possibilities of temptation will certainly be less. Why, it is the promised land.'

'But I have no vocation.'

'I'm not so sure of that.' His smile was confident. 'Your remorse over this sin of thought. I can read detestation of sins of the flesh in your face, in your voice. Don't you feel a sort of natural repugnance?'

'I don't know.' She blushed vividly. 'No,' she corrected at once. But then it wasn't her feelings that mattered, but her will, she thought. 'I don't know,' she added, with a sigh of doubt.

'But you must know. Can't you read your own soul?' he said a little severely. 'You refused to marry a prominent business man. You did not like him, you say. What is this dislike but a shrinking from marriage—its coarseness—its indelicacy?'

'Oh,' she said doubtfully, all her curiosity awake. She felt her face grow hot and hotter. She saw even Joe Duggan in a sort of aura ... But this was madness. Why, she'd die before she'd marry him. It was the devil tempting her again.

'I hate marriage,' she said.

But her vehemence brought her no comfort. She listened vaguely to a long dissertation on the beauties of virginity. It raised men and women to the angelic plane ... She felt cold and lonely. She had not rejected marriage, marriage had rejected her. But it was all the same now. She'd have this empty desolate feeling for ever. Convents were for such as she. She would hide away her broken heart behind a guimpe and veil. And she must make some atonement to God for her wickedness.

He said, austerely, 'It is the will of God that you should take the veil.'

'I suppose it is,' she assented, with a sinking heart. 'And there will be no more horrible temptations?' she asked desperately.

'In a holy convent!' he chided her; 'with prayer and my direction, my dear child—none.'

Chapter 9

Father Burke and Father Dunne knew that Father Brady was in a temper. It was evident in an occasional gleam from under his shaggy eyebrows, a tightening of his lips and a certain sharpness in dealing with their contributions to the conversation. From his transparent efforts to be polite to the guest they also knew that Father Bernardine was the cause. Already there were traces of sarcasm in the parish priest's somewhat excessively deferential voice, and Father Burke looked forward with interest to the breaking down of the dam. Father Brady was seldom able to restrain the free expression of his thoughts beyond the custard and stewed apples. When he had the bishop to dinner, his sense of duty as a host invariably disappeared with the boiled mutton and caper sauce. Yet here was the whiskey and hot water on the table before he had taken down this fop of a missioner a single peg. Was the old man growing dotty? or could he be intending to ask the fellow to give a mission in the town? It was bad enough to have him poaching round at Carrickdhu and at the Mercy Convent, but to bring a Romeo like him into the town … Father Burke looked for sympathy to Father Dunne, but Father Dunne was stolidly intent on squeezing a lemon into his punch.

'So the mission is over,' Father Brady said gruffly, looking askance at Father Bernardine, who was watering his claret.

'Most successfully over, thanks be to God,' said Father Bernardine. 'Allow me,' he added, moving the hot-water jug towards Father Burke.

'No, thanks,' Father Burke said, with a smile of superiority. '*I* never drink.'

Father Dunne smiled at his glass.

'The pride of the cold-water tap,' Father Brady said, with a shrug.

'A little wine for the stomach's sake?' Father Bernardine said, with solemn playfulness.

'Though it's nothing to the sin of watering good claret.' Father Brady gave a moody look at Father Bernardine's glass. 'Tom Curtin's best, too. A successful mission, indeed!' he added fiercely. 'What did you do with his daughters? Tell me that now.'

Father Bernardine smiled, with a tolerant reserve.

'He hasn't sent the second one into the convent?' Father Dunne said, with a faint show of interest.

The knife with which Father Burke was preparing a lemon for lemonade slipped and cut his finger.

'Kitty? Surely not?'

He frowned at Father Bernardine while winding his napkin nervously round his finger.

'Packing her off to-morrow or the next day,' Father Brady said angrily.

'I'm not surprised at Brady,' said Father Dunne, balancing his spoon on the edge of his glass. 'She was his only penitent, one might say. But where do you come in? She wasn't one of your string?' he added, with a questioning look at Father Burke.

'I naturally take an interest in everyone in the parish,' Father Burke said loftily.

'There's news for us, Brady,' Father Dunne chuckled. 'He'll be taking his share of the workhouse calls next.'

'What do you mean by it?' Father Brady said, glowering at the missioner.

'My good friend, my dear friend,' Father Bernardine mildly remonstrated. 'You mustn't blame me if your parishioners have vocations.'

'And he certainly can't blame Burke,' said Father Dunne with a grin. 'Brady has a down on him over the convent, so he tries to keep the girls outside it—except a few he's tired of.'

'Vocation! What's a vocation?' Father Brady snapped contemptuously. 'A young girl gets a fancy for a minute, and you shut her up in a convent for life. She's nearly sure to change her mind the next minute, but there she is behind four walls with the door locked and the key gone.'

'There are too many women in the world,' said Father Dunne, with gloom. 'It's a good job to get some of 'em put safely out of the way.'

Father Bernardine said, 'A vocation is a positive prompting of divine grace in the choice of a state of life.'

'Humph. The prompting of divine grace most young girls have is to get married.' Father Brady meditatively sipped his punch.

'You underestimate the spiritual side of a woman's nature, her longing for Divine purity—' Father Bernardine began, with one of his favourite pulpit gestures.

'I'll be sixty-two in October, and I didn't walk through the world with my eyes shut,' Father Brady interrupted dryly. 'I don't deny there are sports among women—known a dog in my time that wouldn't look at a bone. But what most women want is a husband, and what all of 'em want is a child.'

'I deny it absolutely.' Father Bernardine set his thin lips. 'Woman is a temple of virginity, of holy purity. She fell, of course, with Eve but the fall is more than counterbalanced by divine grace. There is sometimes a struggle with her lower nature, that malign legacy of Eve's sin. But with the example of our Blessed Mother and the saints to sustain her, and the counsel of St Paul, and the aspirations of her higher nature fortified by prayer and grace—'

'And clap-trap,' Father Brady interrupted. 'A few of 'em'll be foolish enough to go into a convent. No wonder so many of 'em go half mad.'

'Don't be too hard on the poor things,' Father Dunne said. 'It's pleasant enough sort of an asylum for a disappointed woman. They can't all get married, and it's not what you might call convenient to have a child without. What harm are they doing to anyone? If it weren't for the breakfast I get at the convent every morning I'd be dead of indigestion long ago. As long as they're able to cook lightly I'm all for 'em.'

Father Bernardine's irritation with Father Brady's interruption gave way to an expression of sadness.

'We can't rival your good *confrères* in facetiousness about holy things,' he said to a gloomy Father Burke who was toying with the rind of a lemon.

'Oh, Brady and Dunne will have their little jokes,' Father Burke said, with a sickly smile. 'I'm all with you, of course, Father Bernardine. Girls hurried into unsuitable marriages by inconsiderate parents! Nice girls brought up in a genteel convent—nice genteel girls forced to marry rough boors! Happily it makes them recognize their real vocation and seek the solace of a convent. Would you believe it that her father wanted that little girl we were speaking of, Kitty Curtin, to marry a regular clodhopper? You must know him? That hulking son of Mike Duggan?' he added, his lips trembling with indignation.

'She seems to have chosen the better part.' Father Bernardine's tone was one of complete detachment.

Father Burke frowned.

'It's true about her, I suppose?' he asked, with an exaggerated assumption of indifference.

'Your good parish priest says so.' Father Bernardine smiled serenely. 'Indeed, there is no secret about it, confessional or otherwise. On my way here I called to see her good mother who spoke freely about it.'

'Between the two girls it'll be a good lump for the convent—they'll be able to build the new chapel now that they have the plans of. We'd have got more out of 'em by marrying 'em off, eh, Brady? Nuns are a caution, to be sure.' Father Dunne gave a shrug of resignation, taking a sip of punch to help him.

'Between her ass of a mother and yourself, ye have made a nice mess of the poor girl,' Father Brady said, sweeping the claret bottle towards the missioner.

Father Bernardine moved the bottle back to the centre of the table with an assured smile.

'Don't,' he said humbly, 'confuse weak instruments with the mighty river of Divine grace.'

'My God, ye took the little girl on the rebound before she had time to find her feet again,' said Father Brady savagely. 'You know it well, Donlevy.'

Father Bernardine shut his lips and stared impassively at the tablecloth.

'Leave all women to God. As He denied 'em common sense, no doubt He has some plan for dealing with 'em.' Father Dunne cheerfully mixed himself a little extra punch in a wineglass.

'It's a queer fool God'd be if He was responsible for every idiocy that's put to His credit,' Father Brady said, with a glare at Father Bernardine.

'It's not often that I can agree with my parish priest in spiritual matters, but I really think there is something in what he said of the rebound.' Father Burke's tone had a blend of condescension and anxiety. 'I bow, of course, to your superior judgment, Father Bernardine. I can't pretend to your experience. Still, in my own small way, I have some knowledge of souls. There was a revulsion from this Duggan. Is the idea of the convent a mere extension of this feeling of revulsion—a refuge as it were, from this purely human antipathy; or, is it the real divine call, on the signs of which we can, so to speak, lay our finger?'

'*If* the young lady consulted me, surely you don't expect me to discuss her?' Father Bernardine said equably, but with a half-reproving smile.

'Ye're making a lot of bother about a girl going into a convent.' Father Dunne yawned. 'Nine chances out of ten she'll regret it. But if she stops out, she'll very likely regret that, too, married or single. So where's the odds? Let's have a walk down by the river, in God's name.'

'I'm not asking your opinion, I am merely giving mine,' Father Burke said sharply to Father Bernardine, ignoring Father Dunne's interruption with a contemptuous shrug. 'I'm an outsider and can speak freely. I've known the young lady, however, for some considerable time, and I've never noticed any of the signs to which I have referred—which were so conspicuously present in her sister Winnie, for example. A strange confessor might easily be misled. One cannot be too careful in things of the spirit; and the consequences of a mistake might be a lifelong misery for the poor child.'

'Quite true, quite true. Very interesting, indeed,' Father Bernardine said, with a smile that suggested the possession of superior knowledge. 'I think I will have a little more of your very excellent claret, Father Brady.'

Father Burke bit his lip and frowned. 'Her parish priest, at least, might do something,' he said pettishly. 'Though she hasn't consulted you itself,' he added, with a sneer at Father Brady, 'you should have tried to prevent the girl from making a fool of herself.'

'Brady can do a lot. But to ask him to work a miracle now—that's entirely too much,' said Father Dunne, with a shrug.

'She's a sensible girl—that's what beats me,' Father Brady said, with a worried frown. 'I went to her the minute I heard it, but she was as obstinate as a brick wall. The convent was stuck in her gullet—what the French call an *idée fixe*. I didn't leave a stone standing on another in any convent in the country, with the abuse I gave 'em, but I might as well have been yelping at the moon. There's no pit of foolishness a woman isn't capable of falling into with her eyes wide open. But it was my friend here on the right that gave the push this time. "Father Bernardine advised me", she said, just as if she was speaking to the Pope himself. "Who the devil is Father Bernardine?" I said, "but Pete Donlevy that I used to thrash every day, and I in the Seminary because he could never decline *bonus, bona, bonum*." She has spirit in her that girl. She laughed in my face and said I was jealous, and all the time the heart was crushed out of her. I had to laugh myself at the idea of being jealous of a tailor's dummy with a gramophone inside him. I'd be just as likely to be jealous of Burke there. May God help the poor girl all the same.'

'If it wasn't one thing, it'd be another,' Father Dunne said, draining his glass.

'Thanks for a most enjoyable dinner.' Father Bernardine spoke with a faint note of injury in his voice and a flush under his ears. 'I'm afraid I have to go.'

'You know you're always welcome, Pete.' Father Brady rose with his guest. 'You're not at all a bad fellow if you weren't such a damn fool.'

Father Burke said a sneering good-bye, which covered an uneasy jealousy. His own success with women always had a relation to sex. Very likely Father Bernardine's were the same. Had Kitty fallen a victim? One could never trust those fellows' pretence of asceticism. Brady and Dunne were dry sticks—Brady was old, too—but a fellow like Donlevy, with half the women in the country after him! Human nature couldn't stand the strain even in a saint. Likely Donlevy made all the hay he could.

'Coming for a walk, Burke?' Father Dunne asked genially.

'No.'

'A tea-party?' Father Dunne surmised, with a shrug.

Father Burke frowned, but he looked at his watch with a feeling of hope. He'd catch her at tea. He must see her to-day about all this. It was the mission nonsense that made Kitty avoid him. He'd soon put it out of her head. He stood at the window of his sitting-room, rattling his keys in his pocket till the three priests had disappeared down the drive. Was it better to make a plan or just trust to chance? If she'd only let him kiss her, everything would be all right. Poor Winnie, he thought, with reminiscent smile, wasn't turning out half bad. But he'd have to be careful of Brady. He hummed a tune and ran lightly upstairs to his bedroom. The Muldoons expected him to tea—he'd have to cut that. And Mrs Cummin—'bother Fanny,' he muttered, 'the staler she grows the more exacting she is.' He put on a pair of white cuffs, brushed his hair and looked at himself carefully in the glass. He was dissatisfied with the hang of the coat from the shoulder, and changed to another suit. He sprinkled eau-de-Cologne on a clean handkerchief and fixed it with careful negligence in his sleeve. He took his newest silk hat from its band-box and adjusted it to a pleasing angle on his head. He hesitated between a silver handled stick and his best silk umbrella with the gold top, and chose the umbrella. He drew his gold chain across his waistcoat and fixed the large gold cross so that it hung well down in the centre. His grey reindeer gloves! No matter where he called now, he thought, with a half-bitter smile, he'd be wearing a gift of the house. Anywhere, except where he was going—from Kitty at least. Damn her! He'd let her go to the devil, and go somewhere he was welcome.

He left the Presbytery, banged the entrance-gate violently behind him, strode forward at a rapid pace, but slackened it when he noticed that his boots were getting dusty. Besides, it would never do to get hot. He went round by Daunt's

Terrace in order to avoid the Muldoons' shop, kept his eyes on the pavement as he passed Rafters, and pretended not to see Bedelia who signalled to him from an upstairs window. He gave curt nods to passing acquaintances. Why should he bother about Kitty with the whole town to choose from? If he did want to see her, it was lucky it was market day … she'd be alone. He turned in at the shop door without hesitation.

'Father Burke! Well, well, to be sure,' Mrs Curtin said joyfully, over the heads of several customers. 'Harry, come up here and finish Mrs Mulcahy's order while I attend to the priest. I know you are, Mrs Greene, but I won't be a minute. The snug, Father.'

She bustled round and opened the snuggery door.

'It's great news I have for you entirely,' she said, in an eager, confident whisper, keeping his hand as she drew him into the little room. 'Kitty is going up above,' with a vague gesture, 'as soon as ever her clothes can be made. The grace of God and Father Bernardine between 'em did it, glory be to God—not to mention your own prayers. I never seen a girl so set on it. No hysterics, no high-faluting, no nothing. It's almost agin nature this taking it so quiet. I half pity Tom he's so broke over it, but we must all learn to bow to the will of God. And them Duggans thought they had her in their pocket! The hand of God is over all, I say. It's wonderful how He led that little girl along the right path. I have every reason to be proud of myself, but I'm a humble woman, thanks be to God. If I had ten more I wouldn't grudge 'em to Him.'

'You're a wonderful woman,' he murmured, with a suppressed sneer.

'I did my best. Though it was a bit of a strain at times. I might be tempted to give in once in a while, but I knew God was behind me, and sure the result proves me right.'

She stood on tiptoe and looked over the side screen. 'But there's Mrs Greene looking as black as pitch. You'll be going up to give Kitty a word in season before she goes? I'll call Peggy to warn her.'

'Please don't take Peggy away from her work,' he protested. 'I ought to know my way up by this,' he added, with a nervous laugh.

'Lighten the poor thing up a bit,' Mrs Curtin said cheerfully, as she held open the door leading to the hall. 'She's more like an old woman than a young girl for the last few days. It's not within reason to let religion hang so heavy on her. There's time and a place for everything, I always say.'

'Trust me,' he absentmindedly replied.

He mounted the stairs slowly, a sinking feeling at his heart. He pulled down his cuffs and the ends of his waistcoat, fixed his hat, gloves and umbrella in his left hand at the most effective angle, patted his hair and assumed the smirk with which he always entered a room. But to-day it was done almost unconsciously. For once he had very nearly forgotten himself. A desirable but unapproachable Kitty mocked his vision and made him tremble. Sphinx-like, with the veiled eyes of the woman in the picture in Dunne's room, she could love. But how to reach her across that gulf?

For a moment he saw himself objectively—stripped of all pretence and hypocrisy, boldly acknowledging his love, facing obloquy even. He saw her approving smile and felt a glow of heroic courage. The world seemed to rock about him. He clung to his resolve, though he knew that his courage had oozed out of his trembling knees. He could do it and he would. He struggled for a moment, but the difficulties crowded in on him and overpowered him. He rested his free hand on the bannister for support. No man could face it. Cut off by an ubiquitous and relentless church that must keep up appearances at any cost. His pleasant, easy life gone … Brady couldn't last for ever. Monsignor Burke was an easy game. And if he played his cards well and was careful … perhaps, a bishopric? Though that would be a heavy strain on one's caution.

He was a fool even to think of the other thing. And her father and mother would cut her off without a penny. It was all so unnecessary, too. She was sure to learn common sense and take what she could out of life—reasonably, of course. And the opportunities were infinite. A priest had a passport everywhere, and was a fool if he didn't make good use of it. He caught a glimpse of himself in the glass of a picture and smirked. He went through his usual operations with his clothes and hair, consciously now. With renewed self-respect he knocked at the sitting-room door, and opened it.

'Oh, it's you,' Kitty said indifferently, without moving from her curled-up position in Winnie's arm-chair, which was, however, turned away from the window. 'I thought you'd never come in.'

'A loosened bootlace,' he said, with irritation.

He was angry with himself for having the feeling of irritation, and tried to overcome it ... She might, at least, have offered him his usual chair. He put his hat and umbrella and gloves on the piano.

'Come now. Don't treat a friend like this.' He held out his hand.

'There are chairs,' she said coldly.

Her eyes moved slowly from his glossy clothes and heavy gold watch chain to the shining hat and the gold handle of the umbrella protruding over the edge of the piano. Father Bernardine was so right, but this man—was he really a priest? There was more in religion than that—was so wrong. It wasn't his dress altogether—that was merely vulgar. It was some combined effect of his leer and his Roman collar. Father Brady hadn't it, nor Father Dunne. But there were others ... And the more repulsive the leer the deeper the collar.

He was conscious of her look as he drew a chair near to her and sat down. He was always conscious of people's looks; of some necessary relation of their thoughts to himself. He was still angry with her for her refusal to shake hands, but he made an effort not to show it. It was, he supposed, because he had once tried to kiss her.

'Admiring my umbrella?' he said, with a nervous smirk. 'These things are thrown at me. I never brought it here before because Winnie never liked me to wear any but her gifts. Poor Winnie! She's such a dear little thing, a bit of a goose, though, don't you think?'

Kitty's frown warned him, and he added hastily, 'Bedelia Rafter gave me the umbrella. It's really rather choice. What?'

She wondered if he had ever tried to kiss Bedelia Rafter. A sharp image of Bedelia Rafter and Stephen Muldoon, in the punt below the bridge, flashed through her mind. For a moment she had a giddy, intoxicating sensation. It must be like that to be kissed. Oh! But it was all right. Father Bernardine said there was no sin unless one consented *after* one was conscious of the thought as sinful. She murmured an ejaculatory prayer and said:

'Wouldn't you like some tea?'

'What on earth put it into your head to go into a convent?' he sneered, irritated by her casual treatment.

'Because I want to, I suppose ... I'd better go and tell Peggy about tea. She won't hear a bell to-day—she'll be in the shop.'

'She saw me coming up,' he said. 'You needn't make an excuse to run away. Ah! That's why you are going into the convent. You are running away—from yourself,' he added, with a sneer.

She winced. Perhaps she had always disliked him because he seemed to know her thoughts.

'I'm not afraid of you, anyway,' she said, defending herself.

'Why should you be afraid of me? I'm your friend—have always been, if you would only let yourself see it.' He spoke gently. 'You're afraid of your passionate heart.'

She flushed. If her heart weren't dead that would be true. He was a beast.

'There's nothing to be ashamed of,' he assured her. 'It merely means that you're a woman. You won't escape your feelings by taking them into a convent. I know it will be worse there instead of better. They want their natural outlet. You can't kill them by repressing them. They only become more active, more violent.'

She listened with a growing interest. His lisp had gone and he seemed more real. He was wrong, of course. The outlet she had wanted was closed to her for ever. If her feelings weren't dead, they were dying. For hours at a time she felt so numb that she had no feelings left. Gradually they would die away altogether. Even now, by following Father Bernardine's instructions, she could direct her thoughts. In the convent, actively working for the greater glory of God, she should be quite safe.

'Take my advice and stay out. You'll only make yourself the more miserable by going in,' he wound up.

'I couldn't be more miserable than I am.'

'Poor little thing. My poor Kitty,' he said tenderly.

She felt his hand on hers, but she was inert, unable to move. Fascinated, she watched him rise from his chair and bend over her. Weak and passive she waited. She could note things: the satisfied smirk on his convulsed face; the absence of struggle in her own will; her feeling of peace and content as once on waking out of a fever; a sort of detached, curious expectancy. A mixed odour of lemon, stale tobacco and eau-de-Cologne awakened her. Mingled with the horrid attraction of his hot breath was the menacing face of Father Bernardine in the very moment of his fiercest denunciation of sin. Feebly and half-reluctantly she threw her hands forward.

'Don't be a little fool,' he said angrily.

'How dare you!' Fiercely she flung him off. She trembled all over. Was there never to be any release? Thank God, she had just saved herself in time. Whether her clothes were ready or not, she'd enter to-night—to-morrow at the latest.

'I suppose you've lost your heart to the pulpit Adonis?' he sneered.

She frowned. What a thoroughly bad man he must be to speak like that of a saint. 'He never forgets that he's a priest,' she said.

He shrugged his shoulders sceptically. 'Anyhow, I can't forget that I'm a man when you're by,' he said bitterly.

'You shouldn't, you know.' She spoke gently now, her resentment ebbing away in a quickened interest. He was suffering, and it was because of her.

'You're a little devil—a heartless little devil. You'll suffer for this yet. By God, how you'll suffer for it. A convent!' he laughed. 'With a temperament like yours you'll soon know what it is to be in hell.'

His words struck her with a cold fear. What if he knew? After all, he was a priest, and didn't some bad prophet once foretell the truth.

'Won't you have some tea now, Father?' she said with a frightened, absentminded stare at a Crown Derby tea-cup on a blue velvet bracket on the wall.

'No, thank you, I'm going to the Muldoons for tea.'

She had a pleasant feeling of relief. He was just Father Burke, after all. She was a fool to think even for a moment that anything that he said could have any weight. Father Bernardine was so different. Handsome, but unconscious of it—just as the angels must be. One could be mistaken as to one's own feelings, but a saint saw straight into one's heart. With a pitying smile she watched Father Burke smirk at the mirror, pull at his cuffs and waistcoat, shake his shoulders into position and pat a lock of hair. He lingered over the arrangement of his hat, gloves and umbrella.

'You won't make friends?' he appealed, turning round and facing her in all his seductive glory.

'It's really long after tea-time.' She only half-suppressed a smile.

'You're choosing a certain road to the devil,' he said furiously.

'I prefer my own road, anyway, to yours.'

He looked at her as if he hated her, bit his lip, turned on his heel, and had assumed his usual pose of deprecating assurance, his head cocked a little to one side, by the time he had reached the door.

She watched him go half with relief, half with regret. If only he didn't make love, he'd be interesting enough when he allowed himself to be real. Was there anything in what he said? Father Brady had hinted at something similar, but he was too angry with her to be coherent. And Father Brady, with his narrow experience, couldn't know as much about the soul as Father Bernardine. She went to the window and looked out idly at the groups of people breaking and re-forming, chattering and bargaining in front of the shop. She turned away suddenly with a shudder. *He* might pass. She couldn't bear that—yet. Father Bernardine had promised her happiness. She must be patient. She curled herself again in the arm-chair and stared at the wall above the piano. It was sure to come—not all at once, perhaps, but some time. Would it take a week, a month, a year?

Chapter 10

The Mercy Convent looked down on Drumbawn physically as well as morally. At its feet were the parish church, the presbytery and the river. It was surrounded by extensive grounds shaded by stately beech and elm. Field after field by the diligent and judicious use of St Benedict's medals, had been added to the original park of the Levis family till no house in the main portion of the town beyond the river escaped observation. The process of acquisition was simple, though sometimes long. The field giving a view of the old whitewashed Dominican convent on the northern outskirts of the town fell in ten years, while the field on the slope of the steep hill that made possible a private way from the convent to the parish church, held out for nearly two generations. Nine days before the feast of St Benedict in each year a medal was thrown into the desired field, a novena was offered up to the saint that God might intervene, and the result was awaited with confidence. The manner of fulfilment varied. A recalcitrant owner died, and his heir was moved to a sense of his religious duty by a substantial price. A novice brought in a field as a *dot*. Bankruptcy made another possible. But the greatest marvel of all was longest in coming. The old reprobate, who for fifty years forced the nuns to walk to the parish church by the public street, died intestate, and his property all came to Sister Angelica, his niece, to whom he had frequently sworn he would never leave a cent. Sister Angelica never walked the gravelled path, shaded by trim juniper hedges, from the convent to the parish church, without meditating on the justice of God, manifested all the more strikingly as her uncle David had left an unsigned will bequeathing in a long clause of derision of the convent, the coveted field to a cats' home.

On a genial morning of May three nuns walked slowly along the west terrace. The external duties of the day had begun. Nuns were busy over their allotted tasks in the schools, in the orphanage, in the house. Reverend Mother, Mother Bursar and the Mistress of Novices had thus a free hour in which to discuss important affairs of direction and government.

Reverend Mother peered over her glasses at the blaze of spring flowers, stooped down with difficulty, now to smell, now to cut off, with a scissors that hung from her leather girdle, a dead leaf or a fading blossom.

'A lot of beds need renewing,' she said briskly. Her slight note of defiance could not be meant for the Mistress of Novices who, looking at her with admiring eyes, hastened to say:

'Indeed they do, Reverend Mother. Badly, very badly.'

Mother Bursar shot an angry glance at the Mistress of Novices, who blushed and added defensively:

'You know, Michael, they're not looking their best.'

'There isn't another convent in the country has a better show of flowers,' Mother Michael stonily said.

'Not even the tulips?' Reverend Mother pleaded.

'As if dear Reverend Mother had to beg for things!' the Mistress of Novices indignantly protested.

'Is it Calixta's business, or is it mine?' Mother Michael enquired, pursing her thin lips.

'Yours, of course, dear Michael,' Reverend Mother answered, laying a benignant hand on Mother Bursar's shoulder. 'You are our trusted guardian of the purse. I'd be very hard myself if I held the purse-strings. How you manage to meet all our wants is a wonder to me.'

Mother Calixta gave a demure smile and a little sniff, applied her blue-and-white check handkerchief to her nose and murmured, 'It can't be hay-fever yet.'

Mother Michael's hard, thin face relaxed a little, and she said, half relenting, half doubtful:

'I've just had to renew all the sisters' summer underclothing—the new gold chalice compelled us to put it off last year.'

'God always provides,' Reverend Mother said hopefully, pulling up a weed.

'And this new Inspector of Orphanages is putting us to dreadful expense—spectacles and teeth. He's even making a fuss about beds and underclothes—it's indelicate.' Mother Michael frowned at a creeper with a calculating air. 'I hoped to be able to pay for the new cope out of the orphans this year, but they'll barely come out even.'

'We live in hard times,' said Reverend Mother cheerfully. 'Inspectors are a scourge. I remember the time when they came in pleasantly to lunch and wrote a few nice words of praise in the book without fussing over anything—quite gentlemen. Thank God the children do no worse now, for all this fuss. You'll manage somehow, Michael? A few pounds would do it. One, two—seven beds here. And we'll want new geraniums and scarlet begonias—I was ashamed of the bedding-out last year. That will be eight beds more in the south terrace. And the greenhouses are a disgrace. We must re-stock the whole of the orchids and primulas. This terrace would be all the better for replanting. I'd run a centre walk up to the dovecote. And that straggling laurel hedge must go.'

'It hides the hen houses,' Mother Michael objected.

'Oh, I'd plant a juniper hedge behind it and let that grow to a certain height before I touched the laurels. Then when we pull up the laurels—thank God juniper doesn't take long to grow—we'd have space for a new herbaceous border along the whole length.' Reverend Mother paused to take breath.

'When I was young,' Mother Michael said, with a set smile, 'I was left a legacy of about eight pounds a year. My mother used to advise me how to spend it. I once added up the cost of her plans—over two hundred pounds in one year.'

'Michael!' Mother Calixta exclaimed, in a tone of horror with an anxious look at Reverend Mother.

Reverend Mother laughed heartily. 'This little calculating machine keeps the roof over us, Calixta. I suppose I'm not to be trusted with trees and flowers. Twenty pounds, Michael? Not a penny more.'

'I know what that means,' Mother Michael said, coldly. 'A hundred pounds wouldn't—'

'How are those children of yours on retreat getting on, Calixta?' Reverend Mother interrupted.

'Oh, beautifully,' Mother Calixta ecstatically replied.

'Let us sit down for a while in the shade.' Reverend Mother looked closely at a rosebud without seeing the grubs. 'We'll let the fowl and the cow-houses pass this morning.'

'It will be cheaper,' Mother Michael said, with a little toss of her head.

Mother Calixta ran forward and drew two chairs close together under a spreading yew tree. 'Please?' she said to Mother Michael, who hesitated to take the second chair.

Reverend Mother sank down on her chair with relief.

'Pheu, it might be July. The sooner we have summer things the better, Michael. Don't crowd in on me, child,' she added to Calixta who had fetched a low stool for herself and sat close to Reverend Mother's knee, looking up at her face.

The Mistress of Novices moved back her seat an inch, blushing prettily. She was forty-one, but did not look it. She was pleased with 'child' as a tribute to her youthful appearance, and as a token of Reverend Mother's affection: the two things, after God—all three were, indeed, inextricably mixed—for which she cared most.

Mother Michael gave a little sniff which quite plainly said 'humph.' She, too, was fond of Reverend Mother but, she told herself, in a rational way. Reverend Mother, with all her carelessness about money, was a woman of sense, for she made her, Michael, bursar, and kept her there in the face of strong opposition. It was all to Reverend Mother's advantage, of course, for no-one else in the convent had her, Michael's, knowledge of accounts and her courage to be offensive. Without her help in keeping things straight the finances of the convent would be in a mess in six months, and the opposition party under Sister Eulalie would at last succeed in ousting Reverend Mother from office. Reverend Mother might have a weakness for sprawling affection like Calixta's, but she could also use her head.

'Are you comfy, dearest Mother?' Mother Calixta asked, laying a hand on Reverend Mother's knee.

'There, there,' Reverend Mother answered absentmindedly, fingering her beads.

Michael smiled down her nose at Calixta, and thought how like a fawning spaniel she looked. It was so much more comfortable and satisfying to one's self-respect to be trusted and feared a little than to be loved and half despised.

'Kitty is all right, but I'm not so sure about Winnie,' Reverend Mother said wearily, pushing back her dimity from her hot brow.

'But, Mother dear, it's all settled. They're in the middle of their retreat for profession,' Mother Calixta said. 'If you said you *knew*, of course, I'd say nothing. But as it is only a feeling—though in these, too, you are nearly always wonderfully right—I must take the courage to say that I think you are wrong.'

'What do you say, Michael?' Reverend Mother asked, with a worried frown.

Mother Michael shrugged her narrow shoulders. 'Winnie is a little fool; but then she's no worse than many of the others we've professed.'

Reverend Mother smiled. 'We can't all of us be wise. It's whether she's going to be a happy little fool or a miserable one,' she said, peering into space over her spectacles.

'Who knows? Anyhow, she's passed her chapter,' Mother Michael said, with a note of finality.

'The gate of heaven!' Reverend Mother chuckled. 'Respect for the sisters' vote is a new thing with you.'

'It gets us the money for the new chapel this time,' Mother Michael said dryly. 'And as you're determined to build it in any case, the Holy Ghost must have been somewhere about.'

Reverend Mother sighed. 'I wish we hadn't to think of money,' she said.

'We needn't if we didn't waste so much on fal-lals. The old chapel is good enough,' said Mother Michael sharply.

'Michael!' Mother Calixta indignantly held up a warning finger.

'The orphans are too much crowded up at the back,' Reverend Mother said.

'The bishop hasn't room enough to show off at ceremonies,' Mother Michael retorted, with spirit.

'A large apse,' said Reverend Mother weakly, 'would be more decorous.'

'Thank God the little Curtins will enable me to balance my accounts,' Mother Michael said, with good-humour. 'I was a little afraid of Winnie balking.'

'It's not at all nice of Michael to speak of my novices in this horrid way. Is it now, Reverend Mother, dear?' Mother Calixta was tearful with vexation.

'I wish I hadn't Winnie on my mind,' Reverend Mother said doubtfully.

'Mr Curtin might throw in the river meadow on the day of the profession, if it was properly put to him,' Mother Michael meditated. 'I could keep five more cows and I can get tuppence ha'penny a quart for all the Guernsey milk we can sell. You could have the shrubbery and the beds and everything if he did,' she added, with an unusual burst of generosity.

'We could run the lime avenue down to the river,' Reverend Mother said.

'Even that, perhaps,' Mother Michael doubtfully agreed.

But already Reverend Mother had extended the lime avenue, and was busy making a path along the river; and growing a hedge—a juniper hedge well back with openings—to shade the nuns from prying eyes while giving access to a terrace on the bank.

'I was keeping the river meadow back as a surprise for dear Reverend Mother … it's sure to come the day Winnie is professed. She and all the novices have been praying for it ever since she entered,' Mother Calixta said.

Mother Michael shot at Reverend Mother her well-known look: 'Don't you admit now she's a fool ?' Reverend Mother's whimsical smile encouraged her to add in words, 'You could come round him if anyone could, Reverend Mother.'

'I might try,' the old nun said reluctantly. 'He's giving us a good deal as it is. And people cling to land. I wouldn't part with a foot of our grounds for its weight in gold. And he's never forgiven us for taking Kitty. There's a real nun for you! But I wish I could see my way more clearly about Winnie. We could have a little summer-house behind the hedge, by one of the openings. I'll get Johanna to influence him. It's not grasping of us, as it must all come to the children one day,' she added, as if pleading with a conscience that hung on a branch of wistaria. 'But I wish we had given Winnie a few months more trial,' with a sigh.

'There's no hedge in the river meadow,' said Mother Michael severely.

'There will be, dear. There will be,' Reverend Mother mused.

There was silence for a few seconds. Reverend Mother was thatching the summer-house. Mother Michael was frowningly calculating the probable losses on her proposed source of profit. Mother Calixta was feeling snubbed. The office of novice-mistress was senior to that of bursar and infinitely more important. Michael, of course, was always horrid. But dear Reverend Mother? She wouldn't mind if they had been alone, but to ignore her before that cat Michael! She felt irritated with Reverend Mother.

'I don't care what anyone says, Winnie has ten times the vocation that Kitty has,' she broke out.

'Ah,' Reverend Mother said sadly, brought back with painful suddenness from a pleasant dream. Most of poor Calixta's swans were geese. Calixta was good, but was that enough? Was she consulting her own ease too much in having her as novice mistress. She sighed.

'Kitty doesn't put ink in the holy water stoup,' Mother Michael said quietly.

'Father Acquaviva did the same when he was a novice, and he became General of the Jesuits,' Mother Calixta retorted. 'It was all dear Winnie's playfulness. She read about it at Spiritual Reading and thought it such simple saintly fun. I like my novices to show signs of Holy Innocence.'

'That's why she runs after Father Burke, I suppose?' Mother Michael gave a keen glance at Reverend Mother as she spoke.

'He's her confessor,' Mother Calixta said, looking apprehensively in her turn at Reverend Mother, who was telling her beads with a troubled face.

Mother Michael made a dive at a wasp with the end of her black veil, and smiled sceptically at the corpse. 'I've wondered till now where our young nuns got their wisdom,' she said pleasantly, whisking the wasp off her lap.

'Indeed, I'm most careful. You know I am, Reverend Mother?' Mother Calixta said, blushing deeply. 'I can't speak frankly of such delicate subjects, of course, but I've hinted, and I've found Winnie as open as the day. The poor child is as easily seen through as a glass of spring water. A real nun to her finger-tips. I've known her to have as many as five novenas running at the same time. And I watch like a sleuth-hound.'

She laughed merrily. 'I once said that to the novices and the dear things call me 'the sleuth-hound' as a pet name ever since.'

'It's so very apt!' Mother Michael said.

'I can't put my finger on anything positive.' Reverend Mother was half-asserting, half-posing a worried question to the gravel at her feet.

'Perhaps if Calixta were to wear spectacles,' Mother Michael suggested, with malice in her shining teeth.

'It's all because Kitty is your favourite,' Mother Calixta tartly retorted.

'My dear child, I've no favourites,' Mother Michael said, with a shrug. 'Winnie has survived her noviceship without making too great a fool of herself, so I'm willing to take your word for the rest. As far as I'm concerned, we haven't had two more promising nuns than the Curtins since I became bursar. Vocations are your business and dowries are mine. In cash they're both equal; and both eminently satisfactory. Instead of worrying about Winnie, Reverend Mother should be blessing her stars. They say Tom Curtin has pots of money, and our purse is a bottomless sieve.'

'We could put the profession off for another three months,' Reverend Mother suggested.

'In twenty years Winnie will be the very same as she is to-day,' Mother Michael decisively said. 'They were both due for profession three months ago, and you've kept them back with no result but to complicate my accounts. It's not fair to Kitty with nothing whatever against her. And Calixta will know just as much about Winnie in three months as she knows now. The profession day has been fixed by the bishop; and we've practically arranged to begin building next week. It means an overdraft unless we have Tom Curtin's cheque at once.'

'She draws a net round me so that I can hardly breathe when she speaks like this,' Reverend Mother said to Mother Calixta, with a sigh. 'You're sure it's all right?'

'Dear Michael takes such material views of things,' Mother Calixta said primly. 'I know my novices. Winnie is a saint if ever there was one,' she continued, with enthusiasm. 'Such acts of mortification, such offerings up, such—'

'I hope to God we aren't making a mistake,' Reverend Mother interrupted. 'If she were only like Kitty I'd feel quite happy. There, if you like, is complete detachment from the world. Well, well, let us hope for the best.'

After a few seconds' silent fingering of her beads she said thoughtfully:

'You must put up an iron paling along two sides of the river meadow, Michael—the sisters would be so frightened of the cows. Perhaps, indeed, it would be better not to keep cows there at all.'

'I wanted to speak to you about the kitchen range,' Mother Michael said hastily.

Chapter 11

Kitty watched the shadows grow darker and darker. The stained-glass window behind the high altar was a black smudge. The little red lamp in front of the tabernacle twinkled more luminously. In the fading light the silence grew deeper. The sacristy clock hammered out the seconds with a force and clearness that added to the stillness. There was something soothing and protecting in the regular, detached, slow beats. Only unexpected sounds, the banging of a door somewhere far away in the convent, a distant burst of laughter, desecrated the quiet and peace.

A sigh from Winnie's stall opposite seemed like a groan of pain. Kitty started and glanced across nervously, but was reassured by the immobility of the dim white figure. She settled herself back on her heels, half kneeling, half sitting, and leant her shoulder against the side of her stall with a sigh. The menacing sound had made her nervous. She smiled wryly as she pulled herself together. The retreat was telling on her, but it was practically over now. The nuns would soon be in for night prayer; then bed, a long sleep in the morning, and her last farewell to the world at eleven.

Could she sleep at all this night of nights? But that was only a scrap of someone else's talk. She just felt tired and languid—not at all exalted, as Mother Calixta said novices felt on the night before their profession. Perhaps the exaltation would come at the supreme moment when she made her vows—those wonderful vows of poverty, chastity and obedience. She murmured the words under her breath in a tone of awe; but sighed at the lack of response in her feelings. Was she always to suffer from this aridity of soul? There was no glow of feeling such as Father Bernardine promised her. Nothing but bleak mountains which she had to climb arduously, cold at heart. And that was only sometimes. Mostly it was merely drifting with the current without any feeling at all. Perhaps the many rehearsals, the effort to remember the proper bow, the right response, had deadened her capacity for feeling. God would one day—perhaps to-morrow—unlock her feelings and allow her mind and her heart to act in unison. It was so hard to go on spurring her mind without any response from her heart. Yet she knew she was right. Father Bernardine over and over again had made it quite clear. God had marked out the path for her. The convent was her only way of salvation and atonement. If only her feelings would for once come to her aid. Even in the presence of the Blessed Sacrament there was only this hard, mechanical belief. She knew God was there now, loving her, helping her. Her mind accepted it, believed in it firmly. She wanted to feel gratitude, but her heart was like a dry well. So with her vocation. It was an eternal truth, decreed, Father Bernardine said, from before time was. But it gave her no emotion.

Not that she had no feelings. Unhappily she had. Feelings that she had failed to bring under the sway of her mind. It was her punishment that the devil had so much power to tempt her through her emotions. Those emotions that she could not subdue to the service of God were easily moved by temptations of the devil. When she thought she had completely mastered them they grew again in strength; and it was only by almost superhuman prayer that she prevented them from conquering her. It was as if she were the guardian of a fragile dyke against which great waves beat: her puny mind and will against the turbid waves of her lower nature. In the crises of furious storms it was only one last, almost despairing, cry to God that had saved her. Even then she could feel no gratitude. She could only thank God with her mind and her moving lips … It was so odd that God should give the devil such power in His own world—but she must not think. That, too, was a wile of the devil. God gave sufficient grace to resist all temptations. And recently, thank God, they had been less active. Perhaps it was the approach of her profession ... Her vows would be new weapons against the devil.

One, two. Half-past eight. How long time took in passing. Half an hour yet before the nuns came to night prayer. What was Winnie thinking of? She might be asleep, she was so still and silent. How little she knew about Winnie! The convent, instead of bringing them closer to one another, had divided them. How little one knew about any of the nuns!

She watched the little lighters attached to the gas-lamps. Soon a nun would come and tug at the chains and the chapel would glow with a brilliant light. One saw little of the convent from the noviceship. It would be different in the professed community room. What matter if it all seemed so trivial? There was the greater glory of God to be worked for, and the salvation of one's own soul.

Nearly three years! It seemed like an eternity. And she might live to be old. Reverend Mother was seventy, and Sister Euphemia was nearly ninety. She shuddered and huddled herself into the corner of her stall.

She remembered so well the blank desolation of the night of her entrance. It might have been yesterday in its vividness; though the chasm that yawned across to it made it seem a hundred years: her anguish when the door was shut behind her. The feeling of despair at the grating of the key in the lock. Her revulsion from those endless kisses that congratulated her on her doom. It was as if grinning devils mocked at her. And in the chapel there was only an angry God who frowned on her and spurned her. And her relief when she fainted. How suddenly the lights danced up and down. The nuns' voices reached her from a distance like subdued music.

The water Reverend Mother put to her parched lips was a heavenly draught, and there was consolation in her kind, 'I know, dear. You'll be all right tomorrow.' Peace came only when she was alone in her little whitewashed cell. How well she remembered sitting on the blue-and-white coverlet of her bed, noting with the peace of exhaustion the scant white-enamelled furniture, the bare waxed floor, the blue-and-white curtains; and the curious sensation she had had as of an emptiness of all sensation, a dead restful feeling from which she had never since quite awakened.

But that was nonsense. She was always quite wide awake. She smiled faintly. She saw all the absurdities of the noviceship!

Her mind moved over the past, to and fro, like a shuttlecock: the peace of the long nights and the times of silence and the agony of the recreations. It was as if she had grown suddenly old and Winnie and many of the novices had gone back to the nursery. They couldn't be as foolish as they seemed. She knew nothing of them, just as they knew nothing of her. Nothing, thank God, of the storms of temptation that left her pale and exhausted. She knew too much of real sin to toy with danger. Winnie was one of the silliest. She spoke of Father Burke as if he were a lover—but that must be the recklessness of innocence. She spoke of half a dozen saints in the same words, and of several nuns. Even Father Brady had his devoted admirers; while almost the whole noviceship was in adoration before Father Bernardine. There was nothing wrong, of course—just mere silliness. But how often their talk, the perpetual comparison of their stages of 'gone-ness' was the occasion of temptation to her. They called her a prig because she wouldn't join in their game of placing the objects of her affections in their order of precedence. But it was only because she was afraid. Her emotions, frigid in her intercourse with God, played her curious tricks when the novices spoke of love. When they boasted lightly of their 'number one,' 'number two' or 'number three,' her set face indicated, not condemnation as they thought, but her effort to guard herself from sin. Nothing in the convent had been difficult except the recreations. Not the obedience, not the work, not the ordered monotony of the daily round, nothing except the constant direct and indirect references to sex. Not even the saints and angels were exempt. St Stanislaus was a greater darling than St Aloysius. One novice was 'gone' on St Vincent, another on St Benedict Joseph Labre. There was open jealousy over the priests. Sister Camilla was accused of making eyes at Father Burke, and Sister Chrysostom of waylaying Father Bernardine in the corridor. A handkerchief of his was put up to auction by a prayer-collecting novice and scraps fetched as much as ten rosaries. She particularly disliked talk of Father Bernardine. God had used him for her salvation; but He was also using him for her punishment—or, rather, He was allowing the devil to use him as a temptation. No, she mustn't dwell on him. It would all be different when she was professed. Her vow would help her.

A quarter to nine. How ghostly the chapel looked in the gloom of the gas lighters. To-morrow her hair would be cut off. If only her ghosts went with it. What was Daisy Thornton's baby like? Had he blue eyes like him—no, no, she mustn't think of that. And Joe Duggan had never married. He was a great man now. She was glad her father had helped him. He dressed more quietly and spoke better. If he weren't so repulsive looking? No, no, she mustn't think of things like that. And Father Burke had changed. She really believed she had done him good. The one good thing to her credit was that she had resisted him and the result on him was wonderful. He seemed to have repented. Perhaps he had never been really wicked. It was not for her to cast stones. He should not have allowed himself to fall in love with her, of course. He cared for her still—she could see that. But she was sure that it was now in a holy way. He did his best to avoid her, and when they met, he was so gentle. He never even tried to hold her hand, and if he held it sometimes unconsciously, she knew from the way he dropped it suddenly that he was fighting a noble battle. He had really good taste in music, and there was something very sympathetic in his singing voice. It was absurd of Winnie to be jealous of her. She had got over her dislike of Father Burke, but he could never be anything more than a friend. Winnie was frivolous and couldn't see that he had grown serious …

She shook herself and knelt straight. She mustn't allow these distractions to-night of all nights! She should be thinking of her vows. Poverty was nothing. Notwithstanding all Mother Calixta said it seemed to be a joke. They weren't poor. And obedience saved one the trouble of thinking. Mother Calixta told one to do some silly things, but that was because she was so silly. Reverend Mother was different. Chastity? Oh, that God would make that vow her strong armour. She wished she knew more about it. But Mother Calixta was always vague. Even Father Bernardine was disappointing in his direction and in his convent sermons. He never spoke to nuns, he said, on gross subjects; never even mentioned hell and toned down Purgatory till it seemed a desirable place to live in … Would her vow remove those horrid temptations of the flesh altogether? restore her to the original innocence of Eve? Father Bernardine said, yes. But then he had said that the convent would, and the convent hadn't. She didn't know. Or would her vow, as Mother Calixta said, be a sort of supernatural help that stilled the passions ? Anyhow, Father Brady couldn't be right when he said she'd be only exchanging a whip for a scorpion. He was getting more crabby as he grew older, and practically all the nuns except Reverend Mother and a few old black veils had given him up as a confessor.

Besides, he had never forgiven her for coming into the convent; and when she went to him with a difficulty he told her cruelly to go out home and get married. It was so odd he hadn't more spiritual discrimination, for he was kind in many ways, and Reverend Mother said he was a saint. Everything was so difficult to understand. Anyhow, he couldn't say that to her any more. Thank God, to-morrow she'd be bound to God irrevocably and the devil would knock in vain at her heart.

She turned her eyes towards the tabernacle and prayed. Her lips were dry. When she thought of God He seemed suddenly to desert her. She had nothing to offer. She was an empty husk without an idea, without words. Oh, for one moment of Winnie's fervour! It was no use, she couldn't pray …

And there were those other images coming again. Why had God given her a body and feeling, and emotions that seemed meant for no other purpose but to offend Him … oh, thank God, there were the lights at last.

She watched the leisurely lay-sister turn on light after light. If the nuns would only come quickly. And she had been so safe all day. Why didn't they hurry? There it was striking nine—two, three, four. She set her lips and counted the strokes desperately. God would surely give her the strength to hold out. Oh, there were the nuns at last. The formal night prayers would be a help. The mere swish of the nuns' trains trailing along the pavement was a help. Oh God, not that. No, no. It was a last effort of the devil, but with God's help she'd overcome him. God was subjecting her to this last trial of strength. She couldn't pray. Her throat was parched. Oh, that wonderful thrill. How beautiful it was—just as if Heaven had opened. No, she hadn't consented. It was the devil making believe that her will had given way. She had asked God to help and He couldn't refuse. She was feeling better already … She joined in the responses. The united prayers of the nuns were a thanks-offering to God for her. They would sustain her now and always. Why did this struggle to overcome the devil always leave her so weak? But she mustn't think of it or it might come on again. If she could only sleep, and not dream … The tabernacle door was a glowing flame, and through it God at last was smiling at her …

When a tug at her veil awoke her, she was suckling a pink-and-white chubby baby with yellow hair and wonderful blue eyes, full of a deep content. A happy smile was still in her face as she turned towards Reverend Mother.

'Bed, now, dear,' the old nun said, with a smile. 'You mustn't even pray too much—the nuns have all gone to bed. You must be strong for to-morrow. I needn't ask if you feel happy. You look it.'

'I am.'

She still smiled, happy and half dazed.

'Good night, dear, God bless you,' Reverend Mother said as she shuffled off.

Kitty stared at the lay-sister putting out the lights. It was such a queer dream to have, yet it gave her a sort of holy feeling, made her feel as if she could really pray. Ah, that was it. Dreams always went by opposites, and God had sent it to console her, to confirm her virginity, to assure her that her vocation was real …

The lay-sister coughed, and Kitty hurried away, murmuring a fervent prayer of gratitude and thanskgiving.

Chapter 12

When Winnie gave the deep sigh that echoed through the darkening chapel and frightened Kitty, she was feeling happy and contented. The excitement of the retreat was practically over, the excitement of the profession was still twelve hours off, and it was nice to have a rest in between.

She settled herself down comfortably. Her mind wandered fitfully back over a happy past and forward to a roseate future: three years of almost unclouded happiness; and the future was even more promising. In the early days there had been difficulties, small clouds that passed as summer showers, but, once she had learned to adapt herself fully to the convent life, nothing really troubled her. Father Burke had been a great help, and Sister Eulalie, but, as they said, she must always have had in her the makings of a sensible nun.

It wasn't God's will to deprive one of everything. The human affections were the best foundation for divine love. Once the great sacrifice had been made, and one had given up one's home and the pleasures of the world for the rigour of conventual life, God allowed one a good deal of latitude. She did not love God less because she loved Father James; indeed, she loved Him more. With a deep human love in one's heart one knew what one was talking about when one prayed. It would never do, of course, to love a layman, but a priest was something sacred in himself. She never prayed with more fervour than when she was feeling lonely for Father James. And kissing him was almost a prayer in itself, it made her feel so happy and so holy ... Mary was exalted above Martha, because Martha fussed about while Mary loved. Mary knew human love and was preferred by God. Such a lot of the nuns were Marthas. They were strict and priggish and self-important and were never satisfied but when they were trying to make life miserable for themselves and everyone else. She knew; for she had almost been a Martha when Father James rescued her …

She'd never forget the night of her entrance: the despair of going into the convent just when she had awakened into life; the first gleam of hope in Sister Eulalie's whisper as they kissed, 'I've arranged about the sacristy—you'll see him in the morning'; the mingled hope, fear and doubt of the night; the bliss of the few minutes after Mass in the back sacristy. And heaven had never entirely shut since. There were scruples she had to fight down before he had fully taught her to walk fearlessly in faith. Like the admiral in some battle one had to shut an eye to rules and regulations. But God forgave minor breaches of the law in the great love she was able to offer Him. Rules were right enough for the Marthas who could never be anything but paving-stones in heaven; but for the elect, as Father James said, they were hindrances that it was often meritorious to ignore. One had to be prudent, of course, for the Marthas were terribly suspicious and weren't spiritual enough to understand things … The risks she ran had often made her blood run cold. But in time all fear disappeared in her great love and she realized that God must have been protecting her … The sacristy was simple enough; but the infant school during the night recreation was worse than the enchanted forest to the princess in the fairy tale. One had to tell white fibs, and might never meet anyone anywhere. But it all made one so brave and wise. That was the wonderful thing about love; how it had made her grow. She used to be so much afraid of a mouse and of hell; but now she was afraid of nothing, not even of waiting for him in the dark in the church walk. Nor of sin; since she knew that there was no sin in the love of the divinely appointed. Why, she used even to be timid of Kitty; and now she felt hundreds of years older and wiser.

She glanced across at Kitty's stall with a satisfied smile. She heard a succession of slight groans and smiled superciliously. There was a Martha if ever there was one … a box of scruples, afraid of her own shadow. It must be that; or why was Kitty such a spoil-sport at recreation? If she only worked up a 'particular' for someone she'd be far happier. For anyone except, of course, Father James. She didn't mind his having some of the older nuns for number two or three; but not Kitty … Strict observance of rule might be all a pose of Kitty's to attract attention. Some of the frumpy old muffs were saying already that Kitty would be a Mother one day—maybe Reverend Mother.

She smiled knowingly. What a sell it would be for the Marthas when Eulalie was Reverend Mother. Poor old Reverend Mother Teresa was a bit of a nuisance. She was nice enough in a way; but she had a disconcerting way of looking at one, and of shooting out an awkward question. And she kept Michael in office who had eyes that could pierce like a gimlet. Calixta was all right and was a bit gone on the bishop and Father Bernardine. For the present, Eulalie said, no-one could be better in the noviceship than Calixta, who was such a softy. When Reverend Mother had gone a little more astray on flowers and glasshouses Eulalie would spring her mine … Eulalie was a duck. She understood things. One didn't tell her everything, of course, though one might, almost, if Father James wasn't so particular about keeping such sacred things, as it were, under the seal of confession. Freedom was Eulalie's motto. When she was Reverend Mother one shouldn't have to run to holes and corners. Unless Kitty changed she'd be a nobody under Eulalie. She'd always have her face, of course; and she'd look still better in the black veil. Even old priests liked talking to her; and the new curate at Derrydonnelly couldn't take his eyes off her …

What had come over Kitty at all? She used to be such fun at school. Still, one never knew with those secretive ones. Once or twice she had caught Father James looking at Kitty in a queer sort of way, but he had sworn he didn't care a pin for her … And Kitty had changed in her manner to him lately. Nothing much to worry about yet; but those saint's eyes of hers were dangerous, and one couldn't help being afraid she'd use them …

It was odd how both she and Kitty had changed. The convent was wonderful. It freed the souls of the chosen, Sister Eulalie said, and tightened up others. While broadening her own soul, it had narrowed Kitty's … She was sorry now in a way that she had prayed so hard for Kitty to come in. Kitty was just a wet blanket of a rule-keeper, and wasn't even really pious. She didn't go in for the rosary competition during the jubilee and had no favourite saints … while she, Winnie, had eleven and Patricia had seventeen. That reminded her … She must finish the novena for the river meadow.

She shut her eyes and prayed for a few minutes with fervour. So much done. St Benedict was rather a muff, but he was an old dear for getting land and things. Who was that new saint Patricia praised for being such a brick? He cured her of toothache, or was it an ingrowing nail? Anyhow, he was wonderful, and as prompt as prompt. Her mother was always on the look-out for saints like that—she'd tell her about him. And he'd do finely for Calixta's novena. Calixta was a dear, though she was a greedy-gut for novenas and rosaries. It was to get her brother an increase of pay this time. That would be easy after getting him the Commissionership with the last novena; and the novices would put their whole hearts into it …

Heigh-ho. What was keeping the sisters? There was no chance of seeing him to-night. But he promised faithfully to come to the infant school to-morrow night. She mustn't forget to unlock the door. And he'd be master of ceremonies tomorrow, and wear the new lace surplice her mother gave him for her. The bishop looked so mean beside him. He'd look so wonderful in a cope and mitre. If priests weren't so jealous he'd be a bishop. It would be wonderful to see him in purple and jewels … a sort of king … god-like …

She held her breath in ecstasy. She shivered a little and frowned. But then, he'd have to live at Caltra … miles away. Never that, never, never. She'd hardly ever see him. No, he mustn't be a bishop. But parish priest of Drumbawn would be lovely—if only God took that dreadful Father Brady. With Father James parish priest, and Sister Eulalie Reverend Mother, the convent would be heaven …

Here were the nuns at last and she hadn't had time to meditate much on her vows. The Finnegans would be sure to be at the ceremony, and the Miss Purcells, and maybe the Thorntons. She hoped nothing would induce her mother to wear that new hat. The poppies would be too awful, especially before the stuck-up Finnegans. The two cakes had come all right. Magnificent … three tiers. It was so much more distinguished to have a cake each. And the dinkiest little ornaments. Powdering her face wouldn't do Stella Finnegan much good. She'd be coming into the convent in despair one day and she'd be very soon taught her place—there were several novices with snubs to pay back. The idea of offering to God what she couldn't get any man to take! But this was envy and jealousy, and she must keep free of all sin to-night …

She joined in a few responses, her mind wandering among the elaborate decorations of the high altar. Eulalie was a dear to have done so much—far finer than when Leo was professed.

There was distinction, too, in having kept their own names. She had never known that to happen before—Kitty had, of course, to change the K of Katherine into a C. Still, they were bringing a great deal into the convent and deserved consideration; and her mother was presenting a new monstrance—silver gilt and beautifully jewelled. And if her father gave the field? Their vow of poverty would mean something; not like Leo's who hadn't a penny … She was glad she was able to give up so much to God. Tomorrow she shouldn't own a penny. It would be thrilling to sign one's will just before one made one's vows. Her mother had promised to keep them well supplied, but, of course, that didn't count. One viewed vows in the spirit and not in the letter, as Father James said. Calixta was rather silly in explaining them just as if they should be taken literally—it was only the Marthas did that, or pretended. But there was no law for the heart except a little prudence, Father James said. And, of course, she was prudent. Even Calixta, who wasn't really a bad sort and might understand, didn't find out much for all her probing. She was more afraid of one look of Michael's. Eulalie would put *her* on the shelf the first thing. Not that Michael saw much either—one was wise enough for that. And dear old Reverend Mother had almost lost her eyesight for everything but flowers. One should have to be more careful in the community room all the same. Some of the black veils had eyes like hawks. The Marthas were bad enough, but one wasn't safe even from the Marys—especially those who were gone on Father James. It was really scandalous of old nuns like Gregory and Martin—forty if they were a day …

She said the final 'Amen' with a snap. Kitty would be such a nuisance, too. If only she'd lose her head on Father Bernardine or someone …

She was half off her knees when she thought of her special intentions. She sank back on her heels and prayed furiously, consulting at intervals a written slip between the pages of her Office book. After a few minutes she put away her book with a sigh of relief, and looked around … There was Muredach going out. She'd catch her up and they'd have a word on the stairs if none of the Mothers were about. It was too dangerous in the cells, the night before profession—a Mother might pop in any minute. There was still the rosary she swapped with Macartan, but that could wait.

She hurried after Muredach, passed her in the corridor, slowed down and coughed.

'What does it feel like, Win?' Muredach said, in a hushed awed whisper to the floor as she drew abreast.

'Tremendous,' Winnie said, with a deep sigh.

'Pie and all that? I never felt a bit when I was received,' Muredach said dolefully.

'Profession is different,' Winnie said, with a sniff of superiority. 'I'm nearly bursting.'

'I had a peep at the cakes. They're scrumps,' Muredach said greedily. 'You won't forget to bag an extra bit for the noviceship, Win? We're all praying for you like mad.'

'As if I could forget! I hope it's to Stanislaus you've been praying, and not to that little prig Aloysius?'

'Of course! And plenty of the almond icing, Win. I could eat tons of it.'

'Mother is sending a special box for the novices,' Winnie said, with condescension. 'Chocs and fondants and marrons glacés.'

'O-oh!' Muredach said, with breathless excitement.

The approach of Mother Michael made them fall apart. Winnie lingered on the stairs, but Muredach doubled back to impart the joyful news to a chum. People with hair like Muredach's were always selfish pigs, Winnie thought resentfully, as she walked slowly to her cell. Little tears gathered on her eyelashes. How stupid of her to remind herself of the one thing she was anxious to forget. Her hair! The only real sorrow of her profession. If it was anyone else but God who demanded it, she'd die first. It was almost cruel of Him. Muredach's hair was beautiful, but it wasn't a patch on hers. And to cut it off with a shears! She groped to the gas jet and turned it on fully. It wasn't for nothing she was named after the holy martyr, St Winifred. It was almost as bad to have one's hair cut off as one's head—especially such hair. But she'd be brave. There was no sacrifice she wasn't prepared to make for God. Besides, very few had seen it, covered as it had been by veil and dimity, for over two years … And Father James said he loved her for herself alone …

She took off her veil and guimpe and let her hair fall over her face and shoulders. She passed her fingers tenderly through the fine strands, let the light play on the gold, and sighed deeply. Who could say that she wasn't making a sacrifice to God? Tears rolled down her cheeks. Would she get the mirror hidden behind the drawer? No, she couldn't bear to look at her glory. Except just this way, with its beauty half blinding her. And her nose would be red and her face blotchy. It was too cruel. She cried quietly, and, after a while, smilingly. God always gave compensations, Eulalie said. If He was taking her hair, He had given her much … her vocation … Father James.

A knock at the door made her start. It couldn't be 'lights out' already.

'It's I—Reverend Mother,' came through the open fanlight.

Winnie made a dash for her guimpe and veil and put them on hastily. She was pushing loose strands of hair up under her dimity as she opened the door with a flushed face.

'Oh, dear Reverend Mother. To keep you waiting like this! I was half undressed,' she said simpering.

'Humph! You look excited, child. What's wrong with you? Shut the door and let's sit on the bed,' Reverend Mother said brusquely, looking over her spectacles.

'Just happiness, Reverend Mother. Profession is so wonderful.'

'What were you crying for, then?' Reverend Mother asked sharply.

'Joy, Reverend Mother, dear,' Winnie said, with that simplicity which satisfied Mother Calixta. 'I *always* cry when I'm happy.'

'Humph. Sit down, child,' Reverend Mother said impatiently. 'It's not yet too late,' she added, after a pause, during which she nervously fingered her beads. 'I should have spoken to you before about it, but one thing and another … Well, to-night, I felt I must.'

'Yes, Reverend Mother.' Winnie faltered. She pulled at her guimpe, stroked the coverlet of the bed in a vain effort to force back a blush that she felt was growing deeper. Was it about Father James, or what? She avoided Reverend Mother's eyes which she was sure were looking at her over the spectacles. One never knew from Reverend Mother's voice whether she was angry or not. Often the more angry she was, the gentler was her voice. If she could only look her in the face, but she dare not.

'I'm afraid my hair is falling down,' she added, with a nervous giggle, running her fingers along the edge of her dimity.

'Have you thought out everything—the difficulties before you—your vows? Now is the time to hesitate, to doubt, to turn back, if necessary.'

Winnie gave a little sigh of relief. She stole a glance at Reverend Mother, who was staring at the polished floor. There was nothing, after all, to worry about.

'Why, goodness me, Reverend Mother, I've never had a doubt in my life. I only wish God asked ten times more of me.'

'Is there nothing you have a strong attachment to? Nothing you find it hard to give up?'

'There's my hair, of course,' Winnie said, after a pause, her head cocked thoughtfully. 'No-one sees it now, but still I always *knew* it was there—such a comfort. You remember how you used to admire it, Reverend Mother?'

Reverend Mother gave a jerk at her beads, pulled them rapidly through her fingers and gave a weary little grunt.

'There's nothing in any of your vows that troubles you?' she asked.

'Goodness, no, Reverend Mother. I love them all. They are as easy as easy.'

Reverend Mother frowned at the floor, sighed, sought inspiration in the ceiling. Her search there ended in another sigh.

'You're sure you wouldn't be happier in the world?' she jerked out.

Winnie's look of open candour became slightly resentful.

'Is it me, Reverend Mother? In the world?' she said indignantly. 'I'd hate it—the roughness, the coarseness, the want of gentility. Never seeing anyone nice. None of the fun—of the spiritual helps of the convent.'

'You might get married,' Reverend Mother said grimly.

'Reverend Mother!' Winnie indignantly flushed. This was an insult to Father James. As if, loving him, she could marry anyone. A priest couldn't marry. 'I hate marriage. I hate it,' she said violently.

'Well, well. Perhaps I'm wrong,' Reverend Mother muttered to her beads, half relieved, half doubtful. 'Vows aren't as simple as you think,' she went on dreamily. 'I'm afraid I sin against holy poverty ten times a day—I'm planning now to try and get the river meadow from your father. It won't be mine—in a way. But is my vow only a subterfuge? It's the same with obedience, and—well, well.'

She roused herself, sat up straight on the bed and peered

at Winnie, whose indignation had given way to a pitying contempt. Eulalie was right. Reverend Mother was becoming dotty. As if a Reverend Mother could sin against obedience!

'Father is sure to give us the river meadow,' she said, resuming the noviceship look of candour.

'So you've never been in love?' Reverend Mother suddenly shot out.

Winnie shaded her glowing face with a movement of her veil. She felt proud and happy. Still, wild horses wouldn't drag her secret from her. And, somehow, it would be a sin against her love to tell a lie. What should she do? She couldn't explain, and if she could, no-one would understand.

'Never wanted to get married?' Reverend Mother said to bridge the pause.

'Never,' Winnie said primly, with an indignation that equalled her relief. 'How you do probe, Reverend Mother. And I answered that before, too. I wouldn't marry a king,' she added, with a heroic effort at truthfulness. 'I want to be a nun.'

'Well, well. Let us hope you'll never be tempted to marry anyone,' Reverend Mother said dryly, snapping a link in her beads. 'That's the third to-day,' she added. 'It's dreadful, I believe, if those feelings come to one after one is professed,' she went on, holding up the severed ends of the beads and staring at them with a troubled face. 'They do, you know, and then it is dreadful—dreadful. Love is a terrible thing, I'm told. In a convent it is hell … Sister Matilda who mends them for me will be in bed,' she added, with a sigh, gathering the ends of the rosary in her left hand, 'but I think I have a pincers in my room. Good night, child. I'm afraid it's long past ten, and our lights ought to be out.'

She got up heavily off the bed and patted Winnie's shoulder. 'God bless you, child. I hope you'll never be strongly tempted.

But everything might turn out for the best,' she said wearily.

'God will help me,' Winnie replied, as she held open the door.

'He might—He might.' Reverend Mother said dreamily, again absorbed in her beads.

Winnie watched Reverend Mother plod heavily down the corridor. It was so dreadful to be old. And she could never have been in love. Hell? Why, it was heaven. She shut the door, undressed and washed quickly, put out the light and slipped into bed. The idea of suggesting that she wanted to get married! If it were to him now, of course it would be different. It would be wonderful to be with him always. But he was a priest. Why had Reverend Mother put the thought into her head—it made her feel so lonely ... She'd see nothing but him on the altar to-morrow. And he'd be holding the book for the bishop while she made her vows. She'd be thinking of him so much that she must be word-perfect. She must go over the words once more in her mind to make sure.

In the middle of a fervent pledging of her chastity to God she dropped off into a dreamless sleep.

Chapter 13

A brilliant May sun smiled on the bustle of the convent. Nuns in blue-and-white aprons and sleeve protectors spoke to one another in hurried whispers, and darted hither and thither with preoccupied faces.

Sister Eulalie, with three assistants, added the last touches to the decoration of the sanctuary, and herself laid out the bishop's vestments with loving care.

Mother Michael superintended the preparations for the *déjeuner* in the big reception room. Mrs Curtin had asked her to spare no expense, and Mother Bursar was not averse from a generous display which entailed no strain on the convent purse. Her only problem was to keep Mrs Curtin's lavish desires within the limits of convent good taste. The huge profession cakes had been placed in position over night. The best table-cloths, the best silver and glass gleamed joyously. The frilling of roast fowls, the jellies, the salmon in aspic contributed, with the flowers and fruit and pastry, to an elaborate colour scheme. Even the hock had been decanted in the interests of harmony; while the more ostentatious champagne was discreetly hidden away under a white cloth on a side-table, humbly awaiting the bishop's special permission (never withheld) for its use. Orphans, their faces shining from a ceremony application of soap, peeped in at the doors, said, 'My,' with greedy lips, scuttled off with an 'Oh' at the sight of Mother Michael, and gathered in groups round the chapel to discuss the relative merits of Sister Winifred and Sister Catherine.

Novices, thinking ahead of their own professions, wandered about aimlessly with an air of suppressed excitement. Older nuns, with no particular duty in connection with the ceremony, made tours of inspection, sniffed at Sister Eulalie's decoration of the altar and Mother Michael's arrangement of the table, fed the doves, said bored rosaries in the beech avenue and discussed pleasantly Winnie's and Kitty's shortcomings. Old Sister Thomasine, martinet and ascetic, whose fever of irritation at the interruption of her regular school duties could only be assuaged by *Tristram Shandy*, sat chuckling over it in a corner of the community room to the fury of Sister Ambrose, who wasn't allowed to read the books in the top shelf and was bored by *The Path of Christian Meekness*.

Mother Calixta flitted about here, there and everywhere, with the excited serenity of a beautiful hen whose chickens were bursting the shell. She said tender words of encouragement to Winnie, and less tender, but still motherly, to Kitty. She approved the work of Sister Eulalie who asked her, for goodness' sake, to keep out of her way; of the labours of Mother Michael, who merely sniffed without lifting her eyes. She saw that the rings, which were to make her dear children spouses of Christ, were in their due place; that their wills were ready for signature. She tested the huge scissors on the hair of a thrilled orphan; and moved the black veils, made ready for the profession, from the back of a chair to a table.

Kitty, alone in her cell, sat on the end of her bed, her face almost rivalling the spotless white of her veil, and stared down on Drumbawn, beautiful in a thin heat haze. She had come out of the night, black with terror, successfully, she hoped. But the long hours of waiting since the dawn were terrible. This feeling of despair, as of a prisoner awaiting execution, must be a temptation of the devil. She was waiting, not execution, but deliverance. The glory of the sunrise, and the glorious singing of the birds, had shouted hope; but there had been no response from her heart. The joy and beauty of the world seemed to touch the outer rim of her senses, but could not penetrate to the desolation that filled her. The pearly softness of the sky, the fragrance of the white thorn, the laughter of the orphans only stabbed her to fresh pain … Or was the empty, aching feeling just hunger?

Winnie stood by the side of her cell window eagerly watching the front drive. It was all perfectly thrilling. Twenty-three priests! And the bishop, and the town priests, and the Dominicans, and maybe, lots more hadn't come yet. There were the Finnegans. Stella had a new hat. Not much. One would think the whole place belonged to her. Was that Mrs Thornton? Yes, it was. And the eldest Miss Thornton, too. Talk of a swell profession. And the Miss Purcells. They were grand, of course, though they came to every reception and profession for the food. If he'd only come before Mother Calixta came for her. Oh, oh! If he wasn't in the carriage with the bishop. Did he look up? How distinguished looking he was … She sighed deeply and moved away from the window. But she'd see him again in a few minutes … One more look at her vows and she'd be ready.

The orphans, in their summer prints and new blue hair ribbons, discussing each fresh arrival, curtsied deeply to the bishop's carriage. Little groups of priests in soutane, surplice and biretta, round the sacristy steps, took snuff, discussed the bishop, the crops, the Misses Curtin's dowries and the luck of the convent.

Subdued cries of 'the bishop', 'the bishop', ran through the convent. Aprons and wristlets disappeared magically. Habits were dropped and trailed. Mother Calixta, shepherding Winnie and Kitty, cried frantically, 'Where's Reverend Mother? Where's Reverend Mother?' The ceremony had begun before she was discovered by two orphans in the North Terrace, bent over a rose bush, fingering her beads with one hand and trimming off dead leaves with the other.

Kneeling on her *prie-Dieu* in front of the Sanctuary Kitty had a feeling of remoteness—as if she sat apart and watched things, herself included, that had no relation to her. Usually at Mass and Benediction, although unable to move herself to fervour, she had a sense of awe, of sharing in some wonderful if impenetrable mystery. To-day the ceremony was merely fussy, a number of unrelated details which she noted clearly, but in which she had no concern. She was indifferent even to the sensuous music, which for once did not give her sinful thoughts. What seemed to matter somehow, but not to her, was the singing out of tune of the priests, their boredom, the length of the lace on Father Burke's surplice, the bishop's cough and the colour of his handkerchief. Father Burke was playing some game with a faldstool, a book, a bougie and a bishop. It was important that he should not get them all mixed up; that the faldstool should be set exactly rightly on the marble step of the sanctuary ... Reverend Mother was in it, too, and Winnie and Mother Calixta. And someone who was vaguely herself, who moved when nudged by Reverend Mother, knelt at the bishop's feet and spoke automatically at Reverend Mother's prompting ... In one of the interminable journeys she signed a paper which Mother Michael said was a last will and testament. Was she going to die? Was that the something that was vaguely impending? But nothing happened. There was a grating sound that took her back to the clipping of the grass on the edges of the garden walk. The two heaps of hair on the table made such a contrast. What was Winnie crying for? The poor thing looked such a fright. What made her head like that? There was some connection between Winnie's cropped head and the fair, golden pile on the table, the gold glinting in the sun, but she couldn't understand ... They were dressing her in black. It was a funeral then. That was Reverend Mother's voice. 'It will soon be all over now, dear.' Was she going to die? The long marching had begun again. There was her mother with red poppies in her hat. Why was she crying? The bald patch on the top of her father's head looked larger as he bent forward over his arms. Who was the bishop talking about … Those two beautiful young virgins who gave their whole hearts to God; who to-day were filled to overflowing with the joy and gladness of divine grace; whose every thought would henceforth be God's. Poor man, what a bad cold he had. Where did the ring come from? She stared at the silver band on the ring finger of her right hand. Why, of course, the bishop had put it there. She remembered now—her vows and all. She must have been thinking of something else at the time. And the wonderful feelings the bishop spoke of? Was it because she was so hungry she could experience no other feeling?

To Winnie the whole ceremony was enchanting. She was conscious of occupying the centre of the stage, of the new episcopal vestments, of Father Burke's wonderful surplice and recent hair-cut, of the two long rows of priests, of the super-abundant flowers, of the visitors at the back of the choir. She glowed with fervour; and her prayers were as intensive as her pride. She had a momentary feeling of jealousy that Kitty shared the stage with her; but she soon forgot this. She was the senior and did everything first … Poor Kitty seemed to be in a maze … It had all turned out just as she had dreamt of it: a brilliant sun, and Father Burke as good as professing her. And eleven priests more than at Finbar's profession—and that was the highest number up to now. Father Bernardine, too. Very likely he came because of Kitty—but there he was, anyhow … She had only one breakdown. She sobbed hysterically when her hair was being cut off. But the thought of the depth of her sacrifice soon consoled her. She even wished that she could walk up the chapel with bared head so that people might know what she had given up. For, of course, with the veil, people wouldn't realize it. *Age quod agis.* Some novices lost their heads over profession, but her motto supported her. She needed no help from Mother Calixta, and gave all the responses with feeling and conviction. It was a slight disappointment that it was the bishop who put the ring on her finger, but by closing her eyes she was able to imagine that it was Father Burke. And once when his fingers touched the back of her hand, her happiness was complete. The sermon moved her to tears of joy. It was so beautiful. And so true. Her heart was all God's. His and Father James's, for was he not a priest of God …

She kissed the nuns with rapture at the end of the ceremony, as if congratulating them on her own happiness. A fat priest said with a snigger, 'I wish we could have a share.' She laughed happily. Poor Father Burke would have to wait for his share till evening, unless … but it was difficult with so many people about. An excited orphan cried out, 'Isn't Miss Winnie—Sister Winifred I mean—looking a duck.' Winnie wanted to kiss all the orphans—they were such dears. But Reverend Mother said sharply to her and Kitty, 'Run away now and have some food, children.'

Outside the door giving on the corridor, Mrs Curtin held out her arms. Winnie noticed the poppies with a pang, but magnanimously forgave them. 'Oh, mother, I'm so happy, so happy,' she cooed, returning her mother's kisses again and again. It was so beautiful to be crushed in somebody's arms after the nuns' pecking.

'My cup is full—I'm that happy,' Mrs Curtin said tearfully, disentangling herself. 'There now. That's enough. I must kiss Kitty. You're like a saint in a picture,' she continued, throwing her arms round Kitty, and pressing her to her breast. ''Tis you were the born nun I always said.'

Kitty, clung, trembling, to the warmth and softness. It was as if the ice that congealed her had suddenly thawed; as if she had been kissed back to life … All she wanted now to make her happy was to go home with her mother and feel her arms always round her … 'Oh, mother, mother,' she cried brokenly.

Mrs Curtin held her at an arm's length and looked from her to Winnie admiringly. 'It's not every mother has two such holy nuns to her credit,' she said, with a complacent sigh.

Winnie simpered.

The little colour that had come on Kitty's cheeks left them again. The convent had closed in on her like a tomb. The nuns moving silently up and down the corridor, made her shiver. She looked at her black veil half resentfully, half apprehensively. That mystery in the chapel had made her one of them. Was it all a dream? She tried to remember, to picture the scene, but it was all a confused blur. Yet, there were her black veil and her ring; and her vows that she could neither see nor feel, nor even remember …

'I wish it was ten pounds of marrons glacés instead of seven,' Winnie said pettishly.

'There's a stone of the best chocolates,' said Mrs Curtin.

'For shame, Mrs Curtin,' Mother Michael broke in, bustling forward and shaking a finger in mock indignation. 'Still keeping these poor children from their meal. Sister Catherine is looking half starved. And his lordship has been enquiring for you. He'll be in a temper if he has to wait for his food any longer. Kitty and Winnie can come in the moment they've eaten something.'

'Eating alongside the bishop'll give me a cold fit. Let ye be quick, girls, and distract his attention from me,' Mrs Curtin urged.

Winnie rushed off towards the refectory. Kitty followed with dragging steps. The long corridor, with its north light, was cold and menacing. It was like a prison; and the north terrace, still in deep shadow, was the exercise yard. Sister

Thomasine, pacing up and down, her head bent saying her rosary, was one of the prisoners. Sister Thomasine was nearly seventy … Fifty years more … And beyond the shadow was the sunlight, freedom … The loud voices and the laughter from the reception-room hurt her. It was like eating and joking at a wake.

'Don't you feel a new woman—something holy, divine?' Mother Calixta said, brushing past. 'I mustn't delay a moment. The bishop! you know.'

Kitty staggered as if from a blow. That was just it.

She felt a woman—for the first time in three years …

At the foot of the stairs Sister Basil waylaid her.

'They've stolen your soul. They hid mine in a well and put lead over it. Deep, deep, deep down,' she said wildly, her eyes like smouldering fires in her haggard face.

Her look of terror made Kitty's blood run cold. For a horrid moment she saw herself with these wild eyes, this accent of despair. Was this the end of a woman in a convent?

'A spider!' she said unconsciously, with dry lips.

The wild mad look changed to one of hunted fear. Sister Basil peered round furtively. 'The devil!' she said, in a hoarse, frightened whisper. 'But I know a place where he'll never find me—under my bed,' she added exultantly, as she scuttled up the stairs.

Kitty bit her lip with vexation. She had resolved never to use the noviceship trick of getting rid of Basil. She didn't mean to. But, for the first time, Basil had made her afraid. Afraid of what? … And Sister Damien was half mad … and some of the others had all sorts of hallucinations. She pulled herself together and tried to avoid Sister Anne, but Sister Anne wouldn't be avoided.

She caught Kitty by the side of her veil and said effusively:

'Rapt up into the seventh heaven, dear! I know. I was myself on that blessed day. I've only time for one word. His lordship has asked for me specially—his nephew married my sister-in-law's second cousin, you know. It's just this; and you'll thank me for it all your life.' She lowered her voice to a confidential whisper. 'You're one of us now, and I can unseal my lips. Have nothing to do with Eulalie and her set—they're cats. Cats, that's what they are. Cats. I'll tell you lots more another time. Only a word now to the wise! Hurry in or the tea will be cold. I said to Angelica: Catherine will be one of us. She has gravity and the grace of God. If you don't be quick you'll miss a lot of the fun in the reception-room. Try and sit near Father Flaherty. He'd make a cat laugh about the bishop. I'll say a rosary for you when the visitors have gone. Prayer, my child, is the light of the soul. I hadn't a chance yet to warn Winifred about Eulalie, but I will. I never shirk an act of charity.'

'I'm dropping with hunger,' Kitty said, with a smile. She broke away from Sister Anne. Food was what she wanted. She'd put away all morbid thoughts. She could be gay and she would.

She ate heartily and withstood all Winnie's entreaties to 'hurry or the bishop would be mad.' It was only when Mother Calixta rushed in and said in a tone of agony, 'Still eating, and the bishop has asked for you both three times,' that Kitty put away her napkin.

'Look pleasant, Catherine,' Mother Calixta said anxiously, at the reception-room door. 'His lordship likes us all to smile. It shows we're happy, he says.'

'The newly professed, my lord,' she said, with smiling timidity into the bishop's right ear.

He swallowed a mouthful of roast chicken, turned half round in his chair, smiled at Winnie, gave her his ring to kiss, blessed her, and said perfunctorily:

'Happy, my child? Sister Winifred, isn't it?'

Mother Calixta plucked Winnie out of the way as the bishop held out his hand to Kitty, with an 'Ah!' which showed that beauty could appeal even to a bishop. He shook her hand warmly, and patted her shoulder with his left hand while he gave her a blessing with his right.

'You've every reason to be proud of your daughters, Mrs Curtin,' he said, still smiling at Kitty.

'God is very good to me, my lord,' Mrs Curtin replied with fervour.

'He has every right to be with the gifts you give Him, ma'am,' the bishop said, with an approving look at Kitty. 'Get a chair for Sister Catherine here between Reverend Mother and myself, Mother Calixta. You'd like to have a word with your mother,' he added, waving Winnie away, with a smile.

Winnie retired crestfallen. It wasn't fair, and she the eldest! She always knew he was a horrid old man. He hadn't even given her time to say how happy she was. And she had intended to make him laugh, too, by being daringly original and replying, 'I am as happy as a bishop, my lord.' And now it would never be said … She had a gloomy vision of Kitty being offered the first place all through their life in the convent. Her eyes filled with tears …

'The other guests are waiting to congratulate you, dear,' Reverend Mother said, patting her hand.

Winnie blushed prettily. Her spirits revived. She gave a rapid glance round the table. She had been so absorbed in the bishop that she had not noticed the pause in the conversation and in the clatter of knives and forks. All eyes were fixed on her. She felt a deep pride. Should she speak first to Mrs Thornton on the left of the bishop, or to Father Bernardine just beyond her mother? Where was Father James? Oh! How could she get to him first and he halfway down the long table? Her father smiled at her sheepishly from behind Father Burke. She made a dart forward and almost upset Sister Francis and a dish of cream tarts … It was the becoming thing to greet her father first. It would be thrilling to kiss him before all the table; and Father James would know why. Oh! if only she could! But she'd give her father two extra kisses for *him* …

While Tom Curtin was awkwardly putting away his napkin and pushing back his chair, Father Burke was on his feet. She held out her hand impulsively. Why didn't he press it more? He was so cold and reserved in public. And there was something worried and distant in his look. Father Flaherty's chuckling remark, 'Burke is in luck,' gave her a thrill of pleasure. Oh, why couldn't she? Even one? She threw herself desperately into her father's arms and clung to him. 'Oh, father, I'm so happy, so happy,' she muttered, kissing him passionately.

'There now. That'll do—that'll do,' Tom Curtin said nervously, half pleased and half ashamed of the unaccustomed display of affection.

'Don't waste 'em all on your father,' Father Flaherty said hilariously.

She smiled through her tears. Father Flaherty was always so pleasant. And not one in the whole room knew whom she had been kissing all the time …

'I've seldom had the privilege of professing two more promising nuns,' the bishop said, smacking his lips. 'I wish I could get as good champagne as that at the Palace, Mrs Curtin.'

'I'll see that you will, my lord,' Mrs Curtin said heartily.

'You are much too generous to us all—much too generous, ma'am. It's dry without being too dry. I noticed their demeanour all through the ceremony. Different, of course, but with qualities in each that make for perfection. Sister Winifred's nice attention to detail. Every word and bow was important and perfect. A veritable Martha. And Sister Catherine's absorption in the ceremony as a whole. She reminded me not a little of her great patron saint, St Catherine of Siena … the same rapt devotion, as if she were treading the mystic way. Another Mary. Yes, Mother Calixta, I think I will take another glass in honour of their good parents.'

'The lord has a good eye for likely fillies,' Father Flaherty said, with a wink at Father Burke.

Winnie tossed her head and barely acknowledged Father Brady's gruff congratulations. She a Martha, indeed! How little the bishop knew. Poor Kitty with all her scrupulosity about rules and things, was one of the worst Marthas in the house ...

'I suppose the champagne will come this way ultimately,' the eldest Miss Purcell whispered to her sister.

'Why, of course. Rich publicans, my dear. I've never enjoyed a profession more ... the chicken in aspic ... simply perfection.'

'I daren't,' Miss Purcell said, with a sigh of regret. 'Nothing else solid.'

'I can manage several dishes yet. Remember, I warned you to go without breakfast, Eleanor,' her sister said severely.

'Nothing is more gratifying than the growth of vocations,' the bishop said loudly, for the benefit of the table, hesitating over an embarrassing choice of sweets. 'I think a few meringues first, Mother Calixta, and perhaps that wobbling thing after. There's no better proof of the strength of the religious spirit. Young girls surrounded by every luxury turn their backs on all the glittering allurements of the world and willingly accept poverty and the other hard abnegations of convent life. I wish I had your cook, Mother Calixta. Yes, two more.'

'They say the young Curtins were bored to death. One might have asked them to tea, perhaps, if it weren't for the shop,' Miss Purcell whispered.

'The dispositions of Providence, dear,' the younger sister murmured. 'And as they were educated above their station the convent is a nice refuge. This trifle is excellent. I wish the dear nuns would share some of their poverty with us. They must be rolling.'

Kitty sat rigidly in her chair, her hands clasped within the folds of her veil. She wanted so much to laugh, but she was afraid of crying. Light replies to the bishop's compliments died on her lips, and she answered in stiff monosyllables. Fortunately he was more interested in his food, and soon forgot her. It was all so comic. The tragedy in the chapel, and then this. It was like the farce that followed *Hamlet* in the Theatre Royal when she went once with Bessie Sweetman. The face of the dead Ophelia had been behind every jest ... But if she laughed now it would be in that dreadful hysteria of Sister Lawrence. It was horrible but intensely funny: the bishop discussing spirituality between huge mouthfuls of food and long draughts of wine; priests gulping down food as if they hadn't eaten for a week ; her mother, her face almost rivalling the poppies in her hat, flushed with contented pride, narrating volubly to Father Bernardine the decisive signs of her children's vocations from childhood; Mrs Thornton blending a respectful deference to the bishop with a scarcely veiled contempt for the rest of the company; Stella Finnegan divided between imitation of Miss Thornton's boredom and enjoyment of Father Flaherty's coarse jests; nuns flushed from the hard labour of cramming sixty violent appetites; nuns brooding over their favourite priests with the watchful anxiety of hens who had each the care of a single chicken; the Miss Purcells heedless of everything but their food; the Rafters, the Devines and the Muldoons torn between the pride of lunching with the bishop and jealousy of the Curtin display; her father making a desperate effort to look as if he enjoyed himself, and all the time longing to be at home behind the counter; Father Brady making no effort to conceal his contempt; Father Burke, looking worried; Father

Dunne, bored but tolerant; Mother Calixta hanging on the bishop's plate and glass, and Reverend Mother, half hidden behind the bishop's chair, gazing absentmindedly at the floor, isolated in mind as in body, her fingers moving with steady regularity from bead to bead as her lips completed a prayer ... Reverend Mother could get outside all this horror and confusion, but then, Reverend Mother had the gift of prayer. Kitty sighed dismally. She could neither be of it nor get away from it. Her vows had done her no good. She had the same empty feeling she had had every day since she entered the convent. Yet she couldn't detach herself from anything. Even this luncheon which disgusted her, interested her. She couldn't philander with priests, but it wasn't entirely because she was afraid of herself. One had to play the game. And she had all sorts of repugnances. But behind was an intense curiosity. Sometimes, when off her guard, she had wished that priests would hold her hand. Yet when they tried to do so she couldn't. It might be that God or her guardian angel came to her help. But why, when she imagined things, did God leave her to fight almost alone? Then her desire knew no limits. She was pushed to the edge of the precipice with a violence that she could not withstand and only saved herself on the brink of a superhuman effort. Had she always saved herself? Father Bernardine said she had. She didn't know. Father Brady said nuns and priests were sending him to an early grave; and gave her penances as if he believed that she had fallen. She couldn't have. She came into the convent to save herself from sin, and God couldn't desert her. He gave her no comfort, and much pain; but He had saved her from herself. He must have ... Yet why did she feel this sudden antipathy to the convent ... to all nuns?

'You ought to become a nun, Miss Thornton,' the bishop said, wiping his mouth with his napkin. 'See how happy and contented Sister Catherine here is.'

'How d'ye do. No, thanks,' Miss Thornton said, with a nod to Kitty, and an insolent toss of her head. 'I know too much about them.'

'Hear that now, Reverend Mother,' the bishop said jocosely over his shoulder.

'You're not thinking of going, my lord?' Reverend Mother, with a sigh of relief, rose hurriedly from her chair.

'God bless me, no,' the bishop said, with an anxious look at his glass. 'Not even in a convent where the Reverend Mother is always praying?' he added, with a wink at Miss Thornton.

'One gets more out of sin in the world,' she retorted flippantly.

'Selina!' Mrs Thornton said severely.

The bishop stretched himself back in his chair, his eyes twinkling.

'Come now, Miss Selina—'

'If you've done with Kitty, my lord, she might, with your lordship's leave, be going round and bidding the time of day to the rest of the company,' Mrs Curtin interrupted deferentially. 'Winnie has near finished her round.'

'Of course, of course. God bless you, my child. May the peace and happiness you enjoy today abide with you for ever. I think I'll try a peach, Mother Calixta. It's seldom I get them so early. And give one to Miss Selina.'

'Here's Father Bernardine dying to have a word with you,' Mrs Curtin whispered, giving Kitty a nudge.

Kitty got up reluctantly and curtseyed to the shoulder of the bishop, who was again fencing jovially with Miss Thornton. Winnie, flushed and triumphant, was talking to Stella Finnegan. Winnie liked the fun and excitement, Kitty thought enviously. If only she had Winnie's spirits or Selina Thornton's calm indifference. Her nerves were so strung that another turn of the screw would make them snap. Yet she must try and talk to all these people who would congratulate her on her happiness. She stood behind her mother and glanced down the long table with a half-frightened, half-hostile look. Why was Father Duffy of Derrydonnelly staring at her with those calf's eyes? Father Brady wasn't approving her. And who was the man beyond Father Dunne? Sister Anne with all her talk of gravity was evidently enjoying Father Flaherty …

Her eyes came back to the man beyond Father Dunne. How was it she hadn't noticed him before? He stood out from the others somehow. It was as if he were outside it, too. There was irony and tolerance in his smile. His eyes caught hers for a moment, and she held her breath … They seemed to see through her …

She looked hastily at her father, who was regarding her with a moody frown. She smiled at him, but he frowned more deeply and turned away to talk to Father Burke.

What was that sudden change in the strange man's eyes just as he had looked at her? The irony was still on his lips, but there was something else. It was only a flash as he withdrew his eyes. It was as if he understood and pitied her. Who was he? He didn't even know her, she thought, with a resentment that quickened her interest. She stole another glance at him. He was listening to Father Dunne with the same half-ironic smile. He couldn't be from the town with those clothes and his quiet tie … and clean-shaven. His eyes must be very dark. Even Bessie Sweetman, who was hard to please, would say he was good-looking.

'I think I have seen everyone before except the man beyond Father Dunne,' she said to her mother.

'Oh, him?' Mrs Curtin said indifferently. 'That's the new organist. He's very select, they say. The whole town is running after him, but he keeps himself to himself.'

'In a moment, Mrs Rafter. I must speak to Sister Catherine now.' Father Bernardine broke off Mrs Rafter's voluble confidences. 'This is a happy day,' he added, jumping up and clasping Kitty's hand. 'A poor Colmanite is thrown into the shade by his lordship. I feared you had entirely forgotten your old friends.'

The complacent smile jarred on her. It was so different from the other man's. She had heard of him, of course. What was his name? Lynch—George Lynch.

'She's not likely to forget you, Father, and you putting her in and all,' Mrs Curtin said warmly.

'A most edifying ceremony. Your quiet, undemonstrative happiness was very grateful to me. It was a more than sufficient reward for my small share in determining your vocation,' Father Bernardine murmured, patting her hand.

She felt suddenly hard and bitter. They were all so foolish. That stranger knew more about her than the whole of them put together. And she had thought that Father Bernardine knew things … She had followed his advice for three years, yet he thought her happy now. Why didn't he do his hair like Mr Lynch? Why hadn't she before looked more closely at his mouth and at the curls trained across his forehead? He couldn't really know. It was his voice and his belief in himself that hid all this shallowness from her … or was it some other glamour? It was a weak face, not strong like the other man's.

'The best of good luck to you, Sister Catherine, though you look peaked itself,' Mrs Rafter broke in cordially. 'Though we've lived in the one town all our lives we've never passed a word before. Not that I bear any malice,' she added, with a hostile look at Mrs Curtin. 'Well, well, if a girl has to be a nun there are worse places than Drumbawn. I had a notion that way myself once, and, now, thank God, I'm the mother of ten.'

'Your father is looking as black as thunder,' Mrs Curtin said hastily. 'Run down, Kitty, and lighten him up a bit.'

They were all little tops spinning round and round and interested only in themselves … If she had made a mistake it was her own fault ... not her mother's, nor Father Bernardine's. She must smile. She smiled and murmured incoherent thanks to half a dozen people in succession.

'I hope you're feeling happy,' her father said, with a look that gave the lie to any such hope.

'It's not my funeral,' she laughed, as she kissed him.

'They've tied you up now. You'll feel that,' he said gloomily.

She winced. But she wasn't going to think of that any more—to-day, anyhow. It must be her father made her feel more cheerful.

'I'm just as I always was,' she said.

'Then God help you.'

'Old crusty face!' she retorted. 'I'm going to be happy.'

'That's the proper spirit, Sister Catherine. We mustn't leave happiness altogether to people in the world. We religious must have our share. My warmest congratulations,' Father Burke said, in a cooing voice.

She gave him her hand, but she was looking beyond him ... Would Mr Lynch speak to her like the others, without introduction, or would Father Dunne introduce him?

'Nothing but changes in the town. Here's Father Burke telling me he's as good as offered Lissakelly parish. He's between two minds whether he'll take it or not,' her father grumbled.

'It's a horrid, gloomy old town,' she said regretfully. But the regret was that her duties did not take her to the parish church. She'd like to hear Mr Lynch play. She was sure he could play well. His eyes *were* brown. Dr Thornton was good-looking, but nothing to ...

'You'd like me to stay?' Father Burke said, in his lisp, with a languishing look.

She smiled at him. Her father was wrong to regret change. A good organist would make—What was it Father Burke had asked her? He'd probably repeat it.

'Yes, yes,' she said.

Father Burke sighed contentedly. She felt her old repugnance revive. Why did he smile in that abominable self-satisfied way ... with that leer that seemed to smirch her?

'There are the cakes still to cut. I'll never be round the table in time,' she said. 'Cheer up, papa. Everything will come right.'

Nothing seemed to hurt her now, not even Father Burke's horrid look. And she could think of Dr Thornton as if he were merely anyone ... Perhaps it was her vows, after all?

The Miss Purcells, who were busy eating—the elder had decided that she could make room for a peach—took no notice of Kitty. Father Dunne smiled satirically and gave her a lazy greeting.

'Well, you've gone and done it, Miss Kitty. Why you did it beats me. I suppose there's a streak of madness in us all.'

'Does it matter what a woman does with herself?' she laughed. She was conscious of the man standing up beside Father Dunne and of the warmth of her cheeks.

'That's true. Still, I thought you had more regard for yourself.'

'He thinks very badly of us poor nuns,' she said, with a smile at his companion. The answering smile pleased her. It said without words, 'We both know Father Dunne.' He understood her.

'You go to the wrong quarter if you think Lynch admires nuns. He can't abide them. But you don't know him? Mr Lynch, the new organist. He has been taking your measure all day. Sister Catherine, is it they call you?'

Again his smile answered her that she was right in thinking that Father Dunne was talking nonsense ... There was something clean and invigorating in the touch of the firm, cool hand.

'I heard you sing at Benediction on Sunday evening. I wish you were one of the nuns who sing for us,' he said quietly.

She knew his voice would have that timbre. It was just right, like his tie and the way he held himself; and the lean brown face was so striking under his dark hair.

'Good Lord! And he's always saying that women ought never to sing in a church. He's all for Palestrina and Orlando di Lasso and boys' voices and all that. Women only pipe out their own little squashy hearts, he says,' Father Dunne jibed.

She liked him for making no attempt at contradiction or extenuation. He merely looked at her with the ironic smile on his lips.

'I know,' she agreed. 'Often at Mass I've only to shut my eyes and I seem to be in a theatre. If they sang the right kind of music it might be different?' she added vaguely.

His eyes had lighted up and the ironic smile was gone.

'There's a convent in Paris where they do it astonishingly well. The nuns' voices are like the wraiths of dead women. Life seems to have been drained out of them. It's beautiful, but too horrible.'

'There's little fear of that in Drumbawn. They're a strapping lot of women,' Father Dunne said, with a yawn. 'These convent lunches upset me. They're too early to have a decent appetite for 'em, and too late to let a man enjoy his dinner in comfort after.'

'It's dreadful, dreadful,' Lynch said, continuing his own thought. 'No, no, anything but that.' He was looking at her again with pity in his eyes.

'I'd like to sing in the church,' she said simply.

'I give you up, Lynch,' Father Dunne said, with a shrug of contempt. 'You're quite as bad as the rest.'

'While we have nuns in the choir it's surely best to have those who can sing,' Lynch said, with a contented smile.

'You'll be liking them next,' Father Dunne said in a tone of warning against the last depth of idiocy.

'No, I hate them worse than ever,' Lynch snapped.

'Don't bite the head off the poor girl. She hasn't done you any harm,' the priest said gently. 'Though I'm glad you have that much sense,' he hastened to add, as if ashamed of his softness.

Kitty laughed gaily. Mr Lynch might look at her as angrily as he liked, but she knew he didn't hate her.

'I'll come if I can,' she said, moving away. She held his eyes for a moment. His anger had completely gone. They were such wonderfully soft eyes, sympathetic and understanding … he was like a real friend.

The guests seemed more human and friendly. Why shouldn't they be happy? She was happy. She answered jest with jest as she made the round of the table. She laughed at Father Brady for saying she had made her bed and now would have to put up with it. She was able to assure Stella Finnegan that there was nothing dreadful 'about it all'. She talked of Daisy and the baby with Selina Thornton as if the past had been entirely blotted out. Something wonderful had come over her … fresh and cleansing as the sea breeze on the top of Dangan hill. Perhaps it was the grace of her vows working at last?

'Where is Winifred?' Mother Calixta asked excitedly. 'I told her to be ready to cut the cake at Father Brady's end of the table. The bishop wants you at his end. Run and find her. That's a good girl. And don't be late yourself. His lordship is getting tired.'

Kitty searched the chapel and the noviceship. She went at last to Winnie's cell and found her, sobbing on her bed. 'Go away. Go away. I don't want anyone. Can't you leave me in peace!' she cried.

'The cakes! The bishop is waiting,' Kitty said in feeble astonishment.

Winnie sat up and said furiously: 'Everyone is down on me. The bishop's cake is my cake. I hate him. Anyone could see he was gone on you. I'll die before I cut Father Brady's cake. Cut them both. I don't care. I don't care.'

She burst out sobbing afresh. Kitty tried to soothe her, but she pushed her aside. 'I hate you—I hate everyone,' she added bitterly.

'Don't, Winnie, dear. You ought to be so happy … Your vows and everything. I'll speak to Mother Calixta. We'll manage somehow about the cake.'

'It's not that. It's not that at all,' Winnie said, in a despairing voice.

'What is it then?' Kitty asked gently.

'Oh, oh, I'm so miserable. I was never so miserable in my life. I know by his look it's true. It's that horrid bishop. Mother Michael told me. The bishop told the Mothers. Those dreadful vulgar nuns at Lissakelly, too. They'll be making up to him. I wish I was dead.'

'If you mean Father Burke, I don't think he'll go,' Kitty said impatiently. 'He's not worth bothering about, anyway.'

'Who told you? Who told you? Did he tell you himself?' Winnie asked, with jealous suspicion.

'Papa said it was doubtful. And Father Burke doesn't seem inclined to go,' Kitty said coldly. 'It seems he has a choice.'

Winnie stared at her with lips apart. Slowly fear gave way to doubt, and doubt to conviction. She heaved a deep sigh of relief which shook her body.

'He'd never leave me unless they made him. He won't go. It was wicked of me to doubt him. That cat, Michael, wanted to spite me. I don't mind about the cake. I really don't, Kitty. My nose will be a fright. I'm glad you're to be at the top of the table. I'll slip in quietly by the lower door. Father Brady won't notice.'

'Do have sense now, Winnie,' Kitty said severely, wiping off the marks of tears with a towel. 'We're sensible nuns now.'

'Oh, I'll be sensible. Let us hurry down. I must make sure there's no fear of his going.'

'Come, my child,' the bishop said impatiently as Kitty entered the reception-room. 'We're all eager to partake of this very excellent cake. Let me help you to perform the last symbolical rite of your complete withdrawal from the world … of your marriage, as it were, with God.'

'Have they all gone?' Reverend Mother asked, half awaking from a reverie.

Chapter 14

Father Burke had strayed into the vow of celibacy without giving it any particular thought. Priesthood was a career and not a vocation. He was an average prudent man of the world who managed a small business with care. He was a teacher of a system of morality which he did not practise. He had never analysed his beliefs; and could not have honestly said how much, if at all, he believed what he preached. The subject did not interest him. He had no embarrassing convictions. He studied religion and morality—just enough to get through—to pass examinations. His vow of celibacy was merely a stepping-stone to a living. His preoccupation henceforward was to make life as pleasant as was compatible with moderate ambitions.

He never had a moment's regret that he had chosen the priesthood as a profession. It flattered his vanity, gave him ease, comfort and scope for the prudent gratification of his passions. His guiding principle was to reap all the pleasure he could without compromising his position, or putting any obstacles in the way of promotion to a parish. Higher ambitions were mere vague velleities which he pictured in his fancy; for which he hoped but could not labour, as they brought no immediate reward to his vanity. But a parish meant security, and could be reached by judicious steering. He took risks, but they were what he called fairly safe risks. He looked on every woman with the eye of desire, but exercised a wise discrimination before going farther. He recognized that some women had stupid affectations of virtue which made them impregnable; but the confessional often gave him a key to more easy virtue, or to the still more attractive innocence; and the freedom of intercourse allowed to a priest furnished almost indefinite opportunity. He seldom dropped the cloak of religion, and his carefully graduated series of affairs, ranging from the holding of hands to adultery, never resulted in scandal.

The bishop picked him up in Bridge Street on the morning of the profession. He appreciated the honour, but with some slight trepidation, for there was always the remote danger of something awkward coming to light. The bishop's cordial manner, however, reassured him. He ventured to enquire how long it had taken his lordship to drive from the palace, at Caltra; and, on hearing that it had taken only an hour and a half, expressed surprise that any pair of horses could do the journey in less than two hours. The bishop said severely that for some time he had been keeping a close eye on Father Burke with a view to promotion, and after careful investigation was prepared to offer him the important parish of Lissakelly. Father Dunne had a claim of seniority, but Father Burke's superior zeal as Director of the Women's Branch of the Sacred Heart Sodality, as a preacher, as head of the Temperance Society, as part confessor at the convent, made him the fitter choice for such a conspicuous charge. Father Burke, with a happy smirk, muttered something about his unworthiness.

'I have chosen you,' the bishop said, with a note of infallibility. 'You'll be careful about the convent there. Women are weak and the world is growing censorious.'

'You can trust me, my lord,' Father Burke said demurely.

He was elated by the news, but had a little undercurrent of depression. He was a kind man and felt for the women who would have to give him up. He was genuinely sorry for them. He must break it to them gently. He hoped none of them would make a fuss. He saw himself explaining to them that he was a soldier who had to obey orders—a martyr to duty. In a way it was a relief. They had become so many that it was difficult to keep the scales even .... and jealous women were dangerous. Partly because he hadn't the heart to do it, and partly because she might let things out, he had never dropped a woman. But this wouldn't be giving them up. The knot would, as it were, be cut for him. He saw them, consumed by grief, performing a sort of suttee. He hoped his successor would be a prig like poor old Brady or Dunne, who didn't know how to get the best out of life. There was no-one in the town who could step into his shoes. Hopkins, the Dominican, would try to make an innings, but wasn't formidable. It would be nice to think that his friends would be faithful to him when he had gone. Lissakelly was a promising parish—and there was the convent. No Brady to interfere with him now! But he'd have to be careful about the convent. Nuns were the devil when they grew jealous. Life was very difficult.

Though he had decided to say nothing of his promotion for the moment, so that the women should hear of it first from himself, he couldn't resist a dig at Father Flaherty, who was said to have expectations of Lissakelly. He waited behind as the bishop passed into the sacristy, took Father Flaherty confidentially by the arm, and said:

'Hullo, Flaherty. You'll be glad to hear that I have a chance of Lissakelly.'

'As much chance as I have, and that's damn little,' Father Flaherty said moodily.

'The old man has given me the choice.' Father Burke was a little nettled.

'He may be a fool, but he's not as big a fool as all that. Try a rise on someone else, my bucko,' Father Flaherty said, with an incredulous grin.

Father Burke looked supercilious. These fellows were so jealous, and never recognized merit. Flaherty might be clever at books, but he hadn't the sense to avoid being found out, and would never get promotion—suspension, more likely. There would be red eyes in Drumbawn the day he'd leave, no matter what the Flahertys thought. It would be all to the good if Flaherty went round spreading doubts. It would open the question. It was rather a pity he had said 'choice'. It would have been better had he said that he had been appointed, and was trying to beg off.

The ceremony embittered him a little. Kitty always rankled. She was one of his worst failures. How he had loved her, too! The thought of all that he would almost have done for her made him shiver. Thank God, her standoffishness had worn out that madness. He ought to have known the type, and never have bothered with her. But there it was, he just couldn't help himself. If he could only take her down a peg? But it was no use. He had tried every way. He could almost hate her for the smile of indifference she sometimes threw him lately. She was nearer to him when she had disliked him.

His resentment against Kitty made him think more warmly of Winnie. She wasn't a bad little thing … A dear, innocent little fool, and she could love. She had developed wonderfully. The more she got the more she wanted. She'd be heart-broken at his leaving … poor little girl. He was very fond of her. If he could only do something to show her how much he loved her before going away … Something that would make her remember him for ever … But he was sure she'd do that … something that would console her. Those snatched hours in the infant school were too short. Ah, there was that, of course! He blanched a little, and the bougie he held shook in his trembling hand. That was the nearest squeak he had ever had. Poor Sister Christina! It was horrible to think of her on the streets in Liverpool. Though she had been horrid to him she had never let out a word. And he'd have helped her if she'd have let him. If he only knew as much as he knew now, the accident wouldn't have happened. The awful things she said to him and wanted him to do! Still, she went off quietly without anyone suspecting anything. It wasn't necessary for her to go to the workhouse hospital. That was her pig-headedness. Though it was a joke that it was run by nuns. He mustn't think of her any more. It was all so harrowing—the child being brought up in such immoral surroundings too ...

He touched Winnie's hand as the bishop was putting on the ring. It seemed to spring to meet his touch. She looked up at him for a moment. He *must* do something for her. There was less danger now that the walk went straight to the church. Poor Christina had to climb over two high fences. And Winnie was cute enough in getting out of the convent and in. It would be more difficult, though, at night. Just when the nuns were going to bed would be the best time; and she could be back at three or four or so. The presbytery was quite safe any night Brady and Dunne were away. The servants slept at the back and could hear nothing. He'd be running a risk, of course, but it would show her how much he thought of her. And it wasn't a very great risk, after all. Why not this very night? Dunne was going to Caltra. And Brady was likely to sleep the night at Deelish—his brother was very bad—coming back for Mass in the morning. But he'd have to make sure of that. He'd have a nice little supper smuggled away in his bedroom—champagne and things.

After Mass he told Father Brady of his promotion. The old priest frowned and said dryly: 'So Dunne is passed over again. Well, well. The strongest proof of the truth of the old church is that she exists at all.' Father Burke was annoyed—no word of regret for his going nor of congratulation. He managed to find out, however, that Father Brady was spending the night at Deelish and would walk back in the morning in time for Mass. He was restored to good-humour by what he felt was an evident intervention of Providence. Father Flaherty's anger, expressed in the violent remark that the church is a bloody pantomime, cheered him. Bedelia Rafter's pale face and anxious enquiry, 'There's no truth in it, is there, Father?'

warned him to keep a veil of mystery over his going, else there might be scenes in public. 'Tell everyone not to believe half of what they hear. I'll explain it all. Will to-morrow at four do?' he said, with a look of tender regard.

He wished he hadn't spoken of the matter so soon, and put on an air of worried reserve. He must put off an explanation with Winnie till to-night. With luck she wouldn't hear the rumours. To the next enquirer he said pettishly that there was no truth in the report. But at luncheon he could not resist telling the Miss Purcells the truth; and was highly gratified that the elder stopped eating for a few minutes to discourse on the decay of manners. She didn't know, nor could the younger sister when appealed to help her out of her difficulty, what the Women's Branch of the Sacred Heart Sodality would do without their gentlemanlike Director. There were priests and priests, and it was possible, of course, to have a religious soul beneath a rough exterior, but that nice combination of both, so happily exemplified in Father Burke, was difficult to get twice. But she did sincerely hope that it wouldn't be Father Dunne. Partly because Father Dunne was so near, and partly because an attractive-looking gelatine caught her eye, she said no more, but her shrug was expressive.

Pleased by such a reception of his news by what he called the élite of the town, Father Burke tested solid business opinion as represented in Tom Curtin on his other side. Tom was in bad humour and resented any change. There were his own daughters, he said, making fools of themselves by becoming nuns. He didn't know what had come over the world, but the one thing certain was that it was going to the dogs; though, thank God, trade had never been better. That, it seemed, was exactly Father Burke's opinion also, and he was glad to have it confirmed from so responsible a quarter. He was extremely worried by the choice put before him by the bishop, torn between his duty to obey what was virtually a command of his lordship, and his own inclinations. Tom Curtin said emphatically that bishops were entirely too interfering, but if the worst came to the worst, the town would give Father Burke a subscription. Father Burke deprecated this with his most gloomy look of surprised pleasure … With a feeling of terror he saw Winnie rushing towards them. No, she didn't know—she was looking too happy. He'd make her still happier when he'd tell her about it to-night. She was so fresh and pink. Was the little minx telling him what was in store for him by all this hugging of her father? She was really pretty to-day; and she put so much of herself into a look and a handshake. Perhaps he was lucky, after all, in having her and not Kitty, who was looking so reserved and cold-blooded up there beside the bishop. It was too late now to try and wake Kitty up. The convent seemed to have frozen her … Yet there was fire in her he knew. Though he had given her up, he couldn't help thinking of her. He was very near hating her, but she could make a fool of him still by a look …

He discussed gloomily the illness of Father Brady's brother, but his spirits revived at the approach of Kitty. She looked brighter. He ventured his mildest method of flirtation and was elated with the result. If he was only sure she was thawing he'd be tempted to refuse Lissakelly. One minute of her would be worth hours of Winnie. She really did seem sorry that he was going …

He broke off a sentence of Tom Curtin's in the middle, saying he had an urgent sick call to attend to. He must get into the fresh air to think all this out. He couldn't talk to Winnie now. He slipped out through the nearest door, got his hat and strode thoughtfully down the juniper walk towards the parish church. Kitty had disappointed him so often that he was a fool to build on a look and a word or two. He couldn't give up Lissakelly, of course. He might never get such a chance again. But he could often come over to Drumbawn. It would be dark to-night without a moon … and the hedges had grown up high. He hoped Winnie wouldn't be afraid—there would be stars in any case. No, he couldn't take the risk of coming to meet her beyond the presbytery gate. If only it were Kitty! He'd go back to the convent in a few minutes, when most of the visitors had gone, and try to have it out with *her*. He'd arrange with Winnie then, too. That reminded him. Had he finished the last of the champagne? It was too bad of Mrs Curtin to let him run so short.

He hurried quickly to the presbytery and satisfied himself that there was a bottle left. There was always plenty of cold meat. And he'd get some of the profession cake from the nuns. It wasn't a bad world at all, though many fools of priests and nuns didn't knock the best out of it. Heigh-ho, there was all the more left for those who had sense. He lit a pipe and glanced idly through the *Drumbawn News*. Next week there would be an article on him. He really must be careful in Lissakelly and not get too much entangled. Perhaps he'd better see the Editor and give him some tips. He yawned, ran upstairs to his bedroom, and hummed 'Coming through the Rye' as he brushed his hair and clothes. He looked round the room with, a satisfied smile. It was fit for a princess, not messy like Brady's and Dunne's. The table near the window would do for supper. If only it were Kitty though. How should he approach *her*? He'd have to make an effort to see her alone. She had treated him badly, but he'd forgive her if she'd be sensible …

He thought of her all the way back to the convent. He cared for her, of course, but it would be a bit of a triumph to humble her. If he were once even with her he could leave Drumbawn happy. Even a kiss would round off his life somehow. But she was the sort that didn't stop at a kiss if they once got so far. The difficulty, he thought gloomily, was to get her there.

He smiled contentedly as he reached the terrace. His luck was standing by him. It was a good augury that Kitty should be the first person he saw. He frowned. How did that organist fellow get to know her? It was all Dunne's fault, taking him up. Anyhow, she had said good-bye to him. He was a cheeky bounder and should be kept in his place. He preened himself and advanced to meet her with a smirk. He pulled at his cuffs. There was actually a glow in her eyes and she was smiling at him in a more than friendly way. He looked about furtively. Nearly all the people had gone. Far down the lime avenue was what looked like Mrs Curtin with two nuns.

'I am looking for your mother,' he said, with a searching look down the entrance drive where a very obvious bishop was talking to Reverend Mother.

'Come with me, then,' she said brightly. 'She's gone down towards the river meadow with Winnie and Sister Eulalie—father has given it to the convent.'

'A generous gift to God will bring reward a hundredfold.'

Unconsciously he lapsed into a professionalism. This riot of late May flowers, in which spring and summer met, was a tribute to her beauty. The dead mask of the morning had gone, and a new life shone in her eyes. If he had ever seen love, this was it. He patted, in passing, the golden hair of a little orphan.

'It's been a wonderful day,' he said cheerfully.

'Wonderful,' she replied, in an absorbed tone.

'You don't think so badly of me now?'

'How could I?' she said, with a happy laugh.

Her joy, confidence, hope intoxicated him. That look in her eyes … that ring in her voice was for him.

She plucked a leaf of lime and pressed it to her face. The sunlight flecking her face through the tender green of the limes, her soft languorous smile, the heaving of her guimpe, the violet depths of her eyes burnt him like fire. Though his heart beat violently and his eyes were blurred, his usual caution did not desert him. He looked furtively back. There was no-one on the terrace or in the avenue. Cows lazily chewed the cud in the fields beyond the iron palings on either side. Ahead, Mrs Curtin, Sister Eulalie and Winnie had disappeared round a curve.

He snatched the hand that held the leaf and crushed it. 'You do love me then, after all?' he said, with a confident leer, though his lips trembled. 'I can't kiss you here—it's too public. You must meet me somewhere.'

She stopped at his first touch and looked at him with the pained, uncomprehending look of a frightened child. Her eyes wandered from his triumphant face to the hand that held hers like a vise. The white of his strained knuckles and the black hair on the backs of his fingers seemed to hold her with a horrid fascination. Suddenly she flushed and wrenched away her hand. She gazed at him with a sort of dull wonder. Slowly the colour left her cheeks and her expression hardened. With a contemptuous smile she walked quickly away.

He stared at her with astonishment. A moody look at the creases in his trousers and at his pointed shoes gave him confidence in himself. She was only putting on. She ought to have more sense now that she was professed, but she was young. They were often like that. He started after her and laughed as he came abreast of her... a shrill laugh, in which doubt and self-confidence struggled for mastery.

'Don't play the injured innocent. You can't deceive me. I saw it in your eyes. I have cared for you ever since I first set eyes on you. Don't be a little fool.'

'You unspeakable cad,' she said, with bitter contempt, without slackening her pace or looking at him.

Her cold, level tone cut his vanity to the quick. He glared savagely at the back of her veil. The idea of a daughter of Tom Curtin's treating him like that. Girls who wouldn't know her had run after him. He thought of Winnie with resentment. He'd have nothing more to do with either of them … But he'd be lonely to-night. Why should he punish Winnie for that cold devil? It would be a blow to her pride that he was able to do what he liked with Winnie. He looked at her sidewise as if expecting his thought to affect her. No sign of it. He continued to look at her half speculatively, half with resentment. She seemed entirely unconscious of him and of what had happened. Her face was again the face he saw on the terrace … with a sort of unearthly expression of joy. Had he made a mistake, after all, and was she one of the religious lot? The thought pleased him. If she was that sort of fool it wasn't because she cared for anyone else that she was nasty to him. One could make allowance for her narrowness of mind. After all, Winnie was worth ten of her. His feelings did not, however, keep pace with his thoughts, and there was resentment in the laugh with which he tried to say lightly:

'It was all only a joke. I did it just to test you—to see if you were the same old spitfire. What a pretty pattern the sun makes on the avenue.'

Her eyes hardened again, and she set her lips. A worried look came into her eyes.

'You'd better leave Winnie alone, too,' she said, with sudden anger.

'My sister's keeper!' he jeered. 'But your Sanctity needn't worry—I'm going to Lissakelly.'

'Thank God!'

He winced, but Winnie's sudden blush, as they turned the corner, restored his confidence.

Mrs Curtin and Sister Eulalie got up, with exclamations of pleasure, from the wooden seat overlooking the river and advanced to meet him, while Winnie shrank shyly behind.

'Talk of an angel!' Sister Eulalie held up a chiding finger. 'I wouldn't have believed it of you, Father James. Throwing us over like this!'

'The whole town'll be broken-hearted,' Mrs Curtin lamented. 'It was the luck of the world I didn't hear it before the ceremony or it would take away my appetite. I can't even take any pleasure in the field Tom gave the holy nuns all on the head of it. It's a good parish, I'm told. And coming on the day it did, isn't it the reward of God for all you did for them girls? It's proud I am that you were able to sign, seal and deliver 'em before you went.'

'How anxious you are to get rid of me,' he laughed. 'But you won't drive me away so easily as all that.'

'You know I don't wish you to go—far from it,' Sister Eulalie said sentimentally.

'Don't keep me on tenterhooks. Is there a chance of your not going, after all?' Mrs Curtin cried. 'It'd be the happy relief and I near torn in two with trying to make up my mind whether I'd go to confession to Father Brady or Father Dunne, and they both without a heart the size of a chicken's between 'em, or wait and run the risk of the new man.'

'Not a word till to-morrow.' Father Burke pursed his lips mysteriously. 'I want to speak to you about the new banners for the Sacred Heart.'

'They don't want us, Kitty,' Sister Eulalie said, with a languishing look at Father Burke, 'And I haven't had a moment with you yet to talk over the glorious day.'

'There, there; say no more about it.' Mrs Curtin said, after a short discussion. 'Buy them and I'll make up the ten pounds difference. If it were twenty it's glad enough I'd be to give it to a saint like you. There's that Kitty away down at the bottom of the field. I'll have to call her and Tom expecting me back to meet Jameson's traveller.'

Father Burke strolled quietly over to the railing where

Winnie, with a flushed, excited face, was staring at the river.

'You couldn't go? I knew it—I knew it,' she said, in a tense whisper.

'What a beautiful view!' he said, watching Mrs Curtin move down the walk.

'Tell me—tell me? I don't know whether I'm dead or alive,' she said miserably.

'What a timid little mouse we are ! Trust me. I'll explain everything to-night.' He brushed her hand with his.

'The schoolroom?' she said eagerly, her face flushing.

'Much better than that. You must be my own brave little girl, but it will be worth it.'

He gave her minute instructions in a low voice.

'It will be the crown of a perfect day.' She gazed at him with shining eyes.

'Be prudent now. Let us walk on to meet them as if nothing was up.'

'You saint out of heaven,' she said fervently.

Chapter 15

Kitty listened to the conversation of her mother, Sister Eulalie and Father Burke with a sort of objective interest. She felt more and more that she was a spectator, rather grimly amused, of a play.

For three years she had been seeing the convent as an instrument of her salvation, as her only protection against sin. She had excused its faults, magnified its virtues, saw in it only what she wished to see. All that the soul needed could be found within its walls; and if she had not found the peace she sought, the blame lay in the immeasurable depth of her own depravity, not in any defect in the convent. The nuns, in their several ways, were aiming at perfection. If she could not always understand them it was due to her spiritual blindness …

Then suddenly, at the luncheon, all sense of sin had fallen from her. An understanding look from a man seemed to have spirited it away. There was some new freedom in her limbs, in her feelings, in her mind. If this was the effect of her vows it was perfectly wonderful. She was rescued from prison and made free of the earth and all its beauty. It was as if she stood outside and above all the bonds that had enclosed her. She had somehow been born over again. She had felt this keenly as she walked by Father Burke's side up the lime avenue. The old self of fear was gone. Prayer was no longer almost a temptation to sin, but a communion with the new God that dwelt in her new heart … Who was all around her in the dappled light dancing on the walk, in the soft west wind, in the glory of the leaves against the sky. To breathe was a prayer. To be out in the open, to smell the fresh grass and the limes, to feel the joys of form and colour was a song of praise. Father

Burke's attempt at love-making had given her a shock, but not for long. He was of the evil things that were now outside her, that could not hurt her. If it weren't for his influence over Winnie she could laugh at him. Not even his clammy touch could now give her a bad thought. Was he evil? or only in bonds as she had been? Anyhow, she disliked him …

She half wished she did not see things so clearly now. She mustn't allow herself to become intolerant. Yet this wide-awakeness of mind was a small price to pay for her lightness of heart. It was more amusing, too, to see the futilities of the convent without rose-coloured glasses. The last scene at the luncheon had been grotesque. The bishop cut such a ridiculous figure, with a glass of champagne in one hand and a huge piece of wedding cake in the other, extolling holy poverty and comparing her, Kitty, in a rather mixed peroration, to the Rose of Sharon, the Queen of Sheba and St Catherine. While poor Reverend Mother sat apart, a tragic figure, saying her beads, and Father Brady glowered and Father Dunne cynically took snuff. The new organist had seemed as much outside it all as she. And she could look at him and think of him without any horrid desire, as a friend. What had wrought the miracle? She was sure he could be a wonderful friend. She felt it in the firm pressure of his hand as he said good-bye on the terrace.

She must have been blind to have thought that Father Burke had changed. He wasn't even a good hypocrite—a sort of pinchbeck imitation. Anyone could see through him. Yet he deceived her mother, and Sister Eulalie. And Winnie was hanging on his words as if her life depended on him. It was dreadful to be in love on the very day of one's profession, and with such a man. It all came of the unreality of the convent life. Sin was fondled in avoiding it, or was given a frill and enjoyed.

'Father Burke is so wonderful—always up to his eyes in some holy project or another,' Sister Eulalie said ecstatically, as she bore Kitty away. 'The nuns will be in despair if he goes.'

'I wish Winnie wasn't in love with him,' Kitty said viciously.

'Not in love, dear—you must never use that word. Nuns mustn't fall in love.' Sister Eulalie spoke in a tone of gentle correction. 'Devoted? Yes, I'm afraid it will be a sad blow for the poor child.'

'Why not call a spade a spade?'

'No, dear, no. Never that,' Sister Eulalie said firmly. 'A certain amount of freedom of speech is, of course, allowable now that you are professed. But never anything so coarse as that. The French have a gift in these delicate matters. *Epris*, if you like. Poor old Reverend Mother has prejudices against these attachments. But to me they are very beautiful—when the object is worthy, of course, and they are the overflow of a superabundant love for God. Dear Winnie is so true and steadfast, and, if the worst came to the worst, she can offer it up. She recalls a sorrowful incident in my own past—'

'Reverend Mother is going to run the avenue down to the river-bank,' Kitty interrupted.

Sister Eulalie sighed. 'Ah, yes, poor Reverend Mother. Her age, I suppose, and overpraying. Her latest is to take the Infant School away from me. I don't complain. But some of the Sisters are saying she's past her work. Some of us have been putting our heads together—nothing but good feeling for dear Reverend Mother, of course … Relieved of office she'd have more time for her prayers and her flowers … and Michael would go. You'll join us, dear? The party of progress we call it.'

'Whom will you make Reverend Mother?' Kitty asked.

'The Holy Ghost will decide,' Sister Eulalie modestly replied, a faint blush on her sallow cheeks.

'He might choose Mother Teresa again,' Kitty said dryly.

'I think not, dear. Indeed, I know He won't. We've counted the votes carefully. God has been very good to us. Darling Winnie is enthusiastic. With another vote or two we'd be quite certain. You'll have yours before the next election. You know how very fond of you both I am, but, naturally, the supporters of the new regime will expect to be the favourites. We'll expect to find you on the side of God's holy will, dearest Kitty. But there's your darling mother calling us back. I won't ask your promise now. With the hints I've given you God is sure to direct you if you pray for guidance and submit your will to Him.'

Kitty was watching with a frown the manoeuvres of Father Burke. She hurried forward, in advance of Sister Eulalie, to meet her mother. Anyhow, the priest was leaving and couldn't do much more harm to Winnie. The poor child was looking like a ghost. Love was such a mystery. How much of a tragedy could it be with Winnie? Was it love at all, or mere convent silliness? Why was she seeing everything to-day in such a hard, clear light? Up to now she had been warding off the convent and all it meant, turning her mind in on herself, so occupied with her own emotions and temptations that outside things passed her by almost unheeded. To-day they seemed to jump at her. It was as if her mind had been asleep for three years and had suddenly woke up. The convent was silly enough as it was, but what should it be under Eulalie? Reverend Mother might be old and past her work, but she gave one a feeling of confidence. One felt in talking to her that she was real, though she seemed surer of the next world than of this. She saw things clearly enough, though she seemed tired and uncertain, as if life was too complex a problem.

'I'll be leaving them with you, Sister Eulalie,' Mrs Curtin said joyfully, puffing and beaming as they joined her, 'and be going home with a light heart. We put the cornerstone on their happiness to-day, praise be. I feel that proud that I could almost fly. Now that they're on the straight road to God they mustn't forget to give their old mother a lift on the way. Not but what I feel miles nearer to heaven already, praise the Lord, and it the best day's work I ever done.'

'You are, indeed, specially favoured, dear Johanna,' Sister Eulalie said, with emotion. 'My own dear mother felt herself blessed in having one child a nun, but to have two—'

She looked soulfully at the sky, as if words were too weak to express such beatitude.

Kitty had not taken her eyes off Father Burke and Winnie, who were coming towards them, Winnie blushing and smiling, Father Burke serious and detached.

'There is happiness!' Sister Eulalie whispered to Johanna, nodding towards Winnie. 'Doesn't it show that the grace of God passeth all understanding?'

'She was peaked enough a minute ago, but Father Burke could always work a miracle on her,' Mrs Curtin said complacently, taking possession of the priest who walked on ahead with her and Sister Eulalie.

'You seem to have recovered. I suppose he was making love to you again,' Kitty said morosely to Winnie, as they followed.

'What language for a professed nun! I'm really ashamed of you.' Winnie spoke reprovingly, her eyes focussed in an absorbed stare on the back of Father Burke's head.

'He's a dreadful man—he'll hurt you,' Kitty pleaded.

'If I were as jealous as all that, I'd try and hide it,' Winnie retorted. 'I hate you. Don't speak to me again—I'm going to say a rosary.'

The bell for the visit before dinner to the Blessed Sacrament began to ring. Sister Eulalie stopped and put her finger to her lips.

'It's really silence, but you can just say good-bye, Johanna,' she said, in a prim tone.

Mrs Curtin embraced Winnie and Kitty.

'You're happy at long last.' She held a hand of each.

'We are—we are,' said Winnie eagerly.

Kitty had difficulty in supressing an almost uncontrollable desire to laugh. Not that she did not feel happy. She had never felt so happy. She was a little worried by Winnie and Father Burke, but that was only on the surface of her mind. Her happiness was something independent of them all, of the convent, too; some secret that she shared with the wind now gently rustling the leaves overhead. Her real self was ranging the far hills while her comic ghost was playing a part in an inexpressibly funny comedy: Father Burke staring at her insolent triumph while he pressed Winnie's hand tenderly; Winnie gazing at him in dumb devotion; old Eulalie ogling Father Burke; her mother's contented smile, approving it all as a manifestation of divine grace arranged by God and herself.

For the first time since she entered the convent Kitty felt at peace during the visit to the Blessed Sacrament. And her happiness came from the feeling, not of being one of the silent worshippers, but of being outside them, as much apart from them as the God to whom they sighed. She was at one with the God who gave her this wonderful feeling of peace. She had no need to sigh and moan … God was in her heart. She had a feeling of looking with His eyes along the two rows of bent, black figures, splashed with mauve and green and red by the light that streamed through the stained-glass windows. Yesterday she had been like them … groaning and moving restlessly. They were torturing themselves, as she had tortured herself, to no purpose, for God only smiled mockingly in the vivid colours that danced on the tessellated floor, on the polished brasses, on their black and white robes.

The black and white, irregular file of nuns moving towards the refectory made her think again of a prison … with a vague wonder that she was there among the prisoners …

Why was Sister Jacoba racing through the Martyrology?

'Conversation at dinner. Hurrah!' Muredach said, in a gleeful whisper.

'And piles and piles of things in the Community Room,' Dolorosa said, with a watering mouth. 'Sweets and cakes and fruit—and peaches,' she added, licking her lips.

'Buck up, Catherine, and don't look like a stuck pig. It's your feast, you know,' Muredach said indignantly.

Kitty shivered. She had forgotten that she was a nun for ever. Every day she'd have to eat at this long table, and stare at the German print of the Wandering Jew on the wall opposite. Though mostly, thank God, she'd be listening to scraps of spiritual reading filtering through the clatter of knives and forks and not to this jabber. She was no better off than the goldfinch in the noviceship who beat his wings helplessly against the wires of the cage.

'Wasn't Father Burke a duck?'

'I wouldn't give one little finger of St John of the Cross for all the St Teresas in the world.'

'When I'm in good form I can say thirteen Hail Marys in a minute … I said forty-seven thousand in a month for the Chinese babies. I was head of the noviceship list. I bet you five rosaries you can't beat that.'

'What'll poor Win do if Father Burke goes?'

'I won't have a word said against the bishop. His face goes beautifully with his purple robes. *And* the heavenly thrill of his voice—*so* spiritual, my dear.'

'Spoons, indeed!—you should see old Anne and Father Flaherty.'

'Father Bernardine spoke for three minutes and a half to me.'

'Talk of icebergs, my dear! You know how Alphonsa would try to get up a case with a broomstick. But not he. Never shakes hands even. I'm sick of singing for a man who won't even look at you.'

Kitty felt a thrill of satisfaction. She hoped Joseph would go on speaking of the organist. She knew he was that kind. She strained her ears, but Joseph had jerked the conversation on to an infallible prayer against toothache.

If the din would only cease, and she could get out in the open! But there was the feast in the Community Room yet to come. Some day she'd grow used to it, be able to withdraw herself from it all, like Reverend Mother, who sat at the top table as if it were her stall in chapel, while Mother Michael and Mother Calixta sparred across her unheeded.

'I'll have no gadders teaching my girls,' Sister Thomasine said sternly. 'What is it to me if she's professed? That only makes her a black fool instead of a white one. I'll give the sixth class to Sister Catherine, and I'll get her in spite of sixty Calixtas.'

'That was meant for me,' Sister Dolorosa whispered, with a giggle. 'But it's really one in the eye for you, Catherine. I wish you luck on old Tom's treadmill.'

'I'll like it,' Kitty said, looking her pleasure ... Thomasine was a strict disciplinarian, and working under her was no sinecure. It was real work—seven hours a day of it ... She should be free in the senior school from the religiosity of Sister Gregory in the orphanage and from the sickly sentimentality that hung round the infant school ... Thomasine sentimentalized saints as little as priests.

Kitty counted hours on her fingers. With Mass and meditation and prayers and the Office there would only be the recreations left ... and these would be more tolerable in the Community Room. And there was her choir practice of course. She must do her very best in that ...

Her life in the convent seemed to stretch out before her like a long, white road, infinitely dreary. Why did she see it like this when she really felt so happy?

'Of the two I prefer Winnie, she's far and away the truer nun. You can see spirituality shining out of her eyes,' came in a clear whisper through the din of high-pitched voices.

That was Immaculata, who was said to have such acumen about vocations. Winnie *was* looking happy. Was that glow in her eyes spirituality? Vocations were queer things. She had never been able to see her own as Father Bernardine saw it. All Father Brady would ever say was that when one took up an oar one had better strive to pull one's best ... She had entered the convent to avoid herself, but she had brought herself with her ... And the torture had gone now. If her vows had done that she must have a vocation ... Yet the happiness she felt seemed to have no connection with the convent. She felt close to God, but the nuns and the convent seemed to come between her and Him. She had no devotion to her habit, or to the holy founder or to the holy Rule. One kept that because it was the decent thing to do. Would she always have this feeling of wanting to be away from the jabber, to be out in the lime avenue overlooking the river; or better, on Dangan hill ... anywhere where there was a wind, and water and trees and gorse in bloom ...

She'd never stand on Dangan hill again. It was chilly in here. She could never go mad now, like Basil. She was too happy for that. She was alive for the first time for years. She wanted to give herself ... but there seemed to be nothing to give herself to ... The only thing she'd really enjoy was her singing. She felt as if she could sing for ever ... only once a week in the parish church, twice or three times a week occasionally? And in between? There was the work of the school, of course. Work was a great help. But she couldn't take Sister Thomasine's interest in sums and geography, and the Office would be more of a bore than ever without her temptations to struggle against …

'Hush! Catherine has joined contemplatives,' Muredach jeered.

'She's dreaming of Father Bernardine,' Dolorosa giggled.

Kitty blushed. She had just thought of the organist … of his rather austere face which one could trust …

'Leave her to the frumps, where she belongs,' Muredach said impatiently. 'Listen. I had such a time with the young priest from Derrydonnelly. He promised me five masses.'

'Mother Calixta says we mustn't discuss men, dear,' Sister Augusta said timidly.

'Who's speaking of men? He's a priest. Such beautiful eyes—as soft as soft,' Muredach said. 'Catherine could tell you all about them—they run miles after her,' she added maliciously.

Kitty tried to make a flippant reply, but failed. There was something more than silly about this sort of talk today. It seemed, somehow, a desecration. There was something lascivious in it, something unclean, something that soiled her newly found purity. No wonder the organist smiled in that ironic way. He seemed so far above all that sort of thing. What did he think of her?

Her eyes ranged slowly over the tables. Was she one of the frumps, as Muredach said? Their holiness seemed as remote from her as the philandering of the others. It was said that Reverend Mother wore a hair shirt, and Sister Genevieve practised dreadful austerities … Yesterday she could have done this, but not to-day. And she wasn't afraid of death like Sister Attracta, who spent all the time she could in the chapel in the hope that she might die there and have her agony under the eyes of God … She was no longer even afraid of hell, so vividly present to Sister Matthew, who was in a cold sweat if her fingers were not touching her beads … who wore them at night tied round her hand …

Was there any common bond at all between her and them? She could not even use the language of the convent. Words there had almost lost their meaning. God was a God of love or an austere demon; a ridiculous image of Father Burke or some other popular confessor or preacher; a plaything, a lover—someone to be cajoled and flattered, loved and feared. After all, was she not like the other nuns in this? Yesterday she had feared God, to-day she loved Him … Perhaps all the nuns, herself included, were drifting about on separate little islands, with only their dress and their humanity in common, never touching, never understanding one another …

Mother Michael tapped the table in front of her. When the confusion of last words, the moving back of chairs, the shuffling of feet in standing up had ceased, Reverend Mother said grace. Kitty smiled as she joined the file to the chapel for the short visit after dinner. Mother Michael called God to attention just as she ordered the nuns about, methodically and with certainty. Reverend Mother spoke to Him as to some far off, impenetrable mystery.

And all the time He was coursing through her veins, singing joyfully in her heart. He was saying something to her, she did not quite know what; something wonderful that needed no definition, which satisfied in itself without bothering about its meaning.

She lingered in the chapel, unwilling to face the distraction of the Community Room. The novices were to come in there to-day for the feast … If only she could fly away and leave it all. Nothing could ever break the spell that now held her; yet the clatter of the nuns would impair it somehow. If only she had joined an Order of perpetual silence! No, not that either. What was it she wanted? She didn't know. She had everything … Happiness welled in her heart, yet she seemed to want more. Perhaps she was becoming a mystic like Sister Stephen …

She stood in the corridor and looked through a window at the flowers ... Once before she had that desire to go away ... to walk for ever along a road that never ended, alone with her heart. But that was when she was in love with Dr Thornton. And she was a nun now ... The empty corridor was more like a prison than ever ...

Reverend Mother came out of the cloak-room, her outdoor boots on, a stout stick in her hand.

'Fie, fie,' she said, with a whimsical smile. 'Not upstairs yet, and it your feast.'

'Winnie is there. Let me go with you,' Kitty said eagerly.

'I oughtn't, you know,' Reverend Mother said doubtfully. 'Well, well, I may as well confess I'm escaping it myself. When you are as old as me even feast days will bore you a little. Slip on your boots. I'm going down to have a look at the river meadow. You'll easily catch me up.'

Kitty caught her up within a few yards of the front steps. They walked on together in silence. Reverend Mother fingered her beads, stooped to touch a flower, stood for a moment to watch the pink May trees, and walked on with a sigh. Kitty sighed contentedly. Reverend Mother didn't jar with the beauty of things. She never talked twaddle about God or the saints and she could be silent. If the convent was always like this. Her thoughts leapt to the river. Once she had rowed down with Winnie to Dunbrack, but a more beautiful stretch was just beyond, skirting the woods of Lavally. To go on and on to the sea was a dream she had always had, and now it could never come true ...

'Have you ever wanted to get out of the convent, Reverend Mother?' she asked suddenly.

'Oh, yes,' Reverend Mother replied, her eyes absentmindedly on the blue of the distant mountains.

'And how did you get over it?'

'It wore off, I suppose. One has aches enough to occupy

one's mind at my age without remembering the old ones. Mercifully one forgets.'

Kitty shivered a little. Ache was the word that described her feeling now … a sharp pain that constricted her breast without diminishing her happiness … astringent but exquisitely pleasant, like lemon on the tongue when one was thirsty.

'Goodness me,' Reverend Mother said nervously, waking up from her reverie. 'You were only professed to-day, child. You're not unhappy?'

'Oh, no. It's the hills or something … the smoke.'

'The only way is to lose yourself in God,' Reverend Mother said, with the air of having lost herself in her plans for the river meadow.

'I feel as if I never knew anything about Him till today,' Kitty said in a hushed tone, as if afraid to break the spell which the afternoon stillness and light had cast on the broad plain.

'Eh, that's a good sign of your vocation,' Reverend Mother said after a pause, in which she had come to a decision about the paths in the meadow beneath her.

Kitty stared at the winding river. The colour seemed to have gone out of everything. It was the talk of vocations that gave her a sort of empty feeling. She felt a slight chill, turned round and looked at the convent, half shrouded in trees. In the shadow of a cloud all charm had gone out of it. The limestone orphanage looked raw and menacing. She shut her eyes with a feeling of revulsion.

'We'll sit here a minute,' Reverend Mother said, sinking with a sigh of relief on a wooden bench.

Kitty sat down, her limbs trembling. She clenched her fingers in the effort to hold something that was slipping from her. She wouldn't let go her happiness. The convent threatened to snatch it from her. She had been dead, but now she was alive. She had tried to escape from life and it had come back to her miraculously … It was surging in her veins now. She opened her eyes, half afraid of losing an illusion, and drew a deep breath of content. The plain was flooded in light. The town smiled back at her peacefully. The river, in a shimmer of silver, seemed to laugh at her fears.

Yet this morning she had renounced life …

The thought passed lightly through her mind. It recurred as she tried to trace the course of the river hidden by the Lavally woods. She played with the thought as with something odd and interesting that had no particular relation to herself.

'I have it all in my mind now. Let us be going back.' Reverend Mother rose with the help of her stick.

Kitty, with a wrench, turned her eyes away from the view that absorbed her, and followed with dragging steps. The sun was now gilding the trunks of the trees and the green lichen-covered slates of the convent. The warm creamy wash of the stuccoed walls glowed in the slanting light. It was what she was going back to behind the walls that gave her this empty ache in her breast and made her limbs like lead … She had entered when she had thought herself dead; and now that she had come to life in the tomb … she had bound herself to stay there for life. People who were buried alive lived only a few hours, but she might live for years and years …

She laughed a little shrilly.

'What is it, dear?' Reverend Mother asked.

'Just a funny thought,' Kitty said bitterly.

Perhaps one day she should be able to forget, like Reverend Mother, who had already forgotten that she had asked a question … She should begin to forget, perhaps, when she was fifty—nearly thirty years more. People lived ages in prison … that old man in the Chateau d'If … the prisoner of Chillon.

She stopped, thrilled with hope. Prisoners escaped

sometimes. She hugged the thought for a moment and rejected it painfully and reluctantly. They were in bonds to men, but she was bound to God … by God …

She stared at Reverend Mother's back, a bewildered look on her face. It was a dreadful thought … yet it seemed as if God had dealt unfairly with her. When she was trodden down, broken, weak, obsessed by fear, He had exacted a promise from her. Then, having bound her in chains for life, He freed her soul from temptation; and, as if to mock her, gave her the power to see and feel the beauty of the world. He couldn't have done it. He couldn't be so cruel … the same God who had given her these new feelings. Yesterday she was a withered branch: to-day she was like that flowering myrtle, bursting into life. The convent, and everything that bound her to it, were only a horrid dream that menaced but could not hurt this new life, which was in every breath she drew, in her blood, in the exultant freedom of her limbs. There must be some explanation, some way out. God could not at once have made her bound and free.

With a light step she followed Reverend Mother through the front entrance.

'We'll have to go up, I suppose,' Reverend Mother said dolefully, as Kitty helped her to change into her house shoes in the cloak-room. 'They moider one so with their chatter.'

So at seventy Reverend Mother still felt this … fifty years more of it … and Reverend Mother was spared the worst. A reaction set in with Kitty. Little things irritated her; the fastening of her shoe, the long rows of shawls and wraps. She felt suffocated in the dim cloak-room, and the hard brightness of the corridor, shining with beeswax, gave her no relief … All her life she'd be half suffocated by the smell of beeswax. On the stairs she shuddered at the shrill notes of Sister Luke's cracked soprano.

'Someone ought to stop her,' she said.

'Eh, eh!' Reverend Mother said vaguely. 'Oh, Sister Luke! It pierces even through the oak door. She's worse, though, in "Who is Sylvia?"'

'We'll have that, too,' Kitty said in despair.

'Let us hope it's over,' Reverend Mother sighed. 'Dear Luke is just a little acid. Even Michael hasn't the courage to give her a hint.'

They waited outside the Community Room door till the last falsetto note was smothered in applause.

There was a hum of excitement when Reverend Mother entered. Her most devoted supporters ran forward to greet her. One got her chair, another her cushion, a third held her footstool ready, while several nuns loaded the small table beside her chair with plates of fruit, sweets and cakes. The followers of Sister Eulalie looked at one another, shrugged and smiled.

'You missed both my songs, dearest Reverend Mother,' Sister Luke reproached her.

'We heard wonderfully through the door. Didn't we, Sister Catherine?' Reverend Mother said, making a nervous dive for her beads.

'Wonderfully,' Kitty echoed.

'I was always told what a loss I was to the operatic stage,' Sister Luke said complacently.

Winnie said, 'You haven't spoken to me, dear Reverend Mother. I'm so happy. I feel a real nun at last.'

'That's good. That's good,' Reverend Mother said wearily. Then, with a happy thought she added, 'Help the novices to more sweets.'

'But, dearest Reverend Mother, I want to tell you about my feelings,' Winnie said discontentedly. 'And they've stuffed themselves already.'

'Then stuff them some more,' Reverend Mother said gloomily, moving away, her hand on Kitty's arm. 'For God's sake, sing something, child,' she whispered. 'Something that will last ten minutes—till the office bell rings.'

'Just a word, dearest Reverend Mother—not more than five minutes,' Sister Anne said, rushing forward. 'Something very droll.'

'Sister Catherine is going to sing to us. Another time, another time.' Reverend Mother escaped to her chair.

Kitty made her way to the piano, more anxious than Reverend Mother to escape the cackle. 'How are you feeling, dear?' in a sentimental whisper from Mother Calixta, almost made her cry. She bit the inside of her lip in an effort to restrain her tears and steady herself. She smiled bitterly at a novice's whispered comment:

'Old prim Catherine is giving herself the airs of a Mother already.'

'Anything with four verses,' she said numbly in reply to the yawning 'Well?' of Sister Columbanus, seated at the piano.

She stood by the side of the piano, facing the room, according to rule. Her own voice and the piano sounded vaguely from afar. Several processes seemed to go on simultaneously in her mind: she was singing in the church choir, and George Lynch was listening with critical approval; she was drifting down the river in the shadow of the beech trees; she was back in St Margaret's impressing her determination never to be a nun on Bessie Sweetman; she was watching, with close attention, the roomful of nuns in front of her. Were they happy or unhappy? Some were and some weren't. One couldn't judge of those like Mother Michael and Sister Thomasine who regarded the convent as a home and a business, who prayed or cut up meat or taught geography as her mother weighed tea and sugar. All that one could say of them was that they were interested in their work and in the daily gossip. The religious nuns, with the exception of Reverend Mother and one or two like her in temperament, were the most unhappy: God seemed to torture those who tried to love Him. The happiest of all, at least on the surface, were those like Eulalie and Winnie who lived in a world of their own, made up of a sentimental God, plaster saints, silly priests and sillier nuns. There was a small group, of whom Calixta was one, who seemed able to combine diluted mixtures of Reverend Mother's religion and Sister Eulalie's sentimentality. And there were others, who hardly made a group, each was so individualized, whose only bond was the look of pain or bewilderment they habitually wore …

To which lot did she herself belong? She hadn't Reverend Mother's sane nor Sister Evangelist's tortured sense of religion; nor Michael's faculty of treating God as one of the daily tasks; nor Eulalie's power of illusion. She must be one of the dazed lot, like Bernard, who was now staring out of the window at the westering sun with pain and hopelessness in her strained, longing eyes …

'Will you sing the last verse? There's only two minutes and no-one is listening,' Columbanus asked dryly.

Kitty nodded 'Yes' with a smile at Reverend Mother, who, with eyes shut, was inflicting silence on the nuns nearest to her. Sister Euphemia, who was stone deaf, was listening intently, her finger to her ear. Novices were munching cakes and sweets, giggling and whispering. Sister Luke was criticizing the singer adversely in a shrill, high-piped voice. Sister Thomasine was reading a book in a corner. Winnie was moving about from group to group with a huge box of marrons glacés, explaining loudly to everyone how happy she was. Sister Eulalie's supporters, massed around her, divided the room into two almost equal camps … Reverend Mother's stalwarts having all edged towards their centre of attraction.

A bell rang. Kitty stopped short on a high note. Reverend Mother stood up with a sigh of relief. Sister Columbanus shut the piano with a bang.

The sound woke Kitty thoroughly. All her illusions seemed to fall from her with the sharp thud of the lid of the piano. She felt alone amid all the hurrying nuns. It was a desperate thing to know on the very day of her profession that she had made a mistake. But she *knew*, and she knew *why*. She looked with a pitiful smile at Mother Michael, who was carefully superintending the putting away of the remnants of the feast. Michael, who would have least sympathy with her, would understand her best. She must be as straight and unsentimental with herself as Michael was with the convent accounts.

It was curious how she felt. She tried to read the secret in the backs of the nuns as she followed them to the chapel for Office. The overwhelming feeling of life and joy that she had felt for the last six or seven hours had changed into something stronger and deeper. It was no longer a vague feeling that made her fanciful, but a hard fact that she had to face.

She opened her Office book, joined in the movements of the nuns, made responses, but there was no interruption in her thought. It was foolish, perhaps, to fall in love with a man because he looked at her. But there it was. It had always been like that: with the painting master, but that was nothing and had passed quickly; with Dr Thornton—who hadn't even looked at her. That was horrid, but this was different. Instead of almost driving her to despair it gave her courage. Courage for what?

She held her breath and could hear her heart beat. She was a nun now and must never love a man again. She waited, as if to hear some confirmation of this, but none came. She was a nun, but she did love a man …

She ought to be afraid of God for having broken her vow, but she wasn't; and He ought to be angry with her, but He didn't seem to be. Even if He were angry she couldn't say she was sorry, because she wasn't sorry, she was glad. She could now even pray, which she could never do when she had fought against love. And she had none of those horrid temptations which always came when she tried to put the thought of love away. She wished she was clever and could understand. Father Brady seemed to know, but she hadn't listened to him. Father Bernardine and Mother Calixta were only echoes of spiritual books, and her own experience flatly contradicted them.

The monotonous chant of the Office gave her a delicious sense of rest. The measured rise and fall of the thin voices made the garish chapel austere. Reverend Mother had advised her to lose herself in God. To-night, she felt in harmony with Him. Love and hope drew her close to Him. She knew she was in complete accord with His will. Yet Reverend Mother had meant something entirely different: that it was only by emptying her heart of human love she could be one with God. But this was the opposite of the truth. So far as she could be sure of anything she was sure that Reverend Mother was wrong.

Where was all this leading her to? All her life she had craved for love. In the shock and misery of a disappointment she had sought peace where there was no peace. In her madness she had promised the impossible. Almost at the moment in which she tried to deny she was a woman nature had reasserted itself. Sexless women might make good nuns … Even she could go on trying to live as a nun with her heart and her judgment pulling against her … She might forget like Reverend Mother, or go mad like Basil, or live in misery like Bernard … But she couldn't philander—madness, rather than that. She'd get out of the church choir somehow … As long as she wore a veil she'd avoid *him* …

There was a shuffling of books and a banging of stall seats. She held her hand to her panting heart. A feeling of suffocation gave way to one of intense relief … She could leave the convent … God wouldn't hold her to a promise she made in ignorance …

Her heart fluttered timidly. With a shy blush she joined the nuns who were leaving the chapel. It would be so wonderful meeting him out in the world where one could breathe … The convent looked so friendly now. Even dour Sister Thomasine was smiling at her … She clasped her hands under her veil to preserve her secret which every glance seemed to threaten.

'Look over the sixth class geography. You're coming to me to-morrow,' the old nun said gruffly.

'How jolly!' Kitty said, smiling inanely.

She hurried away, clutching her happiness to her heart.

The old nun stared moodily after her and muttered:

'I hope the black veil isn't turning her into a fool.'

Chapter 16

Winnie sat on the end of her bed listening intently. When the sounds had almost ceased, but not quite, would be the best time. They were fewer now but appallingly loud and menacing. The banging of a door made her heart jump to her mouth; a creak made her blood run cold. A footfall lengthened out till it seemed to reverberate all along the corridor. The watch in her hand ticked quickly, but the hands took ages to go round. At ten minutes to ten she'd start—five minutes more. Time would have passed faster if she had not begun the rosary for Muredach's intention so soon. And it was too late now to begin the rosary she had promised Sister Euphemia. It wasn't even worthwhile to begin darning her stockings. She had planned everything out so carefully—there was no reason to be afraid. Blessed Joan of Arc had no fear of the dreadful noises of battle; and the Curé d'Ars was calm when the devil, in the shape of a mad bull, raged about his house smashing the furniture. There was nothing to-night beyond the ordinary sounds she had heard, almost without noticing them, hundreds of times—nothing at all to worry about. In fact, everything had been providential: Muredach getting a headache—no wonder, and all the sweets she ate—and herself breaking off the arrangements after lights out: Mother Calixta giving her an extra long sleep in the morning. She wasn't really afraid. Her guardian angel might be a bit fussy over her breaking so big a rule, but she'd make it up with him again. One Hail Mary and she'd start, in the name of God, and trust to the Divine protection. But first she must rumple her bed—someone might come in. It would appear as if she had gone out of the room for a few minutes.

She murmured a Hail Mary as she threw back the clothes. A sudden shock of memory made her stand erect with a blanched face. Tears welled in her eyes and she trembled with emotion. Her hair! If it had only been last night or any other night, she thought despairingly, wringing her hands. But she had given it up to God; and she mustn't spoil a perfect gift by her regrets. She rushed distractedly to a drawer, feverishly uncovered a hand mirror and laid it on the bed. Unloosening her veil and guimpe she exposed her hair, took up the mirror nervously, screwed round her head to get the best reflection, muttered a horrified 'Oh!' Her hair that had been finer than the Magdalen's, more beautiful than an angel's aureole! God had never got such a gift before. She looked again, held the mirror farther away, and screwed her head to a new angle. Her face became more composed. It was different, of course, and nothing to what it was, but, thank God, in the hurry they had not cut much of it. In fact, her face had a new attraction. As a child she had worn her hair bobbed like that, and it had been much admired. God was very good to her. Her eyes fell on her watch. Nine minutes to ten. She worked feverishly and in two minutes was holding the handle of the door, a strained look on her face. She must be natural. She steadied herself, stepped out, looked up and down the corridor, went back to her room, put out the light, shut the door of her room noiselessly behind her, and walked boldly towards the stairhead. The lights would be on for at least seven minutes yet. With luck she wouldn't meet anyone. They'd probably take no notice in any case, and if they did she could easily explain.

She sighed with relief at the head of the stairs. God *was* good to her—the lights in the lower corridor were out. Once she got beyond the bend of the stairs she'd be quite safe. She muttered an ejaculatory prayer and stepped cautiously over the second step which often cracked. Thank God, it didn't creak, and no-one could hear her now in her lightest house shoes. She fingered her beads, murmuring a prayer of thanksgiving. At the foot of the stairs she leant against the newel-post to steady her nerves. Once she used to be so timid, but she knew now that the devil could not hurt her, with such a pure love in her heart. Father James had explained it all so beautifully. Not even a ghost could harm her.

She groped in the half-light to the cloak-room. It was so dark inside, but she wasn't afraid. Her shawl was on the first peg. Yes, there it was. But she'd have to wait till the lights of the corridors above were put out. It was God's will that her cell was on the first floor—it would have been so much more difficult to get down safely from the top floor. If anyone came now she could hide behind the pile of chairs at the back. She'd say the rosary for Sister Euphemia's intention while she waited. Love was so wonderful for driving out fear … not entirely, but it almost did. The Scriptures said it. The faint light at the foot of the stairs was a great comfort. Suddenly her teeth chattered and the beads shook in her fingers. That awful sound was only the Sister putting out the lights. She mustn't stir yet till all was quiet.

She shut her eyes and prayed. He'd be waiting at the presbytery gate. It was all so wonderful. He'd give up promotion for her sake. It was wicked of Kitty to throw doubts on him. Kitty was jealous … that was it. Sin was a dreadful thing and deserved eternal punishment. But things that were sins for some people weren't sins for others. The spiritual bond between him and her was purer and holier than marriage. It purified everything and made things that seemed coarse, beautiful. And tonight it was to be more wonderful and beautiful than ever.

How still it was, and how dark. She groped her way to the door, her heart beating fast. It seemed darker than when she had shut her eyes. She blinked at the window which she knew was opposite. There was a star, several stars. It was being false to feel afraid. Love was courage. It wasn't quite so dark now.

By crossing over she could grope from window to window. It was such a ghostly, grey darkness. The main entrance door was the nearest, but it wouldn't be safe. Besides, the key was usually taken away. The key was never removed from the inside of the sacristy door. And there was no danger that a creaking door or her footsteps on the gravel would be heard in the cells from the chapel side.

The cool iron knob of the door leading to the chapel gave her a sense of relief. Once that was open and shut she should be safe. It was miraculous that she had never once knocked against a picture. Her guardian angel hadn't deserted her after all. If she had only had the chance to test the hinges before supper. She must only risk it and pray. The knob turned and the door opened and shut almost without a sound. She hardly deserved her luck her faith was so weak. She fell on her knees and prostrated herself in thanksgiving. The little red light in the sanctuary was so comforting after the darkness of the corridor. It was as if God Himself was smiling on her. Tomorrow, when she had more time, she'd thank Him properly. It must be long after half-past ten—it had seemed an age in the corridor—and she had promised to be at the presbytery gate by then. She prostrated herself again as she passed the high altar, opened the sacristy door with a sigh of expectation, and stood for a moment on the threshold, her heart beating fast, blood mounting to her cheeks. He was so much a part of the sacristy to her that by shutting her eyes she could feel his arms pressing her to his breast, and smell eau-de-Cologne, his favorite scent. Trembling, she lit a match. The white face of the clock stared at her—twenty-five past ten. It had seemed countless years. She must hurry. She mustn't give way to foolish fancies with such wonders awaiting her. The flame caught her fingers, and she dropped the match. No matter, she could find the door easily now. But it would never do to leave the match on the floor. She groped with her open hand on the polished parquet and found the unburnt wood and, near it, the charred tip. She stood, undecided, and felt with her hands. The loud, measured ticking of the dreadful clock was threatening her with disaster. The darkness was alive and threatening. Her legs shook. She must either sink on the floor, or run for her life. She told herself that she was too weak to move; but she rushed blindly towards what she thought was the door and stumbled against a press. The cool, polished wood steadied her a little. She moved her hand along the top. It was the big vestment press. She mustn't be afraid. There was nothing to be afraid of. She held on to the bevelled edge with twitching fingers. Her lips felt dry and cold, and her cheeks drawn, as if they were about to crack. She'd never get there. And he was waiting for her. He had often leant against this press, his elbows resting on it. In this very spot he had often kissed her. The blood came back to her cheeks. Her hands suddenly became hot. She pressed them and her hot face against the wood. The clock, striking half-past ten, made her jump with terror. But when she realized it was the clock she grew calmer. She knew her way now. She could find the matches if she wished, but she didn't need them.

She groped her way towards the door leading to the back sacristy. Three short steps and she should be at the outer door. Her hand found the key at the first effort. She sighed contentedly as she arranged the bolt so that she could open the door from the outside. She stood for a few seconds on the doorstep. It was so bright after the shuttered sacristy. Anyone could see her. But the gatekeeper always went to bed at nine, and this was the blind side of the convent. She moved forward quickly, then stopped abruptly. The crunching of her thin shoes on the gravel was like a blare of trumpets. What a fool she was—no-one could hear. She walked on tiptoe. The rough gravel hurt her feet. What queer shapes things had. What awful black thing was that? It was only the cedar tree;

and once past it she'd be at the top of the juniper walk. What a black chasm it looked … but the stars would protect her. They were smiling on her, blessing her. She shut her eyes and ran. The thumping of her heart and the intolerable anguish of the sharp gravel piercing her feet through her thin shoes, only made her run the faster. She must escape this black terror. Her shawl fell loose. It was like some horrid monster hissing along the gravel behind her, yet if she let it go she was lost. She prayed to the Blessed Virgin and all the saints to protect her. Only by God's aid could she avoid rushing into the hedge, yet she couldn't stop. What had happened? She slackened her pace. She was no longer going downhill. She must be there. She stopped abruptly and peered round anxiously. Her thumping heart almost ceased beating. It was the mercy of God that saved her. Another step and she'd have been on the railings. She was bathed in a cold sweat. Her limbs shook and every nerve vibrated. Her heart beat more loudly than the ticking of the church clock. The Blessed Virgin *had* protected her. Pantingly she muttered a prayer of thanks. But she mustn't delay. Nothing could happen to her coming to him. She searched for her handkerchief, dried her face and her wet hands, and looked around to take her bearing. God be praised for making the stars shine so bright. She walked back slowly, bowed reverentially as she passed the front door of the church. She couldn't be so very late, after all, she had run so quickly. How her feet pained her … but that didn't matter. She must steady her breathing. What would it all be like? It had been so easy coming, after all. It was as if she was walking on air she felt so happy. There was the white gate.

'Winnie!' came in a hoarse whisper.

'Oh,' she said, with a deep breath.

She clung to him and kissed his lips again and again.

'Happy?' he said lightly.

'In heaven,' she murmured.

Father Brady's brother died at half-past three. At four o'clock the old priest was walking in to Drumbawn, reading his Office. He'd have a few hours' rest, arrange with one of the Dominicans to supply his Mass in the church, and come back and say Mass at Deelish at eight o'clock, or so. These details ran, through his mind over and over again. He shut his breviary with a sigh. God deserved more than his second best, and He couldn't give Him more with all these distractions running in his head. Poor Tom had lived honestly and had gone to his God. He was a bit peevish at the end, but that was the pain. They had bickered every day they ever met; still, there was never such a friend born ... And the world went on just the same. A man dropped out and another took up the spade. It looked sad enough in the bleak dawn when Tom was breathing his last; but here were the birds singing now and the glitter on the hedges, and the flushed, laughing sky as if there was nothing but joy in the world. And how else could it be and God above it all, only that men were so perverse, running after this and that? It was a queer world, Church and all, and God had His work cut out for Him to manage it all. There was the bishop now sending Burke to Lissakelly. But who was he to throw stones at Burke or the bishop? He had spent his own life trapesing round Drumbawn, and sorra much more he had done than to wear out his shoes. Still, it might be worse with a man like Burke. He had nothing much agin him ... but there he was. The fellow wasn't wholesome somehow ... Well, well, when his own time came he hoped he'd have as peaceful an end as poor Tom. And who knew but the bishop'd have sense for once and give the parish to Dunne? Dunne might be a bit hard on women, but what of that? It was safest in the end to give the poor, misguided creatures a wide berth ... Nuns, too ... for what were they but flesh and blood in a veil and guimpe, instead of a hat and feathers? Poor Tom! No doubt he could read all the riddles by now. No man grew better crops or turned out a better beast to market. He did his day's work and went to his rest. Could more be said of any man?

He opened his breviary again and began to read. He knew the accustomed words by heart. His lips moved in prayer; but his eyes wandered over fields swelling green with corn and grass between hedges white with hawthorn, while the shrill beauty of soaring larks woke all sorts of vague thoughts and memories: quarrels with Tom as a child, his ordination, the profession yesterday ... God was like this, full of the freedom and freshness of a spring morning and made men to His own image; but they were always making a hash of themselves and of one another. Nothing'd satisfy them till they made God into a sort of mixture of a fool and a tyrant like themselves. There was Johanna Curtin driving them two innocent young girls into a convent, and thinking she was pleasing God by it, too. But was she to blame after all when it was the Church put it into her head? It wasn't for him to question the wisdom of the Church, though often it was hard to see it ... He hadn't much of a bent that way himself, thank God, but he wouldn't like to have his life before him again and go through the struggle he had to make to keep his vow of celibacy. It was hard enough when it was your own free choice. But them young girls weren't free; not one in twenty of 'em. Fellows like Burke and the bishop painting the life in the colours of the rainbow ... It's little they bothered about the strength or weakness of human nature. It was a queer kind of vanity, glory be to God, to be pretending that black was white. Celibacy came easy enough to a few; and a good many more strove as best they could. But what about the rest—the half of them or more? Decent men and women, too, many of 'em to start with, but caught up in a net from which they couldn't escape ... condemned to misery and pretence and hypocrisy ... and all the harm they were doing … Well, well, it wasn't for him to judge. He had his own sins to account for, and heavy enough they were. Though, thank God, he had never advised a young girl to become a nun or a boy a priest. What was Tom thinking of it all now? It was hard to know anything on this earth …

He leant heavily on the umbrella as he descended the steep hill past the convent, and stared moodily down the empty street. He knew every man, woman and child behind all them dead walls, everything about them except the things that mattered. Once in a way he could help one of them by agreeing with them or not meddling, and that was about all. But even then he wasn't sure whether he did right or wrong …

There he was thinking of other things when he ought to be saying his prayers. He'd have to go back on his Office and say it again. He put his breviary under his arm, watched a salmon rise and the eddies die away, as he turned down by the river. He yawned as he unlocked the side gate opening into the churchyard. He'd throw himself on the bed for a few hours first and then arrange about the Mass. He stood and frowned at the draggled shrubs. He'd have to get them trimmed. The Portugal laurel was the worst. And the nuns kept their walk in such great order, too. He moved a few paces and followed the trim lines of the juniper hedges with an absent-minded glance. He had moved away a few steps when he remembered something he had seen. He turned back and peered closely up the gravelled path. Ah, he was right! There was something. A black bundle of some sort, about half-way up, on the grass in the shadow of the hedge. He'd let it be—something the nuns dropped, no doubt. He looked at it again and it seemed to move. He'd have to go and see what it was. It had such a queer shape, too, and was so big. He had too much curiosity in him at his age—to climb another hill, too, and he dog-tired. He pursed his lips as he came nearer and emitted a soundless whistle. Some tramp or other! But how did she get in and the gate locked? Poor thing! Maybe she hadn't a bed to go to—but he'd give her a talking to. He stood still and stared incredulously. He put down his umbrella and breviary on the gravel. What in the world was a nun doing there? It couldn't be she was dead? He ran forward quickly along the grass edge, and stood for a moment, undecided, over the crouched figure. There was no trouble, she was sleeping like a baby. One of the young Curtins—Winnie. What was the meaning of it all? Her shawl all over dust, and her slippers almost in flitters. He passed a hand over his troubled forehead and frowned. Was it running away she was? Thinking to get out by the church gate, and finding it locked? Did anyone ever see the like? If it had been Kitty now he wouldn't have put it past her. But Winnie had seemed happy enough. For that matter she looked happy now, with that innocent smile on her face.

He touched her shoulder. She turned half round and snuggled into the grass. He shook her gently. She yawned and looked up at him with a smile.

'What in the—' he began, but he stopped suddenly.

Every trace of colour had gone from her face and she was staring at him in terror.

'The grass is wet with dew. You might get your death of cold,' he said gently.

She was not listening to him. Her eyes wandered in terrified wonder from her dust-covered shawl to her torn slippers, to the sun blinking with a myriad golden eyes through the top of the hedge. She gave a sigh of relief and sat up suddenly. Terror had not quite left her eyes and a furtive expression was now added to it.

'My shoe hurt me. I sat down to rest. I must have fallen asleep,' she said, measuring out the truth carefully, and watching its effect on him.

'It was a nice morning for a walk, anyway,' he said cheerfully. 'Trying to run away you were, was it?'

Her face relaxed. The frozen look of terror which constricted it disappeared. She blushed deeply. Her eyes looked up at him with the open candour of a child.

'That was it,' she said eagerly. 'I was running away.' Her expression changed again. With a dazed look of pain she added brokenly, 'But I'll never do it again—never.'

'So she wasn't running away,' he said to himself, stubbing the edge of the path, a puzzled look on his face. 'Well, well, the poor girl is hurt, anyway, and there's no use in me pumping more lies out of her.'

He wagged his shaggy eyebrows fiercely at the toe of his boot and said, 'Well, well,' aloud.

She watched his eyes. Slowly her look of fear came back. 'I turned back at the bridge,' she said.

'You did, did you?' he said, with stern sarcasm, taken off his guard by the superfluous lie.

'You don't believe me, but it's the truth—it's the truth.' Despairingly she struggled to her feet.

'There now, there now. A couple of hours' rest'll do you all the good in the world. Let me give that shawl a shake for you.' He spoke absently, trying to drive off suspicions that were crowding in on him.

'The poor thing—the poor innocent little girl,' he muttered under his breath.

With a look of despair she walked beside him up the path. She looked at him furtively now and again. Her lips moved as if to speak, but no sound got beyond them.

No wonder his face frightened her. He was thinking fierce thoughts and looking them. There was nowhere she could get to but the presbytery; and Burke was alone in the house. He clawed the air with his right hand, as if to rid himself of the thought. Burke might be light in his manner with females, but he couldn't do the like of that. The girl was a little off her head or something and was only stravaging round, not knowing what she was doing. There were priests who did the like … no, he wouldn't think it. He was just a nasty minded old man, belying people like that, and there was no more harm in that innocent child than in a babe unborn …

'Are you coming in?' she asked, choking with fear, at the top of the walk.

'You can get in the way you got out, I suppose?' he said harshly.

She said feebly, 'I can.'

'Listen to me now. Say your prayers. That's it. Say your prayers,' he said, staring over her head at the stuccoed chapel.

'A layman wouldn't do the like, let alone a priest,' he murmured, as he turned on his heel.

❧

Winnie's dominant feeling, as she walked away, was fear. Did he know? Would he tell? The convent was more than ever necessary now to her happiness … and this horrid old man threatened it.

Sitting on the edge of the path in the dawn, in the bitter, grey light which was so soothing to her lacerated heart, she had planned her martyrdom. She would spend the rest of her life with a secret sorrow in her heart, an example to all the nuns of patient suffering. The halo she had seen gathering on her brow had stilled the anger, the resentment, the awful desolation that had made her sink to the ground in weakness. Soon all the horror of the past had been blotted out. She had succeeded in forgiving Father James, in decorating him with all the attributes of a fellow-martyr. He was to be a beautiful memory, just like Sister Eulalie's friend. She would drop a hint now and again to sympathetic nuns, and they would speak of her sorrow enviously, in hushed voices ... She hurried to the sacristy door with a quaking heart.

Her beautiful vision was torn to bits. Anything might happen. Even the door might be locked. She gave a sigh of relief when it opened easily. Perhaps he didn't know, after all? Father James always called him an old owl. Yet he looked so fierce and knowing. He must have known something. His version of it would go the round of the convent, and the nuns would speak of her, behind her back, as they did of Sister Clothilde who had been caught doing something terrible ...

She stared vacantly at the clock. Would they send her away? No, thank God! She counted five strokes mechanically. There were those horrid birds singing and she so miserable. Reverend Mother would be kind. But that sort of kindness from Reverend Mother was terrible, worse than Michael's bitterness. And Mother Calixta was always put out when her charges were discovered doing anything wrong. There was nothing wrong in what she had done, but they'd never understand that. They'd just judge by appearances like the rest of the world ... Censorious cats, Father James called them.

She leant on the vestment press and wept in pity for herself. To have come like this, too, when all was over, when she had made her great sacrifice. She had put it all away as a bad dream; but this shock brought it all back again. Not the happiness, she never could or would forget that. But her rage when he told her he was going, the fury with which she hated him, the things she said to him. It was the champagne, of course, that had gone to her head. But to fall from heaven into an icy cold hell in one moment was more than flesh and blood could bear. And he had been a saint through it all. It was just as hard on him; harder, perhaps, as he said, but he had borne up wonderfully. It was all the cruel bishop. And she had left him in anger. It was so wrong of her to feel so desperate, not to care what happened to her ... to wish herself dead. And when he warned her at the door to be careful, how she had sneered at him. God had been merciful to her in the dawn, cold and lonely, as if in sympathy with her misery; and in the rosy colour of the sky afterwards that gave her hope, and showed her the true way to bear her suffering ... She must send a little note to Father Burke to tell him that she saw everything as he did, beautifully.

She shivered. And now Father Brady had spoiled it all. If only she hadn't been so tired and sleepy. God was punishing her for her carelessness. She had never liked Father Brady; how right she was. She couldn't understand Kitty's liking for him. Kitty?

She started and stood erect. Could Kitty help? She looked hopefully at the sunlight penetrating a chink in the shutters and followed the little shaft, with brightened eyes, to its playground on the distempered wall. Kitty might be able to do something! She looked at herself in a small mirror and shuddered. She must get the dust off. There was the priests' clothes brush. She took off her shawl and veil, brushed them and her habit carefully. How lucky that Father James insisted on having a looking-glass in the sacristy. Her clothes were damp, but Kitty wouldn't notice that, and she'd change her shoes before going in to her. She'd hate telling Kitty anything, she was so prim and particular, but it was her only chance. Not everything, of course, but just enough to make her see that she was in trouble. Father Brady looked on Kitty as a rock of sense. If only she could get Kitty to speak to him before he'd have time to tell the Mothers ...

The stroke of the quarter made her put aside the brush hurriedly. With another look at the glass she rushed from the room and across the chapel. What should she tell Kitty? She opened carefully the door giving on the corridor and breathed more freely. It was a dreadful mess to be in, and Kitty wouldn't believe just anything. Besides, how much did Father Brady know? Oh, that God might direct her to say just the right thing and no more. She put away her shawl in the cloak-room, and crept softly up the stairs. She couldn't think. She'd have to leave it to God and the inspiration of the last moment. Running away would never do with Kitty, who knew she was so happy in the convent. She opened her door noiselessly, changed her shoes. She felt so much better that God must be less angry with her. Perhaps Father Brady knew nothing at all? Still, he caught her asleep in the juniper walk before five o'clock in the morning, and that *must* look odd. Why had she said she was running away? If she had only said she was walking in her sleep or had a toothache or something? But Kitty would get him to keep his mouth shut.

She tiptoed quietly along the corridor and up the stairs to Kitty's cell, and murmured a prayer for light and guidance as she turned the handle of the door.

Chapter 17

Kitty woke to find Winnie standing inside the door, her finger to her lips, curiosity almost overcoming the fear in her eyes. For a moment it was no surprise to Kitty that Winnie should be in the boat under the trees of Lavally. But what was a nun doing there? A blink and a look round the dimly lighted room made her sit up with a start. She blushed vividly. Had Winnie surprised her secret?

'You'd think they had cut it on purpose. You look better than when it was long,' Winnie tragically whispered.

'What do you mean? Oh, my hair! I haven't looked.'

'You're like a beautiful boy,' Winnie said, half jealous, half admiring.

Kitty put up her hands, felt her hair and blushed again. Under a hat one would hardly notice that it had been cut.

'You're always showing off your arms,' Winnie said, and flopped down on the bed with a sigh of misery.

'The bell hasn't gone? What are you doing here?' Kitty asked severely. 'What's wrong?' she added anxiously, as Winnie began to cry.

'It's old, deaf Euphemia who's next you, isn't it?' Winnie said, with an anxious look at the wall, 'and it's the stairs on the other side? I've had a dreadful, dreadful time,' she added, allowing herself a few choking sobs. 'It's that dreadful Father Brady. You must get him to promise not to tell.'

'Tell what? The difficulty would be to get him to tell anything.'

'You think so? You really think so?' Winnie eagerly clutched Kitty's hand, pulling it towards her. 'It was nothing, of course. But it might look strange if the Mothers heard about it. And I wouldn't like the nuns to know for anything. They might pass remarks. The fussy old Marthas, I mean.'

'It's a way they have,' Kitty said unfeelingly. 'But what about? It must be nearly six o'clock,' she added, with a yawn.

'It's not. You've no heart. Wait till you hear—then you'll be surprised. He caught me asleep on the grass under the juniper hedge over half an hour ago—before five o'clock,' she whispered.

Kitty's start and her surprised 'What?' made Winnie give a deep sigh of satisfaction.

'What in the world were you doing there?'

'Just asleep. You should have seen me. I got all wet, too. The dew.' Winnie had recourse to her handkerchief.

'But why—what brought you there?'

Winnie dabbed her eyes for a few seconds, sighed and looked into Kitty's surprised eyes with innocent candour.

'What, indeed? That's what I can't make out. Do you remember when Laurence walked into Mother Calixta's cell in the middle of the night? Dressed and all, too. And she never remembered a word of it afterwards. I had all my clothes on—even my shawl. Wasn't it queer?'

'Sleep-walking?' Kitty said, with relief.

Winnie gave a pleased nod.

'You think so? But wasn't it queer? I was dazed when he spoke to me. I said such a funny thing. He asked me if I was running away, and I said I was. Did you ever hear anything so funny?'

But Kitty didn't think it at all funny. The words reminded her of her own decision to leave the convent.

She looked at Winnie anxiously. Winnie had been in love for years. With that dreadful man—but still, it was love.

'In the church walk, too,' she said, continuing her thoughts aloud.

Winnie dropped her eyes and nervously fingered the bedclothes.

'You didn't go to meet anyone?' Kitty asked doubtfully.

Winnie gave her a quick, half-frightened look, buried her face in her check handkerchief and sobbed. 'To say such a thing to a professed nun! And you said yourself it must be sleep-walking,' she said brokenly into her handkerchief.

'I'm sorry, dear.' Kitty patted her hand 'I don't know what I thought. Father Burke leaving—and you are in love with him, you know. I shouldn't have said it.'

Winnie's sobs ceased suddenly when Kitty began to speak. She sniffed a few times and said with pained indignation, 'Indeed, you shouldn't. You almost make me blush with shame. I have a deep regard for Father James, of course, but I trust it is in a nun-like way. I must say I'm surprised at you, Kitty. And you a nun, too. Why, one would think you were out in the world you speak so grossly.'

'I almost am,' Kitty said, with a happy laugh. 'I'm going to Reverend Mother after Mass. I suppose there'll be a lot of fuss with the bishop and things, but I ought to be able to clear out in a few days. You can't imagine what it is to feel that you're so near freedom,' she added, lifting up her arms with a sweep that sent the loose sleeves of her nightdress over her shoulders.

'Don't do that. It's so immodest,' Winnie gasped, in a shocked tone. Her look of surprise changed to one of horror, and she edged away from Kitty. 'You wretched girl; what are you saying? And you only professed yesterday? Are you mad?'

'I was; but I'm sane since yesterday,' Kitty said, looking at her bare arms with a sigh. 'Some day I may even wear a low dress.'

'There wasn't a scandal?' Winnie asked, breathless.

'I'm just sick of it all,' Kitty said, with a yawn and a lazy smile.

'You're as mad as you used to be at school. The devil has got hold of you, or you wouldn't speak with such levity of holy things. Say you're mad, Kitty darling. I'd rather you'd be mad than to give such scandal. The nuns will always be pointing to me as the sister of the nun who ran away. What will darling mamma say?'

'What, indeed?' Kitty winced a little. 'There'll be the devil to pay. But papa might stand up for me.'

'Such language! And your deception! Pretending to be strict about things! I must say I always suspect that sort myself. Why, they were all saying you'd be in the running for office before long. Anyone who could pretend to so much could conceal any depravity. I shouldn't be at all surprised if there was something.'

'Perhaps.'

'Oh, tell me,' Winnie said eagerly. 'I'll be able to help you. I'll never tell anyone. I'll pray for you. Prayer can move mountains. Though your sins are as red as scarlet they'll be made whiter than snow. I'll keep it a dead secret.'

'It's only that I'd rather make love outside than in the convent. I never could stand priests. Run away now, Winnie dear, and don't be a fool. You're breaking the rules by being here.'

Winnie blushed furiously. She leant against the end of the bed for support and glared at Kitty.

'No rule stands in the way of saving a soul,' she said. 'Though you hint things at me itself, I'll do my duty and warn you. You are a bad nun; but, thank God, you can't escape from your vows. The bishop won't let you go. He didn't let Clothilde go. I don't know what you've done, but it couldn't be much worse than what she did. And if he let you out itself your vows would still cling to you. You could never have anything to do with the degrading passion lay people call love. Or if you did, you'd be living in sin.'

Kitty smiled happily at her extended hand. Winnie was talking such nonsense. Love was purifying and not degrading.

The degradation came when she tried to crush love out of her heart. She felt now as if she could float out beyond the convent walls; fly without moving her wings. Locks or walls or bishops or nuns could not stop her. A bird must feel this freedom. She was no longer caged. She could soar and sing like a lark, proclaiming her happiness.

'Poor old Winnie. We never got a chance,' she said, patting Winnie's hand in an overflow of sympathy.

Winnie resented this ignoring of her superiority. 'A chance of what?' she asked angrily.

'Of knowing ourselves, life, anything—the beauty there is in the world.'

'How can you say such things, you wicked girl, after all that Sister Eulalie and St Margaret's and God and mamma and the convent did for us ? I often warned you that you were neglecting the divine knowledge and the safeguards God surrounded us with. You may not know yourself and the world, but, thank God, I do. I know everything that God wishes me to know, and I trust for guidance to His holy will.'

'There's the bell. Cut away now. I want to dress and make sure of seeing Reverend Mother,' Kitty said, throwing back the bed clothes.

The bell startled Winnie into a recollection of her own trouble.

'You won't forget about Father Brady, Kitty dearest?' she implored.

'No. Do run off,' said Kitty impatiently. 'I hope to goodness you won't get cold or anything. You ought to see the doctor about that sleep-walking.'

'No, no,' Winnie said in alarm. 'I'll pray. Be sure not to forget, darling.'

She tiptoed towards the door, turned round when she got half-way, and whispered impressively: 'And I'll pray hard for you, too, that God may save you from your wickedness. I'll offer up for you a great sacrifice I'm going to make. You'll see that He'll listen to me, and you'll be a good nun yet. Think of the disgrace. I'd be dead ashamed; and the nuns would be so much put out. And to go back and live over the shop—it's all too dreadful.'

Kitty jumped out of bed. 'If you don't hurry you'll be caught rule breaking,' she said, preparing to wash.

'The seventh rule of modesty, Kitty darling,' Winnie said, in a shocked tone, turning away her eyes.

She stood, listening, with her hand on the handle of the door.

'There's such a lot of noise. Do look out, Kitty, and see if the corridor is clear,' she whispered.

'Like this?' Kitty laughed, splashing the water in her tiny basin.

'Oh, no, no. I'll risk it and trust in God,' Winnie said nervously.

Kitty, an amused look in her streaming face, watched her leave the room. As the door shut noiselessly she threw back her head and laughed aloud. Nuns were so funny. They weren't all as funny as Winnie, of course. Still, some were even funnier. The funniest of all was Sebastian who was in love with St Aloysius and fought with any nun who dared to pray to him. But that was a tragedy. She rubbed herself with her little towel till she glowed. What seemed so comic must be a tragedy for so many. Not all of them could satisfy their hunger for love in a saint. Sex was so much stronger in a convent than outside …

Her mind wandered back over her past life as she put on her habit. Unlike Winnie and so many of the others she hadn't been ignorant when she entered. Not that she knew much of the world. She knew little of it except what she picked up from Bessie Sweetman and Daisy Thornton; but, little as it was, it made her resent the glosses and evasions of the nuns at St Margaret's. Their attempts, direct and indirect, to persuade her that she had a vocation had made her definitely hostile. The confidences of an unhappy nun made her almost hate the convent. The passionate devotion of some of the nuns, instead of evoking any response of affection, gave her acute feelings of uneasiness. The austerity of some of the nuns appealed to her even less than the sensuousness of others. And all combined in trying to catch her in a net. Nuns who were unhappy in the convent were as eager to have her become a nun as those who were happy. It was as if decoy birds really enjoyed inducing others to share their unhappiness. How often she had laughed with Bessie Sweetman and Daisy Thornton over the efforts that were made to entrap them. The easy capture of Winnie made her dislike nuns all the more. The one fixed resolution she had carried away from St Margaret's was never to become a nun. Yet the convent must have influenced her all the same. When she got into that dreadful state of mind over Dr Thornton a convent seemed the only refuge. All her actual experience of convents was forgotten, and the accumulated suggestions of years drove her to the veil. From a child the convent had been dinned into her ears as a haven of peace and freedom from sin. She had had no call, no vocation. She had entered the convent to escape from sin. Ever since she had been so preoccupied with temptation that she had given little thought to her vocation, and had taken Father Bernardine's word for it …

She said the angelus to the sound of the bell and hurried down to the chapel for morning prayer. In passing Reverend Mother's stall she asked if she could see her for a few minutes after Mass.

'Eh, eh?' the old nun said, after a few seconds' struggle to recall her mind. 'Why, of course, child. Come to my room about a quarter-past eight.'

She said morning prayer with a glad heart. At meditation her eyes wandered, and her thoughts. The nuns, huddled back in their stalls, made such a restful picture. It was all so beautiful, so quiet, so dead. Winnie was asleep in her stall, her head swaying gently, a peaceful smile on her lips. They would go on being dead like this for years and years, and she should be out in the world, alive. It was selfish of her to think like this. And some of them would deny that they were dead. They would say that they were full of a life that was higher and far nobler than hers. Perhaps they were. But she could never be of those few. She could respect them and admire them, could understand them even, but she could not be of them. What was it George Lynch called them? Wraiths of dead women. There were a few in St Margaret's, there were a few here, there were some in every convent. The futilities of the others obscured them, but they had a beauty of their own as an orchid has. Thank God, she no longer believed that God took the trouble to form her wonderful body in order to give Himself the pleasure of seeing her trample on it much less to see her make believe …

She joined in the Office as in a hymn of thanksgiving, and felt, as Father Dunne reverently said Mass, that God was adding new strength and courage and hope to her already overflowing heart.

She caught up Reverend Mother in the corridor near her private sitting-room. The old nun smiled, led the way into the room without speaking, sighed as she pointed to a cane armchair for Kitty, and looked a little worried as she sank into her own chair.

'Well, now?' she said, grasping her beads.

Kitty looked at the inkstain on the red table cover, at the bowl of tulips in the centre of the table, at the crucifix above the *prie-Dieu*, at the few dozen books on an open shelf.

'Before I forget it, Sister Thomasine wants you for the sixth class—and she generally has what she wants. You'll find her strict, but straight,' Reverend Mother said, with a sigh.

Kitty looked at the few austere chairs along the distempered wall. It had always struck her, too, that so many of the nuns weren't straight ... little petty crookedness that sickened one ...

'I want to leave the convent, Reverend Mother,' she said, looking up with a feeling of relief.

The old nun's florid face went grey about the eyes and she suddenly looked older and feebler. She looked down at her rosary, watched her fingers twirl round and round a single bead till the wire snapped.

'I always do that,' she said, holding up the rosary with a wry smile. 'My God, child! What put that thought into your head—and the ink hardly dry on your vows?'

'I must have been mad. I was a fool, I didn't know what I was doing. It was all a dreadful mistake.'

'It isn't twenty-four hours ago yet,' Reverend Mother said vaguely. 'It's all this might be the mistake. Everyone agreed that you had every mark of a true vocation. It's the excitement or the devil tempting you; perhaps your stomach is upset. There's the bell for breakfast. We must be going down or the nuns will be asking questions. Say your prayers and it will all pass away. Come to me again to-morrow and tell me it's all right,' she added, with a hopeful sigh, putting her hands on the arms of her chair as if about to rise.

'Please don't go, Reverend Mother. We must settle it now. I have no vocation. I never had a vocation. I don't even know what's meant by it—it's meaningless to me anyhow. I want to go home, to go out into the world, to live. I don't want to be a nun.'

'My God, my God! But you are a nun, child.' the old nun said feebly, with a supplicating glance at the crucifix. 'This is dreadful—dreadful. Poor child, poor child. What can I do? It's all my fault. I'm not fit to rule—I never was. It's all a bad dream. If it was Winnie now … but I was so sure of you. I thought to myself she's coming to ask me to be allowed to practice some austerity, but I won't let her. Perhaps later, I thought—the scourge once or twice a week, but not yet, not yet.'

'It has been all my fault. I'm sorry to give you pain. I've been such a fool, but I must go—I must go,' Kitty said brokenly.

'But I can't let you go, child.' Reverend Mother dropped her hands on her knees with a helpless gesture. 'You must satisfy the bishop. He may not let you go at all. He's against letting nuns out into the world again. It gives scandal, he says, and is a reflection on the Church, and must be avoided at all costs. I don't know. Often when I see their misery inside I think they'd be better out. But when I think of them out in the world, bound by their vow, and without the safeguards of the convent, I'm inclined to think the bishop is right. It's all a mystery, and I'm not fit to deal with it.'

The feeling of the prison house came over Kitty again. But she was now conscious of the bars without any fear of them. They stifled her and she was going to break them. Whatever the bishop said she'd go out. And she'd leave all her chains behind her in the convent.

'But one is free to marry?' she asked coldly.

'It's that, then?' Reverend Mother said, with a sigh. 'No, no. You'd go out with your vow of chastity. Sometimes, very rarely and with the greatest difficulty, one might get permission to marry, but under onerous conditions. It hardly ever happens, the Church is so much against it. Your vow is perpetual. Don't go out into temptation, child. This must have happened very suddenly. You haven't had time to pray yet. You haven't even consulted your confessor. We'll get Father Bernardine down for you. Believe me, you'll be happier in the convent.

No-one will marry you—there is a strong feeling against it. And even if you met someone who did wish it the Church would put every obstacle in the way. One can withstand these temptations. They pass off.'

'But I have no temptations,' Kitty said. 'I've had none at all since I made up my mind to leave. I want to be free.'

A feeling of rebellion surged through her. A sense of injustice rankled in her. Reverend Mother, with all her gentleness, was one of her gaolers. Her life from a child flashed through her mind in an instant. Always she had been pushed into the convent. Her first memory was of being called 'Kitty Nun'. She played nuns with her dolls. In the infant school she was the little nun. Her nurse hardly ever spoke of anything else. And always her mother was pushing her relentlessly into the convent. Her revolt before was only half-hearted. She hadn't burst the bonds with which she had been secured so remorselessly. Her mind had been so filled with the images of what she was not to think or do that the inhibitions themselves drove her to madness about Dr Thornton. Father Brady would have saved her, but her whole training made her turn to the convent, led her to listen to Father Bernardine and accept his final push into misery. George Lynch's look was only the occasion of her rescue. She wasn't sure if she was in love with him at all. It was just that she had burst her bonds. She was in love with life, with love, maybe. But her mind and emotions had, for the first time, some sort of balance.

'No-one can be free in this world,' Reverend Mother said, with a sigh, after a long pause in which her mind seemed lost in the blaze of flowers in the bowl.

'But I am free, Reverend Mother,' Kitty said happily. 'I can't tell you how free—as free as the air, as the sunlight, anything.'

'Your vows, dear?'

'I don't believe God cares a pin about them. I'm sure He never meant me to take them, and doesn't wish me to bother about them.'

Reverend Mother, horror-stricken, with half-open lips, stared at her. 'Blasphemy!' she murmured weakly. 'Kitty, darling, pray, and pray hard. I never dreamt the devil had got such a hold on you.'

'He hasn't really, Reverend Mother. I'm sure he had for the last three years, but not now. Now I'm sure it's God.'

'That's the worst temptation of all. Oh, Kitty, that you should have come to this. There's no more subtle snare than to think that God approves of your sin. I don't know what to think. I'm bewildered by it all. You're a good girl, and you're all wrong. You must lay bare your soul to your confessor. And the bishop may be able to help. Above all, pray. I'm too old and too confused even to understand, much less to help. You want me to speak to the bishop?'

'Oh, yes, yes.'

The old nun's lips trembled. Tears fell unnoticed on her guimpe. Kitty threw herself impulsively at her feet and wept.

Reverend Mother patted the head in her lap with one hand and fingered her beads with the other. 'There, there, now,' she said softly, after a few minutes. 'We must be going down to breakfast.'

'I'm so sorry to hurt you. You forgive me, Reverend Mother?'

'It doesn't matter about my hurt. It's the hurt to God that matters. Of course, I forgive you. I can't understand you, but I forgive you all the same. Let us pray that God may. Whatever you do, may you be happy. Run away now, child, and God bless you. Your tea will be cold.'

Chapter 18

Reverend Mother forgot her breakfast. She looked out at the trees and flowers with eyes that held the vague wonder of a child. It seemed impossible that sin could exist where every leaf and bird spoke the goodness and love of God. All nature praised Him. Man alone sinned, tried to deform this beautiful world. Why God allowed sin was one of the mysteries she could never fathom. As nothing could detract from His infinite goodness, sin was in some way connected with His inscrutable wisdom. Sin could even enter a convent. It had always come as a shock, but she had been forced to recognize that nuns sinned. That they actually had passions like women in the world. Before she entered the convent she had had vague curiosities, but no real temptation. As a novice and a young nun she had had regret for her horse, for her own room at home with its flowered chintz curtains and valences and chair covers, for her 'coming out' ball which had never taken place, for her amber necklace. And once, when her younger sister married, she had sinfully longed to be out in the world, not that she might marry, for the thought of marriage had always been repugnant to her, but to see the Pope and the sky and colour of Italy, where her sister was to spend her honeymoon.

She sighed as she watched nuns pass to and fro on the terrace, their eyes fixed on the ground. It was impossible to believe that sin could enter that peaceful garden. But, alas, it had entered often and often. She had tried time and again not to see things, to find excuses, to refuse to listen, to forget. God was punishing her now for her sins of omission. She was seventy and she had never even tried to understand. It had been so easy to run away to her prayers and her flowers.

She had been twenty-five years Reverend Mother, yet she knew less of the convent than when she was a novice. Kitty Curtin's madness convinced her of her unfitness to manage the convent. God knew she had never sought office. All she ever wanted was to be let say her prayers in quiet; and, perhaps, to be allowed to tend the flowers if God willed it. The nuns would never have elected her Superior. She had been appointed by the old bishop, largely because she was a De Lacy of Cleggan; and she had been reappointed, time after time by the old bishop and the new, because the nuns had never been able to agree, and it came easier to a bishop to appoint an old Superior who gave no trouble than to risk a new choice. A nice mess she had made of it. After Kitty Curtin anything might happen. And the worst of it was she couldn't even understand this scandal. In the other cases, horrible as it was to remember, the nuns had been found out doing wrong or had confessed to human weakness. But here was a girl who denied that she was committing sin at all, gloried in her action as if it was a virtue, and even denied the validity of the sacred laws of Holy Church on which the whole idea of the conventual life depended. It was as if the convent was toppling to the ground. Here was gross sin and scandal. Yet the girl didn't seem to be a sinner. She was frank and honest. She had kept rules with scrupulous exactness. If she had any fault it was in praying too much.

She walked up and down the room, tried to say her beads, but the thought of Kitty kept intruding itself. She knelt at the *prie-Dieu*, but it helped her less. The gentle, thorn-crowned face on the crucifix seemed stonily indifferent. 'It was all my fault, all my fault,' she said, in a voice shaken by sobs. 'Father, forgive her, for she knows not what she does. It is I who have been remiss. I don't know how, but I always am. Visit her sin on me'—she paused and added vaguely—'if it be a sin.' Kitty's cheerful, happy face seemed to smile at her as it had smiled when she was saying things that should have distorted her face into some black image of sin. She was glad the child wasn't unhappy. It was all so hard to understand; but, perhaps, Michael and Calixta could throw some light on it. Anyhow, she mustn't neglect her duty so much.

She sternly put away her beads as she walked down the stairs. She must keep her eyes about her. Not that she ever saw anything till after the harm was done. She turned back with a frown from the step of the door leading to the terrace. Flowers were an indulgence, and she'd have to give them up. She passed several nuns, their eyes demurely downcast. Having given so much to God, if they had only given a little more! They committed none of the grosser sins, of course, and had made great sacrifices, but if they didn't squabble so, what a blessing it would be! It seemed as if grace sharpened the tongue in some natures, made them what might almost be called spiteful, if one weren't sure that it must be all quite unconscious. Even holiness was a mystery in its manifestations.

'What are you doing?' she said, in gentle reproof, to an orphan who was leaning idly on a long-handled polisher.

'Helping Susy, ma'am.'

'And what is Susy doing?'

'Nothing, ma'am.'

She stood at the reception-room door and watched eight orphans sitting on their heels in a close circle engaged in eager, whispered discussion.

'Old Reverend Mother never sees a thing,' one said disdainfully.

'Busy, children?' she asked, with the little irony she could bring herself to use.

'Polishing the floor, ma'am,' they said, in chorus.

In the corridor three novices were busily dusting one picture, with an absorption the task didn't seem to demand. She passed on with a sigh. If they would only not practice these small deceptions. Rules and regulations tempted the young. This thought led her too far, and she put it aside hastily. They broke small rules like the rule of silence, but they wouldn't break the bigger rules …

She met Winnie at the entrance to the covered passageway leading to the school.

'How are you getting on, child?' she asked, as they walked on together.

'Oh, beautifully, Reverend Mother. I feel wonderfully strengthened by my vows.'

'Hum. Has Kitty said anything to you?'

Winnie hesitated, but plumped, 'No, Reverend Mother,' candidly. 'Is there anything?' she added.

'I hope you'll be a good nun,' Reverend Mother said, breaking a long silence, as they entered the hall of the school-house.

'How could I be anything else, dear Reverend Mother, with all the blessings that surround me?' Winnie said warmly, but with a slight tinge of reproach. 'You need have no fear of me, dearest Reverend Mother.'

'God bless you, child. I hope not, I hope not.' Reverend Mother gave a pained smile as she noticed Sister Eulalie's rapid glance, her frown, her perceptible stiffening and immediate absorption in her class.

'Reverend Mother, Sister,' Winnie said, rushing forward.

'Oh!' Sister Eulalie said, with a start of surprise, 'Stand up, children, in honour of Reverend Mother.'

Reverend Mother motioned them back to their seats.

'This is indeed an unexpected honour, Reverend Mother, dear,' Sister Eulalie said through her teeth. 'The children sometimes ask "What has become of Reverend Mother?" I explain to them that naturally you are busy over the new flower-beds. They are too young to understand that a Reverend Mother has so many important duties. They upbraid me for being about to leave them after so many sweet years. As if I would do anything so cruel of my own accord! I try to explain that it is your will and God's; but the poor wee mites aren't as consoled as they might be. Won't you have a seat, dearest Reverend Mother? You must find standing very trying at your age.'

'Don't let me interrupt your work, Sister,' Reverend Mother said, making an effort not to betray in her voice the wriggle of the worm.

Sister Eulalie sniffed. 'Read, Pat Rafter. Let us show dear Reverend Mother that we don't spend our time in idleness.'

Reverend Mother listened for a while, said a few words to the assistants, Sister Anastasia and Sister Laurence, and made her way towards the senior school. She sought refuge in her beads, but, remembering her resolution, dropped them suddenly. Was she right in changing Sister Eulalie? Where, after all, was she likely to do less harm than in the infant school?

She hadn't solved the question when she entered one of the senior class-rooms. The children stood up, but Sister Thomasine rang them back into their seats at once.

'Visitors are such a nuisance—always interfering with work,' she said, with a bleak smile.

'Could you fit in Eulalie?' Reverend Mother asked timidly.

'I couldn't. There are limits—Why, yes, I can. Anything to move her from messing about in the hall with visitors. To give her her due she can sew. A back room where she'll see nobody.'

'She'll be troublesome,' Reverend Mother said apologetically, but with a sigh of relief.

'Not to me,' said Sister Thomasine grimly.

Reverend Mother sighed, 'I wish they made you Reverend Mother.'

'God forbid. Anyhow, they won't. They know I'd send half

of them packing and make the rest work. By the way, that's not a bad worker you sent me to-day. She started in well—no nonsense about her. She has the makings of a good nun in her, Sister Catherine. But we've wasted enough time. I must go back to my work. What does that silly Calixta mean by rushing in and disturbing my school like this?'

Reverend Mother gave a sigh of relief.

'Your breakfast, Reverend Mother, dearest,' Mother Calixta whispered breathlessly. 'I've only just heard. Not even a cup of tea! Why, you must be starving.'

'No wonder the novices have no sense,' Sister Thomasine said, with a frown at the nearest class, in which a novice was struggling with the divided attention of the girls who were trying to listen to the whispered conversation of the nuns.

'Find Michael for me, Calixta,' Reverend Mother said moving hastily towards the door. 'I want to consult you both. Something dreadful has happened.'

'But your breakfast—your breakfast?' Calixta said anxiously, when they reached the hall.

'Run on, child. Meet me under the yew tree,' Reverend Mother said sharply.

Calixta hurried away offended. On the terrace Reverend Mother, stooping down to examine a flower-bed, tried to avoid Sister Gregory. But Sister Gregory rushed towards her and exclaimed: 'Oh, Reverend Mother, it's all over the convent that you have been in the schools. The dear orphans will be deadly jealous if you don't come and see them. I want you to admire the new scapulars they're making. They'll be such a help to them when they go out into the world. Blue—the Immaculate Conception. They'll wear them in addition to the brown, of course.'

'Another time, another time.' Reverend Mother made her escape with a weary smile. She ought to go to the orphanage, but she couldn't face it this morning. Some day she'd have to look into it closely … So many of the children went to the bad when they left the convent. Everything seemed such a failure to-day. Even the flowers seemed less attractive. She fingered her scissors and beads restlessly and sank, exhausted, into a chair.

'Not one word till you've had this.' Mother Michael firmly held out a small tray on which was a cup of tea and two thin slices of bread and butter.

'Drink it, dear,' Mother Calixta, hovering in the background, said with emotion.

Reverend Mother took the cup and sipped the tea slowly. There was an explanation to make, and she was no good at explaining. They would ask questions which she couldn't answer. She lingered over the bread and butter, her eyes fixed thoughtfully on the ground. But she was only shirking thought. What was the use of thinking out the unintelligible.

'What is it, dearest Reverend Mother?' Calixta asked eagerly, taking a seat beside the old nun as she finished the last mouthful.

Mother Michael took the tray and put it on the ground, drew forward a chair and sat down. Reverend Mother shook some crumbs off her dress and said with a moan:

'Kitty Curtin—Sister Catherine wants to leave the convent.'

Mother Calixta flushed a deep red. 'It's not my fault. Indeed, it isn't, Reverend Mother. She got every instruction. But she was always reserved and deep and wouldn't open her heart to me. The Sisters will say things, but it's not my fault. You won't blame me, Reverend Mother?'

Her voice trembled and she clutched the old nun's arm appealingly. Reverend Mother shook her off gently … Should she have to change Calixta, too? And who was there to put in her place?

'There, there, don't cry. It's all my fault. I don't blame anyone but myself,' Reverend Mother said, with a timid look at Michael, who was frowning at the gravel. 'What are we to do, Michael?' she added feebly.

'This must be stopped,' Michael said, with decision. 'Our whole financial arrangements would be upset. It's not only that we'd have to give up her *dot*. With the two girls here there is the whole of the Curtin money to look forward to; but with Kitty out we'd probably never see another penny. You must act, and act firmly, Reverend Mother. It means peace of mind or anxiety for years to come.'

'I never cared much for her,' Mother Calixta said, with an air of parading her own virtue.

'Can't we leave money out of it?' Reverend Mother groaned. 'It's the poor girl's soul that matters.'

'Souls are all very well in their own place, but you can't run a convent without money,' Michael said, adding with a spice of malice, 'and it was you who would have the new chapel, Reverend Mother.'

'I agree with dearest Reverend Mother. You always bring your horrid money into everything, Michael,' Calixta protested. 'What hurts me is the girl's wickedness in daring even to think of throwing away the graces of a nun's life.'

'Don't be a fool,' said Mother Michael curtly.

'I'm a miserable woman,' Reverend Mother said, looking around, as if seeking some means of escape.

'It's a desperate business.' Mother Michael thoughtfully rubbed her sharp chin with the middle finger of her right hand. 'Her *dot* is as good as spent already. I suppose there's no fear of that little goose Winnie going?' she suddenly asked Calixta.

Calixta frowned. 'You've no discrimination in souls, Michael. And I'm not the only one who's remarked it. Dearest Winnie—a model novice and a model nun!'

'Then, if it's put properly to him Tom Curtin may not ask back Kitty's money,' Michael said, in a tone of relief. 'If the worst comes to the worst that would be something to fall back on. Even half of it wouldn't be too bad. I hope the bishop won't interfere too much at the money end. He's so keen that he puts people off. You are the person for that, Reverend Mother. Indifference to money is one of the best assets in things of the kind. But perhaps we're making mountains out of molehills,' she added cheerfully. 'I have known many a nun who wanted to leave who's still wearing the veil. What has happened?'

But Reverend Mother had got hold of her beads and was lost to the world.

'You haven't told us what's at the bottom of all this—what Kitty said?' Michael repeated more loudly, shaking Reverend Mother's veil.

'The poor girl—the poor, miserable girl. And she as happy over it as if she was doing God's will. She—but I'd better begin at the beginning.'

She told the interview simply, but with frequent reflections on her own unworthiness and lack of spiritual understanding.

'That's all, I think,' she wound up sadly. 'I never felt so helpless. Can either of you throw any light on it?'

'I never heard of such wickedness. Just as if I had never lectured her on our Holy Rule,' Calixta said indignantly. 'I must say I always suspected her—she's so secretive—never ingenuous and open like darling Winnie. And to wait till after her profession—just as if she intended to strike a blow at me. I may have been a little cold to her in the past—I admit that. There is just one chance. I might try and be nice to her—appeal to her better feelings.'

Reverend Mother stared at the eager, appealing face, as if she had seen it for the first time. Why had she got Calixta made novice-mistress? Because she liked her face and her childish ways?

'I never before felt such a fool, Michael,' she said.

'It's a bad business—worse than I thought,' Michael agreed, with a wry smile. 'I'd face even the loss of the money if I thought the poor girl was going to be happy. But she's not. She's only exchanging one illusion for another. I'll do my best to make her stay.'

'The world is coming to an end the day Mother Michael gives up caring about money,' Father Brady called out from some distance, as if to give warning of his approach.

'He needn't be told yet. He'd only be sarcastic with me,' Mother Calixta whispered, blushing prettily.

'As for illusions, sure they're what ye all live on, God bless ye. Don't stir, Reverend Mother, I'll be glad to rest my legs,' he continued, pulling a chair towards the group.

'I'm sorry about your brother,' Mother Michael whispered. 'Father Dunne told me.'

'I never heard,' Reverend Mother said.

'Poor, dear Father Brady, what you must be feeling,' Mother Calixta sympathized. 'May God in His infinite mercy give him rest and peace.'

'Poor Tom—he went off this morning,' the priest said hurriedly. 'What a nice shady place ye have here for managing the affairs of state.'

'The Sisters will pray for him,' said Reverend Mother, interrupting a prayer which she had already begun.

'Thank ye, thank ye. A prayer'll do no-one any harm. What's ye'er best news?'

'A very great trouble,' Reverend Mother said, with a sigh. 'I'm glad you came. You may be able to help us.'

The priest said an almost inaudible 'Pheu!' and looked stonily at the gravel.

'One of the Sisters wants to leave.'

'Ah!'

'It's a great blow to us. One of the young Curtins—Kitty.'

The priest started. 'You mean Winnie?' he said, with a puzzled frown.

Reverend Mother shook her head. 'Poor Winnie is quite settled down. No, unfortunately it's Kitty.'

Father Brady took off his silk hat and mopped his brow. 'The poor thing, the poor thing. Well, if that doesn't bang Banagher.'

His eyes gleamed as he replaced his red and yellow handkerchief in the crown of his hat. 'Tis you're the great hand at rearing novices, Mother Calixta,' he said fiercely, clapping the battered hat askew on his head.

'I did everything to lead her to grace,' Mother Calixta defended herself. 'I admit she deceived me, though I always had my suspicions—she was so unresponsive to affection. So unlike darling Winnie, who was an example to the noviceship.'

''Tis you're the great judge entirely, glory be to God,' he said moodily. 'What a hearty laugh God must have over the whole thing now and agin—not that it isn't enough to make a devil cry. Well, well. Tell me about the poor girl, Reverend Mother. What's at the back of the little fool's head?'

He listened, drawing circles and triangles on the gravel with the tip of his umbrella.

'I don't know what to do. I'm in a fog—up against a blank wall. What are we to do?' Reverend Mother ended with a moan.

'We've tied the poor girl up in a nice knot,' the priest said. 'We all have a lot to answer for.'

'We showed her the way to perfection—I'm sure I did my very best in that—and she's wilfully rejecting it. It's unfair to tax us with responsibility,' said Mother Calixta primly.

'Can't you suggest anything, Father?' Reverend Mother asked.

'Sorra bit. The harm is done now. If ye don't let her out

she'll have a bad time. And if ye let her out with that vow tied round her neck, she'll likely have worse.'

'If only one knew what to do,' Reverend Mother said. 'May God guide us to what is right. But will she stay if we try to keep her?'

'Now that you ask me I'm afeard she won't,' the priest said. 'She's a stubborn girl. She defied me in coming in and she'll likely do the same about going out.'

'She won't disobey his lordship. His persuasive eloquence would move a heart of stone. And I'll get the novices to pray. I'll pray for her myself, though she hasn't shown any consideration for my feelings,' Mother Calixta said.

'You must do your best to make her stay, Father Brady,' said Mother Michael, in a business-like tone. 'You can guess yourself the loss she'd be to us if she goes. Put everything straight to her—I'm going to. If she has made a mistake she must grin and bear it. What has she to go out to? She'd be like a prisoner let out on a ticket-of-leave with a life sentence hanging over her. Her own mother would be down on her. People will think she has done something dreadful. If she were the greatest saint alive and put off the veil, she'd be looked on as a criminal.'

'Dress makes the saint and want of it the sinner,' the priest hummed.

'It's to our advantage, anyway, that we hide our sins and our squabbles behind our habits and our high walls,' Mother Michael said, with a shrug. 'I don't know what whim has come over her. If it's love it will wear away. Work on her sense of honour. She has given her word and she ought to keep it. What is a little pain? In or out she'll have that. And there are fewer to see it here. And pain, too, wears off. She's not sentimental, thank God, and I'll see that she gets plenty of work. You'll find she'll be a sensible nun one day.'

'I'll see. I'll see. Ye're wonderful people, God bless ye.' The priest screwed an eye to examine the branches of the tree.

'Mother Michael puts it all on too low a plane,' Mother Calixta said, with a toss of her little head. 'I always appeal to the novices' good feeling. Sister Catherine unfortunately hasn't much, but we might rouse it. I'd put before her the pain she's giving to dear Reverend Mother and all the Sisters—I leave myself out though I feel it intensely. And there's the Blessed Virgin, and her guardian angel, and all the saints, not to speak of our Divine Lord Himself. She's making them all blush with shame.'

'Convents, convents!' Father Brady gave a covert glance at Reverend Mother, whose body swayed gently, her lips moving in silent prayer, as her fingers slipt past bead after bead in rapid succession. 'I suppose they have a meaning?' he added, with a shrug.

'I often wonder myself. But a bursar has to keep the place going,' Mother Michael said, with a grin. 'You're always too hard on us, Father Pat. And if you can't keep that obstinate girl, look out for another postulant for us with three or four thousand, or my books won't balance this year.'

'Oh, you'll get plenty,' he said morosely. 'Mad as ye all are, the world is madder still. It's the habit I suppose that throws such a glamour over ye. I'd feel it myself if I didn't know ye so well. But it's past a joke to be tying up young girls before they know their own minds. I wish to God ye let Kitty Curtin alone and didn't induce her in here—and many another, too.'

'I never heard such talk,' Mother Calixta said. 'It was God who led her in—God and her own free choice.'

'As you're so deep in His confidence you might find out whether He isn't leading her out again,' said the priest dryly.

'We all know that's impossible. It's the devil and her own wicked will,' Mother Calixta affirmed.

'QED, as we used to say when we did the Asses' Bridge and proved that two and two made four and the like,' the priest said. 'I'm only an old man, Mother Calixta, with nothing like your knowledge of God and the devil; still, I have picked up a grain or two of some sort of knowledge of men and women. Now if I had my way I'd not let a woman enter a convent till she was thirty, anyway—forty or forty-five wouldn't be too high for some. Age is the best test of a real vocation. And even then—'

'Vocation?' Reverend Mother said sharply. 'Are you speaking of her vocation? I'm sure Kitty—'

'He's been saying horrid things, dearest Reverend Mother,' Mother Calixta interrupted. 'Speaking of vocations as if they were something human and not the divine call they are.'

'Oh, no, I didn't say that. Far be it from me to say there is no divine call, and that many a woman isn't capable of any sacrifice in answering it. What I meant was that I'd rather run the risk of keeping women with vocations out of convents than let in, or coax in, girls with no sort of vocation at all—the very opposite, maybe.'

'We are very careful,' Reverend Mother said nervously.

'There's Kitty—and the rest,' he said.

'I sometimes think if they had more work to do—if we could keep more of them busy. If we got up a secondary school or some industry,' Reverend Mother suggested, in vague distress.

'There's something in that,' Mother Michael brightly agreed. 'Some convents make a lot of money that way.'

'I'm afeard you can't dodge human nature by making lace, or teaching French,' the priest said, with a shrug. 'And the more you take on yourselves the more nuns you'll need. You'll want money for this and that. It would break Mother Michael's heart not to see a vocation in any girl with a few thousand pounds. And Mother Calixta there would play on the feelings of a turnip if it had a suitable fortune.'

'Oh, no, no,' Reverend Mother said, horrified.

Father Brady laughed. 'Perhaps that was a poor attempt at a joke. But I'm not at all sure that I didn't mean something even worse. There's something wrong with the whole system. The natural calling of women is to have children.'

Mother Calixta said, 'Oh,' and blushed. Mother Michael smiled grimly. Reverend Mother shook her head. 'Celibacy is the higher life,' she said gently.

The priest shrugged his shoulders. 'If you stopped at that I'd be satisfied. But you know well, Reverend Mother, all nuns don't stop at that. Ye hide from grown girls the meaning of their natural functions. They often come into a convent never dreaming what's before 'em. It's nuns and not me that make out a vocation to be something natural. Girls are supposed to be some sort of sexless angels. Their bodies are something degraded and vicious that are outside them. Instead of knowledge ye feed them with hints and insinuations. Things that no woman can avoid appear to be mortal sins. Many nuns live in a haze of ignorance and religiosity. They can't distinguish vice from virtue, what can be controlled from what can't be controlled. In the end anything might happen. An extreme case is a sexual pervert who firmly believed she was a saint.'

'It is not true. It is not true. I feel it's not true,' Reverend Mother said appealingly.

'We never think of these things, much less discuss them,' said Mother Calixta. 'Nuns are specially protected. I get special novenas said for my novices as a shield of holy purity and they never fail—that is, hardly ever. There may be an occasional case of obsession by the devil.'

'Nuns aren't all as ignorant as all that,' Mother Michael said, with a thoughtful frown.

'They aren't,' Father Brady said grimly. 'Thank God you'll find as good women in a convent as out of it. Women with their eyes open who choose a hard life and live it decently. But I'm thinking of them that come in ignorant, and of others, whether they're ignorant or not, who wake up after they come in. Some of 'em get on all right. But the rest—well, well, it's a topsy-turvy world.'

'Poor things. Poor things,' Reverend Mother said, distressed. 'But God is by their side. He always helps. They have only to pray. It may be a hard struggle, but they overcome themselves.'

'Always?' the priest said.

'Don't remind me,' Reverend Mother appealed. 'I try not to think of it. Life is such a mystery. I could have done more. I've been too careless. If only I had been more watchful. But they all seemed to have such good vocations. I always knew I wasn't fit for my office.'

'If you had a hundred eyes on you you couldn't alter people's natures,' the priest said. 'As long as you have convents these things'll go on. You can prevent this and that,' he smiled. 'By locking up the convent well at night you could stop nuns from going out to meet people. But what good'll that do you? It's what's going on in their minds and wills that matters. And who knows that? Do we know ourselves, let alone know anyone else?'

'I know my novices,' Mother Calixta said, with confidence.

The priest looked at her for a moment in silence.

'We must only do the best we can. We can't shut up the convent,' said Mother Michael dryly. 'On the whole, we do very well.'

'But there are real vocations. I know it, I know it,' Reverend Mother said.

'There are, and in Drumbawn convent, too, thank God,' the priest agreed. 'But you don't give a girl a vocation by telling her she has one, or by putting a black veil over her head. How many of the young postulants that come to you share your ideal of a vocation, Reverend Mother ? They come in for a hundred and one reasons: because some foolish nuns have put the idea into their heads; because they're in the way at home and it's easier to persuade them that they have a vocation than to get anyone to marry them; because a mother or father wants to make a vicarious sacrifice for their own sins; because a vain priest wants to boast of the number of vocations he has made; because of the sort of education you give girls that makes them bored with their own homes and unfits them for making one for themselves. There are as many reasons as there are nuns, and most of them are wrong ones. And at the end of them all an illusion. The wonder is that things aren't worse than they are.'

'I'm sure it's not as bad as that. I'm sure you're wrong. If only there was another Reverend Mother!' Reverend Mother lamented.

'Eulalie?' Father Brady said, with a shrug.

'No, no. She's not quite—' Reverend Mother said feebly. 'But God will be sure to choose the right nun. Someone who—'

'Can work miracles,' the priest interrupted, pushing back his chair, as if to relieve his feeling. 'I'll have to go now. There's no hurry yet, I suppose, with Kitty Curtin? Some day when I'm less moidered I'll come and speak to her. If I had an ounce of sense I'd let her be. We're all only the blind leading the blind.'

The three nuns watched him cross the terrace, his head bent and his feet dragging from age and fatigue.

'I never heard such talk. Sheer impertinence. Talking of nuns as if they were ordinary women,' Mother Calixta said angrily.

'I don't know. Sometimes I have doubts. But he must be wrong. A few, perhaps, but oh, not so many. I don't know. I don't know. Yesterday I could have sworn by Kitty,' Reverend Mother muttered to her beads.

'I must go and see after the dinner.' Mother Michael looked at her watch. 'I'll give that foolish girl a talking to and try and teach her common sense. It must be his brother's death that has upset poor Father Pat. We must take things as we find them and keep going. But what the convent would be under Eulalie I can't even imagine. I'll put a spoke in that lady's wheel.'

'We must be charitable,' Reverend Mother sighed.

'There are limits even to charity,' Mother Michael said, with a firm setting of her lips, as she walked briskly away.

Chapter 19

For a week Kitty was reasoned with and prayed for. The orphans and the nuns made novenas for a very special intention. Only the Mothers were supposed to know that she wanted to leave the convent, yet, in twenty-four hours, every nun and novice knew at first, second, or third hand. She felt she was the subject of discussion in every group. Nuns waylaid her under the stairs, in the cloakroom and offered advice or condemnation. But mostly they showed an excited curiosity and resented her refusal to discuss herself. It was no use for her, they said, to try and hide what was up. They all knew: she was going to join a strict contemplative Order; she had done something unmentionable; she was going to run away with the doctor, with both the school inspectors, with the orphanage inspector, with the new organist, with whom she had been seen speaking twice in the day of her profession. The loathsome Clothilde made overtures of friendship; said one was a fool to leave the convent where one could enjoy oneself when one knew one's way round, just as well as out in the world, and began a lewd story.

The solidarity of the convent gave Kitty a feeling of helplessness. Reverend Mother, Sister Eulalie and Sister Clothilde were at one in urging her to remain. Faith, hope, love, religion, purity, hell, heaven, fear, piety, honour, comfort, public esteem, good luck, were all used as weapons to hold her in the prison into which she had strayed. Even Bernard, who sympathized with her, begged her not to leave. No woman had the strength to face the isolation, the desertion by her relatives and friends, the misrepresentations entailed by the step. She once thought she had the courage to go, but, at the last moment, it failed her. Every day she wanted to, but she knew now that it was a mere purposeless wish, a daily drug that soothed her for a moment with hope, only to plunge her almost at once into a worse despair. It was as if everyone who spoke to her was adding a brick to the opening through which she hoped for release. She had a stifling feeling as if air was gradually being withdrawn. A heavy weight seemed to press her down. She started from her sleep at night with a feeling that she couldn't breathe. Some terror seemed to await her round the corner of the shrubbery, behind a tree. Yet beneath all this fear her resolution remained firm, had even grown stronger. It was as if she had a double personality. One side of her could be depressed by fear, responded to the accusations that she was a lost soul, that she had offended God grievously, that she was obsessed by the devil. But this self was dominant only when she was semi-conscious, when the other self, newer, more active, was not wide awake. The passive self was weak, cowardly, afraid. It stored all her old memories of hell, of the devil, all the fears of her childhood, of her youth. It was a sort of trail in her consciousness. It was there even when her new self was in command, but with little strength to worry or to hurt her. She could examine it, question its pretensions to guide and rule her life, laugh at it. It called itself her conscience, but it was only a collection of bogies with which her mother, nuns, confessors, had frightened her. Men had made it and not God. It was something imposed on her from outside, something against nature, against God. It tried to tie her down, to put her in unnatural bonds, to keep her in them by terror and fears that had no real existence. It told her she was in sin when, for the first time in her life, she had shaken herself free of sin; that she was offending God when she knew she was pleasing Him.

For days she oscillated between half-conscious fear and a belief that she was above all fear. Fears which felt formidable faded away when she thought them out. Yet always they came back to torment her when her mind was inactive. Even the warnings and advice of the nuns which seemed so futile while she listened to them, made her tremble at night when she was half asleep.

Every day she asked Reverend Mother when the bishop was coming, but was always relieved when she heard that he was delayed in Dublin. She was feverishly anxious that he should come, yet she shrank from seeing him. Like the others he would ask explanations and not listen to them. He would judge her by some set formula and condemn her. Perhaps he would refuse to let her go? What should happen then? She had a curious feeling of being swathed round and round with bonds. They crushed her, yet she felt free. Everyone refused to release her and told her she could not release herself; yet she knew she could. She could hardly breathe; yet with a movement of her hands she could tear away all her bonds.

After the first day Winnie never spoke of Kitty's leaving. Something seemed to have happened to her. She had become quieter and more gentle.

'I forgot to tell you that I spoke to Father Brady about your sleep-walking on his way in to see Reverend Mother the very day it happened, and he promised to say nothing about it,' Kitty said to her one day.

'Did you? It doesn't really matter,' Winnie said listlessly.

'Don't you mind my going?' Kitty asked.

'Oh, you won't go. I'm praying for you. Let us say a rosary now,' Winnie said, with a smile.

If only the others, too, let her alone. But Mother Calixta told her at every turn that she had no heart, and Sister Thomasine said several times a day that she had no sense. Reverend Mother asked hourly if she had yet heard the voice of God. Mother Michael gave her what she called 'a man to man talk' every day. Sister Basil warned her that the devil was crouching behind her. They all warned her of death and hell, but what she longed for was life; the life she had never been allowed to live. They asked her to forget the world. But she longed for things to remember; to fill her empty heart; even to stand on a hilltop, as she had once seen a woman stand in a picture, her hair streaming in the wind, and drink in, with parted lips and glowing eyes, the joy and the glory of life.

'Go into Father Brady, dear. He may give you some light,' Reverend Mother said one morning, with a sigh.

'And Father Bernardine is coming this afternoon and the bishop to-morrow.'

'Must I see them all?' Kitty asked, with a shudder.

'I can't believe you're bad at the bottom,' Reverend Mother said sadly. 'You mustn't neglect any opportunity of grace. I don't believe in pressure, but some chance word may soften the hardness of your heart. Try and respond, dear, Father Bernardine is so kind—he's rushing down in the middle of his retreat at St Margaret's.'

Kitty smiled drearily. What, she wondered, would the nuns call pressure? For days every conceivable form of pressure had been brought to bear on her. She had been praised as a saint and denounced as a sinner; reasoned with, cajoled, hectored, treated alternately as a reasonable being and as an irresponsible child.

She found Father Brady at breakfast. Mother Michael, who was in attendance on him, stood up when Kitty entered.

'I have to go away for a few minutes. See that he wants for nothing,' she said, with a smile, patting Kitty on the shoulder and pushing her into the chair beside the priest.

Father Brady went on eating a mutton chop in grim silence. He put down his knife and fork when he had thoroughly cleaned the bone and said with a sigh: 'My teeth aren't as good as they were. What's this madness you're up to? I hear they're bringing down Pete Donlevy to work a miracle on you. I once thought you were a girl of some sense.'

'Shall I pour out your tea?'

'Do, then. No—none of that cream. I wish they wouldn't be skimming it off the orphan's milk. Commend me to nuns for that sort of piety. What's putting it into your head to leave the convent where you have every comfort for this world and the next?'

'You told me not to come in.'

'I did. And I'd tell you the same to-morrow. But you're in now, and I tell you not to go out.'

'But I have no vocation!'

'You never had one. What has that got to do with it now? You're not the first man or woman that made a mistake. You have taken your vows and you'll have to keep them. You're a straight girl and you'll do your best, I know. What is forty or fifty years compared with eternity?'

'It's my life,' she said dully. She stared at an engraving on the wall—a straight, bleak road, without shelter or shade, stretching on and on interminably.

'What are we all but leaves blown about in the wind?' he said gently.

'I don't believe it. It's because you are old and forget,' she cried. 'I was never alive till now. God didn't give me life to stifle it. You say you knew I never had a vocation. Didn't God know that better than you? Would you hold me to a promise I made through a mistake? Is He likely to?'

'Whist, girl,' he said, with a pained frown. 'I'm sorry for you from my heart out. There's the law of the Church and we can't go agin that. It may look foolish enough at times and it may be hard to see the meaning of it, but we know the Holy Ghost is behind it.'

'I don't believe God is like that. I know He's different. You make Him out to be a narrow-minded, tyrannical man, only worse. You say He wants to strangle me, but I feel He wants me to live. I can't explain, but I know it, I know it.'

Father Brady ran his fingers through his thick hair, a worried frown on his face. 'That can be all explained, child. I wish I studied my theology more and I could make it as plain as A, B, C to you,' he said, scratching his forehead. 'You're trenching on some heresy or other, if I could only lay my hand on it. People that want to do wrong always try to invent some new kind of a God. He's a God of infinite love, of course, but there are things about Him that we must take on trust. If He seems to be hard, we may be sure there's kindness behind it. And the Church has the last word on Him. I admit it's a bit hard on a girl to hold her to vows she took in ignorance; that, in a way, she was fooled into taking. I wish myself there never was a convent in the world. They're foolish things at the best; and, at the worst, they don't bear thinking of. Still, a vow is a vow and we must abide by the law of the Church. Where would we be at all if we didn't hold tight to its infallibility with the power of things it lays down that sounds so foolish. Be a good girl now and stick to the cross you've made for yourself. Everything'll be clear to you when you get to heaven. And if you'll have to suffer a little misery in the convent itself, you'd have to put up with more outside.'

She felt depressed and miserable. Even Father Brady was against her. When she had freed her soul, had begun to live for the first time, they tried to bind her, hand and foot. It was as if a snake was slowly coiling round her … She stared at the priest, at his kind, pippin face. A lark began to sing over the terrace. She watched it soar higher and higher and disappear, but the piercing call to her heart still lingered.

'Outside it'd be the very devil,' the priest said sadly.

She half opened her lips to drink in the exquisite sound. It was life calling to life. Somewhere beyond the elms the lark was still calling, 'Come away, come away and live.' Through the open window the wind among the leaves called her, and the infinite blue of the sky.

'Out there somewhere one could live,' she said, with a sigh.

'Your father and mother will be agin you. Your friends won't know you, or'll look down on you. People will avoid you. You might just as well be dead.'

'I must live,' she said simply.

He dashed his cup and saucer aside impatiently. The cup rolled over on the tablecloth.

'Is there a man in it?' he asked fiercely, as he mopped up the tea with his napkin.

She watched the brown stain spread on the cloth. Was there? She didn't know. She saw George Lynch's face take shape against the white of the cloth. It still wore the understanding smile. But she had no particular feeling for him except, perhaps, gratitude. He was the instrument that had awakened her to life. He would not look down on her, or avoid her. He could be more to her, perhaps. But he was not necessary to her life now. At least not yet.

'I don't know,' she said, with a smile.

'You're a romantic little fool,' he exclaimed angrily. 'Remember the last time.'

She laughed. 'The convent has taught me sense.'

'Give it a chance of working a second miracle then,' he said derisively. 'Take my word for it, girl, you'll sup sorrow if you leave all this.' He waved his hand, and she followed the movement with critical eyes. The shining furniture, the polished floor, the crude German prints on the cold walls had never seemed more repulsive.

'I've been taking other people's word for things all my life. I'll try following my own judgment for once,' she said bitterly. 'Though I'm not so sure,' she added, with a smile, 'that all the time you haven't been telling me to go.'

'No, no, no!'

'But you've often told me yourself what convents are. They haven't changed because I want to leave. Do you want me to be as miserable as Bernard? Or go to the devil like some of the others?'

'No, no,' he said, with a pained frown; 'and you know well that the bulk of 'em are good poor women enough.'

'But I don't want to be a "good poor woman enough",' she said derisively. 'You've often said yourself that the best of them are half-dead. They were born half-dead,' she went on, with growing anger. 'I was born alive and you have all tried to kill me—not you, I must say, till now. My sort who stayed on in the convent are most of them above in the graveyard. You can see their tombstones—whole rows of them, just about my age. If I live all you can promise me is a living death. And you want to put it all down to God. Because I'm not willing to commit suicide, you say God wants me to. I don't believe you.'

She looked at his drawn, pained face, stopped suddenly and burst into tears. 'It's not you, Father Pat. It's only the priest in you,' she said, with an attempt at a smile. 'You're too kind for that. And God is at least as kind as you are. It's all lies, lies. And if people believe these lies out in the world, what do I care? It won't hurt me to be treated badly when I know I'm right. And even if I have to starve, I'll die free.'

'My God, my God!' the old priest groaned. 'I wish there wasn't one convent in the whole world. Don't cry, girl. Don't cry.'

She wiped her eyes with her check handkerchief and smiled pitifully. 'I'm only being sorry for myself when no-one else will be sorry for me. I'm really very happy,' she said miserably. 'Won't you have more tea?'

'Nuns. Nuns,' he said angrily. 'Do you want to choke me?' He stood up, seized his hat and umbrella and fiercely frowned at her.

'There's no changing you out of this foolishness?' he said, rubbing the nap of his silk hat the wrong way with his sleeve.

'No.'

'God help you then—and you'll need all He can give you. I don't know which of us is the biggest fool—you for going or me for trying to keep you. There, there. Don't cry again. God bless you, and always remember that you have a claim on me—I should have kept you out of this place by main force. Wait till I meet your mother and Peter Donlevy! And if they're too hard on you at home, come and tell me, and I'll read the Riot Act to your mother in a way she never heard it before. There, there. What would you thank me for? For thinking you near as big a fool as myself? Run and see if the road is clear for me to the front door. If I had to listen to any more nun's gabble this morning it's tempted to break my umbrella on 'em I'd be.'

Chapter 20

The interview with Father Brady renewed Kitty's courage. She walked along the corridor towards the chapel with a light step and a smiling face. She should have at least one friend. Two, for she was sure that her father, no matter how he might bluster at first, would never condemn her. And there was always Bessie Sweetman who had no illusions about convents.

'A moment, Sister,' Sister Evangelist said mysteriously, beckoning from the entrance hall.

Kitty's heart fell. There was to be no respite. The unceasing attack was to begin afresh. It had little effect on her resolution, but it was wearing her temper very thin.

'Come out in the porch. Something overwhelmingly important—a miracle,' the old nun said, in a hoarse whisper. 'We must shut the door. I wouldn't tell anyone—not even Reverend Mother—it is so dreadful. A revelation! I was on the look-out for you. I saw Father Brady go out. Poor man. I saw failure written on his face. Her heart will not yield to human persuasion, I felt—not even to a holy priest. She is waiting for a special communication from above. "Humble an instrument as you are, you must deliver your message, Evangelist!" I said to myself. It came in a dream last night. I saw you as plain as you are now, and a loathsome serpent with the devil written all over him was creeping up your guimpe—slowly, slowly, making for your mouth. I couldn't move with terror. I had a sudden illumination. The devil will enter her mouth and possess her eternally the moment she throws off the blessed protection of the holy convent. It is a warning straight from God,' the old nun added, with tragic sincerity.

'You'll take it to heart, dearest Sister?'

'Thank you, Sister.' Kitty shuddered, and gave an unconscious look at her guimpe.

'Thank God, thank God. I can see the warning has touched your heart,' the old nun said excitedly. 'I am blessed forever; who knows but God in His Divine mercy will cure my indigestion at last and prevent the devil worrying me. You'll pray for me, dear Catherine. God will listen to you. There is more joy in heaven, you know, over one sinner that repents, than over ninety-nine just. Not a word to anyone. We'll keep our little secret between God and ourselves. Immaculata would be jealous—she thinks no-one gets a revelation but herself.'

'Well, well, I'm really surprised.' Mother Michael opened the door. 'A senior, like you, Evangelist, breaking silence.'

'God forgive me. But it was something transcendently important,' the old nun said.

'It always is,' said Michael. 'Would you mind feeding the doves for me to-day? Laurence is ill.'

'Oh, thanks, Mother,' the old nun said gratefully. 'I'll do my very best to fulfil the important trust.'

'Was she throwing the devil at you?' Michael asked, when the old nun had hurried away.

'Very gently,' said Kitty.

'Pickles,' Mother Michael said cryptically. 'There's no harm in the poor thing, but she has no stomach. I'm as strong as a horse myself, but cold meat and pickles make me see visions.'

'The Sisters weren't to be told about my leaving. I'm getting tired of everyone lecturing and advising me,' Kitty said.

'A secret—about another person—in a convent!' Michael said, with a shrug. 'Women! my dear. Anyhow, it has its uses. Constant dripping often wears away a stone. Did Father Brady knock any sense into you?'

'He did—to leave as soon as I can.'

'Men are such softies, especially the fierce ones like Father Pat. I told Reverend Mother he'd do no good. Bernardine will do better.'

'You've often said he hasn't two ideas in his head.'

'That's why, maybe. And the bishop will put down his foot. Don't be a fool, Kitty. What are you going out to? If you defy the bishop your mother must be told to-morrow and she'll be demented. You can't live at home with her.'

'Father Brady will speak to her.'

'He might as well speak to the moon. All her life she dreamt and schemed to make you and Winnie nuns. It's not religion with her, it's a monomania. The moment her dream comes true you want to smash it to bits. She'll never forgive you. Here at least you won't have people barging you all day long.'

The sitting-room over the shop loomed before Kitty in all its appalling loneliness. Without Winnie to fight with it would be worse. And that hard steely glitter in her mother's eyes when she was crossed!

'You don't really know anyone in the town. Besides, all the other girls were always jealous of you—they'll be glad to have a hit-back at you. You'll be Tom Curtin's daughter that was turned out of the convent,' Mother Michael said, in a businesslike tone.

'But I'm not,' Kitty protested.

Mother Michael shrugged her shoulders. 'People will believe what will tell most against you. Legends will grow up about you—to your discredit. All sorts of things will be said and believed. The most charitable will put their fingers to their foreheads and say you are mad.'

'You're horrid.'

'Before you're out a month you'll wish yourself back again and we can't take you. You can't even come up and see us or see Winnie—we can't have you giving a bad example to the young nuns. At home you'll have black looks and hard words. You can't go for a walk in comfort. You'll be pointed to as the spoilt nun. You know the sort of thing—averted looks, shrugs, whispering.'

'I can go away.'

'Your mother won't let you have a penny.'

'I can work.'

Mother Michael looked her all over, not unkindly, and shrugged her shoulders. 'And put it out of your head that you can marry. Not a man in Drumbawn would have the courage to do it. He daren't, even if he would.'

'We're not living in the Dark Ages,' Kitty said indignantly.

But her tongue was dry and she had an uncontrollable feeling of depression. 'I shall be free, free.'

'God help your head, child. Don't believe in empty words. I'm telling you the facts. We're in possession. We're protected by the prejudices of generations. No matter how right you are you'll be put in the wrong. There's only one thing to do when you make a mistake in this life, and that's to make the best of it. Some of the happiest nuns you see here went through what you're going through now. Had they done what you're bent on doing they'd be mad or in their graves.'

'I don't believe it. I don't believe it,' Kitty cried hysterically. 'It's more devilish than I thought—devilish—devilish.'

'Be a good girl now, and have sense,' Mother Michael admonished sympathetically, taking her hand.

Kitty shook her off and with tears blinding her eyes groped her way into the corridor. She stood for a while at a window. Slowly the blurred haze gave way to light and colour. The flowers smiled at her. The deep, peaceful blue of the sky dissipated the suffocating feeling that oppressed her and gave her an acute longing, half pleasant, half painful. Sister Thomasine passed, with bent head, telling her beads. Near the cote doves fluttered round Sister Evangelist, perched on her shoulders, pecked off her hand. How peaceful it was, and beautiful! Sister Bernard walked down the centre path, her face pale as a Madonna lily, her eyes staring, unseeingly, with a look of unutterable anguish, at the brilliant flowers.

Kitty shuddered. It was as if the riot of colour decked the bed of a corpse. Death itself was preferable to this living death. Her tears fell freely. The warmth coursing down her cheeks comforted her. Michael had the jaundiced view of the slave who had submitted—the sort of fossilized fear that posed as common sense.

'Cry, dear. Let the tears flow. God is at last unlocking your heart,' Mother Calixta cooed in her ear.

Kitty started and stiffened. 'I must be going out to my work,' she said coldly, drying her eyes.

'Thank God. Father Brady has started the good work. Only a tiny candle yet, perhaps. He's not very spiritual. Wait till Father Bernardine turns on the light fully. He'll penetrate your soul—and the bishop,' Mother Calixta said ecstatically. 'I don't speak for myself. But I have done something. Haven't I, dearest? And darling Winnie is praying for you. There's a saint if ever there was one. As open as the day and obedient to the slightest hint of the Divine will,'

'Sister Thomasine has gone to the school—I must go,' Kitty said.

'That's a sign that God is working in you—your anxiety to fulfill your duties. But a little word from a poor novice mistress may be a still higher call. Tell me how you feel the grace acting. I may be able to give it a little push. A word in season may make all the difference. A stitch in time saves nine. I've known a good start from tears end in heaven. All your life you may have cause to bless me for this providential opportunity. Thank God, Father Brady opened the floodgates of repentance. I'm dying to know what he said to you. Don't leave out a word.'

Kitty gave a sigh of relief at the approach of Reverend Mother.

'I found her in tears. What a blessing, dear Reverend Mother!' Mother Calixta said.

'Humph!' said Reverend Mother dryly, with a sharp glance over her spectacles at Kitty. 'Run away now, Calixta. Your novices are waiting for you.'

'I thought of a little lecture at the opportune moment,' Mother Calixta moved with reluctance. 'She was just going to tell me what Father Brady said. I'm sure I could throw some light—'

'Run away now. There's a good child,' Reverend Mother said dreamily. 'Come, Kitty. Let us say a prayer together in the chapel.'

Mother Calixta frowned, and walked away slowly with much dignity.

Reverend Mother sighed. 'He didn't do you any good? Well, well, Father Bernardine might,' doubtfully, 'or the bishop,' she added, still more doubtfully.

'I'm sorry, Reverend Mother. I'm afraid no-one can,' Kitty said affectionately.

'God can,' said Reverend Mother.

'He always tells me to go—I'm often afraid of myself, but He gives me courage.'

'Hush, dear. That's the devil. A prayer from your heart now and I'm sure all will come right yet.'

They knelt in one of the benches at the back of the chapel. Reverend Mother's eyes were fixed on the tabernacle door in a rapt gaze. Kitty asked God to guide her aright. The loud ticking of the sacristy clock seemed to say, 'Go, go'. There was something hard and stern in the command as if a difficult task were imposed on her. That was it. It was a duty. She had been shirking life. Not of her own will—at least, not altogether. But now that her eyes were open, no matter how difficult was the road, no matter what obstacles stood in the way, there must be no faltering, no drawing back. She shivered slightly. She knew so little of life, of the world. The future stretched out before her, black and forbidding.

Bessie Sweetman lived in rooms in Dublin, was a secretary or something. Bessie would help her to find work. What if Bessie wouldn't? She had a momentary feeling of weakness, of giddiness, and clasped the back of the bench on which she leant. She mustn't give way to cowardice. This weakness was due to the pictures Michael and the others had drawn of her future. They were true to some extent, but surely there were many people who were not blind worshippers of convents? Mother Michael said they were in possession. Father Brady, when he was not trying to be official, thought them ridiculous. George Lynch killed them with an ironic smile. Many of the girls at St Margaret's thought them silly and futile. Bessie Sweetman went farther, and hated them. What was it she called them? Vampires that fattened on the blood of illusioned fools, and for the disillusioned, hells on earth. How Bessie used to rage. Always, almost from her birth, she said, she had felt the tentacles, as of an enormous octopus, groping round to clutch her and suck her blood.

Kitty gave a deep sigh of relief and felt as if she had herself escaped a horrible disaster. Her strength came back, and her courage. If the difficulties were ten times greater than Mother Michael pictured them, nothing could stop her now.

A feeling of peace possessed her. The quiet of the empty chapel, the twinkling light before the tabernacle, the colours playing on the tiled floor, Reverend Mother's absorbed face, the white and black of her dress made a sensuous appeal. Pleasing images passed rapidly through Kitty's mind: Evangelist feeding the doves; the chant of the Office in the mirk of a winter morning; the gliding movement of white and black figures to and from their stalls; a white and black line of nuns on the hill above the river, their veils swept back by the wind, giving the life and movement of a Greek frieze; a nun saying her rosary in the dappled shade of the beech avenue.

She sighed. It had an attraction—to look at, when one knew one was outside it. But to be of it? She looked affectionately at Reverend Mother. For Reverend Mother, perhaps, and for some others the outside beauty had its reflection in an inward peace. But for the rest? Make-believe, dull resignation, despair or a seething anguish.

Chapter 21

'I never knew such nonsense,' Sister Thomasine grumbled. 'In the middle of a geography lesson, too.'

'But Father Bernardine, dear Sister. And he *must* catch the mail back,' Mother Calixta said meekly, 'with, we hope, a soul rescued!' she added with a sigh.

'Stuff and nonsense. Give her a dose of castor oil. If ye only let the child alone she'd settle down. They all do. Souls, indeed! I warn you this is the last time.'

'*Except*, of course, for his lordship to-morrow. Unless divine grace acts sooner.'

Sister Thomasine contemptuously shrugged her shoulders. 'Thank God, I never knew I had a soul. I never saw anything but gallivanting to come of 'em. If you want to fool about with a priest invent a soul for him to meddle with. They're all alike, bishops and all. If she wasn't good-looking it's little bother there'd be about her. Sister Catherine, come here a moment. You can go with Mother Calixta for half an hour,' she continued, with a frown when Kitty came near. 'There's a play-actor within in the parlour that wants to doctor your soul. See that you're back in time for your arithmetic class.'

'Poor Sister Thomasine has no spirituality,' Mother Calixta said, with a sigh, as they descended the stairs.

Sister Eulalie rushed out of the infant school and put an arm round Kitty's shoulder. 'I saw *him* coming. I have the infants praying hard already. Thank God,' with a spiteful glance at Mother Calixta, 'I'm not snatched away from the dear angels till to-morrow.'

'I assure you, Sister, I did my best to stop it,' Mother Calixta nervously protested.

'I know what I know. I take note of everything and treasure it up,' Sister Eulalie said darkly. 'If a Mother was my friend,

I'd expect her to *act*. Dearest Kitty, remember *I'm* praying for you. And I'll take it so badly if you disappoint me. Perhaps if you'd been better instructed this would never have happened.'

Mother Calixta, deeply blushing, with little resentful lines at the corner of her lips, kept silent till she reached the corridor.

'The cat!' she murmured, taking Kitty's hand. 'Courage, dearest. Open your heart wide. Winnie is in the chapel praying for you. Let the good seed sink in. I'll be in the chapel, too, all the time you're in with him, watering your change of heart with my tears and prayers.'

She patted Kitty's hand and pushed her towards the reception-room door.

'My dear Sister Catherine.' Father Bernardine stepped forward briskly to greet her.

He dangled a purple stole in his left hand while he shook hands. 'Do you prefer here or the confessional? Perhaps you'd like to get rid of some of the burthen first by an absolution?'

'No, thanks. I prefer, if it must be, just to talk.'

'Let us make ourselves comfortable. It is not for everyone I'd come away right in the middle of a retreat. But when you sought me—'

'You were sought for me,' Kitty said coldly, taking the chair he offered her.

'Ah!' He frowned slightly. 'You won't mind my taking this arm-chair? The journey down was rather fatiguing. A mere trifle, though, in a good cause,' he added, with a smile, settling himself well back in the chair with graceful negligence.

He rested his elbows on the arms of the chair and joined the tips of his long, slender fingers. His hair hung a little down on his forehead and gave him a look of fatigue. He gazed thoughtfully at his nails, frowned, sighed, smiled again and said with a nice blend of interest and affection:

'Now, my dear child, what is this temptation?'

Kitty gave a slight start. He had placed her chair straight in front of him, and in the short silence she watched him closely. How exactly would he begin? She knew most of his poses by now, but this was something new. The tightening of his lips helped to conceal the weakness of his mouth and gave it a note of sternness that was not yet severity. The general effect of the set of his head, of his tone, of his half-averted eyes was a slightly pained surprise. There was no doubt about his good looks. No wonder so many of the nuns were in love with him. When he spoke she was wondering vaguely if she had ever been in love with him, if that was why she had listened to him, been led by him?

'It's just that I grew up suddenly,' she said lightly.

For a moment he was disconcerted. Then the look of pain deepened. He turned his big brown eyes fully on her and said sadly and a little reproachfully: 'You mean you have allowed the world to whisper to your heart, to dim its beautiful freshness. A Greater than I has said, "Unless you become as little children you cannot come unto Me". But, thank God, the insidious temptation cannot yet have gained much foothold. We must strive with God's grace to restore your heart to its original innocence. You must again become as a little child with all its trust and confidence. Such only is the kingdom of heaven. Now what is the particular trouble?'

'It is everything. The whole life here. I don't believe in it. It's not life at all, but a mockery of it.'

He pursed his lips and frowned. 'The evil has gone deeper than I thought,' he remarked regretfully to a print on the wall. 'But we mustn't despair. We must try and get at the root of the trouble.'

He smiled. 'What is it *you* object to in life consecrated by the lives and deaths of innumerable saints of God?' he asked, with patronizing, half-bantering sarcasm.

'I'm not a saint of God—I'm only a woman,' she said bitterly.

His complacency annoyed her. For a week she had been subjected to hourly doses of intensive pietistic talk. It had come to seem a mere patter of meaningless words, repeated by rote. 'So are the others,' she added resentfully.

He looked pained and hurt, shuddered a little, closed his eyes and rested his hands on his knees as if making an effort to recover from a shock.

'This is serious.' he said. He joined his fingers again, looked at the ceiling with the expression of one of Guido's saints, and said: 'A convent to me is a vase of beautiful flowers filling the ambient air with the odour of their sanctity.'

She laughed. Half the nuns had this silly phrase from one of his sermons written in their Office books.

'Then when one of the flowers goes bad, the best thing to do is to take it out of the bowl and pitch it away,' she said.

He frowned and said in a piqued tone, 'Please allow me to complete the figure. One mustn't deal crudely with metaphors. There is, perhaps, as yet only a slight wilting of a leaf, a tiredness in a petal. The precious flower of your vocation—'

She gave a sigh of relief, caught at the word, and interrupted eagerly: 'You were wrong about that. I never had a vocation.'

'Please allow me to be the judge of that,' he said sharply. 'I never make a mistake. The decision of your superiors here in admitting you to profession confirmed my judgment. You, yourself, are the final proof. Why else did you enter, take your vows?'

'Why, indeed?' she wondered blankly. 'I don't know. It was some sort of blindness. You all told me things that weren't true.'

He sat erect in his chair. His figure stiffened. He tried to smile, but his lips and eyes expressed anger and resentment.

'You were the worst,' she said, her anger kindled by his.

He laughed harshly. 'This is very serious, indeed, very

serious. After all my prayers, my labour. The careful study I gave to your soul. The counsel I've expended on you.'

'It was my own fault to be such a fool,' she returned. 'However, it is not yet too late. I can go.'

'It is too late,' he said sternly. 'I have no wish to be hard on you. But you speak foolishly. The Church can't alter its laws for the whim of a foolish girl. You've made a vow of obedience to your superiors, to your holy bishop, to our holy Church. I can't speak for his lordship, but I certainly could not recommend a dispensation in your vow of obedience. Your most excellent mistress of novices thinks there is some temporary aberration. You haven't given me one solid reason to justify your extraordinary conduct. Your superiors agree with me that you had a real vocation.'

He stretched out his hand and took the stole off the table. 'You must have fallen into some sin. Come and remove the burthen from your soul. In the serene light of God's holy grace you will repent of this madness.'

'But I have committed no sin,' she protested. She felt as if she was being enclosed in some new net.

His smile, half of superiority, half of pity, made her angry.

'You want to keep me here against my will,' she said.

He smiled again for a moment, and then said solemnly, 'My dear child, your will is no longer your own. You have given it up into the hands of your superiors, of your good bishop, of our holy mother the Church. You say you have committed no sin? You have already gravely broken your vow of obedience—at least in intention. If you leave this sanctuary of God's love,' he waved his hand towards the walls, 'you will sin daily against your vow of holy obedience. In a short time your soul will be a mass of corruption. *Facilis est descensus averni*—hell will yawn wide in front of you. An eternity of torment for the gratification of a mere whim!'

She shut her eyes with a shudder. All the devils of her childhood seemed to rush at her. She put out her hand to ward them off. It fell limply through the empty air to her knee. She opened her eyes and smiled.

'I am counting the hours till I go,' she said.

He shrugged his shoulders. 'This hardness of heart is only adding to your sin. Is my troublesome and inconvenient journey to be fruitless? Is this your gratitude? Have you no thought for all the hours I have spent on the cultivation of your soul? What will his lordship say but that I have been remiss in my duty?'

His lips relaxed and hung loosely, revealing the weakness of his mouth. His eyes glowed with self-pity.

She felt hard and bitter with herself. If he was acting at all it was quite unconscious. What was life or death to her was to be determined by his vanity. And she had listened to him for three years, believed in him, subjected herself to the tortures of the damned on his advice.

'Is there any use in continuing this?' she asked, and smiled, half in pity, half in wonder, at his self-centred face.

She stood up to go. He rose, took her hand and patted it.

'For my sake?' he appealed.

'Good-bye,' she said, and abruptly snatched away her hand.

'Then your sins be on your own head.' he said bitterly, with a melodramatic gesture.

She hurried out of the room and along the corridor. She hesitated for a moment at the turn to the chapel. Mother Calixta and Winnie were in there praying, waiting for her.

'Let them pray,' she muttered recklessly, and shot into the passage to the schools. She was too confused to pray; and she needed prayers with all the booby-traps that were being set for her. At the foot of the stairs Sister Eulalie waylaid her.

'I felt as I prayed that a miracle was being performed. Was *he* very divine?' she asked, with ecstasy.

'For God's sake leave me alone,' Kitty said rudely, rushing up the stairs.

Sister Thomasine met her inside the door of the classroom, pointed accusingly to the clock, and mumbled: 'Five minutes late. Thirty-five minutes wasted in talking to a fool. Made you worse, very likely. Father Brady isn't good enough for 'em. They must have frilled idiots of special confessors. They can't spare time for their work with all this play-acting. In my time nuns used to have some sense.'

Kitty went cheerfully to her class. Sister Thomasine and arithmetic were a welcome relief from her soul. If only the convent were always arithmetic she might put up with it. But to-day arithmetic was not a relief. What if the bishop prevented her leaving? The thought recurred again and again. Sin and hell kept obtruding themselves among fractions and made a mess of a complicated sum to the amusement of her pupils. She blushed and wiped the figures hurriedly off the blackboard, half fearful that the children had read her thoughts. Was it a sin to want to live? She had given up her will, Father Bernardine said. Yet she was never more conscious of it. She wanted to do things, anything—but of herself. To have freedom to choose: that was life—to feel that one was free. She might make a muddle of things, but there would be the joy of effort, and the experience, and the knowledge for the next time. To give up one's will to Mother Calixta! If it were only to poor Reverend Mother or even to Michael? Yet that was what the rule of the convent came to. Calixta was God to whom unquestioning obedience had to be given. It couldn't be a sin to laugh at this nonsense, to deny that God ever intended it. The opposite must be true. It was a sin to give up one's will to women who were more muddled and sillier than oneself. Always her will had been outside her, tossed about from hand to hand, from her mother to the nuns, and back again; to some confessor; and then to the nuns again ... to Mother Calixta ... for ever. And always, of course, her will never had been outside her. It was always in her to prick against the goad, and now it revolted. It was something that couldn't be given up. The whole meaning of life was in one's own mastery of it. Perhaps they had invented hell, too? She dabbed the blackboard viciously with her chalk. If only she were clever and could understand things. Yet, somehow, she knew. They were trying to hold her by bonds that did not really exist. Hell, too? She shuddered. But that was so much a part of her life that it must really exist. Yet what was the hell she feared but a threat of her mother and the nuns and her confessors? The only hell she had really experienced was the discord in her own soul when she had tried to carry out their will ...

The bell for the break-up of school sounded. On her way to the chapel she met Mother Calixta who frowned at her and passed by with her head in the air. That was Father Bernardine. Other nuns looked at her curiously and questioningly, frowned and gathered their skirts as if to avoid her, or smiled encouragingly. They all knew about the interview. She couldn't stand this much longer, the perpetual discussion and whispering, this exhibition of herself—what Muredach called 'a perfect godsend to the monotony of the convent'.

After dinner Winnie came up to her and asked her to come for a walk on the hill above the river meadow. Kitty looked at Reverend Mother, who smiled encouragement.

'I have special permission,' Winnie said mysteriously. 'Let us say a rosary as a preparation,' she added, when they reached the terrace, 'that God may unlock your—our hearts.'

Along the beech avenue they half chanted the monotonous prayer. Some new change had come over Winnie, Kitty thought. She seemed more excited, yet more settled. Her eyes glowed with some sort of exaltation. The listlessness of the past week had all gone and she walked with a springing step, her cheeks slightly flushed.

'God often works a miracle through the humblest of his instruments,' Winnie said, with emotion, as they sat on a bench overlooking the river.

'They have begun to trench for the hedge,' Kitty said, wondering vaguely what was this new move in the game. Poor Winnie wasn't a formidable obstacle.

'I feel for you from my heart. I, too, have been through the slough of despond,' Winnie said tenderly.

Kitty smiled at one of Father Bernardine's favourite phrases. 'You've been to confession to Father Bernardine,' she said.

'Who told you? Who told you? How did you find out?' Winnie asked resentfully. She bit her lip and added, 'Forgive me, dearest, for being so petulant. In future I'm going to be absolutely even-tempered. I have been to confession to that saint. Oh, why did I never discover before to-day what a saint he is! I was blind, blind. I seem to have stepped on to the ladder of perfection for the first time.'

'Have you fallen in love with *him*, too?' Kitty unfeelingly asked.

Winnie flushed, bit her lip again and said meekly, 'Even if you tried to hurt me now I could bear it without getting angry. I have the most beautiful feeling for him, of course. Something pure and holy, like worship of the angels. I could kneel down and kiss the hem of his soutane in gratitude and—affection. He rescued me from the slough—from despair. Oh! so beautifully. Not a harsh word. If he told me to walk across the river there I feel I could do so without wetting my feet. It was like that.'

'Last week it was Father Burke.'

'Don't mention him,' Winnie exclaimed, forgetting her equability for a moment. 'He never came to see me! Not a word, not a line. Off he went to Lissakelly without ever even saying good-bye to me.'

She bit her lip again and pulled herself together. 'I'm not angry with him. It's only excitement at the memory of the despair I was in. And, imagine! what I thought horrid of him turns out to be the beautiful working of God's will. Father Bernardine explained it all so beautifully, but I'm no good at remembering. And I was going to offer him up in any case—for you. That God might speak to your heart. And though he didn't come to see me itself Father Bernardine says it's all right. That God will take intention for the deed. Do you feel anything working in you yet, Kitty darling?'

'No,' Kitty said harshly, smothering an inclination to cry.

'But you must, you must,' Winnie urged. 'I'm going to be absolutely unselfish from this out. And I can't be happy unless you share with me. Everything is so wonderful. Listen to what I went through first. But God rescued me. I made a clean breast of it all to Father Bernardine, but he made me promise never to mention it to a living soul again. So I can't tell you what it was. It was some horrible danger—I don't quite know what. He has a beautiful way of saying a thing without saying it. But out of evil, he said, good may come. That I can make a stepping-stone of my dead self to higher things—I'm not quite certain, though, but it was Father Burke once said that. But you know what I mean. My experience has given me a fuller heart to offer to God. I feel it already. I have a sort of divine pity for Father Burke instead of being angry with him for not coming to see me. And just at the end of school the young priest from Derrydonnelly, who has taken Father Burke's place, came in. He looked so lonely that my heart went out to him. Though I knew he had a "particular" for you, I forgave him. I spoke to him nicely and let him hold my hand for a bit—not for long, of course, for the children were there—and he cheered up wonderfully. I feel as if I could be kind to everyone. My heart is overflowing. But always Father

Bernardine will be first. He made my soul white as the driven snow. The horror and the despair have all gone and only the beautiful memory remains. I know now what makes Eulalie so kind. It is all wonderful, wonderful. I feel a real nun at last—as if I could be a saint!'

Kitty was bewildered. She watched in wonder the ecstatic face gazing dreamily at the blue mountains that stood out vividly against the golden haze of the plain. What did the girl mean? Still, though less coherent, it was much the same sort of nonsense that many of the nuns talked. Anyhow, a Winnie who wasn't always flying into tempers was a pleasant change.

'Did Father Bernardine speak about me?' she asked.

'Oh, I forgot,' Winnie said penitently, with a start. 'That was what I asked you up here for. To make a sisterly appeal to you, out of the depths of my own joy. You can't look at the change God has worked in me and keep a hard heart. You owe that much to God and to me. I gave up Father Burke for you, you must give up your evil intention for my sake.'

'I'm getting tired of all this. Father Burke gave you up—thank God. He never even came to see you.'

Winnie flushed angrily, but with an effort restrained herself. 'You can't hurt me now,' she said gently, her lips twitching a little. 'I can't explain fully. He didn't give me up. Father Bernardine explained it all. God spoke to Father James, too. That was why he didn't come to see me, I'm sure. If you knew everything you'd understand what a beautiful miracle it all was. That very morning I came to see you before rising bell I offered him up for your sake—that God might give you light. I suffered horribly—his not coming to see me, and everything. I didn't know what I was doing. When I heard he had gone to Lissakelly I thought I'd die. But all the time I knew my sacrifice would save you. I was praying for you in the chapel to-day when in came Father Bernardine—just after seeing you. I never noticed before what beautiful eyes he had. He looked sad and put out. But really noble-looking, with his brown curls going a little white at the tips. A sudden thought struck me—it was from God, of course. And I went straight up to him as he knelt on the altar steps and asked him to hear my confession. His beautiful smile nearly took my breath away, and I knew then he was a saint. Making my confession to him was heaven itself. Your heart must be as hard as stone not to have been moved by him. His voice was like the new gong at the consecration—it sank into me like the most beautiful music.'

'Oughtn't we to be going back?' Kitty suggested.

'You won't leave the convent, Kitty?' Winnie pleaded, laying a hand on Kitty's knee to prevent her getting up. 'I am thinking only of your happiness. I want you to be as happy as I am.'

Kitty shivered. It was useless, she thought, to say anything of Winnie. She could not even begin to understand. Her own life had been unreal in many ways, but she had occasionally looked a fact in the face. But Winnie had never even tried to do so. The pettiest of convent pieties and the most foolish of convent romances were her favourite food. Winnie could believe black was white, preferred to believe it.

'I'm so glad you are happy,' she said, with an attempt at a smile.

'Happy? I never felt so happy in my life,' Winnie said, with rapture. 'When I knew Father James was going I thought I'd die. But now, by the will of God, it's all for the best. With Father Bernardine for extraordinary confessor, what more is there to desire? And my devotions, of course, and my duties. Don't tell any of the others, but he's going to write to me every week—spiritual instruction. He's going to take a very special interest in me. The Mothers won't read his letters, of course. They'll be marked "spiritual matters" on the inner envelope. I can't believe you think of going. There's no life on earth as happy as a nun's. I was often jealous of you, but I'm so happy now that I want to share with you. I'll be sorry, of course, if you go—and ashamed and all that, but I can never be really unhappy again. I want you to feel that I want you to stay entirely for your own sake.'

'I know that,' Kitty said listlessly.

'We've been so happy all our lives together,' Winnie went on. 'I feel you had a hand in waking me up to the perfection of that saint in human form. I looked round all the pictures before dinner and there isn't a single saint or blessed or beatified half as good-looking. I don't mind sharing him with you. And the nuns will be so put out if you go. Calixta says you have no consideration for her feelings. And I can't help feeling badly towards you if you hurt Father Bernardine after advising you to come in and all. And I won't neglect you like I did for the last few years, and I'll get some of the young nuns you don't really know to take you up—the really good sort. We'll have the time of our lives. And we can often talk of *him*. Some of the others will be mad jealous when they know he has taken me up—but I must say of you you're not that ...'

Winnie went on and on, in an unending stream.

Kitty watched the smoke curl lazily above the drab roofs of Drumbawn. She could make out the shop by the six red chimney pots in a row. Father Bernardine was safer for Winnie than Father Burke. There was no reason to bother about her now. Her religion was so inextricably mixed up with the worship of handsome priests that a convent was the best place for her. She clenched her hands. Good God, the tortures she had undergone to fit herself for these futilities! And the net in which she had entangled herself. If her father went against her, what should she do? She hadn't the price of her railway ticket to Dublin—not even a penny ... Still, the loneliness of the drawing-room, with its view of the dreary street from behind the rep curtains, was better than the talk of Winnie and her friends.

'And when Eulalie is Reverend Mother, it will be heaven on earth.'

Winnie's exultant words made Kitty think of Reverend Mother, her kindness, of her utter bewilderment in the midst of the convent she was supposed to govern; of Michael keeping a certain external order; of this nun and that, happy or miserable, whose only common link was a uniform dress. Tears came into her eyes at the memory. All the nuns she had known seemed to twine into an immense tree against the smoke screen that hung over the river. Faces hung out; the patient, the resigned, the heroic, the stunted, the rebellious, the indulgent, the repressed, the merely futile; those who loved God in fear, the sexless, the sexed; many lovable. All seemed so much human waste. And, with a slight shifting of the screen, tortured as well. She shuddered … A tortured human waste heap …

'I told Father Bernardine you often had these mad fits against nuns at school. And that I was sure God would help me to get round you. You'll stay for my sake, Kitty darling?' Winnie babbled.

'I'd die first,' Kitty said fiercely.

The river smiled invitingly up at her. Nuns had done that, she thought, setting her teeth. But that was for the cowardly, the despairing. And she wanted to live, would live.

Winnie had a struggle with anger, but her newly found meekness triumphed.

'I'll pray. I haven't prayed at all yet really—not, I mean, since I got real grace.'

'Pray till you're black in the face,' Kitty returned.

'Wait till mother talks to you,' Winnie said, after a long

pause, during which she fought valiantly against a temper which she did not entirely succeed in conquering. 'She's coming after the bishop and'll be tearing mad.'

For a few seconds an intense hatred burned in Kitty—of Winnie, her mother, the bishop, the convent, the whole system that tried to crush her. Then she laughed a little shrilly. 'You fools,' she said, rising, and walked off towards the convent.

Chapter 22

'The Bishop. And he hasn't a minute. He's due at Thornton Grange at one for lunch,' Mother Calixta whispered excitedly. 'I've told Thomasine that you must come at once.'

Kitty put aside her book and followed Calixta listlessly. Thomasine grunted contemptuously as they passed her desk.

'Your dear mother has come, too just by accident. You can have a nice comfortable talk with her after his lordship has gone.'

The 'just by accident' roused Kitty to the ghost of a smile. The sooner it was all over the better. She was too tired to be afraid, too tired even for courage. Half awake and half asleep, the whole night long, the phantoms of all the fears of a lifetime had battered her. She had seen herself dead and judged and damned. Devils who assumed kaleidoscopically the features of the bishop, of Father Bernardine, of her mother, had mocked at and scorched her. They had stamped on her quivering flesh with red-hot irons thoughts, words and actions that she had considered innocent, and labelled them 'sin' in fiery letters.

'Our love and prayers are telling on you. You're coming round. You look like a saint,' Mother Calixta said, as they walked through the covered passage to the convent.

Kitty smiled and walked with a lighter step. It was so that people were encouraged and prayed for on the way to the stake. The humour of it appealed to her.

'Is it worth while taking all this trouble with me?' she asked gaily.

'Not a sparrow can fall to the ground—' Mother Calixta said, making a desperate effort to remember. 'Scripture—you know.'

'But I want to fly. And you're all trying to clip my wings.'

'Hush, dear. You must be humble in speaking to his lordship. You were looking nicely miserable a minute ago. It's not becoming to look so happy and you in sin. When he has advised you and you have seen the error of your ways, then it would be quite fitting. Try not to smile, dear.'

Kitty tried not to laugh, but without success. A broad smile was still on her lips when she entered the reception-room. The bishop put down his tumbler and mulled claret, wiped his mouth with a napkin, shot a quick look at her, smiled jovially, squeezed her hand, turned to Reverend Mother, who was sitting at the corner of the table, and said, with a smile of contempt: 'This is another of your mare's nests, Reverend Mother. You'll find this girl has no notion of leaving us.'

'I'm sure she won't when you've spoken to her, my lord,' Mother Calixta said unctuously.

'Hum, hum.' The bishop pursed his lips and expanded his chest. 'Leave us now, Mothers.'

Reverend Mother sighed, got up heavily, looked at the bishop's red face over her spectacles, sighed again, took Kitty's hand.

'God bless you, dear—whatever you decide to do,' she said quietly.

'Now, Reverend Mother. I have no time to lose,' the bishop said impatiently. 'What's all this about?' he added, as the Mothers left the room, pointing to the vacant chair. 'These women think a bishop has no important work but attending to them. I'll be late for luncheon. And this claret has got quite cold.'

He finished his glass, smacked his lips and smiled benignly. 'You look as happy as the day is long?'

'I am.'

'Then what the—then what's all the fuss about?' he asked angrily. 'There, it's ten minutes past twelve and I have six miles to drive.'

'Because I'm going to leave, I suppose,' Kitty said.

He stared at her with a deep frown.

'You're going to leave, are you?' he repeated, with a not unkind jeer.

'And I want you to dispense me in my vows.'

'To dispense you in your vows?' he repeated, with the same jeer. 'Is there anything else now?' he added, with heavy sarcasm.

'To annul them if you can,' she said desperately.

He laughed heartily but with a display of some temper.

'I'm not the Pope—yet,' he said, with more enjoyment.

'And what for now?' he added sarcastically. 'No, no, you needn't waste any more of my time,' he continued, with another look at the clock. 'I could dispense you in your vows, but I won't. I've heard about all you said to Reverend Mother and Father Bernardine—they were both much too soft with you. And when I have more time to spare I'll let them know it. I have also had a talk with your good mother—a good religious woman who knows her duty and is prepared to do it. Go back to your work and give up this nonsense. You're a good-looking girl and will make an excellent nun in time. But there must be no more of this foolishness or I'll come down severely on you. Even your good looks won't save you a second time,' he added, with a smile.

'I'll go,' she said timidly, shivering under the smile, which, on the swarthy aggressive face, seemed more threatening than a frown.

'You'll go out into the world in sin, with your vows slung to your back, with your mother's door shut in your face, without clothes to your back or a penny in your pocket?' he said, in angry derision. 'My good girl, when you think it over, you'll think better of it,' he added, more kindly. 'I must be off.'

He felt the outside of the silver claret jug with his hand. 'I have a bad cold,' he said, with a friendly smile. 'And this is still warm. You have all made me hoarse with all this talking.'

He poured out half a tumblerful and drank it. 'Goodbye now and God bless you. Pray for me. Send in those foolish Mothers to me.'

He squeezed her hand. 'Have a talk with your good mother and then go to the chapel and say a few prayers as a penance. No, don't say any more, I haven't another minute. You'll make a fine nun yet, God bless you. A horse often goes all the better in his second wind. But don't let this happen again, or you'll see the hard side of me.'

He gave her hand another squeeze and pushed her gently away.

'Did he make everything all right? He can be so beautiful,' Mother Calixta said, rushing up to Kitty in the corridor.

'He wishes to see you both,' Kitty said to Reverend Mother, who was staring through the window at the doves on the terrace walks.

'Again?' Reverend Mother gave a shuddering sigh.

Kitty stared at the doves. She laughed. Turtle doves were like holy nuns—always pecking at one another. She heard the bishop's hearty laugh and Mother Calixta's thin giggle. Doors were opened and shut. There was the bishop's laugh again, and her mother's boisterous roar in chorus. They were laughing about her—over the bishop's easy triumph. Why should she not laugh, too? She laughed till tears came into her eyes.

'Hush, Sister. The rule of silence is no joke,' Sister Laurence said, with a frown, in passing.

'It's a much better joke than the rule of silence,' Kitty said gaily, but with a sudden feeling of lead at her heart.

The bishop's coarse, strong face seemed to look down on the quarrelling doves with an amused, jeering smile. She was just one of the old community shawls that one pitched anywhere in the cloakroom. Her feelings were nothing, her mind, her will were nothing to him. She blushed vividly and her lips stiffened. He was her superior … represented God to her … that coarse, rude bully. He, the director of her soul, the arbiter of her will …

'She'll be like putty in ye'er hands after the lambasting I gave her,' came with a hoarse laugh from the entrance hall. 'You must keep your young stock better in hand, Reverend Mother, but you'll find she'll answer to the curb now. Goodbye to all of you, and God bless you. My luncheon'll be stone cold or done to a cinder. Be stiff with her, Mrs Curtin.'

Kitty walked quickly towards the entrance. They wanted not only her mind and will, but every vestige of her self-respect, of her pride, of her vanity, even.

'You darling thing!' Mother Calixta said, with outstretched arms. 'I knew he'd come round you.'

Kitty pushed her aside and looked stonily at her mother's hand.

Reverend Mother sighed and lumbered dexterously between mother and daughter.

'The bishop is rather a tornado,' she said, with a sigh. 'We must bear up under him, Kitty. Quietly, my dear, quietly. It's something to know one's own mind. I never did, God forgive me. Everything will come right in the end. But I've come between you and your mother.'

She moved aside with a smile. With an answering smile Kitty suffered her mother's embrace.

'Shook off my feet I was with the bad news Mother Calixta there gave me, and I standing on the doorstep and me not knowing why in the world she sent for me; and it a market day and all. But all's well that ends well, as the Prayer Book says. Sure if a bishop couldn't work a miracle, who could?'

Reverend Mother prayed desperately, her eyes fixed on Kitty's face. 'Just a moment, Mrs Curtin,' she interrupted. 'The reception-room is a little less public. Shall we leave you?

I'm sure you wish to speak to Kitty alone.'

She smiled appealingly at Kitty. But Kitty was beyond all smiles. Her face was drawn and rigid, her eyes glowed.

'There's nothing mother has to say to me that everyone may not hear,' she said bitterly. 'You heard her get her instructions.'

'Is the girl demented? And me thinking the bishop had sobered her,' Mrs Curtin cried.

Reverend Mother shepherded them into the reception-room and shut the door. Mother Calixta soothed Mrs Curtin. 'It's all right now. She has yielded to nice feeling. And his lordship was so very kind and considerate. God was so good as to listen to my poor little prayers. We'll all take her back into our hearts again.'

'I'll leave to-day,' Kitty said.

'Against the bishop's express command! His lordship! who represents God, whose spouse you are! Your vow of holy obedience, your religion!' Mother Calixta gasped.

'We must pray for him,' Reverend Mother said vaguely. 'God will soften his heart. But there is your vow of obedience. It would be a mortal sin to go against his will.'

Kitty laughed. 'If there was any sin it was in taking a vow that meant obedience to him,' she said wildly. 'And it would be a greater sin to keep it. I feel soiled, I shall never feel clean again as long as I stay here. I'd have no religion if I believed that that man represented God.'

'His lordship! His lordship! Blasphemy! Reverend Mother, dearest, can't you do something?' Mother Calixta said, putting her hands to her ears.

Mrs Curtin's florid face had been gradually growing purple. She stared at Kitty with wide-open eyes that changed from bewilderment to anger and then to hate. Her jaws that had at first hung open shut tight in a malevolent expression.

'Leave her to me, Reverend Mother, leave her to me,' she said violently. 'It's no daughter of mine at all that's in it. It's the devil that's in her. A devil out of hell, I say. Tie her to the leg of her bed, Reverend Mother. Put her on bread and water and starve the devil out of her. And we'll get masses said for her by every priest in the town, and far and wide. I don't care what the bill is so long as she gets back her seven senses.'

'Do keep calm, Mrs Curtin. Let us pray,' Reverend Mother said, patting Kitty's hand.

'Don't I know my duty and my religion? 'Tis I was always the good mother to her and she to stick a knife in me at long last!' Mrs Curtin swayed in her chair. Her features worked convulsively, the red poppies in her hat bobbing jerkily from side to side.

Mother Calixta with a terrified look at Reverend Mother put a restraining hand on Mrs Curtin's arm which was raised as if to strike Kitty, who sat quite still, her face as white as a sheet, staring at her mother as if fascinated.

Mrs Curtin threw off the nun's arm roughly, flung herself passionately on her knees in front of Kitty, embraced her legs and kissed the hem of her habit.

'God forgive me for speaking badly of a holy nun,' she said. 'Sure 'tis you're miles above me on the steps of the throne of God. I promised you to Him and I in my agony. Is it to break my word you would, and bring bad luck on me now and hereafter? The little money we have'd wither up, and the business'd go to pieces. Though it's not that I'd mind, but the loss of my soul. I didn't leave a stone unturned to give you to God, but I must have left out something. Don't break my heart and me on my knees before you? Your mother that bore you and tended you night and day when you couldn't fend for yourself?'

Kitty sat stiff and rigid. Tears coursed freely down her cheeks. She had an impulse to throw herself into her mother's arms, but she seemed tied to her seat. She couldn't move her hands that were clasped within her wide sleeves. It was as if her feelings were sealed up by something hard and bitter in her mind. Then suddenly her feelings, too, were frozen. That was it. All her life she had been fattened for sacrifice. She was the victim of her mother's selfishness. A feeling akin to hate burned in her, but only for a moment. After all they were both victims alike of some fate, of some horrible system that had no pity. If she suffered, her mother suffered, too. She shut her eyes and felt as if she were sinking into a quicksand. She grasped the sides of her chair to save herself from being engulfed. The hard wood gave her a feeling of security. She opened her eyes with a sigh of relief, but could hardly see her mother through the haze of her tears.

'God has unlocked her heart,' Mother Calixta said.

'I'm sorry, mother, but I can't. I must go,' Kitty said gently.

'You refuse the mother that slaved for you?'

'I must.'

Her mother stared at her in horror. Then anger blazed in her eyes and she groped round with her hands as if seeking a weapon with which to strike. 'I hope it's out dead before my eyes you'll go,' she shrieked, foam gathering at the corners of her lips. She raised her hands and with eyes upturned hissed, 'The day you cross the threshold of this holy house may God blast you with his seven curses. Amen.'

Reverend Mother stood up, horrified. She caught Mrs Curtin, who was struggling to her feet, by the arm, muttering, 'Oh, that it should have come to this! What shall I do? What shall I do! I'm not fit. God forgive me. God forgive me.'

Mrs Curtin shook herself loose. 'It's no use, Reverend Mother. I'm the bereaved woman this day and I must have my say. From this day out I have only one daughter.'

'Poor darling, innocent Winnie,' Mother Calixta said. 'She'll be always a comfort to you.'

'She will, the saint. And I'll need all that even she can give me,' Mrs Curtin gave a breathing space to her anger, which, however, in a moment, broke out afresh. 'As for you, you hussy, you changeling, you, you'll never darken my door. Not a penny-piece of my hard-earned money will you ever touch. It's God's money and not for the likes of you. I know my religion better than to encourage sin that's as black as hell.'

'This has gone too far. You must stop. It's very wicked of you.' Reverend Mother spoke with authority, but added weakly, 'It's all my fault. It's all my fault.'

'I beg God's pardon and yours,' Mrs Curtin, somewhat taken aback and half shamefaced, said. 'But I couldn't stand by and see God and my holy religion trampled in the dust by my own flesh and blood.'

'A wounded mother's feelings, Reverend Mother, dearest,' Mother Calixta said sympathetically. 'But if the wicked girl repents, Mrs Curtin?'

'Then I won't be behindhand with God. I'll call back my curse and give her my blessing.' Mrs Curtin glared at her daughter.

Kitty sat quite still, her eyes closed. She had a curious feeling of being a ball which people were playing against a wall. She heard distinctly every word that was spoken; but her mother's voice gave only the impression of the hard thud against the wall, and the nuns' voices the soft thud of the rebound.

She felt Reverend Mother's hand on her wrist and stood up mechanically. 'I can't see any way out, God help me. But I'll pray again. Go to your cell, child, and lie down. You look done up,' the old nun said affectionately.

Kitty went to her room half dazed, and sat on the end of the bed. The one fixed idea at the back of her mind was that she must go. She was tired, but she dared not sleep. She might sleep on into the night, till the convent was shut up. She sat erect in the effort to keep herself awake. Soon a lay sister brought a bowl of beef tea and some dry toast.

'It's many a holt they have on you in a place like this,' she said, eyeing Kitty curiously, as she arranged the tray on the bed.

On her way out she stood for a moment with her hand on the handle of the door, half turned her head and said musingly: 'What's to prevent anyone walking straight out that has the mind for it? And who could say "boo" to her?'

'Thank you.' Kitty smiled at her.

'With all their bishops and Bernardines,' the lay sister muttered cryptically, with a series of nods, as she shut the door.

Of course, that was the thing to do, Kitty thought. Her distaste for food passed away and she attacked it briskly. With the last mouthful her spirits fell a little. She couldn't go down through the market in her nun's clothes. Would her mother let her in? And she hadn't a penny to take her to Bessie Sweetman. Would her father help her against her mother? He might, but she wasn't quite sure. And even if Father Brady would do anything it would imbroil him with the bishop. She nodded with sleep. The difficulties seemed to grow insuperable … Everything depended on getting down a hat from the top of the wardrobe in her bedroom at home. With every effort it receded farther from her grasp … She was on the bank of the river. It seemed to beckon, but she drew back with a loud, 'No.'

Mother Calixta stood beside the bed. Kitty rubbed her eyes and smiled.

'You have repented? God be thanked. You said "No" quite plainly to the devil. It was the voice of God,' Mother Calixta excitedly said.

Kitty laughed.

'I wasn't thinking of God or the devil or my soul—but just how I'm to get away.'

'Of all the depraved girls I ever knew, you're the worst!' Mother Calixta exclaimed, shocked and angry.

'I wonder if Peggy could smuggle up my old clothes. Mother said she had kept them all. And if Reverend Mother would lend me a few pounds—'

'You're mad!' cried Mother Calixta. 'To make me a partner in your sin! What a blessed relief it would be if you did die,' she added vengefully.

'I never felt more alive,' Kitty said. 'You might just as well give in. You can't make me out mad. I defy you to keep me here.'

Mother Calixta flounced out of the room. Kitty went to the window and lifted the blind. Her eyes wandered over the terrace, the wide-stretching park on her left, the river flowing quietly almost at her feet on the right. It had its charm. And there was a beauty in many of the futilities. She loved Reverend Mother. And Michael was a good sort, and Thomasine. Dozens and dozens of 'em. She drank in the pungent smell of the pinks glowing beneath the window. It all seemed so peaceful now: the long shadows of the trees, the sleek Guernseys lazily cropping the lush grass. Was she just a misfit? It was more than that, of course, but she was liking them now that she was going. Why was she going? She hardly knew. Only just that she must. Goodness, there was the sun low down. She must have slept and slept. She must see Reverend Mother and cut the ridiculous knot.

The door was flung open and Winnie rushed in. 'Oh, Kitty, poor dear Mother Calixta is in despair. You can't … '

'I can.'

'You aren't?'

'I am. Don't be a fool, Winnie.'

'I'll never speak to you again.' Winnie proudly drew herself up. 'Don't make me forget that I'm a holy nun. You wicked, wicked girl, giving up the sanctity of the convent to steep yourself in the sin and wickedness of the world. I might have known the kind you were when you resisted the entreaties of that blessed saint on earth.'

'Who gave *you* permission to be here? Be off to your work,' Mother Michael said sharply, from the door.

Winnie blushed and bit her lip. 'I just felt the inspiration—I couldn't resist it,' she said, with uplifted eyes.

'Be inspired now to go off about your business,' Mother Michael told her dryly.

She watched Winnie's pouting side face till it was hidden by the door, sighed when the door closed with a bang and said:

'I wish it were *you* who was staying.'

'Winnie is the saint of the family,' Kitty said, with a shrug. 'You have made up your mind I'm going then?' she added, smiling.

'*I* have. Calixta is weeping in the noviceship, smothered in the smelling-bottles of her little fools. Reverend Mother is in bed. Her conscience won't allow her either to keep you or let you go. She thinks she'll be damned if you're made to stay; and that you'll be damned if you go without the bishop's permission. And as she knows he won't give it she has nervous prostration.'

Two lay sisters brought in a trunk and a hat box.

Kitty held her breath. 'Did you do it?' she asked brokenly.

'No,' Michael snapped. She waited till the lay sisters had gone. 'I think I would have when all failed—and by all accounts the bishop cooked our goose this morning but I didn't get the chance. You've put me in a hole, you know, unless your father is generous. He did it. Blew your mother into fits. Came up here with your things ten minutes ago and threatened to pull down the convent, choke the bishop and every nun that stood in your way. Luckily he saw me. The game was up, and I tried another tack for holding on to your money. Butter wouldn't melt in my mouth. He's coming back for you at nine o'clock. It's eight now. I'll send you up your supper. Eat a good one, for you're going a long journey. All your clothes are there.'

'Not home?'

Michael laughed grimly. 'He was brave enough with me, but he's afraid of your mother. Between ourselves I think he and Peggy Delaney packed the things and stole away with them while your mother was busy in the shop. Dublin—by the night mail. I'll come up for you when the sisters have gone into night prayers—no good-byes. You're a fool, you know, but God send you'll be no worse off outside than you'd be here,' she added, with a frown and a slight break in her voice as she hurried out of the room.

Kitty unpacked quietly. All emotion seemed to have dropped from her. She had a vague curiosity as to what clothes her father and Peggy had chosen, and a keen regret that they were so old-fashioned. She saw mirrored on the dress she held up to the wavering light a smart Selina Thornton as she appeared on the day of her profession ... This was dreadfully old-fashioned and she'd look a fright. But it would be dark when she was on her way to the train. She took off her habit and dressed quickly. Happily she hadn't a glass in which to see herself in that hat with her short hair. But whoever brought her supper would tell her whether she was even passable.

It was the same lay sister who had brought her lunch.

'Then that's that,' she said, without surprise, when she had put down the tray, looking at Kitty approvingly.

'How do I look?'

'A bit dowdy, but you have the youth. I used to be in the dressmaking and millinery before I came in, and I keep up with the fashion papers. If I had an hour or two at you I could smarten you up.'

Kitty shook her head.

'It's an easy life you're leaving to face the world,' the nun said, as she went heavily out.

Kitty ate her supper, standing by the window. The red light in the north-west shone through the branches of the trees. Was she a fool, as Michael said, to go out into that darkening world, hardly knowing why? The voices and laughter of the nuns floated up from the community-room. The cracked voice of Sister Luke sang, "Who is Sylvia?" Kitty waited for the usual little flutter of applause and sighed tolerantly when it came … She had never been of them. And now she was going to live …

Two lay sisters came and took away her boxes. Kitty stayed on at the window staring at the black, blurred trees. She did not even know where she was going to in Dublin. Not that it mattered. Nor what she was going to do. She had a momentary ache for the familiar lights of the town which shone with an unusual brightness, and a timid fear of the darkness beyond. A fresh voice whistled cheerfully. She could hear the tramp of youthful footsteps on the pavement outside the convent gate, and the echo of happy laughter. That's what mattered to be free, to live.

'Come, dear,' Mother Michael said gently.

They went down the stairs without a word. In the hall Mother Michael kissed her on the cheeks and mouth, whispered 'Be happy,' and held the front door open.

'Hurry,' her father said, from the foot of the steps. 'It's not too much time we have.'

'This is a bad business, a bad business,' he added, halfway to the gate. 'It's women, women, convents and nuns, priests and bishops. The town'd be poisoned agin you. Dublin is, maybe, best. Religion has put a queer twist in your mother. She might sober down. But not yet. Oh, not yet, by any manner of means,' he added ruefully. '"Johanna", I said, I'd rather be dead than be a slave in my soul." And that's why I won't let nun or bishop say a word agin you, Kitty. But the poor woman couldn't see it. Let us keep on the dark side of the street. There's Joe Duggan, now, that I thought the world and all of. An hour ago I asked him if he'd marry you, and believe me or no, he shirked it. I could see the desire of it in his eyes, but the courage failed him. And he thinks he's a free man, chairman of the Town Board now and a desperate politician that'd die for the rights of man and all that. Offered to pay me back to-morrow what he owes me—all in deadly fear. "A vowed nun", he said, green in the face. You'll have a hard time, girleen.'

'Poor Joe,' she said lightly. 'Where am I going to, father?'

'Here—put that in your breast, and there's more and regular where it comes from. I made my own way in the world and I won't be browbeaten. Work, girl. It's the great thing for filling the heart. And here's an address to stay at in Dublin. You have some friends in Dublin—girls or the like?'

'Oh yes, I'll be all right.'

'I was at my wits' end trying to know where to lodge you in Dublin. Where I stay myself, off and on, is rough and ready. By the luck of the world I thought of the new organist, and he a Dublin man and all. You don't know him. I told him everything and he took a power of trouble. Wired himself to a decent woman whose lodgings he knew of, asked her to meet the train. Could he do more if he were my own son, and he almost a stranger, so to speak?'

'Almost,' she said vaguely.

'Be careful of men,' he said, as he hurried her into the waiting train. 'I'd go myself with you only your mother is in such tantrums—but she'll quieten down. Good-bye, and remember I'm always at your back.'

She smiled quietly and often as she lay huddled back in the corner of the compartment. Should she ever see George

Lynch again? Hardly. Had she ever really forgotten him? He seemed to have passed out of her mind. Yet it was he made her decide to leave. Was there anything in that? She didn't know. But she would never be a fool again. He remembered her, bothered about her, did not condemn her … Bessie Sweetman would know lots of nice men. She slept with a smile on her lips.

THE END

Notes

BY KATE MACDONALD

Chapter 1

age quod agis: 'do well whatever you do', in the sense of focusing on the task at hand. This reflects Winnie's fervent discipleship in the Catholic way of life as taught by her school.

rep: a type of woven cotton fabric with ribbing running across the breadth, mainly used for upholstery.

frieze: a sturdy woven fabric of wool, with a raised and trimmed nap, used for outdoor garments.

sorra: dialect term; a negative that reverses the intention of the succeeding phrase, for example 'Sorra step further' means 'Not a step further'.

whatnot: a set of free-standing open shelves designed for the display of small ornaments.

trapesers: derogatory dialect term for people the speaker despises.

snuggery: the den, the private office attached to the business, reserved for intimates and for business conversations.

Chapter 2

switch: a hairpiece, made of a fall of hair attached to the crown to increase the wearer's own hair volume. In the Victorian period women would collect their own hair brushings to make a switch for themselves.

agra: dialect term of endearment and approval.

warm: well-off financially.

voteen: dialect term for a woman particularly noted for her devotional practices.

ducks and drakes: the game of skimming stones across still water to make them jump. In this context Tom is anxious that the calm progression of his business may be disrupted.

inagh: dialect term of derision and rejection.

hedge school: an institution unable to offer more than a very basic education, with no cultural refinement or intellectual prowess.

counter-jumper: slang for a man who has crossed the class divide, figuratively jumping over the counter of the shop which is his proper social level, into the ranks of the gentry where he will never truly belong.

handsel: dowry.

maggot: madness, a foolish obsession taking over her mind.

Chapter 3

green and red ribbons ... blue ribbons of a child of Mary: awards signifying levels of educational attainment or good behaviour in a Catholic school.

dolman: a tailored shawl or mantle worn over a dress, often in matching fabric.

guimpe: the starched (usually white) garment covering the chest and neck, worn by nuns with the coif (tight head-covering) and the wimple (the looser head-covering).

the Blessed Sacrament and Our Lady of Good Counsel: sites of devotion in the church where particular objects and images of religious significance are placed to concentrate the worshipper's prayers. In this case, the Blessed Sacrament would be the consecrated wine and wafers used for the Eucharist, and Our Lady of Good Counsel would be a portrait or image of one of the incarnations of the Virgin Mary.

feast: in this case, the celebratory meal to commemorate the liturgical feast of the saint after whom the Reverend Mother was named.

manage her cup: to drink from her cup according the etiquette in which her daughters were being educated by the nuns, rather than her own, more comfortable, probably more slovenly manners.

more vocations to his credit: a central theme in the novel is the culture of competition between convents and priests as to who can bring in the most well-dowried women as nuns. Each woman's adoption of an enclosed life as a nun is claimed as evidence of a religious vocation, whereas in fact the process was as often an economic or social choice as a religious one. The reputation of a priest who brought in many vocations was ostensibly based on his holiness.

Chapter 4

missioner: a priest conducting a Mission, a programmed campaign of public sermons, intercessions and opportunities for private confession, intended to bring people to the Church, and to encourage them to acknowledge a vocation for the religious life. The role required charisma and theological knowledge as well as performance skills.

cap: slang name for a novice, a junior nun in the first three years of her training before she takes the final step of profession.

Chapter 5

delisk: dulse, an edible kind of seaweed.

poor gom: affectionate dialect term for 'poor fool'.

soft clauber: mud, or farmyard muck.

Lisdoonvarna, Malahide, Bray: Irish towns noted for their social and leisure activities in the Victorian period. Lisdoonvarna still holds an annual matchmaking festival.

magrim: a megrim, either a type of bad headache or migraine, or an obsession bordering on illness.

senachie: dialect term deriving from the Gaelic for storyteller, meaning here a conversation or a cosy chat.

Chapter 6

lowest tariff: the lowest amount in a girl's dowry for admission to a convent, the term (used here by a shop-keeper) points up the overtly financial basis for admission, predominating over the religious vocation.

bangs Banagher: referring to the fabled reputation of the Irish town, meaning to beat everything.

readamadasy: a generic instruction book for learning to read, its title of *Reading Made Easy* corrupted though wide usage into this portmanteau term for a reading book.

Passionist: a priest in an order with a particular devotion for the Passion, Christ's death on the cross.

Chapter 7

antistrophe: term from classical Greek theatre and poetry, in which the chorus sings portions of the ode (in this case the laudation of Winnie's vocation by Father Burke and Mrs Curtin) in two parts by turn, strophe and antistrophe.

antimacassar: the ornamental mat placed on the top of a chair back, to protect the upholstery from repeated applications of hair oil (macassar oil was very popular in the Victorian period) from men's heads.

Chapter 8

'My name is Norval': from the noted eighteenth-century play by John Home, *Douglas*.

covered car: a horse-drawn carriage for hire, probably similar to a brougham.

Confiteor: a prayer said at the beginning of the Mass or other service, that begins with a general confession of sins.

Chapter 9

watering his claret: diluting wine with water at the table was a prudent practice to avoid drunkenness (and also a Classical convention), but by the eighteenth century it had acquired a sense of penny-pinching (watering the wine to make it go further, and to cheat customers) and unnecessary prudence for a gentleman who ought to be able to hold his liquor.

string: term from horse-breeding meaning a collection of young horses being trained. In this case its application to the women with whom Father Burke was known to be flirting, or worse, suggests the casual contempt with which the women were regarded by some of the priests.

sports: term from animal husbandry meaning a throwback, an individual that does not exhibit genetic norms, in this case a woman who does not want to marry and have children.

good lump: a good lump sum, an amount of money as capital or to produce invested income.

Chapter 10

dot: French for dowry; British and Irish convent terminology often used French words from the fashionable French traditions.

Michael: nuns conventionally took the name of their preferred saint on entering their Order, and were called by that name for the rest of their lives.

passed her chapter: passed a novitiate test.

fal-lals: nonsense, frivolities, unnecessary rubbish.

day of the profession: the day a novice became a nun by professing her vows.

Chapter 12

spring her mine: to explode her mine, to release the planned attack on Reverend Mother's rule.

Chapter 13

faldstool: portable folding chair in a church for the use of a bishop officiating at the service in a church not his own.

bougie: French for a candle, a lamp held by non-officiating priests during the Mass.

maze: in an amazement, dazed, not herself.

Chapter 14

velleities: very faint wishes or desires.

cute: acute, clever.

augury: pagan term for a forecast of the future.

Chapter 15

that old man in the Chateau d'If: the prisoner in Alexandre Dumas' novel *The Count of Monte Cristo.*

the prisoner of Chillon: the title of a poem by Lord Byron (1816).

moider: to pester, annoy, get in the way of.

'Who is Sylvia?': Sister Luke is singing Schubert's setting of the Shakespeare poem.

Chapter 16

the Curé d'Ars: an eighteenth-century priest (beatified in 1905, canonised after the publication of this novel) with particular powers to endure poltergeists and give clairvoyant spiritual advice.

stravaging: to roam aimlessly without intent, a purposeless activity.

Chapter 18

the Asses' Bridge: the fifth proposition in the first book of Euclid, on the geometry of the isosceles triangle.

Chapter 21

***Facilis est descensus averni*:** from the Aeneid, the descent to hell is easy.